Winter Twilight

Fiction
Adventures in Heaven
When I was a Boy in Boston
Journey to the Dawn
In the Morning Light
The Sun at Noon
Between Day and Dark
Something About My Father and Other People
The Bitter Spring
Summer Storm
Memory of Autumn

Nonfiction
A Literary History of the American People (Vols. I and II)
The Book of Libel
Palestrina
Fathers of Classical Music
H. L. Mencken: A Portrait From Memory
The Tone of the Twenties
George Sterling: A Centenary Memoir—Anthology

Editor
Arsenal for Skeptics
(under the pen-name of Richard W. Hinton)
Stradivari by Helen Tinyanova
The World of George Jean Nathan
Stories From the Literary Review

Co-Editor
The World Over 1938
The World Over 1939
The American Mercury Reader
Modern Stories From Many Lands

Poetry
The Bell of Time
Memoranda For Tomorrow

Plays
Something to Sing About
Moment Musicale

Charles Angoff

WINTER TWILIGHT

South Brunswick

New York   •   Thomas Yoseloff   •   London

Thomas Yoseloff, Publisher
Cranbury, New Jersey 08512

Thomas Yoseloff Ltd
108 New Bond Street
London, W1Y OQX, England

SBN: 498 07489 7
Printed in the United States of America

Winter Twilight

One

It was Saturday afternoon, in March. David, his wife and daughter Anne were at the dinner table. Saturday dinner after *shul* was the main meal on that day. It had been so for about five years now, and David was glad. It was a lovely affirmation of their Jewishness, on the kitchen level to be sure, yet there was something warm and binding about it. David always felt this way on Saturday at this time, and he was also glad because it rounded out his life. It brought him back to his childhood days in Boston, when the whole family would be together after *shul,* and then Father would go off by himself to the front room, gently close the door and sing to himself lovely religious hymns and Yiddish songs and Hebrew songs and a few Russian songs—after all, it was Shabbes.

David, his wife and daughter had come back from a *bar mitzvah,* and they all felt good about it. The services had gone off with ease, the boy had sung his blessings calmly and clearly, and his last chant, with the whole congregation standing, was especially moving. It brought tears to David's eyes, which he tried vainly to control He was sure that his wife was also trying to control her tears, and he was even more sure that Anne was deeply moved. He was very glad that Anne was the sort of person who was sensitive to such occasions—this brought him very close to her.

David and Anne were sitting at the table waiting for Mother to bring the food and then sit down herself. They would all eat together. David was attracted by Mother's apron. It was freshly laundered, it was neat, it, too, was Shabbesy, he said to himself with a smile—kindly cleanliness and calm and inner contentment hovered over the room.

"I was thinking, Daddy," said Anne, "how really good and wonderful Jewish synagogue music is."

"It is, Anne," said David.

"And Hebrew is a wonderful language," said Anne.

"I'm especially glad you feel that way, darling," said Anne's mother. "Even before you were born, darling, I was hoping you would learn Hebrew and speak it, along with English, of course, and Yiddish, and French and whatever other languages you wish to learn in high school and in college."

"I love French, too, Mommie," said Anne, "you know that. I'm so glad I'm taking college French already at the High School of Science. Madame Hopmayer is a doll. And I'm studying a little Latin, by myself, you know. Thank you, Daddy, for helping me. That first lesson you gave me early this week was good. So many English words from Latin, as you said, I never really thought there were so many. But Hebrew, that's different, it seems so close, you know."

"It also helps you to understand the prayers, darling," said the mother. "So many of the prayers among the Jews are poems and lyrics, very beautiful. If you don't undrestand them, you miss much of their beauty. Some are also in Aramaic, but even with Aramaic Hebrew helps."

"I know," said Anne, and a quiet descended on the table.

David looked at his fourteen-year-old daughter, and was amazed at her many aspects. Sometimes she would be like the child she had been eight and nine years before, and sometimes she would be as adult as any of the people who came to the house—thoughtful, logical, considerate, like the proverbial chameleon. But maybe all children of her age were this way. Really, all people were that way . . . all men and women, all children have many faces that speak for varying inner beings, and yet there is a persisting core of personality. And now Anne was serious, enthusiastic, and David thought how intense and

8

warm and all-out youthful enthusiasm was. And he was especially glad that she had so much enthusiasm for Jewish things—for Hebrew, for Jewish history, for Jewish music, including synagogue chanting. For David, as he was getting older, had the notion, perhaps it was mystical, that Judaism was at the center of the world thought, that it contained all that was beautiful in other ways of life and combined them in a pleasing and orderly and magnificent structure that was at the same time a poetry and a music, and that was also a beacon of some sort for the whole world. And, he thought, it was no accident that Judaism was the mother of Christianity and Mohammedanism and of many other religions with smaller followings.

David had dreamed that his home would be deeply immersed in Judaism, for thereby it would be most human, most universal, most inclusive of all that was loveliest in the endless and caressing mystery that was this life. And David thought that some of this mystery was now at this very table, and that his Anne was expressing it.

"I was thinking, Daddy and Mommie," said Anne, "while we were in the synagogue, about God. I'm always, lately, thinking about God."

"What have you been thinking, Anne?" said David.

"One minute, please, Daddy, it's sort of hard to say. I always feel when I'm in the synagogue, when there is a *bar mitzvah* or a *bat mitzvah,* that I really am close to God. And I think how good God has been to me. I really am having a ball in this world, I know that's not the way to say it, but you know what I mean."

"Yes."

"I just don't see how anybody can say he doesn't believe in God, I just don't see it. With everything, the beautiful days and the nights and all the music and school and boat rides, and friends, especially, well, the whole world, it's so really wonderful. And that's what frightens me."

"Why, Anne?" asked David.

"I mean, it's wonderful. I hate to think I might lose it. I mean, I'm afraid, well, you know, just afraid. All little girls think about that, if they'll grow up to have children, you know, everything is so wonderful that you think funny things. Did

9

you have such thoughts when you were my age, Daddy and Mommie?"

"Of course, darling," said her mother. "It's nothing to be afraid, it's all perfectly natural. In psychology, you'll have it in college, it's called youthful *Weltschmerz*. That means the sadness you've been thinking of, telling us about. The literal meaning, it's a German word, is world pain, but it means the sort of sadness that you are speaking of. So don't think you're unusual, or something's wrong, it's all natural."

"Daddy, were you afraid when you were my age?"

"Of course, I was," said David. "As Mommie told you, we all go through the sort of sadness you are speaking of. As a matter of fact, I was probably afraid of more things than you are now."

"Like what?" asked Anne.

"Money, finances, health," said David. "I came from a poor family, seven children, I the oldest. My father seldom made enough for us to live on with any real decency. Oh, we ate and lived, but close to the edge, so when I was little, your age, I used to wonder what would happen to my high school education and what would be my chance for college if anything happened to my father. I never really got over that worry, not till I was twenty or older."

"I see," said Anne, as she sank into a thoughtful silence. Then she said, "Remember what you said, you'd take a walk with me after dinner, while Mommie went to see Mrs. Goldberger of the Parent Teachers Association."

"I'll keep my promise," said David.

"Only one thing, Daddy, before we walk, we'll play on the machine *El Hanegev* and *Shir Hapalmach*. I love them. The Israelites have such wonderful songs. You know, it must be very exciting to be in a country that has just been founded, is only ten or eleven years old. I sometimes think, Mommie and Daddy, how wonderful it would have been if I had lived at the time of George Washington and Thomas Jefferson and all the others, and Betsy Ross and Benjamin Franklin. It already makes me sad I didn't know Chaim Weizmann, the first President of Israel. That's a nice thing to say, I mean it makes me feel good

10

all over, the first President of Israel." Anne smiled then said, "I only hope Ben Gurion doesn't die before I see him."

"He's very healthy," said Anne's mother. "He exercises, he stands on his head, he works on the farm, but, of course, he is over seventy. If Churchill has lived to, what is it, David, eighty-four?"

"I think so," said David.

"If Churchill can do it, then Ben Gurion can do it," said Anne's mother. "I'm that much of a chauvinist."

"I don't feel like eating any more, Mommie, I'm excited," said Anne.

"That's not a reason for not eating," said her mother. "Finish all that meat. I gave you little enough as it is. You ate all those cakes and cookies and sandwiches at the *Kiddush* after the *bar mitzvah,* that's why you're not hungry. Well, young lady that's not food what you had over there, you finish every last piece of that meat."

"Please, Mommie, I'm full. Please."

"Then finish that big piece of meat, and the potato and the carrots. Next time I'll forbid you to eat more than one cookie at a *bar mitzvah* before dinner."

Anne looked at David, and smiled, happy over her victory over her mother, then she went at the meat and the vegetables.

"And you've got to have a peach and a plum," said her mother. "Then you two can go, and I'll rush over to see Jean Goldberger. Every year I tell myself not to get mixed up in these community affairs, and always I give in and say I'll serve as a vice-chairman, and always it ends up by my doing most of the heavy work. I urged Jean to take the presidency of the PTA, thinking she would really make a good president, but she's so rattled."

"I think you'd make a wonderful president, Mommie," said Anne.

"Frankly, I think I would, but I'm sick of all the petty jealousy, and all for what? I've had enough of this public work."

"They all say you're marvelous," said David.

"Mommie, Daddy, I was sad about something else at this morning's *bar mitzvah.*"

"For a happy day, you had a lot of sadness," said David.

Anne smiled. "Oh, Daddy, you say it in such a funny way. It was a happy sadness. Look, Daddy, I've just said something you could have said." Again a smile spread across her face.

"Now tell us what's the other thing that made you sad," said David.

"Well," began Anne, "it'll sound kind of strange, but I'll say it just the same. I was sad because I already had my *bat mitzvah* and I won't have it any more."

A warm sorrow, but a sorrow nevertheless, suddenly coursed through David, and he saw in his wife's eyes that the same thing happened to her—there were a few moments of deep silence at the table. It was a silence that brought them all together in a rare and wonderful intimacy. They were all present at a lovely and somewhat crucial moment in the family history. They were seeing time passing them by, and their love for each other was making this passage easier to bear. This is what made family life so precious, and it all added to the wonderment and the soft grandeur and the ineffable centrality of Anne in this family, at this very table.

"I never realized before," said Anne, "that what has happened once can't happen again, I mean many things. And that is why I'm sometimes sorry that I'm getting older."

"You're only fourteen, Anne," said David.

"I know. But fourteen is a year older than thirteen, and thirteen gets farther and farther away, the way eleven or ten is far away now. It's wonderful to have birthdays, but they go away."

"Birthdays do go away," said Anne's mother. "But new ones come. Maybe you ought to think about those that are coming. You're young enough to think about a lot of birthdays coming."

"I know," said Anne. She looked at the peach and plum that her mother had put before her. "I'll eat them. I was just thinking about something else." She took some bites of her peach, then of her plum.

Her mother smiled. "You're the only person in the whole world who eats two fruits at the same time."

"No, everybody does," said Anne. "I can prove it."

"Prove it," said her mother.

12

"Let's have a bet," said Anne, with an excitement that was reminiscent of her excitement when she was about ten.

"Prove it, smartie," repeated her mother.

"Well," said Anne, with determination in her eyes, "when you eat fruit salad, you eat many fruits at the same time. So . . . "

Anne's mother looked at David, and David looked at Anne. David and his wife smiled at each other.

"I win, don't I?" said Anne.

"You win," said her mother, "but I still think that it's strange to eat two fruits at the same time. Well, I have to clean up in a hurry," and she was off to the kitchen. David and Anne remained at the table. He was sorry his wife couldn't be at the table a little longer. He thought of calling her back, and his only explanation would be, "Please, dear, let the dishes wait . . . this is a good time to be together at the table, just talking." But before he had a chance to get up and walk to the kitchen, Anne said, "Daddy, I'm glad I was *bat mitzvah*. I'm glad we belong to a synagogue where not just boys but girls, too, are *bar miztvah*. I was thinking while we were in synagogue what I thought when I was *bat mitzvah* a year ago. I was proud, really proud that I sort of really became a member of the Jewish people. That's what reading the Torah does, and what the blessings do. I felt I could now feel I was sort of related you know, to Abraham and Jacob and Isaac and Joseph and Bar Kochba and Chaim Weizmann and, you know, all the Jews and all Jewish history. I was just thinking, Daddy, Jewish history is one of the oldest in the whole world, and that's a wonderful thing to be a sort of member of. It really made me feel wonderful when I was up there, reading the Torah. And you know something else, Daddy?"

"What?"

"This will sound silly, Daddy, but I want to say it. I can hardly wait till my children are grown up and they are *bar mitzvah*."

"Will you invite Mommie and me?"

"Why, Daddy!"

"I look forward to it, so does Mommie."

"And I'll remember everything that took place at my own

bat mitzvah, I'm sure I will, Daddy. But, Daddy, there's something I still wish I knew, I wonder about it."

"About what, Anne?"

"Where does time go, Daddy?"

David was startled by the question. There was such maturity about it, it opened up such a bewildering world of other questions that David didn't know what to say first. In fact he wasn't sure he knew what to say at all. Where does time go? Where, indeed, does it go? Where does so much of it come from, and where does it finally end up, or does it keep on going round and round in circles? He looked at his daughter and he wanted to press her close and bury his face in her head of hair and say nothing and hope that out of this embrace would come some answer for her question. And he saw the tender and pleading look in her eyes, and he saw the sorrow all over her face—the sweet, childhood sorrow, and he wished he could say something, but his mouth wouldn't open. Finally he did manage to say, " I don't know, Anne, I don't even know exactly what time is. It's something that flows, that comes and goes on. I know I'm not saying very much or anything, really, but I just don't know, Anne dear."

"Do you think God knows, Daddy?"

"I suppose so, but that, too, I don't know, Anne."

"You know something else, Daddy?"

"What, Anne?"

"I was thinking that at the same time life gets more and more exciting it also gets more mysterious and a little sad, in a good way, you know. You know what I would like to do?"

"What?"

"Walk on Broadway today, not in the park. I feel like being on Broadway. I like it when people walk up and down, it's exciting."

It was a bit chilly on Broadway but the brightness of the sun made one forget some of the chilliness. David felt holidayish, and he sensed that Anne did also—and Broadway itself seemed to be in a holiday mood. Anne was holding him by his arm, hopping up and down, pulling him this way and that, and David was delighted by her exuberance. Through the corner of

14

his eye he saw how warm and bright and clear her eyes were, how glowing her face was, and he felt grateful to God that he could be so close to so wonderful a child. Always when she was this way, she appeared to be filled with the secrets of all creation, with all its warmth and wonderment and all its regard for mankind. In his college days David had thought, now and then, that nature was indifferent to man's wishes and hopes most of the time, that man was a sort of accident in creation enjoying no more privileges than a stray bit of newspaper tossed here and there by the breeze. But as he grew older David was not so sure, especially when he looked deep into the eyes of those who loved him and whom he loved—his wife and daughter. Therein he saw some profound, though inexpressible, assurance that man was more than an accident, that there was some sort of purpose behind his creation, and that in some strage way man was specially chosen by the Creator for some special purpose. David didn't know the purpose, he doubted any human being possibly could know the purpose, but he was profoundly convinced of the existence of such a purpose. Perhaps, he thought, this was the essence of all religions, a profound conviction of a purpose in the creation of man and in all life, that this purpose was good, and that doing good was therefore in agreement with the overall purpose, which was divinity.

David felt himself being pulled to a store window. "Daddy, isn't that green dress in the middle wonderful? It's a little too old for me, but next year it will be just right, won't it?"

"I guess so."

"I like the combination, green and white, don't you?"

"I do."

They were walking again, up Broadway. There seemed to be fewer people, and David didn't know whether to be happy or sad. The chill in the air seemed to be a little sharper now, but David was sure that Anne didn't feel the slightest bit colder. If anything she seemed a bit more thoughtful. "Daddy, I was just thinking about Franklin D. Roosevelt, I think he was the greatest President we ever had. Know why?"

"Why?"

"Well, he took a country that was just crumbling, we learned in Social Studies at Science High, it was just going to pieces, the banks closing, everything, and he put it back on its feet. I think he was just as great as Lincoln. A man like Hitler I don't understand at all, or Stalin or Khrushchev. What pleasure is there in killing people? They must be crazy. I never feel good when I've had an argument with somebody, like with Kathi or Linda or Stevie, and I can't wait to make up. Imagine being angry with the whole world, and wanting to kill people!"

"It was pretty terrible, Anne, but you were little then, you weren't even here yet. When President Roosevelt died you were less than four months old."

"I know. Daddy, was the world always mixed up, like it was then, and like it is now, with all the conferences going on, in Geneva and other places, and everybody worried about a war coming?"

"I'm afraid so, Anne. The world generally is what you call mixed up. When you get to college and study history a little more deeply than you are now, you'll realize that even when there is outward peace, it is only outward, and that actually there are tensions between nations, one wanting what another has. I supose nations are like individuals, they're never satisfied, that is, most of them, they're never satisfied with what they have, even though it's plenty for them and their children. They want more and more and when they see a neighbor or even a country far away that has more than they do—more land, more trade —they get jealous and start maneuvering to get some of the other country's land and trade, and one thing leads to another, and soon there is a war."

"But nobody really wins in a war, that's what we learned in Social Studies," said Anne.

"You must have been studying Norman Angell's *The Great Illusion.*"

"Yes, the teacher mentioned it, Miss Gordon."

"There have been wars, I guess, that you might say have been beneficial, such as our War of Independence, and don't forget what the Maccabees did in Jewish history. And I think that the First World War did some good, and the Second World War, too, but there are many wars where the victors and the vanquished are not much better off, I mean, when the

16

victors have to support those whom they conquered, and that brings about depressions, and so it goes."

"You could have mentioned Israel, Daddy. They had to fight the Arabs, and if they didn't there would be no Israel. The Arabs wouldn't accept the decision of the UN, and they attacked Israel, so the Israelis had to fight back."

They walked on, Anne was occupied with her own world of thoughts, and David was wondering what that world was.

"Let's go to Riverside Drive, Daddy," said Anne suddenly.

David was delighted, for to him few things in this world were as soothing as the sight of a large body of water, and he had a special liking for the Hudson River. He had sailed up the river many times, in the winter and in the spring and in the summer. It was a river of many beauties and of many varieties of comfort and contentment. During the day, even at its mouth, in the bay, it was a constant reminder of the ease and grace of nature, and quietly it seemed to be saying to the people high up in the office buildings, "Do not hurry . . . do not hurry . . . persistent ease is more consonant with the will of creation, and it gives more delight . . . remember the slowness with which I come from the mountains far up north . . . do not hurry . . . do not hurry." The river was a belt of healing thoughts and reminiscences.

David and Anne were sitting on a bench and looking down on the Hudson. They were saying nothing to each other, they were relishing the very sight of the river, they were warm and content in its arms of comfort and loving stillness.

"I love it," said Anne.

"I do, too," said David.

"Daddy," said Anne, gently interrupting David's thoughts, "I wish it would snow now. I love it when it snows on the river. It's so soft watching the snow fall on the river, much softer than when it falls in the street, you know what I mean, Daddy, don't you?"

"I do," said David, and hugged Anne close to him, for she was saying things that were welling up within him.

"Snow is special, isn't it, Daddy?"

"It is, Anne."

"The river is special, too, isn't it, Daddy?"

17

"Yes, Anne."

"And I think snow talks, Daddy, it has a speech of its own, we don't know it, just as the snow doesn't know our speech, that's the only difference, but snow has speech, rain has speech, and water, everything. Wouldn't it be wonderful if we knew what snow was saying, what rain was saying, what the river was saying?"

"It would be very wonderful," said David . . . and again he and Anne became silent.

David's mind went back to the days of 1945–1948. Anne's questions about Franklin D. Roosevelt and Hitler directed his mind to those years. They were salient, leaping, tense, vibrant, history-packed years. The war in Europe ended with a crushing defeat for the Nazis, and the war in the Pacific ended with an equally crushing defeat for the Japanese. The overwhelming nature of both defeats gave them the aspect of preordination, there was something Biblical, in fatefulness, in them. Every day had size and stature, every newspaper every day was a chapter in history, and somehow the world seemed to be shaking itself down to a chapter even more historic, one felt it as one read one's newspaper every morning. One felt it as one listened to the radio and watched television. And Russia, a darkness was coming from there, a creeping, insidious darkness, as evil, in many ways, as Nazism.

As one thought of those days one had to recall the face and the speech of President Franklin D. Roosevelt—his fireside chats: "My friends . . ." . . . and his death, the way it shook the country . . . and President Harry Truman . . . he looked good and worthy and sound even as he took the oath of office. The prairie and the Middle-Western rivers and the sprawling but powerful communities spread low and calmly across the spacious states pushing farther and farther west and north and south. The tang of the air in those spaces was in the man and in his speech, in the set of his jaw, in the straightforward look of his eyes. And David recalled what the wife of a man close to President Roosevelt had said about President Truman: "Don't underestimate that man. Truman is perhaps more of a Democrat, more of a progressive than Roosevelt was. Truman has skipped meals, no one ever forgets that. All our truly great Presidents have skipped meals, and Washington, who didn't, is only an exception who proves the rule."

In David's own life there were encounters with shabbiness in people and in situations. He saw a maneuverer flourish and climb on top of other men's ideas and other men's money, and win for himself the respect of many for enterprise and knowledge and wisdom . . . and he met men of the cloth who were little better than merchants of dubious medicines on circus grounds . . . and he met women who appeared to have no souls . . . but he also encountered women of great depth and vast comfort, for all their bewilderment with the ways of the world and even with the ways of their husbands . . . and he encountered men of great spirituality who gave luster to the words rabbi and minister . . . and he met men who were helping build a new nation on an ancient foundation that was still strong, as strong as it had been for nearly two thousand years . . . and there was a glorious Saturday in 1947, on a November evening, when Israel was born. Now it was still only a dream, now it was a lusty, vibrant being, mature enough to have powerful enemies eager to see it die, and strong enough to fight these enemies with a determination that dismayed the enemies and the rest of the world . . . and the dancing in the streets that Saturday night, dancing in the very heart of New York City and in the streets of many other cities and towns and in the homes of Jews the world over. The incredible became real, the impossible became true, and every Jew the world over grew an inch taller. It was the longest and most glorious evening in two thousand years. David was elated and uplifted to new levels of being and feeling, but the memory of a personal agony dampened this holy evening.

"Daddy," said Anne, "I wish I knew as much as God, don't you?"

David smiled and was overwhelmed by the novelty of Anne's wish. He took her hand in his and a goodness went through him, and he said, "Yes, I do, too, but maybe we do know at least some things that God knows. After all, in the Bible it says that Adam ate of the tree of knowledge, so man knows some things."

"I know, Daddy, but I mean I'd like to know what the future

19

will be like, how everything will turn out, what everybody will be doing, what man I'll marry, what my children will look like."

"I wish I knew these things, too, Anne," said David as he caressed her hand, "especially I would like to know about you."

"But God already knows."

"I suppose He does, Anne."

And once more the two were silent, taking comfort in being near each other, and in watching the river flow.

Two

The death of President Roosevelt seemed to put the whole nation in a historic frame of mind. People already were placing him on the same plane with George Washington and Andrew Jackson and Thomas Jefferson and Abraham Lincoln and Woodrow Wilson. Some said that, in certain ways, he was superior to them in influence, since he had an effect not only on American history but on world history. The whole anti-Nazi world looked to him for leadership, and he supplied that leadership in his peculiar, almost off-hand, yet enormously effective way. He who had originated the phrase the Good Neighbor Policy, as expressing our relations hereafter to the Latin American countries, himself seemed to be the good neighbor of all the peoples of the world. The very aristocracy of his bearing, the Harvard yard atmosphere in which he always seemed to be moving, somehow added to the authenticity of his devotion to the Good Neighbor Policy in all things. He was a democratic aristocrat. He seemed to have a high sense of honor, as democratic aristocrats often do.

David recalled the one time that he had been at a press conference of President Roosevelt. It was in the spring of 1935. David had been in Washington, looking for possible articles for the *American World*. Morton Jackson, the successor of Harry

Brandt as editor, had suggested that he go there "and look around, there must be some writers who have off-beat articles or ideas, human things, we want to make the *World* a family organ, dealing with public affairs, of course, but lightly, and especially do we want to give the woman's angle. I do believe that this is a woman's world, America is a woman's country. Anyway, wander around, and see what you can see." David was depressed by the assignment, as he had been depressed by Jackson's whole program for the magazine . . . he was slowly turning it into a cheap, semi-popular monthly that would appeal to all groups and end up by appealing to none. He was very enthusiastic about his new departments: "The Mother of the Month . . . the Bride of the Month . . . How to Conquer Fear Through God's Power . . . " David was sick at heart whenever he thought of these and similar departments that Jackson had installed. Still, he jumped at the idea of going to Washington, but for reasons that were wholly different from what Jackson had in mind. David wanted to see the Washington where so much had lately happened, where so much had happened in the recent past and in the not-so-long distant past.

He also wanted to be away from New York for a while . . . he had been in Washington before, but only now was he there on an official business trip and on an expense account. He registered at the Willard Hotel, and was delighted later to learn that President Lincoln had stayed there when he came to this city just before his first inauguration. The hotel undoubtedly had changed much since Lincoln's day, and yet it was exhilarating to know that Lincoln the man had once walked and eaten and slept and breathed here.

That first night David went to the cocktail room at the Willard to meet some people he had written to: They were reporters and correspondents of various newspapers and magazines, whose writings had interested him. He doubted very much that they could write the things that Jackson had asked him to hunt up, he wasn't at all sure that he would ask them about such things, he would just talk to them about things in general. The cocktail room was rather small. Hard liquor was still difficult to obtain, but there were plenty of cocktail and highball glasses on the tables. David ordered a beer.

People were talking all around David and he listened: "That man in the White House is killing all the initiative in the country, hell, if we lose that, everything we stand for is gone, the very thing that built up the nation."

"That may be so, but you got to protect the people somehow, they have a right to live at a minimum basis."

"Well, who said they have a right? I'll tell you. By just being human beings they have that."

"Yah? How about the people who start businesses, invest thousands and millions of dollars, and then lose it, because they guessed wrong? Does the government owe them anything? Hell, no, they took their chances and they lost. The same way with smaller people. Just being born a human being doesn't mean that you can coast along on the government bounty . . ."

"Who's talking about coasting? A man gets sick in the street, and an ambulance comes along and takes him to the hospital and there they fix him up, and generally the matter of money doesn't come up at all. I say a man should have the same basic right to minimal subsistence for himself and family."

"Have it your way, all I say is that this is rank socialism, and what built this country up is not socialism but free enterprise, and you can laugh all you want about Hoover and his rugged individualism, but he's right. You start giving the people something for free, and pretty soon there isn't very much left worth giving to anybody."

"I say Harry Hopkins is a cheap politician, all he can do is spend and spend, and for this future generations will pay . . ."

"Well, I like him, he may be a little high-handed, but I like to see a former social-worker high-handed once in a while, it's a change from seeing a mogul, a moneybags like Judge Elbert Gary being high-handed, Judge Gary who thought that it was written in the Bible that it is mandatory for men to work not less than twelve hours a day. I may be wrong, on second thought I believe he said that the Bible was for four-teen hours a day. Yes, sir. Jesus was anti-union, St. Paul was for filling the coffers of U. S. Steel, St. Francis was for pro-tecting the big banks against the little banks. From all the yelling that went on at the time the SEC Act was up for con-sideration in the Congress, you'd think that the country was

23

about to be destroyed, just because Roosevelt wanted to make sure that the stock swindlers in Wall Street found it a little harder to steal money from poor people. If I had my way, I'd abolish Wall Street . . . "

"I can't make out that man in the White House, he seems like such a happy-go-lucky fellow, without a worry in the world, yet somehow history has chosen him to be the guardian of all the little people of our time, at least in this country, and by example, it could be, also all over the world. In Albany he was only a so-so Governor, good but not brilliant. Al Smith was a bigger man, with a more developed social instinct. He was brought up in the slums and he never forgot it. And that's where history works in a strange way. Al Smith, the slum boy, is head of the Liberty Leaguers, they who want to save capitalism, I mean the Old Line Capitalism, the Du Ponts and the Carnegies and the Rockefellers, and the man who wants to save the little fellow is a born capitalist, a millionaire. Why did history pick Franklin D. Roosevelt instead of Al Smith or some other man born to poverty? Who knows why?"

And so the talk went on and on, all of it heated, some violently against what was going on, and some enthusiastically for what was going on, but all of them clearly conscious that these were historic times, that a historic man was guiding the destiny of the people . . . politics and economics and government had come within the four walls of every kitchen and every living room in the land. The President's voice was frequently heard within the same walls. Government truly, at long last and on such a scale, had become everybody's business. David felt exhilarated to be in this stuffy, smokey, crowded cocktail room. Here was reflected what was going on across the whole nation.

Someone tapped David on the shoulder. "David Polonsky?"

He saw before him a tall heavily bespectacled man, who was an editorial writer for one of the Washington newspapers, and also a writer for a New York monthly magazine. With him were two women. David recognized one of them, a columnist for a string of Middle-Western newspapers. The editorial writer introduced the other woman, a smallish woman, with rather sleepy eyes. She was one of the Washington correspon-

24

dents for the New York *Daily Truth,* a newspaper that pretended to be objective in its news reporting but actually was prejudiced in favor of Communism. The editorial writer found a table for the four of them, and before David knew it there was a bottle of whiskey and a bottle of gin on the table. David and the editorial writer each had a whiskey and water (David didn't have the courage to order another beer, he merely took what the editorial writer said he was going to have), and the two women had straight gin with beer chasers. The editorial writer was pretty much of a New Dealer, as David himself was, so was the columnist. He wasn't sure about the *Daily Truth* woman: she could be a Communist or she could be a fellow traveler, of whom there were many in the country at the time.

The editorial writer said, "I suppose one of the questions future history will ask will be whether FDR and the New Deal went far enough. At this time I'm writing an article on that theme—it's really foolish, in a way, to write such articles now, since all that's going on here is experimental, by rule of thumb, and only time will tell, yet one can't help thinking. I personally am glad he didn't go any farther, indeed, he may have gone too far already. I personally am a little worried about the NRA, the Blue Eagle and all the other forms of regimentation of our economic life. They've done some good, perhaps a lot, but only in the short run. The long run, that's what worries me. The NRA is too much like the corporate state in Italy, and that's fascism."

"Not while FDR is in the White House will we have fascism here," said the woman columnist. "But you've raised a point. Under another man it could lead to fascism or to communism."

"Basically, there's no difference betwen communism and fascism, is there?" asked David.

"There's a world of difference," said the *Daily Truth* woman firmly. "The Russians fought Hitler, they didn't join him."

"They were friendly to him, had a pact with him, didn't they, while the Western Powers were fighting Hitler," said David.

"For a magazine editor you are most naïve," said the *Daily Truth* woman. "You confused liberals of the *Globe* variety! Maybe I should say all American liberals are confused, without the courage to go all the way."

"Well," said the editorial writer rather sadly, "isn't that a rather old-fashioned phrase, *confused liberal?*"

"I've been called that any number of times," said the woman columnist. "I guess I am a confused liberal, but I see nothing to be ashamed of."

"I don't either," said David.

"Confused liberals have held back progress, they're blind to the forces of history," said the correspondent for the *Daily Truth,* "Its their confusion that makes them the tools of the capitalist forces."

"Now, now," said the editorial writer, "I'm not a tool of capitalist forces and my two friends here are not, either. I incline to think that it's confused liberalism that is responsible for much, perhaps most, of the progress in politics and economics that the world has made in the past 150 years—better working conditions, the right of franchise, free speech, free press . . . "

"What free press have you got here?" asked the correspondent for the *Daily Truth.* "Remember Upton Sinclair's book, *The Brass Check?* He proved that the American press is corrupt, plays right into the hands of its owners, is the tool of capitalism, is . . . "

"One minute, my dear friend," said the editorial writer. "That Sinclair book was an important book. He highlighted some real evils in American journalism, but he also scandalized a good deal of the truth, I mean he exaggerated, and in some cases he just didn't know what he was talking about. Anyway, the press is a lot freer now than it was twenty-five years ago. I can tell you that department store owners now are more afraid of newspapers than the other way around. The American press is the freest in the world. And may I add, it is certainly a lot freer than the press in Russia, which is truly a kept press, kept and controlled and wholly owned by the Communist party, no, by Stalin himself."

"That's slander, a brazen lie," said the *Daily Truth* woman. "The Russian papers print the truth."

"What would happen," asked David, "if one newspaper in Russia criticized Stalin, how long would the paper last?"

"No paper would do it, they all agree with Stalin," said the *Daily Truth* woman.

"That's a laugh," said the woman columnist.

And so the talk continued, now mounting in intensity, now subsiding to a polite level. David had heard all these points of view before, he had read them before. At bottom, he wasn't too interested in the finer points of difference between the two opposing sides. There was something about most political discussion that offended him. He had only one political principle, namely, the utmost freedom of expression in every media, with its corollary, the utmost freedom for the individual that is consistent with social life. David did not discuss with the three people at his table any specific articles for the *World,* he merely said, "Well, if you people ever have any ideas that you think would be right for the *World,* write to me, or get in touch with me before I leave Washington." That satisfied his sense of moral obligation to Jackson.

The following morning he went to the Presidential press conference in the White House, but as he entered the large room where the President was sitting, this sense of history appeared to vanish. The press conference began. One reporter asked whether taxes were to be increased, and the President said, "I wish I knew how to keep them down. I wish I knew how we could pay for all our projects without money," and the room burst into laughter. The President pulled at his long cigarette holder and turned to hear a woman reporter ask, "Mr. President, what about the persisting rumor that Mrs. Roosevelt is your eyes and ears over the country, that she is your best reporter?" The President laughed and so did the rest in the room, and then the President said, "Well, her hearing and sight are very good, and as a married man I learned long ago to listen closely when my wife is talking." . . . again the room burst into laughter . . . There were more questions, none of them very important. David was astonished how like his pictures President Roosevelt in the flesh was. He also noted that, like Lincoln, he too had a rather large wart on one of his cheeks, and he noticed an appealing boyishness in his eyes, that was in marked contrast to the firmness of his chin . . .

27

his hands were very powerful, so were his shoulders . . . and his head seemed to bespeak a certain spaciousness and ruggedness in his mental outlook.

When David returned to New York he wrote a long and exuberant letter to his mother and father about the Presidential press conference, and even as he wrote it, he couldn't help feeling that this very letter, too, was a historic document . . . one of the Polonskys, an immigrant and the son of immigrants, had been a member of the press questioning the President of the United States. David himself had asked no question, but he was free to do so . . . and David knew, and he knew that his parents knew, that what he had seen and heard and participated in was America, was the very heart of Americanism, and he was profoundly thrilled.

All these and related thoughts and memories came back to him now, as they came back to so many others after President Roosevelt's death. There was something haunting about these memories. They even seemed to take precedence, in some strange way, over the war news. There still was a war, as President Truman reminded the country, and yet people seemed to feel that it was only a matter of a few weeks before the war would be over. The Germans appeared to be at the end of their resources. The Jewish people were sad over the death of President Roosevelt because of his friendship for Jews . . . he had been close to former Governor Lehman, he had appointed Professor Felix Frankfurter to the United States Supreme Court, he had appointed Henry Morgenthau as Secretary of the Treasury. Yet, there were some Jews who couldn't forget that not long before his death President Roosevelt had had a conference with the King of Saudi Arabia, and there were rumors that the President had made some secret promises to the Arabian King . . . whatever these promises were, if there were such promises, they couldn't have been friendly to the Jews. Jews wondered why the Presdient had done this. After all, the Arabs were so openly pro-Nazi, indeed, the Mufti was a personal friend of Hitler's. But some Jews said, "President Roosevelt knew what he was doing, he probably told him all sorts of things, who knows what he told him? He was playing politics, he had to, when you're in politics you have to be a politician, so that's how it was, he figured later he would see, what's later would be later. But, of course, he died, and that makes a difference. But, then, even so, President Truman doesn't have to do whatever President Roosevelt promised, if he did promise. It may also be that President Roosevelt only saw the Arabian King socially, and he made no promises. After all, who knows?"

In the Jewish world there were other speculations . . . President Roosevelt and Prime Minister Churchill had discussed the formation of a United Nations Organization, to take the place of the defunct League of Nations. Along with the formation of this new world league there had also been talk that the German leaders would be brought to trial for war crimes, and among the crimes for which they would be judged by an international tribunal would be the murder of six million Jews. At long last, said Jews, the world would do something about this crime. "The Christian lands were not concerned with our welfare at the time the Nazis were killing our people. They could have offered European Jews, especially German Jews, asylum when it was still possible for Jews to leave Germany. England and the United States were deaf to the pleas of the European Jews at that time. Very few of their statesmen or ministers of religion showed any genuine desire to help. That is a difficult thing to forget. Now, at least, they seem to have awakened to their responsibility."

Then there was something else that was occupying the minds of many American Jews . . . one of the results of World War One was the Balfour Declaration that for the first time in nearly two thousand years stated that the Jews have a right to the re-establishment of their ancient homeland in Palestine. What would now happen to this age-long dream of the Jews? Will they at long last achieve the restoration of their land? The future was highly problematical. England was now revealing its anti-Jewish aspect. It seemed to be siding with the Arabian countries, it put obstacles in the way of large-scale immigration of Jews to Palestine. The English White Paper putting a virtual stop to further immigration shook the Jews the whole world over, and when the British Navy intercepted various "illegal" vessels carrying refugees to Palestine, thereby dooming thousands of men, women and children to virtual extinction, the dismay of world Jewry turned to bitterness. As for the United States, it was hard to say. The oil interests, said some, would surely try to influence the State Department to do nothing that would in any way alienate the Arab countries within whose borders was so much of the available oil of the globe. On the other hand, there was President Truman who was presumed to be friendly to the Jews. The more Jews thought about him the more they liked him. He appeared to be so *haimish,* and his wife seemed to be such a *balaboste.*

Then there was President Truman's friend, Eddie Jacobson. They had met in World War One, when they had served in the same company overseas. Later they were partners in the ownership of a haberdashery store in Kansas City. The business went into bankruptcy, but the two remained friends. It seemed to many Jews that this friendship indicated that the new President had no anti-Jewish feelings.

Thus the future for the Jews in so far as the re-establishment of Palestine as a Jewish state was concerned was something of a puzzle. There were good forces at work, and there were also unfriendly forces, but Jews sensed that something historic was about to happen. David noticed that Jews were becoming more Jewish-conscious, at least many of them were becoming less ashamed of being Jews than they used to be, and many of them in time became active Jews, or they began to read more and more about the people they were part of. The killing of some six million Jews made them bristle with bitterness inside, not only at Hitler but at the apathy with which the bulk of the Christian world reacted to the killings. When a much smaller number of Armenians was massacred by the Turks after World War One there was a world-wide protest, but there was no such protest with respect to the killing of millions of Jews.

The Jewish-Jews, so to speak, while profoundly dismayed and hurt, were not entirely disappointed, for they never had put very much trust in the "goodness" of Christians or in the "humanity" of the people of the democratic lands. Many of them had come over here with the feeling (engendered by their sorrowful lives in Russia or Rumania or Poland or Galicia) that there probably are no "good" Christians, so many of the "good" Christians whom they had trusted, in "the old country," had turned out to be *pogromtchiks,* or had stood by silently when a wave of anti-Semitism had hit a community. They feared that "if you scratch any Christian you will find an anti-Semite."

When these same people came to this country they were not so sure, for a time, about their old feeling with regard to Christians. Americans were really tolerant, it seemed to them. In some neighborhoods there were Catholic churches and Protestant churches and synagogues situated almost in the same block, and there was no violence or any hostile feeling toward the Jews. But as their stay in this country became longer, they became doubtful again. It was better here for the Jews than anywhere else in the world. At the same time they began to note instances of anti-Jewish feeling, not too serious, to be sure, but who can say when a not-so-serious expression of anti-Jewishness will flare up into something terribly serious. The younger children began to complain about being called *kikes* and Christ-killers, and the older children, those already in college, even in city-supported colleges, began to tell disturbing tales about this or that professor who "hates" Jews, professors who openly complain "about you people who are too smart for your own good . . . don't be so eager . . . don't be so aggressive . . . don't be so loud." The wealthier of the recent immigrants heard complaints from their children that they were not admitted to certain fraternities and sororities solely bceause they were Jews.

There were rumors—they were more than rumors, really, they were said by such reputable people as education editors of large newspapers, eminent rabbis, several non-Jewish professors, that one had to accept them as virtual facts—that there were quotas running from about 8 per cent to about 15 per cent for Jews in medical schools, in law schools, and even in some liberal arts colleges—especially in medical schools . . . very few of the medical schools denied this, they maintained a proud and aloof silence. Then some of the deans of the medical schools, while denying the charge of quotas, admitted that they were guided in their choice of students "by the policy that ours

31

is a national institution, which should represent every section of the country, every basic element of its population in more or less its present proportion of the over-all population of the country. Naturally, scholarship is important, very important, but other factors are also important." This sort of obfuscation convinced Jews that there definitely was a quota system against Jews. The tales of personal experiences, spread far and wide in the Jewish Community, only reinforced this conviction. There were scores of cases of brilliant boys, with grades well up in the nineties and with Phi Beta Kappa keys, who were refused by one medical school after another, whereas non-Jewish classmates of theirs in liberal arts college, with grades far lower were admitted into some of the best medical schools.

The horror of the Leo Frank case in Georgia—a Jewish factory worker, wrongly accused (as many competent reporters and investigators claimed) of attacking a young non-Jewish girl, was kidnaped from the jail where he was being held and lynched —though it happened in the second decade of the century did not entirely leave the Jewish consciousness. There were also persisting rumors that there were quotas for Jews in several of the largest book publishing houses in America, and that some of the largest insurance companies and banks had very few Jews in their employ.

So the immigrants began to feel keenly that the tragedy of the Jews is that even where it's much better, as in America, it still isn't really good for them. These immigrants, however, did not stop with their mood of resignation. They became more active Zionists, because "only in our own land can we be completely free and safe." They followed with heightened interest the news of the Jewish Agency for Palestine, an organization recognized by Great Britain and other Powers as representing the interests of the Jews in the Holy Land, and they also began to give more attention to the doings of Dr. Chaim Weizmann, the head of the Agency.

What happened to these immigrant Jews happened, in a somewhat different way, to their sons and daughters. Many of these younger folk, who had enjoyed the advantages of American education and opportunity, had for long looked upon their parents as old-fashioned, and upon their devotion to Judaism and Jewishness as forms of vulgar parochialism. But the Hitler horror had made them reconsider their attitudes, and the callousness of the humanitarian, democratic countries to the plight of the Jews had shocked them. These intellectuals had put pretty much all their faith in the decency of the civilized world, in the rising education of the masses and their consequent greater enlightenment, so that these same masses would raise their voices in protest at whatever inhumanity was practiced anywhere in the world.

Alas, nothing of the sort happened. The young Jewish intellectuals saw little proof of any deep sense of outrage on the part of these people at what Hitler had done; indeed, they seemed to welcome, at least to sympathize with, the more than half anti-Semitic and certainly anti-democratic views of men like Father Charles Coughlin and Gerald L. K. Smith. There appeared to be a feeling among many of these people that what Hitler was doing was not entirely bad. Hitler was somewhat "extreme," but, as some of the more vulgar said, "the Jews had it coming to them." What was even more disturbing was the general apathy of many so-called intellectuals. It was difficult to put into words the attitude of these intellectuals, they said the right things about Hitler and the Nazi atrocities, but such feelings as they had about both were on the surface. They just didn't care enough; even the editors of the *Globe* didn't care enough. David had been deeply hurt by this attitude at the *Globe*.

Soon there developed a lost generation of Jews—Jews who had strayed from the beliefs and customs and traditions of their parents and grandparents, believing that true civilized living was to be found in the "outside" world, and then they discovered that this "outside" world was not their world either. It was a period of great disillusion for many Jewish men and women, a period of rethinking of positions, a period of agonizing reappraisal. For some time they were so dismayed they hardly knew what to do. There didn't seem to be any salvation for them. Their whole body of faith seemed to have crumbled. Slowly, almost unconsciously, they veered in the direction of the very traditions and customs and beliefs that they had rejected, and soon they were listening with more respect and concern to what their fathers and mothers and uncles and grandparents were say-

33

ing about the Jewish situation in the world. They began to read books with Jewish content, histories, biographies, political commentaries, novels, short stories, and they began to go to lectures in Jewish centers and synagogues and temples and lodge halls.

They discovered several things that comforted them. At these gatherings they were among their own kind, and in that alone they found an almost animal peace and ease. They liked the humor of these very people at whom they had sneered, in one way or another, a decade or two before; they liked their general lack of hysteria in the face of what was happening in the world—they were shocked, of course, but one got the feeling that they had been through such situations before and would somehow extricate themselves from this one, too; they were surprised how well informed these people were—how well informed, especially, the rabbis were . . . and as they listened to the rabbis they were pleased to note that these men were not obscurantists, but well trained, most of them, well read, and in general of superior intellectual bearing.

The musicians and the sculptors and the dramatists and the novelists and poets among these intellectuals began to find rich material for creativity in the Jewish life to which they were returning. The painters among them realized what Marc Chagall, in Europe, had known for decades, that Jewish lore was full of wonderful material, and they began to plan Jewish works of their own. Some of the Jewish dramatists had already used Jewish material in their plays, but now they began to think of entire plays devoted to Jewish life. But it was the fiction writers who were probably the first fully to avail themselves of the rediscovered resources.

The intellectuals now wondered whether Zionism really was the parochial and backward philosophy that they had thought . . . on the contrary, Zionism began to seem as a realistic philosophy, perhaps the only solution to the world-wide Jewish problem. Some place had to be found to give homes to the refugees, a place that belonged to the Jews, a place that was real home to whatever Jews wanted to come there, and that place clearly had to be Palestine. For two thousand years Jews had been praying to return to their former homeland, for nearly two thousand years Jews had been buried with little pillows of Palestine soil under their heads. Palestine was the only place. Dr. Herzl and Nahum Sokolov and Shmarya Levin and Max Nordau were right, after all. Thus the older generation and the younger generation of Jews came together, at least, approached each other.

David was very sensitive to what was happening in the Jewish community. Even Feivel (Phil) Sirkin, an old "liberated" Jewish friend of his, who still objected to "nationalism of every sort, and Jewish nationalism is no different," wasn't too violent about the resurgence of Zionist sentiment in the United States. "I suppose we need it, for awhile anyway." David was now more determined than ever before to devote his writing largely to Jewish themes, there was an intimacy about such themes that more general themes did not have. He was filled with a deep sorrow when he thought of Sylvia, how she would have been delighted with all these developments, how comforting to both, it would have been to discuss them. . . "Our Sylvia is no more," her mother had written to him from Arizona . . . he still didn't quite believe it. He must get in touch with her parents again, he hadn't seen them or written to them for so very long now. He had postponed seeing them again from week to week, he was ashamed to think exactly how long.

His irresolution was interrupted by a telephone call one morning at the office of the *Globe*. He recognized the voice at once. It was a voice out of a past so distant that it seemed decades since he had last heard it. It was the voice of Alice Cohen, the girl whom he had first met in Hebrew School Yvrioh when both of them were not yet in their teens, she was the girl the very thought of whom had given him so much comfort in his bewildered days in high school and in college, and the girl who somehow drifted away from him not long afterward. He was glad to hear from her, and he was also embarrassed, though he didn't know exactly why in either case. She seemed a little excited. She and a girl friend were going on a short trip to the South and then to Mexico, and she added, "I happened to see a copy of the *Globe* on the newsstand, so I naturally thought of you, and I thought you wouldn't mind if I called just to say hello."

"I'm glad you did," he said, and didn't know how to go on . . . somehow an anger was rising up within him.

"My girl friend, you don't know her, has to visit some relative in Brooklyn, and I thought, if you're free, that is, we might have a coffee or something, if you want to, that is."

"That would be nice," said David, "very nice, but lunch, I'm sorry to say, is out, I have another engagement."

"Oh, no, no, I don't want you to put yourself out in the slightest . . . "

David was annoyed at the tone of self-pity in Alice's voice. "It just happens," he began, "it's something . . . but maybe we can have a coffee about three, anywhere you say."

They agreed to meet at the Savarin cafeteria in the Pennsylvania Station. "That will be fine," Alice said. "Gertrude, that's my girl friend, will be at the station at 3:45, our train leaves at 3:50, so that will work out fine."

David had no lunch appointment, but he couldn't get himself to have lunch with Alice. In two, three minutes of talking on the telephone she managed to irritate him. Her manner was strange, there was something belligerent in it. For a moment he wished he hadn't made any appointment with her.

He recognized her at once at the cafeteria, and his heart sank at the realization of what the years had done to her. Her face was pretty much the same shape it was when he had last seen her, but now she was using more make-up. Her lips were bright red, and he wondered whether she hadn't done something to her eye-brows, and her forehead seemed to bulge out more, and to shine unnaturally. Her bosom now was quite full, and her body below her hips was also fuller than it used to be . . . he looked at her and he saw that her hair was a dark brown, he remembered it as being more black than brown.

"Hello," he said, hardly above a whisper. "It's nice seeing you."

"Nice seeing you. For a while I thought you were going to give me a complete physical examination."

They sat down for coffee and cake. David noticed that Alice's fingers had become rounder than he remembered them, and the new roundness didn't please him. She appeared to be staring at him as they talked. She now had a permanent job in the Bos-

36

ton public school system, she was teaching English and American history, mostly English, which was her major in college. She already had her Master's degree, which was also in English. She didn't seem to have anything more to say, and David wondered precisely what had prompted her to call him. A certain pity for her was coming over him, though he wasn't sure why he pitied her. She said she had read his articles in the *Globe* and elsewhere, she also said that she read some of his poems and stories which were appearing in various magazines. "A girl friend told me about them," said Alice, "so naturally I read them. Very good. I suppose you're writing a book?"

"Yes, I am, a novel, I hope it will be a novel."

"How nice. I'm sure it will be good."

There were several silences between them . . . now and then Alice would look intently at him, and then she would look down at the table, brushing away imaginary crumbs . . . he himself was conscious of roving, with his eyes, over the restaurant.

Suddenly Alice raised her head and looked straight at David and asked, "Are you happy?"

David smiled. "That's a big question. It's hard to answer with a yes or no. It's hard to say. Are you?"

Alice smiled, and David recognized something . . . there was a hint, in that smile, of the loveliness and the warmth and the wonderment that had been Alice so many years ago. An ache of recollection ran through David's heart and mind. "As you say, it's hard to say," she said. "I like teaching. I go to lectures, read, but whether that's happiness I don't know. What is happiness?"

"I don't know," said David. "I guess it's something you remember." He stopped suddenly. He had said more than he had wanted. He looked at Alice. She obviously realized that he had said more than he probably had wanted, that he had unwittingly touched upon something in their past, something that was still too tender even to recall in any detail, something that was both wonderful and sorrowful.

There were a few moments of tense silence between them. David was sure that Alice still was unmarried, he was sure she knew that he was still unmarried. He wondered if she knew about Sylvia . . . somehow it didn't really matter to him either way . . . Sylvia was in no part of Alice's life . . . and yet Alice, in some wisp of a way, so to speak, was still part of David's life and he was part of her life, total strangeness and indifference had not yet come between them, though a good deal of both was already there.

"Have you ever been in the South?" asked Alice.

"No, not farther South than Baltimore."

"Mexico?"

"No."

"My girl friend, Gertrude, has been to Mexico several times, she says she loves it there, she even speaks a little Spanish. I don't know a word she says in Spanish. Do you know Spanish?"

"Only one word, *hoy,* which means today."

Alice laughed. "Know what I'm going to do before I get on the train?"

"What?"

"I'm going to buy for myself as many mystery novels, you know the paperbacks, and mystery magazines as I can, and I'll read all on the way down, and on the way back I'll buy another batch."

"Why?" asked David in great surprise, which slowly turned to vague sadness.

"They make me forget everything, they're so wonderful. I love them, don't you?"

"Well . . . "

"Too lowbrow for you?" she said, smiling.

"No, it's not that, it's only that there's nothing in them, read one and you've read them all, I mean . . . "

"Well, Christopher Morley and Marlene Dietrich and people like that find them good reading," said Alice, with a trace of belligerence in her voice.

"I know," said David, finally.

"Don't be so sad," said Alice. "It's not so bad, really, the world won't come to an end."

"No, it won't, I guess. Still, there are things . . . "

"I know, the war, the Jews, President Truman. I'm not saying they're not important, but they get me all confused, so I read mysteries. Do you like science fiction?"

"I know very little about it."

"That's good, too. It's getting more and more popular, really, did you know that?"

David looked at her . . . this was an Alice entirely different from the quiet, tender, warm, sympathetic girl he had known, a girl to whom mysteries and murder stories were entirely alien.

"I know, it is getting popular, science fiction. I did read a story or two by, is there a man called Clarke?"

"Yes, he's wonderful, and there's a man in California, Ray Bradbury, he's probably the best of them all. Some of his pieces appear in the women's magazines, they're very good. You really should read them, David, they'd be quite a change from Dreiser and Hemingway and Faulkner and Sherwood Anderson."

David was annoyed by her argumentative spirit. "I have read some science fiction," he said. "I don't think I've read anything by Ray Bradbury, but I will."

"You won't," Alice said. "I know you. You're still a cultural snob." She smiled, "Now, I don't mean anything personal."

David wanted to ask her what she did mean if she didn't mean it in a personal way, but he was too irritated with her to want to enter into an argument with her. Somehow he began to smile.

"Is there something funny about what I said?" asked Alice, who was beginning to smile also.

"No, nothing funny, except it was funny to hear myself called a snob of any kind. Still, maybe I am."

"Maybe I shouldn't have said it," said Alice.

He said nothing.

"A penny for your thoughts," said Alice.

"I'm sorry, I was just thinking."

Alice put her elbows on the table and her face in her hands. "About what, David?"

David looked straight at her, and he had the feeling that she wanted very much to talk about themselves, about what they had meant to each other in the past, about how much comfort they had given each other . . . she seemed so eager and so defenseless at the same time . . . but he couldn't get himself to say what was on his mind. Alice would be offended, they would argue, and there was no sense in arguing now, after all these years of not even writing to each other.

"Is it a secret?" she asked.

"No, nothing secretive. I'm sorry."

"Oh."

"I've just read a good book," said David. "You might be interested. *Focus,* by Arthur Miller, it's about anti-Semitism. Did you read it?"

"No. Frankly, I don't think I would be interested. Anti-Semitism is an old problem, and a novel won't solve it," said Alice rather emphatically.

David was deeply disturbed by this remark. Alice really hadn't changed since the days when she had labeled his interest in Jewish things as a form of parochialism, when she had defended her brother's opposition to "Jewish nationalism and the special brand of Jewish superstitution that makes them think they are the Chosen People." David was surprised he remembered these words of her brother's, word for word . . .

"Novels don't solve problems," said David, with determined calmness. "They highlight them, they humanize them, they shed light on them, and *Focus* is a good novel. You don't have to read it, I was just saying I found it very interesting."

"It probably is," said Alice, "but there are more important things to read now."

"Yes, there are, I suppose, from one point of view. Still, when six million people are killed, massacred by one man, one nation, isn't that important, too?"

"A whole world, millions of workers massacred, not just six millions, but dozens of millions, in flames, that's important, too," said Alice. "I don't claim to know very much about it, I admit, but you always were a little narrow-minded about the Jews, you concentrated so much attention on them. There are other people in the world, you know."

"There are," David said.

"Is your novel about Jews?"

"A good deal of it is," said David.

"Oh."

"Why do you say, Oh?"

"Goodness, you're still sensitive. I just said Oh, I meant nothing by it. Well, you write well, I'll say that."

"Thanks."

"Oh, there's Gertrude. Hi!" Alice raised her arm.

Gertrude was somewhat taller than Alice, but otherwise they could very well be sisters, thought David.

"Gertrude teaches in the same school I teach in, Roxbury Crossing High, she teaches French and Spanish."

"That's two more languages than I know," said David, in a lame attempt to make funny conversation.

"It must be wonderful to work on the *Globe,*" said Gertrude. "Meeting all those people, and Alice told me about your working with Brandt on the *World,* that must have been really exciting."

"Yes, it was."

"Well, Alice, we better rush along, our train is leaving in exactly seven minutes," said Gertrude.

"Have a good time, both of you," said David. "I envy you the trip."

David and Alice shook hands. Her hand was dry.

"It was nice seeing you," said David.

"You look very well, David. Don't work too hard."

"I won't."

"If I come across a specially interesting card in Mexico I'll send it to you at the *Globe* office, will that be all right?"

"Yes, very much, thank you," said David.

He watched Alice and Gertrude run off to the train. He watched Alice especially. The whole station seemed to be filled suddenly with sorrow. He was sure she would not send him a card, he was sure he would never see her again.

Three

Events moved swiftly in the summer and early fall of 1945.
People expected some of them, and when they came they were,
in a sense, taken for granted. But two, three, four, five weeks
later, their enormity came to their consciousness, and the feeling
of just having witnessed occurrences as tremendous as the
coming and going of the Ice Age or the Age of the Dinosaurs,
made people tingle all over. Germany surrendered, Eisenhower
didn't think enough of this, to go to accept the surrender himself, he sent General Bedell Smith, his Chief of Staff. Hitler,
Goering, Goebbells, Von Ribbentrop and Streicher were fleeing
and hiding like the proverbial rats. Some were apprehended and
held for trial: there would be War Criminals Trials.

Russia joined the war against Japan. On the very day this
was announced in the newspapers and over the radio David,
along with others, had the feeling that Russia was taking advantage of a sure victory. Most people felt that Japan couldn't
possibly hold out now that Germany was defeated, and then
there was the dropping of the Atomic Bomb on Hiroshima and
Nagasaki.

The dropping of the first A-Bomb on Hiroshima sent a
shudder throughout the nation. People were glad that the United
States had such a weapon, which most likely put an end
to the war in the Pacific, and at the same time probably saved

a million American lives, as spokesmen for the military forces said, but they were not exuberantly glad. The weapon was too powerful, too dangerous for mere man to possess.

People began to feel sorry for the Japanese; they had to be defeated, they deserved punishment, but this appeared to be too much. There was, in short, the moral question: all may be fair in love and war, as the saying goes, but it began to appear that some things, in war as in love, aren't fair, but dreadful.

The American people, David sensed, were happy that little of the devastation heaped upon Europe and Japan had come upon them, but there was concern about the future. After all, it would be the United States that would have to supply the major share of the money and the materials for the rebuilding of Europe and Asia, and the giving of such aid, as the aftermath of World War One showed, can be very bitter indeed. The beneficiaries resent their benefactor, they who had been life-and-death friends during the war become suspicious of one another. There are political upheavals in these countries often caused by contests, among the politicians, as to who can call the United States the worst names. There are repercussions in this country, inflation and unemployment. In two decades there is another world conflict. It's all so apparently hopeless, and perhaps inevitable. So it has been down the ages. And now there was another worry. Russia, our former ally, was beginning to sow hatred for us within its own borders and within the borders of its neighboring countries—Poland and Rumania and Bulgaria and Czechoslovakia and Yugoslavia and even Albania. Thus in the peace there was an almost certain promise of darkness to come. The only light was the projected United Nations Organization, but it was a thin, flickering light. After all, the League of Nations established after World War One had also been looked upon as such a light, yet it died of ineffectuality.

David's emotions were in a constant turmoil. He found himself spending hours reading *The New York Times,* eager not to miss anything, and when he finished he was more confused and exhausted than before. The periodicals were seldom of much more help. His own magazine, the *Globe,* merely pontificated. Bourne and Loring and the various contributors generally moralized about what was going on in the world. "The United States should exercise greater forebearance in its dealings with some of the less vehement of the Nazis in conquered Germany . . . General de Gaulle reflects the spirit of La France, and as such must be handled with creative imagination. . . . Stalin is not overly trustful, it is true, yet it must be remembered his land has suffered severely. . . . Let us all live in the hope that this time we shall try to create One World, and until it is created let us live accordingly. . . . It seems to us most unrealistic that now of all times Russia should wish to play *Realpolitik*."

Slowly David began to lose some of his compulsion to follow the events of the world diligently. The dizziness of these events was becoming too much for him, besides he had never really been interested, he had merely been temporarily obsessed, and as his obsession subsided he delved more deeply into the world of his imagination upon which he was drawing for his stories and poems and the novel that was occupying much of his mind. It was a world of Jewishness and of contemporary America, closely linked yet separate and different. What was Jewish and what was American had a common ancestor in the distant past, but then came something that led ancient Americanism, so to speak, in one direction and ancient Judaism in a different direction. David felt himself the very center of this continuing attraction and divergence . . . his Judaism called to him from a great and loving depth, and his Americanism was also near to him, but Judaism had the strength of blood, with all its silent and wholly involved acceptances, whereas Americanism was largely still a matter of conviction.

David was now writing stories based on his great-grandmother and several of her children, on his great-grandfather and his ways, on the many cousins and aunts and uncles and friends and acquaintances of the family-at-large and on his own immediate family, also stories based upon his father's brothers and sisters, and of the life they led back in Russia. He was writing stories about boys and girls he dimly remembered in his childhood in the little village in Russia where he was born—very faint memories: snatches of talk, turns of face, recollections of the appearances of fields and hills and cattle grazing in the distance . . . and the village square, vast, muddy, echoing with horses' hooves . . . a bakeshop, a shoemaker's shop, an apothecary . . . small

44

and clean windows looking out into the square, with mysteries inside, mysterious quiet soft talk indulged in by people that David knew and didn't know, people somewhat older, some not too much older, some very much older, but of his own world . . these memories and all their emotional garlands tumbled over one another in David's mind, filling his heart with love and sorrow for times gone by.

And he remembered a small orchard of fruit trees, on top of a hill not far from where his family had lived. The orchard was surrounded by a high wooden fence, with holes that made wonderful means for peeping within. It was a quiet orchard. David and some of his playmates used to peep into the orchard, taking turns and looking at one another with wonderment at what they had seen and saying nothing, for what they had seen was nothing and it was everything . . . it was quietness punctuated with trees growing and spaces between the trees and around them, and it seemed that the spaces were quiet too, and that there was some invisible growth in them, too . . . and the quiet and the spaces and the growing trees all seemed like from another world, and the whole orchard was embraced in a warm mystery, and David and his friends loved to be embraced by this mystery . . . it was a mystery from a strange past and it was a mystery that also spoke for the strange present, for to little boys the present and the past are close and the mystery of the one overflows into the other, and life is one continuous warmth and mystery overflowing into a life that seems to be flowing along with it.

There were apple trees in that orchard, one could see the apples that had fallen on the ground . . . they were red apples, firm and round apples, and the apples still on the trees seemed to be looking down on them . . and David recalled, vaguely, that his heart yearned to touch and fondle and just keep these apples in his blouse pocket . . . and then he didn't see the apples on the ground . . . someone had taken them away . . . and David was sorry, he didn't want his apples to be taken away . . . then, one day, he saw tall young men, in uniforms, walking in the orchard, holding young girls by the hand . . . he didn't know where they came from . . . and he looked at them and especially at the girls, they had a loveliness that was all their

45

own, and David had never before encountered such loveliness . . . and he heard some of their soft laughter . . . and the couples walked round and round, now disappearing from his view and now almost walking right into the wooden wall where he was . . . then he saw them no more for a long, long time . . .

David thought much about them. They were not like the men and women and boys and girls that he knew in his daily life, in his home, in the synagogue, in the village square . . . they were different, and he asked his mother and she said, "Oh, that orchard, that belongs to the *portiz* (nobleman) Paritsky, he has a house there, and his daughters and sons sometimes use it, but he lives in another place, mostly there is a caretaker there, nobody else."

"I want to go in there, mother, and walk around, like I saw some people, young people, walk there, in the orchard, I mean the young men were in uniforms, I want to walk there too, and pick apples, it looks so beautiful."

Mother smiled and said to David, "I know, I used to look in there, too, through the holes in the fence, it is beautiful, but we mustn't, they are not our people, they are Christians, whatever little we know about Paritsky is not bad, but a Christian is a Christian, and we associate with them mostly during the day, mainly in matters that are not social. We leave them alone, and we are glad if they leave us alone. That's the way it is. When you grow up, you'll know better what I am trying to say to you. But the orchard is beautiful. Trees make any place look beautiful, trees and grass and fruit, and a beautiful apple is very beautiful."

This David never forgot . . . "We leave them alone, and we are glad if they leave us alone . . . they are not our people . . ." As David grew older, here in America, and as the years of association with Jews and Christians multiplied, he changed many times his views of what he recalled his mother saying those many years back in Russia. He had thought that what she said was untrue and unjust and the result of deliberate parochialism on the part of Jewish people of "the older generation." In a democracy, he was convinced, all people are our people, and it was wrong even to think otherwise. Then he began to doubt his own former doubts about what his mother had said. Even as a little boy in Boston he had sensed, somewhere in the inner-most recesses of his boyish heart, that non-Jews were different, in some way or other, from Jews . . . that there was some reservation in the friendship of non-Jewish boys with Jewish boys. David sensed a coolness, slight but evident, even in the way the parents of the non-Jewish boys greeted David and his Jewish friends. David dug deep into his memories, and he was astonished how much he remembered about the way he had felt then. Impressions were beating upon him, in the gentle way that impressions beat upon the heart of a young and exuberant boy, eager for one excitement after another.

All America was a huge excitement to him, exactly the kind of excitement that suited him. America was new and vibrant, its history was so much like the history of the Jews, and later on in his life he began to see specific events or groups of events in common between the two histories. The heroes of American history were so much like the heroes of Jewish history: Paul Revere was like Bar Kochba in some way, Thomas Paine was like Moses, and so, it seemed, were Thomas Jefferson and George Washington, the first more so than the second. There were many Moseses in American history. The early New England divines were so much like the great Jewish rabbis: there was Jonathan Edwards, a great philosopher, who was a combination of Rabbis Hillel and Shamai . . . and Benjamin Franklin was a sort of kindly prophet . . .there were times when David, as a high school student, used to have fleeting notions that Franklin was something like the Vilner Goan (the great rabbi of Vilna), learned but not fanatical, inflexible as to principle but not at all unmindful of the weaknesses of the human heart and mind.

These and so many other excitments ran through his young mind and heart, and they remained there and they grew there and they became clearer with time. But, back then, David used to sense that while his non-Jewish friends were receptive, so to speak, to his excitements, they looked upon him as, somehow, strange, they seemed to think that he was overly excited, they loved America, of course, but they didn't seem to be able to understand why David loved it so much more, why he thrilled so to the whole American story. And then when he went to college he noticed the same difference. The non-Jews accepted Amer-

47

ica, he and other Jews were openly and continuously delighted with it. That was the difference, and it was a big difference; perhaps, David thought later, this was in part what the non-Jews really meant when they spoke of Jews as being aggressive.

In college he came upon what was till then the worst type of what he thought of as anti-Semitism: he had overheard a secretary in one of the college offices, where he worked as a scholarship student, call him "a grease-faced Jew." David never got over the hurt that that remark gave him. He thought he also saw a bewilderment in the eyes of some of the professors when dealing with Jewish students, they seemed troubled by the complexity of their questions and by the persistence of their questions. Jews were a questioning people, David began to think, always questioning, taking nothing on faith, questioning their rabbis and their other leaders, questioning the Bible and all the interpretations of it, questioning and studying and questioning some more. But non-Jews, it appeared, while also questioning, nevertheless were more often inclined to accept ideas on faith or on authority.

Now and then David did think that perhaps he was being "overly sensitive," as some non-Jews and even many Jews said about Jews in general—"You people see anti-Semitism where there simply isn't any, you take every honest and constructive criticism as a sign of anti Semitism, you mustn't be so sensitive . . ." David had often thought that there was perhaps some truth in this criticism of some Jews and of himself in particular, but as he grew older he wasn't so sure about the justness of the criticism. More and more he began to wonder whether it was possible for any non-Jew ever not to have some slight amount of anti-Jewish feeling . . . they seemed to look upon the Jew as a constant stranger in their midst, different from them, destined always to be different from them. So perhaps David's mother was right after all, and this was one of the things he determined to write about. It was this resolve that lifted David above the bewilderment of his day, that gave him a wonderful sense of dedication and determination.

He was confirmed in this feeling by his experiences at the home of the Tobiases. He was deeply attracted to and impressed by Mrs. Mary Tobias, from the first time he met her at the New

Year's party that Edith Loring of the *Globe* gave . . . She appeared to be the ideal Jewish-American woman, totally Jewish and completely American at the same time. She seemed to be the contemporary American counterpart of his own Alte Bobbe, perhaps not as profound but very nearly as understanding. Raphael Tobias, not so appealing to David as his wife, nevertheless was good to come back to, so to speak, now and then.

Mary Tobias had also done something else of great importance to David, she had openly expressed the belief that he should write about Jewish subjects, for they were so close to him. This belief had been unconscious in his mind, but as soon as she had told him how she felt about his future writing career, he knew at once that she was right.

The Tobias home was a gathering place for leading Jews of New York and for some out of New York. Mary's parents had been active in the Conservative movement in American Judaism; her father, in fact, was one of the founders of the Jewish Theological Seminary and was a friend of Dr. Solomon Shechter, the great scholar who did so much to shape the Seminary. Mary's mother had been a friend of Henrietta Szold, founder of Hadassah. Towards the end of his life, Mary's father had lost some of his interest in the Conservative movement, because he thought it didn't go far enough in its adjustment to American life, so he became a member of Temple Emanuel, on Fifth Avenue in New York, largely because he was an admirer of the then rabbi of the temple, Dr. Judah Magnes. He was now a member both of a Conservative synagogue and a Reform temple, he contributed to both movements. For a long time he was doubtful of Zionism as a solution to the Jewish problem, and thus disagreed with his wife, to whom Zionism was the chief solution, but not long before he died (and his wife died shortly afterward) he changed his mind and looked upon Zionism as the only major hope for the Jews of the world. The Tobias home thus became the gathering place for Conservative Jews, Reform Jews, Hadassah women, and Zionists. About the same time that Tobias Senior became a Zionist he joined the B'nai B'rith lodge, with the result that functionaries of B'nai B'rith would also come to the house.

David's first impression of the Tobias home was one of amazement at the great interest in Judaism that was taken by almost everybody who went there. As a boy in Boston, as the son of an Orthodox father, and as a resident of the slum area of Boston, David had somehow got the idea that only, or chiefly, Orthodox Jews had real interest in the welfare of the Jews, that Americanized Jews and certainly Reform Jews, had only a mild interest in Jews. David had no facts upon which to base this misconception, but is was a misconception that was quite prevalent in that part of Boston David lived in. It was reinforced by the little that David did know about Reform Judaism. Many Reform temples conducted religious services on Sunday, an appalling thing to David, for to him Saturday was the true Jewish weekly holiday, and Sunday was the Christian weekly holiday. Then Reform Jews were, as a group, against Zionism, and this made no sense to David, for he had been brought up in a home where a picture of Dr. Theodor Herzl was hung directly above the kitchen table, and David had never met intimately anybody who was not a Zionist. As for Conservative Jews, David had barely heard of them, and he knew of no Conservative temple in Boston—he had heard of Temple Mishkan Tefila in Roxbury, a Conservative temple, but David had never been there, and what he had heard about it gave him the impression that it was little different from a Reform temple.

After leaving college and while working on the Hancock *Register,* in a suburb of Boston, David had got to be better acquainted with what Conservatism stood for, and he also became better informed about Reform Judaism, yet it was a long time before he could accept either of them, especially Reform Judaism, as authentic Judaism. When he came to New York City, he became still better informed about both Conservative and Reform Judaism, had gone to services in both types of synagogues and been moved by them, and he was enormously impressed by Rabbi Stephen S. Wise, whose sermons in the early 1930's calling upon Jews and Americans alike to wake up to the menace of Hitler had stirred David profoundly. But so conditioned had David been by his youth that, despite all this, he was still in doubt about the complete Jewishness of non-Orthodox or non-Zionist Jews. David's attitude was a maze of contradictions. Jews who were not Zionists were not real Jews, and yet Orthodox Jews who were not Zionists (and many of them were not) were Jews, but this did not apply to Reform Jews who were not Zionists. Rabbi Wise was a Reform Jew who was a Zionist and who was vigorously anti-Hitler, but to David he was an exception.

It was at the Tobias home that David finally saw how wrong he had been. There he saw that the Jewish world was far more inclusive than the small part of it he had inhabited. He saw for the first time that one could be a very good Jew and not subscribe to all the rules that some Orthodox Jews thought were all-binding. He saw for the first time truly that there was such a thing as cultural Judaism, and nationalistic Judaism, and what might be called scholarly Judaism. It was at the Tobias home that he learned for the first time that Dr. Max Nordau's wife was a non-Jew, and that Saul Tchernichovsky's wife was also non-Jewish, and that so was Israel Zangwill's wife. The knowledge disturbed him at the beginning, but then, he began to accept it as a fact and not allow it to color his views about Nordau's and Tchernichovsky's and Zangwill's Judaism. These men were Jews of great value to Jews, and their private lives were of minor, if any, importance. And it was at the Tobias home that he saw how wrong he had been about the Conservative and Reform rabbis—many of them, he was delighted to learn, were men of great learning and great spirituality.

David's sense of the grandeur of Jewish life in the modern world grew in the Tobias home. There he heard discussions of Jewish life in relationship to Roman law and Babylonian law, which he had never heard in his home or in the little *shulen* where he had gone as a boy in Boston; there, also for the first time on such a scale, he heard discussions of Jewish music as a great art in itself, as an influence on early Christian music, as a molder of much of modern European and American instrumental music and choral music, and he also learned much about the position of the cantorial art in Jewish life and of the cantor in religious life down the ages; and there he also heard much about Jewish archeology and dancing and painting and sculpture and architecture and ceramics—and as he heard such things his heart expanded with pride in his heritage. David now thought he knew better than ever before why Jewishness has managed to survive so many persecutions.

One of the men he met at the Tobias home was Dr. Shmaryahu Nichtenhauser, a short man with a clubfoot, who always seemed to have a smile in his eyes and around his mouth and who had an impressive forehead, and who seemed to know the world of the Middle East, especially that around Palestine, with encyclopedic scope and depth. He spoke Hebrew, Yiddish, Turkish, Arabic, French and German. He played the volin and the piano and he was well versed in musical history. There was, one night, a piano concert at the Tobias home, and afterward at the table there was a discussion of the music of Mozart and of Beethoven, and Dr. Nichtenhauser said: "Mozart is the lovely woman of music, he is the Mona Lisa who talks and sings, especially sings, he is the dream in every woman's heart, he is the dream in every beloved woman's heart, for he knows the glories of being loved, as a beloved woman knows, and Mozart, like the beloved woman, also knows that with love comes a silent sorrow, for the beloved woman knows that love is not immortal, it cools with time, and it cools with age, it brings only memories later, and a memory can never approach a quiet kiss at midnight. Mozart is therefore the perfect composer for men and women alike, and he is the composer for all ages, young and old, for whoever is capable of love is always capable of realizing its evanescence, and this women know better than men, perhaps, and this is why I say Mozart is the lovely woman of music.

"Beethoven, he is the strong, sweet man of musical history. He is superhuman, I mean, he is less interested in men and women, and more in God, and, of course, since he sings about God, he has to sing about men and women at the same time, since man is God's image. But the singing is not direct, as it is in Mozart's case, I mean the singing about men and women. And love to Beethoven is something special. He loves woman not for herself, but for what she reveals about God. That is, woman is God's chief vehicle of expression on earth. In Christian mythological language, Beethoven seems to say that there is no Jesus, there is only a Mary. But, of course, Beethoven was not a believer, for that matter, neither was Mozart. Mozart was so otherworldly, so much of a non-believer that he belonged at the same time to both the Catholic Church and the Masons, and the Catholics hate the Masons like poison, but that didn't bother Mozart, he hated nobody. Beethoven was a metaphysical composer, as say, John Donne was a metaphysical poet, whereas Mozart was the John Keats of music. In Jewish terms, perhaps it would be correct to say that Beethoven was the Rambam of music, whereas Mozart was the Hillel. Mozart was a *Chassid,* Beethoven was a *Mithnagid,* the one a lyricist, the other was an intellectual. Of course, this is over-simplifying the matter, but there is some truth in it."

David had never before heard such marvelous talk about music. It was philosophical and literary and worldly. It dealt with music as an aspect of life lived by men and women of culture, and it was, in some mystical sense, also Jewish talk—it roamed over the whole realm of human history, it was in-stinct with cultural allusiveness, it was sensitive to the nuances of the human soul and of every art form, and always it ques-tioned and generalized and sympathized and yearned for every expression of love, and for every echo and aroma of the glory of existence in every area of creation.

Dr. Nichtenhauser was a new type of Jewish intellectual to David. He was worldly, yet he was deeply Jewish. David learned that he had been born in New York City—and this surprised David, for he had thought, somehow, that only Jews born in Europe could really be interested in Jewish affairs, those born in this country were Jews chiefly by birth. Dr. Nichten-hauser went to the public schools here, then to City College, then to law school, but he was in the practice of law only one year, deciding to abandon the law entirely and become a high school teacher of English. He worked up fast in the ranks of high school teaching, so that in about five years he was an assistant principal.

His interest in Jewishness began at a very early age. His own father was a Zionist but he was also religious, belonging to a Conservative synagogue. Young Shmaryahu did very well in Hebrew school where he studied *Yvrith 'bYvrith* (literally, Hebrew in Hebrew). He belonged to the Zionist club there, later becoming its president. He also was one of the editors of the school Hebrew magazine, contributing fiery articles and editorials in favor of Zionism and the "sacredness of the Hebrew language as against Yiddish, which is a mere jargon, a hodge-podge, without a history and without a tradition." Shmaryahu naturally continued his interest in Zionism in City College, and after college he joined the Zionist Organization of America. He was elected a delegate to local conventions and later to national conventions. He wrote more and longer articles for such magazines as the *New Palestine,* and soon he was called upon to address organizations of Jewish men and women on the Eastern seaboard. His success in the Zionist movement continued to grow and his fame as a writer and speaker spread over the country. Then came the day when he was proposed for the presidency of the Zionist Organization of America. He wanted the post very much. If elected he would have to make an important decision. He now was the father of two children and he had tenure as a high school teacher. If he took the job of president of the Zionist Organization, his economic status would be jeopardized, for all he could be sure of was a job for one year, with the possibility of being elected for another year or two. Those who sponsored him promised him "some kind of job or other when you are through being president, don't worry about earning a living, rich you won't be from us, but starve you never will either." His wife, who was as dedicated to Zionism as he was, urged him to take the chance. He ran for president and was elected, and for the past twenty-odd years he had been in and out of one office or another in the ZOA.

David had heard from the Tobiases that Dr. Nichtenhauser (he had been given an honorary L.H.D. by one of the Jewish theological seminaries) was "a shrewd politician who knows what he wants and knows how to get it. He can be tricky, and he can smile like a first-class Tammany man, and he can make fantastic promises, a few of which he tries to keep, but his ability to get money for Palestine is phenomenal. You have to hear him shame a rich Jew into giving money for this or that Palestine fund to believe how tricky he can be. But he's honest, absolutely honest. And he's so shrewd that if shrewdness will get the Jews back their homeland, then Dr. Nichtenhauser will do it. Some people say that if necessary he will convert the Pope to Zionism, that's the kind of talker he is."

Dr. Nichtenhauser was the chief representative of the Jewish Agency for Palestine in America. The Agency was a sort of *de facto* government for the Palestinian Jews—actually, it could be said, for the Jews the world over—set up by England with the open or tacit consent of the other democratic nations. Dr. Chaim Weizmann was the president, and Moshe Shertok (who later became Moshe Sharett) was a sort of executive secretary. In many respects the Agency was a truly functioning government. It had representatives in various capitals, it had a central treasury, and, perhaps most important of all, it had high-grade propagandists everywhere, and Dr. Nichtenhauser was one of them. American Jewry came out of the Second World War as the most affluent and the most influential segment of Judaism in the whole world. It was in a position to help its less fortunate co-religionists in the rest of the world, and Dr. Nichtenhauser and his associates saw to it that the American Jews were constantly reminded of their duty.

Will Frimmer, a journalist who was an editor and roving correspondent for *Carousel,* a digest-size magazine that tried to compete with and "improve upon" *Reader's Digest,* once said to David, in a whisper, at the Tobias home, "Nichtenhauser is one of the great mysterious men in contemporary American Jewish life. If Palestine once again becomes the Jewish homeland, it may well be that the chief credit, from one point of view, will be due him. Look at it this way. It will be the American Jews who will put over the deal, one way or another. And Nichtenhauser has the American Jews in the palm of his hand, especially the rich Jews. You know what I mean. Then he knows Washington through and through, every Senator and every important Congressman, and he knows every important Governor in the country, no, every Governor, because to him there is no such thing as an unimportant Governor, because when a Governor talks, even if he is the Governor of Wyoming or Arizona or North Dakota, he is listened to all over the country. After all, a Governor is a Governor.

"If you pick up the *Times* or the Chicago *Tribune* or the Boston *Herald* in your own home town, and you read a pro-

Jewish speech by some big shot, you may be sure that Nichtenhauser has been working on him. And, of course, Nichtenhauser is very friendly with Eddie Jacobson, President Truman's former business partner. Eddie and Harry are very close, you know, and that doesn't hurt the Jews. But one thing you must always remember, and that is that Nichtenhauser is always honest when it comes to Palestine. He'll be tricky, hell, he'll be as tricky as a ward heeler when it comes to keeping himself in a good job in the Zionist organization or the Jewish Agency for Palestine, he loves power, and having a clubfoot he loves power more than does an ordinary man, but he doesn't care much for money. I don't know exactly what his job is now, but I'll bet he doesn't make more than $10,000 a year, and I'm sure he steals nothing on expenses, he's very scrupulous that way. He lives in an ordinary apartment somewhere in Washington Heights, it used to be pretty swell, but is run down now, the building and his apartment, but he still lives there, because the rent is low, he has six rooms that need painting badly, but his landlord won't paint it for him, some legal loophole, and Nichtenhauser says that he can't afford the $400 or so that it would cost him to paint, and I believe him. And have you seen his car? A 1930 Chevrolet! Yes, a piece of junk, but he says it runs, and that's all right with him."

David learned later that Will Frimmer was one of Nichtenhauser's chief advisers and most trusted ghost writers. Will got virtually nothing for his services, and no glory whatever, because it would have hurt his professional standing on his magazine if it were known that he was deeply involved in Zionist activities. Will was tall, bald, middleaged, usually silent, and on first meeting he gave one the impression of being very calm, but as soon as one got to know him a little better one realized that he was a mess of neuroses. Indeed, once Will got to feel intimate with one he was very happy to tell one of many of the things that troubled him. He boasted of not remembering a single day in his life when he felt completely happy for as long as one hour. "I'm afraid of everything and everybody," he once said to David, half smiling but obviously telling what was substantially the truth. He was born in a little town in Nebraska, not far from Omaha. There was only a handful of Jews in the town, so whatever Jewish education the Jewish children obtained they had to get in Omaha, which was almost 10 miles away. Will's parents were second-generation Jews and not too eager about giving their children a thorough Jewish background, so that when Will was bar mitzvah he could barely read the Torah, and the event was more a social occasion for him than a religious one.

For two years Will went to the University of Nebraska, majoring in English. At first he wanted to be a teacher of English, and he contributed a half dozen fair poems to the *Prairie Schooner,* edited by Lowry C. Wimberly, one of the professors, who conducted the magazine not as a college periodical but as a general literary magazine of the highest standards and who was a discoverer of several writers who later on achieved national reputations, the most important of them being, perhaps, Eudora Welty. It was thus a great honor for Will to appear in the *Prairie Schooner.* But then his parents moved to Chicago, so Will finished his bachelor training at the University of Chicago, still as an English major. He was at a loss what to do now: whether to go on for an A.M. in English, thereby assuring himself a position as a full-time regular teacher of English in the public school system of Chicago or virtually any other major community in Illinois, or go on to New York City, find a job on a newspaper and write the great American novel and epic, for Will now felt himself skillful in both prose and poetry.

In New York he met only disappointment. The one newspaper job he could get was on a tabloid. There he began as a reporter of fires and police arrests in the Bronx, and all he was allowed to do was to state the facts as briefly as possible, the bare facts and nothing else. As he wrote to his fiancee in Chicago, "I feel like a merchant of paper or of pencils, it's most frustrating." His fiancee whose name was Phyllis Ackerman and who came from a much more Jewish family than his, encouraged him: "It's only a makeshift, dear, so take it only as a job. I'm glad you're writing, on the side, what you really want to do. I have every faith in you."

He wanted her faith very much, since he had little faith in himself. He did write on the side, had been doing so for almost six months, and hadn't sold a thing, not a single poem, not a single story, not a single joke. His heart was set on "making" the *New Yorker,* he was sure that his poetry and his fiction were of the same tone as the fiction and poetry that the magazine printed—he was sure that he was almost as good as, sometimes better than, E. B. White and Wolcott Gibbs and James Thurber and Russell Maloney and Dorothy Parker and Robert Benchley. His favorite two phrases were "well of time" and "cold as limitless space." He wanted to establish both phrases as, so to speak, his trade-mark, he was sure nobody else had ever used them. He once wrote a story about a Park Avenue young girl (he had never been to a Park Avenue home, but he had seen pictures of their interiors in some of the women's and society magazines) who couldn't make up her mind whether to become the mistress of a married young stock broker or an engaged young, struggling poet, who frankly loved her for her body, and said so bluntly. In the end she decided to become the mistress of a young high school teacher, who drank heavily because his young wife wanted to be, in his words, "a fake Park Avenue duchess," whereas he wanted her to be "a real woman," and this was something that the hesitating Park Avenue girl understood fully. Will ended the story with the observation, "Even in the high-school teacher's real arms, Emily still didn't feel truly real, but she felt that if this too was failure it at least was real failure." . . . this "typical New Yorker short story" came back within three days, with no more than a printed rejection slip. He had got several pencilled comments ("Sorry" . . . "Try again" . . . "Not for us" . . . "Thanks") on stories that he had considered much inferior.

Will wrote poetry like William Carlos Williams', and it came back. He wrote poetry like Léonie Adams's, and it came back. He wrote poetry like E. E. Cummings', and it came back. He wrote poetry like Karl Shapiro's, and it came back. Deep down he really didn't like the poetry of any of these writers, but he thought that if he imitated them, he could get into the *New Yorker.* Then he tried writing poetry "like myself," as he told a barroom acquaintance (he was now going to bars on Third Avenue, for he liked some of the stories and sketches of life in Third Avenue bars that appeared in the *New Yorker,* and he thought he might pick up some *New Yorker* atmosphere in them). He wrote free verse about "The Cool Breezes of the Third Avenue Express," "The Ghost of Verlaine Visits Mc-Tavish's Tavern," and "Sappho the Jazz Baby." But they, too, came back. He decided that his fiction was "too vigorous" and his poetry "too blunt and daring" for the "strictly commercial magazines or the Nice Nelly periodicals," in which he now lumped the *New Yorker.* So he sent all his rejected short fiction and verse to several of the "little magazines," such as the *Kenyon Review,* the *Sewanee Review, Tanager,* the *Rocky Mountain Review,* and the *Prairie Schooner,* and again his manuscripts came back, with barely a note on them. What hurt him especially was a brief note from Professor Wimberly of the *Prairie Schooner* attached to one of his stories: "This doesn't seem like you at all, Will, but it's always a pleasure to hear from you."

Will didn't tell his writing disappointments to Phyllis, he was ashamed, and then his shame intensified because he felt he was somehow being unfaithful to her trust in him . . . "a hell of a way of beginning a life together," he said to himself. When she asked him outright how he was doing with his "real work," he would answer, "Marvelous. I'm filling pages upon pages with *real* stuff. If the editors will want it, I'll be pleased. If they won't I'll at least have the satisfaction of being honest with myself, of writing the truth." Phyllis answered, "I love you for saying this, for being yourself, I love you, darling." Now he was still more ashamed of himself.

He got a new job, on the *Evening Express,* which was a notch above the Hearst papers in New York City. He was quickly put on the rewrite desk, which he liked better than reporting, but then he realized that, for him, being on the rewrite desk was not really a promotion but a demotion. When he was a reporter he at least wrote his own lifeless stuff, now he added lifelessness to the lifeless stuff written by others. He felt trapped. Now he could barely write any of his own "honest, real" stories and poems. Soon he stopped writing his own things altogether, for he sensed that he was only filling pages of poor imitations of the work of people whom he didn't especially like, and that he couldn't write his own stories or poems because he had spent so much time being other people that he had lost contact with his own soul. What he wanted most of all now was to find himself, but a new-old obstacle had come his way. He knew it was coming, and it really wasn't altogether an obstacle, because, in a sense, he desired it.

Phyllis had made him agree to marry her on a certain date, and she had gone along and made "preparations," and he had never realized what such preparations were till two days before she came to New York: she had bought a half dozen bed sheets ("We'll need more, dear, of course, but this will do for the beginning"), two dozen face towels and a dozen and a half Turkish towels ("the best fluffy kind, dear, like you once told me you liked"—he did not remember ever saying this to her, but if she said so then it was true, Phyllis had a remarkable memory), she was "just thrilled with a simple Gorham silver service that mother gave us as a grand surprise, she's such a dear, and with the proper initials, too, dear, when mother does something she does it just right, she loves you"), and there was a cake mixer, and several kinds of cooking pots. Will wondered how she would get all this material into the little two-room apartment that he was living in, and that she had agreed would be "perfectly darling for both of us" . . .

His head swam from sheer bewilderment. He loved Phyllis, he had promised to marry her on the date that she remembered so well but that was in a sort of lonesome corner of his mind where it could barely make itself known to his full consciousness. He wrote back to Phyllis glowing letters expressing his delightful expectations. Phyllis had generously promised to marry him "just us, with nobody, by some rabbi, at least a Conservative rabbi, dear, and mother says she's sure you won't mind that when we both come back home for a visit, which she hopes will be in three, four weeks, you won't mind, if she arranges something just a little more elaborate, with Rabbi Goldman of our temple, another wedding, for the family, yours, too, of course, in fact, mother has already written your folks. Being married twice will be simply grand, I'm thrilled at the thought." There was something about this arrangement that Will didn't like, but there was nothing he could do. What surprised him most of all was the sort of girl that Phyllis was revealing herself to be. This was hardly the girl he had fallen in love with, this was hardly the girl who had written him those lovely and loving and encouraging and soft letters in the early days of their engagement. She wasn't loving him now, he felt, she was managing him . . . he was in a confusion of emotions about her, about himself, about their marriage, about his immediate future and his more remote future. Then, one afternoon, he found himself a fully married man. That night he felt more helpless and more hopeless than ever before in his life.

They had planned not to have children for about three years so that Will could get "established" in his writing and so that they could save up some money. Phyllis had a Chicago teaching license which could easily get her a job as a substitute teacher in the New York public school system. She did get a job, but four months later she discovered she was pregnant. She was delighted, but Will was terrified, though of course he did not say so.

Phyllis told him before marriage that she wanted to run a kosher house "for my mother, and, frankly, for myself, too, and I want our chaldren to go to Hebrew school, and for them to get a little more Jewish education than you got, dear, you won't mind, will you darling?" He agreed, as he agreed to virtually everything that she suggested, she was so lovely, so desirable, so genuinely in love with him, so devoid of any other interest in life except him that he could not say no to nearly anything she wanted. And yet he resented her hold on him, he felt that with her love for him she was draining his strength, and his talents, whatever they were.

He had hardly written a line of his "real" work since his marriage, he complained mildly to Phyllis, and she said that she understood perfectly and that she herself had thought about it, and she promised that she wouldn't ask him any more to go with her to buy things for the house—but she did ask him over and over again, and he didn't know what to do about it. He didn't want to begin his marriage with a serious battle.

Meanwhile, he was shifted from the rewrite desk on the *Evening Express* to the special features section. This pleased him. Now he could occasionally write an article of some length, say, 1,000 words, or even a bit longer, and that made him feel he was a writer, after all. He did feature stories about a Spanish-American War veteran who had reached the age of 100, he did another about an ancient woman—she had no idea how old she was, and neither did her oldest daughter, who seemed to be well in her seventies—who had seen President Lincoln's funeral train pass through Albany, New York, and he did a third one on a young girl, Thelma O. Roy, who made the ballet at Roxy's Theatre at the age of twelve. Somehow this last went over with the proverbial bang, and he got a five dollar a week raise because of it. He then suggested that he do a piece on Gwen Dudley Powers, a very much married actress of sorts who had some notoriety on Broadway and beyond. The managing editor was in doubt: "Hell, what's there to write about her, she's been written about so much, besides, who cares? Another woman who can snare 'em but can't hold 'em." Will persisted: "I think I got a new angle on her, I don't know exactly what the angle is, but I feel it inside." The managing editor looked at him, then told him to go ahead.

Will wrote an article about Gwen Dudley Powers that created even more of a stir than did his article on the twelve-year-old ballet dancer. He had unearthed few new facts about her life, but he did have a relatively new angle on her, as he had told his managing editor. He presented Miss Powers as a sad and lonely woman, who wanted emotional stability so hysterically that men were afraid to give it to her, she was simply incapable of quiet, pervading love. She was something of a child emotionally in that she asked of love that it be always at white heat. Money actually was the least of her desires, she had simple tastes in food and clothing and was content with a modest home. There was one thing she wanted very much, to the great surprise of her many husbands, and that was children. At the moment she appeared to be relaxing between husbands—and one point Will made was that she was not laying a trap for still another husband, as some columnists hinted broadly, but she was bemoaning her fate that genuine love had evaded her, that she had achieved a reputation for being something she was not—and, most of all, that she was rapidly approaching an age when the begetting of children would no longer be possible.

This was a relatively fresh attitude toward Miss Powers, and Will wrote with just enough *schmaltz* to make people think they were reading a truly profound literary work. Will himself began to think that perhaps his piece really was literature. His managing editor told him so, Phyllis told him so, many unknown correspondents told him so, so perhaps it was so. There was one sentence that Will liked especially: "Miss Powers is lonely, which, alas, is the lot of all women; she is also very unhappy, which need not be the lot of any woman." Will expressed his delight with this sentence to Phyllis, and she said, "Darling, I'm so glad to hear this. When I first read it, I cried, it was so beautiful. You sort of got right into that poor woman's soul. You have every reason to be proud. You're a real writer."

He now was the father of two children, with a third on the way. In the three and a half years of his marriage he had written one and a half short stories, he somehow couldn't finish the second. He had sent the first one to the *New Yorker,* and it came back with a printed rejection slip, and he was so discouraged that he sent it nowhere else. In the same period of time he had started a half dozen poems and finished none. He felt he had to write another piece on the order of his article on Miss Powers to be able to live with himself, for he was a very unhappy man, as unhappy as he said Miss Powers was. Phyllis was a good mother and a good wife, but a rather obtuse companion, she seemed to have little idea of what was going on in his mind. Yet he loved her, and he was fond of the children. He liked especially the Jewish atmosphere she had brought to the house—the candles she lit every Friday night, the Hebrew and Yiddish songs she sang to the children, and he was glad that she joined a neighborhood temple. At first, he had no intention of going there more than three times a year, the two days of Rosh Hashonoh and the one day of Yom Kippur. But when the Adult Education Program of Lectures was announced he decided to go to some of them. One of the lectures was Dr. Shmaryahu Nichtenhauser. He spoke on "Zionism and the Destiny of the Jewish People." Will was impressed and stirred. The Jews did seem to be a People of Destiny, and Zionism, as Dr. Nichtenhauser explained it, made a lot of sense. Will had heard of Zionism before, of course, but he had looked upon it as something that only elderly people from Eastern Europe concerned themselves with. He decided to look further into Zionism, and also to hear Dr. Nichtenhauser whenever possible. He liked that man.

He suggested he do an article on Dr. Nichtenhauser for the *Evening Express,* but the managing editor would not permit him. "Nobody knows him," he said. "Besides, I think your strong point is women. It's a hunch I have. Think of some other woman, and I'll probably say yes." Will was both offended and delighted—offended because he wanted very much to meet Dr. Nichtenhauser and really get to know him, and delighted because the managing editor had such confidence in him. Then again, he had the feeling that writing about women, as he did, was a form of creative writing: one really had to be an artist to understand women. Men were all right for straight articles, but women demanded deep analysis, and one could write about them only as a poet. Will wondered whether the article he did on Gwen Dudley Powers wasn't really a prose poem. Phyllis as much as said so, and her mother, in a letter from Chicago, came right out and said, "That article is as beautiful as a poem, just beautiful." Perhaps Phyllis's mother had more sensitivity than he had given her credit for.

One evening Phyllis came home from a Temple Sisterhood meeting and told about a movie actress, Hilda Kahn, who had for years been an alcoholic and worse, and then, through Alcoholics Anonymous, had lifted herself from the gutter back to stardom in a forthcoming picture. "She's a Philadelphia girl, Jewish, her people are Orthodox, she was really quite a tramp, as I understand it. She got converted to the Methodist religion or denomination, or whatever you call it. We were just thinking of making an affair out of it, I mean we thought of buying a block of tickets for the opening of the picture, to make some money to buy books of Jewish content for the Sisterhood library. We haven't decided, because many of the girls feel we shouldn't do this with a picture where the leading woman, a Jewish girl, got converted, the picture doesn't say so right out,

64

but it's there. I feel the same way. And I don't think it's being narrow, like one of the girls, Mrs. Tenenabum said, you don't know her."

Will didn't know what to say. He agreed with his wife that it would be funny for a synagogue group of women to make money out of a picture where a convert to Christianity was the star. At the same time he didn't like the idea of boycotting a work of art of any sort because of the religious convictions of one of the participants. It looked too much like the obverse of anti-Semitism. But Will didn't say all this to Phyllis, except, "I guess you're right, darling."

His mind was already working fast in another direction. Hilda Kahn would be a good subject for an article for the *Evening Express*. The managing editor readily agreed. The result was a full-page feature on her, and it was discussed in the whole entertainment world. It was done in pretty much the same subdued, *schmaltzy*, sad-and-simple style of the Gwen Dudley Powers article, but in this case Will really spread himself out. Again Will pleaded with the managing editor to let him do an article on Dr. Nichtenhauser, but again the managing editor said no: "For Christ's sake, haven't I proven to you you're good on women, so stick to them, besides, who the hell gives a damn about this Nichtenhauser?" The managing editor asked for another piece on Hilda Kahn, which Will readily supplied.

It then occurred to Will that there might be a saleable autobiography in Hilda Kahn, and he wanted to ghost it under his name. Hilda agreed. But Will found great difficulty in selling her story to one of the bigger publishing houses. One thought she had no public appeal, another said her story was too sordid, a third said that the public wouldn't buy any book about a former drunk and tramp who changed her religion, a fourth publisher said he wouldn't "dirty" his list with such stuff (he was the same one who made a fortune by publishing the pornographic "novels" of Dick Grazin, who in his fiction specialized in describing minutely the physiology of women). Finally, Will came upon a small publisher who had been in business for only five years, and who frankly was out to make money. A ghosted autobiography of Hilda Kahn appealed to him. "The woman's crazy," he said to Will, "but so is everybody else nowadays. She'll probably go back to drink and to sleeping around, I don't trust re-formed women anyway. I trust them a damn sight less than re-formed men. I'll take a chance." Will was a little upset by the calibre of this publisher, but he was glad that somebody was willing to gamble on his idea. "I'll make something really creative out of this," he said to himself. "Outwardly it will be a ghosted autobiography, but actually it will be a novel." He said this to Phyllis, who replied, "Of course, darling, that's exactly what I was thinking."

The book was a tremendous success commercially, and was bought for the movies for $250,000, of which half went to Will. The reviewers were rather unkind. One called the book "a barrel of schmaltz herring," another said, "It proves that a man can be as much a sob sister as a woman," and a third said that "This tawdry and sleazy 'life' of Hilda Kahn reveals not only the poor subject but also the ghost, who is probably more to be pitied." Will was deeply hurt by such criticism—not one review, even in the Hearst press, said what he wanted it to say, that the book was an honest, probing effort to dig into the soul of a lost woman. All that these Hearst and similar reviewers said, at best, was that the book was "very readable, and should appeal to many movie-goers," a form of praise that did not please Will at all. But as the sales mounted and the requests for serialization came in, Will's hurt to his artistic soul was somewhat dulled. Phyllis was in the proverbial seventh heaven: "It's just marvelous, darling, simply grand. It's almost as good as *Anna Karenina* really. As for the critics, don't pay any attention to them. They don't know everything, and they can be wrong."

Will found it hard to forget the critics. He yearned to do another autobiography for someone. By this time he had resigned his position on the *Evening Express*. He now ghosted the autobiography of Rita Pendleton, the mistress of a celebrated poet who had died in mysterious circumstances in Greenwich Village. This book, too, went over very well commercially, but the reviews were just as poor—and there were fewer of them. Hollywood paid $450,000 for this one. Then Will ghosted the autobiography of Kiki Pam, a second-class Rumanian actress who was plying her trade of courtesan in the more affluent sections of American society. Again Will scored a commercial success —Hollywood paid $500,000 plus a cut of the net, and Will got half of everything. For this book there were hardly any reviews in the better newspapers and magazines—and those that did appear were dreadful. By this time Will had become a bit more accustomed to such reviews. But often, late at night, he would break out into a cold sweat, and his wife would be so frightened that she pleaded with him to let her call a doctor. He told her not to. "It will pass over," he said. She didn't understand what was troubling him. "You are working too hard, dear, you are," she said. "I won't let you. You don't have to, dear, we're well provided for for life. Let's take a long vacation in Europe, in England, anywhere, you owe it to the children, to yourself, to myself." The only vacation he would agree to was a three-weeks cruise in the Caribbean.

There was one thing that Will especially wanted to do: he wanted to prove to the managing editor of the *Evening Express* that he was also "good on men," not just women. He selected a former immigrant from Czechoslovakia, who was now well in his sixties and who still had difficulty with reading, writing and speaking English, but who was a member of the boards of trustees of a large Eastern university, a theological seminary of his faith, two hospitals and a half dozen savings banks. He had given a great deal of money to all these institutions—he made his fortune as an operator and chief stockholder of a chain of grocery stores over the country—and he had a dozen honorary degrees. Will thought that this man personified the story of American opportunity as it had seldom been personified before. He talked the matter over with Phyllis, and for the first time in their married life she hesitated in agreeing with him. "I don't know, darling," she said. "He doesn't appeal to me, but I really don't know why. I just don't think people will be interested, but don't take what I say seriously, you know how little I know about what people want. The other books you wrote, about those women, I was enthusiastic about, as soon as you told me, darling, but this—I don't know. You do what you want, and I'm sure I'm wrong, maybe I shouldn't have said anything, but I would have felt terrible if I didn't."

This opinion troubled Will, but so strong was his desire to prove the managing editor of the *Evening Express* wrong, that he pushed aside Phyllis's doubts. The Czechoslovakian was delighted with Will's proposal. Not long after Will began work on the new book, Phyllis said one evening, "I was thinking, darling, I mean I was wondering why you haven't done a book on Dr. Nichtenhauser, whom you like so much, it would have given you a chance to write about Zionism, about Palestine, and about Jewish affairs in general. But I suppose you did think about it."

Will was startled by what his wife had said. Her suggestion was a perfectly natural one. He was happy that she had thought of it. He was ashamed that he hadn't thought of it—and this very fact made him realize how shabby ambition had pulled him away from what he really wanted: to make some contribution to the understanding of Jewish affairs, particularly Zionism. By this time he had read a great deal in Zionist literature, and he had met Dr. Nichtenhauser several times—and yet he had, so to speak, done nothing about it. Well, he would do a book on Nichtenhauser after the Czechoslovakian book. He said so to his wife, and he thought he noticed a doubt in her eyes—and this hurt him deeply. It was the first time that Phyllis openly, so to speak, did not believe him, and he wondered whether she still believed in him. Now his home, his wife, his last haven of refuge in a world he really couldn't cope with had become a little alien to him. He began to sense some hesitation in Phyllis's kisses and embraces, he thought she was holding things back from him, though he didn't know exactly what she was holding back. Again he remembered, as he had done so many times during the past six years, that he had really done no writing of the sort he wanted: stories, poems, novels, sketches . . . all he could show for the years since he left college was a heap of sneering reviews of his books and close to a million dollars.

Will finished the Czechoslovakian book. It was virtually ignored in the press. The popular newspapers and periodicals, like the more intellectual ones, treated it like a piece of public relations. Worse, the book barely sold. The publisher had put out a first edition of 50,000 hoping to go back to press within two or three weeks after publication, but the book simply didn't move in the bookstores. Only one motion picture company made an offer for it, and the offer was insultingly low for a Will Frimmer book: $50,000.

Will decided that he would write no more "hack stuff," by which he meant the very books that had brought him so much money. From now on he would write only things he truly believed in. But to his dismay he discovered that try as he would what came out was hack stuff: facile, glib phrases that gave the appearance of saying something but actually said nothing.

He sought aid from a psychoanalyst—Phyllis objected to this vigorously: "You're not crazy, darling, I tell you you're not, those psychoanalysts do more harm than good, they'll milk you. What you need is a good long rest and then do just what you want to do. It will be hard at first, darling, but in the end you'll win. You don't have to worry any more about making a living. You have plenty of time. You're only forty-four. Please, darling, don't let those frauds ruin you." Will was impressed by Phyllis's argument, but he just couldn't face himself all alone now, something he didn't dare to tell Phyllis. He needed someone to help him, to be around, when he was looking into himself and seeing what a shambles he had made of his life.

He picked a psychoanalyst who did, as the saying goes, a land-office business with executives on *Life* and *Time* and *Fortune* magazines. He charged Will $35 a fifty-minute hour. This was a steep price, especially when the analyst told him that at the beginning ("for a number of weeks") Will would have to come every day, but Will was so eager for someone to listen to him that he went. For about a month he was exhilarated by the experience: the analyst let him talk to his heart's content, and in that alone there was relief. But then the analyst began to hint to Will that there was an abnormal attachment between Will and his mother. This shocked Will: he loved his mother, but he was sure that there was nothing abnormal in his love. The analyst insisted. Will became angry, and one afternoon he walked out of his office, vowing never to return.

Now he was at a total loss as to what to do with his life. He began to drink secretly—at home and in bars. He joined various clubs chiefly to have a place where he could drop in and drink to his heart's content and with the assurance that if he became a bit intoxicated he would be taken care of. His wife noticed his absences and asked him where he spent his time. He said he was looking for "material." She sensed she better not ask any more questions. Then she smelt liquor on his breath and found an empty bottle of Scotch in his bookcase. She did not let on she had seen it. She was worried but she didn't know what to do. Then she suggested that he go for a general checkup. He went and the doctor told him he had a "nervous heart, nothing organically wrong as yet, but if it persists there may be organic symptoms." He gave him some tranquilizing pills. The doctor also told him his pulse was rather high and his pressure could be lower. "Better drop in every two weeks, for a while, for me to check your pulse and pressure. Nothing wrong, but it's best to be safe." Will did as he was told for a couple of months. Will now found himself taking his own pulse at all hours of the day and night. Then he went into a medical supply store, said he was a doctor, and bought a stethoscope and blood pressure gauge. Now he could take his own pressure and listen to his own heart. Phyllis was appalled. She asked the doctor what she should do. The doctor smiled and said, "There's nothing to do. Now he's in competition with me. Don't worry. He'll get tired listening to his own heart. Just make sure he sees me now and then, say, once a month."

Suddenly Will gave up his heavy drinking and put away his blood pressure paraphernalia. He began to read deeply in Jewish history and philosophy, and he became active in the Jewish Agency. Dr. Nichtenhauser spotted in him someone he could use. He set him to work ghosting pro-Jewish and pro-Palestine speeches to be delivered by Senators and Governors and big businessmen. Will was a superb ghost writer. He was a master of the cliché, and he could weave banalities around a subject with such skill that the listener or reader for a while thought he was learning something. He also made speeches of his own sometimes in behalf of this or that drive, but he didn't like that. He was happy with his ghosting. Apparently that was to be his fate, he said to himself, to write the speeches and articles and books of others. He still yearned to write something "real"— at least one good short story, some good poems, perhaps one novel of quality. He made fresh attempts at a story, but nothing happened. The words came only with great difficulty, and he knew that they were poor anyway. He decided to "take my time. I won't push myself. I'll wait till I really feel I can do it." Meanwhile he would become a better and better Zionist. He was happy that Dr. Nichtenhauser was entrusting more and more important ghosting jobs to him, but he was even happier that he was now on such intimate personal relations with the Zionist leader, who invited him to come along with him to many of the places he him-self was invited to. That was how Will happened to be so much at the home of the Tobiases. They had heard about him from Dr. Nichtenhauser.

By the time David met him Will had a steady job as an associate editor of *Carousel,* a digest-size picture magazine that attempted to rival the *Reader's Digest.* Actually he did little editing. Now and then he would rewrite an article to make it suitable for *Carousel.* He was an excellent rewrite man. He seemed to have an instinct for writing for "the man in the street and the woman in the bathrobe," as one of his superiors said. Now and then he would ghost an autobiographical piece by some actress prominent at the moment. He could come and go as he pleased, and very often he didn't show up at the office for weeks, but nobody said anything. "We get our money's worth out of him," said the chief editor.

Will and David met now and then for lunch, and Will used these occasions to tell and retell to David his whole life, down to some very personal details. Will, it seemed, was getting a little tired of Phyllis, but he didn't have the courage to do any "exploring." Besides, as he told David quite frankly, "I may be ashamed of having failed her, as far as my writing is concerned. To put it bluntly, she knows I'm a hack, and she expected better things from me. But if God chose to make me second-rate, there's nothing much I can do about it." Will was beginning to look upon his ghosting with humor. One afternoon he said to David, "Yesterday I reached a new low even for me. You know the autobiography I ghosted for the big Czechoslovakian tycoon? Sure. It did poorly, I know, and hardly anybody reviewed it. But a business magazine, the *Over-the-Counter-Man,* asked some other moneybags to review the book, and he came to me, asking me to ghost a review for him of a book that I had ghosted originally! How do you like that? I might do it at that, just for the hell of it. After that I don't think I can sink any lower, do you?"

David said he was forced to agree with Will's analysis of the situation.

One of the other people David met frequently at the Tobias home was Rabbi Dr. Joshua Halevy Korngold. He was like no other rabbi that David had ever met socially. He was tall, well-groomed, completely shaven (he didn't even have a mous-tache), he was almost completely bald, but what little hair he had he parted in the middle, and he spoke good English. Though he was born in Germany, he went to England as a young man, and there he studied in the University of London and in Leeds University. He couldn't decide whether he wanted to go into teaching philosophy or becoming a rabbi. His mind was largely made up for him by an American girl he met in London. They fell in love with each other on first sight. She was the daughter of a high executive in the American Jewish Congress, and herself was involved in Jewish affairs. She confided to him that secretly she had always wanted to be a *rebbitsin,* the wife of a rabbi, and it would please her enormously if Joshua went into the rabbinate. That decided it, especially since he himself was veer-ing in that direction.

He and Miriam went to the United States, were married, and he became a rabbinical student at the Jewish Theological Sem-inary, where he made a brilliant record. Indeed, so good was his record that on graduation he was asked whether he wanted to stay on as a teacher, with an eventual professorship, or whether he wanted to become a practicing rabbi. He thought he could always come back to the faculty, and he did want some experience "in the field." He quickly obtained a very fine position, as the rabbi of a small but influential Conservative temple in Chicago. While acting as a rabbi he pursued his studies for the D.H.L. (Doctor of Hebrew Letters) degree at the Sem-inary. In five years he was asked to become the rabbi of one of the most influential Conservative temples in New York City, and hence in the United States. He accepted at once, first be-cause, as he said, "there was a greater challenge in the new post," and also because Miriam wanted very much to live in New York City. Not long after he came back to New York he got his D.H.L. with a thesis on "Hebrew as the Catalyzing Language of the Diaspora." It was a learned dissertation, and when it was published as a book it brought forth highly favorable comments from some of the leading scholars in America, both Jewish and non-Jewish. They all predicted a brilliant future for Dr. Korn-gold in the field of Jewish scholarship.

His scholarship and his excellence in the pulpit aroused the interest of Dr. Nichtenhauser, who called upon him to "lend your talents" to the cause of Jewish public affairs, particularly Zionism. Dr. Korngold felt complimented, and soon he was making speeches for the Jewish Agency and for the Zionist Organization in America. His congregation was delighted: their rabbi was "a public figure," and that made every member of the Board of Trustees feel good—and it also brought in many new members in the temple. Dr. Korngold was now making two and three speeches a week, so the Board of Trustees decided to relieve him of some of his synagogue work by appointing an assistant rabbi, who would do much of the preaching and visiting, and take care of the detail associated with bar mitzvahs. The assistant would also take care of many of the weddings and burials, though Dr. Korngold, of course, would officiate at "important" weddings and funerals and bar mitzvahs.

Dr. Korngold was delighted with the new arrangement. He could now be more than just a rabbi of one congregation. He could now be truly a leader in Israel. Now and then there passed through his mind the thought of giving up entirely his post as a rabbi, but something held him back. A rabbi who didn't have a temple somehow didn't have real status—at least in his eyes. Such a non-preaching rabbi gave one the impression of having failed somehow. Dr. Korngold knew that he had not failed as a rabbi: on the contrary, he was a great success as a preacher, he knew he had commanding presence in the pulpit. He knew he had the respect of his congregation, especially of the Board of Trustees. He was especially proud of what the president of the Board of Trustees had once said in his presence: "Rabbi, I don't mind saying to you, within your hearing, that we are delighted that you are an administrator as well as a man of God, you know what I mean. We always wanted somebody who wasn't just a rabbi, you know what I mean, we wanted somebody who was somewhat more human, you know what I mean, a man who realizes that a synagogue, a temple, has to pay its way, you know what I mean, and that business methods applied to a temple just as they applied anywhere else, you know what I mean." The president also told Dr. Korngold that he was delighted, "and I know I speak for every single member of the Board of Trustees," that his speeches were reported in *The New York Times* and that always the name of the temple was mentioned in connection with Dr. Korngold's name.

Miriam was pleased for her husband, she was, perhaps, even more delighted than he was. Now and then she would notice a strange doubt enter her husband's eyes whenever she spoke of something "especially nice" that had happened to him, such as being invited to address a state convention of Hadassah, or to represent "the Hebraic attitude to morals and ethics" at an interfaith group, or to give the invocation at a local civic function, or to give the chief address at a Knights of Pythias installation of officers, or to be "one of the three dominant religious leaders" at the ground-breaking of a new community playhouse.

"Goodness, I don't understand you, dear," Miriam would say. "This is all wonderful, and all you do is grouch, well, not exactly grouch, but you act glum."

"I'm not glum, I'm just wondering," Dr. Korngold said.

"Wondering about what?"

"About whether this is really what I want. At first I used to be glad, that's true. Seeing your name in the paper is pleasing for a while, people speak to you as if you've really done something when *The New York Times* reports something ordinary you've said, such as the Jews are steeped in ethical values and believe in applying their religio-ethical values not just on Saturday and Rosh Hashonoh and the other holidays, but every day in the year. I don't see why saying this makes me any more prominent than when I didn't say it in public, but from the pulpit, it's commonplace, it has to be restated, of course, and repeated, but, if it appears in the *Times* I become like Aristotle or Maimonides. I don't like it."

"I still think it's good for you, Joshua," said Miriam. "Of course, it's not very new, but the fact that you were picked to say it means something, it means you're a leader."

"I know, but . . . "

"But what?"

"Well, I really want to be a rabbi and a scholar, I want to write some books and articles, especially books. There's a book I want to write on Rabbi Kuk, the founder of modern mystical Orthodoxy, perhaps I should say one of the founders, a fascinating man. He was a very flexible man, but in the good sense, very rational, yet very wonderful, his influence on Orthodoxy was tremendous, but he also influenced Conservatism and Reform. He, I don't know exactly how to say it"—he hesitated, so many things were running through his mind . . . as he looked at his wife he was shocked by the feeling that she appeared impatient with him for reasons of her own. He wanted so much to talk to her now about ideas and hopes and dreams of his, but he realized that her heart was elsewhere . . . he began to wonder whether she was more interested in her social standing as the wife of a man who was quoted in *The New York Times,* who dedicated playgrounds, who represented Judaism at interfaith gatherings; was it possible that his Miriam was that kind of woman? Had he been so terribly wrong about her when he fell in love with her? . . . and who was he, Dr. Joshua Korngold, to "represent" Judaism? There were so many rabbis and scholars who had a much better right to do so . . .

"Your mind is wandering, Joshua," said Miriam. "What really is wrong?"

"Oh," said Dr. Korngold. "Nothing, I guess my mind did wander off. I was thinking about the book on Rabbi Kuk that I want to write."

"That's fine. Then write it," said Miriam.

He smiled bitterly at her total failure to understand him.

"But I can't and at the same time do all the other things. Writing a book requires concentration, study, meditation, time, no distractions. I can't run around from one dedication to another, one speech after another on Zionism or this or that appeal, and attend to my temple duties, and write a book at the same time."

"I don't see why not," said Miriam. "You have an assistant rabbi now, and you yourself said that Milton is good, and takes many burdens off your shoulders."

"Yes, he is fine. Milton Barak is a real help to me. He's eager and he's just fine. But I still have to watch his every step. I only mean that he's a fresh graduate of the Seminary, and naturally he needs guidance."

"But he is a help, isn't he, Joshua?"

"Yes, he is," said Dr. Korngold. "He is a help."

He wished he could tell his wife how much heartache Milton had given him . . . Milton conducted services efficiently, he had a good head, he delivered an acceptable sermon, the people liked him, but that's where the trouble lay, the people liked him too much, and Joshua was ashamed that he was jealous of Milton. He was especially jealous of his sermons, which at times were more than acceptable, they were truly scholarly. One sermon in particular impressed Joshua. That was Milton's sermon on Franz Rosenzweig and his contribution to Conservative Judaism. Milton clearly had done deep study into the life and writings of Rosenzweig, and he also knew his Spinoza well, and Maimonides, his quotations were apt, his organization was excellent. Joshua wondered whether he himself could do so fine a job, it was a long time, in fact, since any one of his sermons had approached Milton's. There was something else. Joshua had asked Milton several times to get references for him in preparation for sermons, and Milton had not only looked up the references, he had also supplied some ideas of his own, and Joshua had incorporated these ideas in his sermons and taken the credit for them. This was shameful and it rankled. Joshua had not told Miriam about this, he was ashamed, and he wasn't sure that she would feel the same way he felt about the situation. Lately she had become too logical, too "reasonable" about many things that he couldn't be "reasonable" about. Recently Milton had shown him two articles which he, Milton, had contributed to two magazines, and the articles were first-rate as writing and as scholarship. *The New York Times* did not quote from Milton's articles, but they should have, thought Joshua, they were far better than anything Joshua himself had said in two, three years. This reminded him, he had not written a single article in all that time, and he sighed.

"As I said, Milton is a help," he repeated, not very eager to go on with this discussion.

"So you can write," Miriam said.

"I suppose I can find time," he said, hoping that this remark would please and quiet her, and she would drop the subject.

But Dr. Korngold did not find the time, he spoke more and more before all sorts of gatherings, he helped open bridges and tunnels and hospitals and insane asylums and public schools. He welcomed visiting Jewish dignitaries from France and Germany and England and South America, and also from California and Texas and Canada. He was home less and less often, and officiated at the temple only once in three or four weeks. His name was often in the newspapers, his telephone was busy, asking him to appear at still more "functions," a word that now had a foul smell to him. Then, out of the proverbial blue, he was elected, on the same day, chairman of one of the most important committees of the Zionist Organization of America (generally the chairman of this committee succeeded to the presidency), and chairman of a very important committee of the Rabbinical Assembly of America, the chief organization of the American Conservative movement. He knew he was fitted to head the first committee, it involved nothing more than a thick skin to take the insults of those who were jealous of him or who merely found pleasure in making the life of a chairman difficult, and of course it called for a certain pomposity of manner, which he had a great deal of.

But the election to the chairmanship of the important committee of the Rabbinical Assembly of America troubled him. He had accepted the election with ostensible pleasure and gratitude, but deep down in his heart he wondered why he was elected. The committee was concerned with important matters of philosophy and ritual and social relations, and he was really not equipped to make any contribution to any of these realms. He had read very little for some five years now in any of these subjects, he had done very little meditating . . . he just didn't have the time or the energy. After a day of making invocations at three or four dinners and suppers and lunches and eating at "functions" where some other poor rabbis made the invocations, he was too tired and unhappy to sit down and study. Besides, the very thought of an invocation bothered him, most were so mechanical, so profoundly offensive . . . he began to wonder whether it wasn't somehow blasphemous to call upon God to help out with this or that project, be it a school or a community center edifice. He was elected to the chairmanship of the important Conservative committee, he was sure, because he was now a "name," and for some reason, not a very honorable one, the Conservative movement, or a few of the important men in it, thought it would be "good publicity" to have Dr. Korngold as head of the important committee: "he'll draw attention to our movement, he'll get us notice in the newspapers." My tragedy, thought Dr. Korngold, is that, in a sense, they're right, I will get them publicity in the newspapers, but I won't make any contribution to the discussions. Milton would have been much better, but he has no "name."

77

There was still something else that was troubling Dr. Korngold: his knowledge of Yiddish and of Hebrew, especially Hebrew, was getting very feeble, simply because he was reading little of either language. There was a bitter irony in that. One of the burdens of his many talks before Zionist organizations was that every "self-respecting Jew, with a genuine regard for the immemorial culture of our people, should become familiar with the language of the Bible and of the prophets," but he himself was getting less and less familiar with it. The Palestinian newspapers were coming regularly to his study, and merely piling up on his desk or in the bookcase, such reading as these newspapers and magazines got was from Milton, his assistant, in fact, he now generally came on the days they arrived and asked for them, and in that way Milton managed to humiliate Dr. Korngold still more, unwittingly, of course, but very effectively just the same. Dr. Korngold had also been one of the earliest subscribers to *Hadoar,* the oldest continuous regular Hebrew publication in the United States, ably edited by that fine scholar, Menachem Ribalow. Dr. Korngold had looked forward to getting it even when he was in England, and he prided himself upon his ability to read its fine Hebrew, but now it was months since he had done much more than open it. Only a few days ago he had attempted to read an article in it, and found to his dismay that he had difficulty in following it.

As a leader in Israel Dr. Korngold was often invited to the Tobias home, which was a sort of social center for some of the most important men in Jewish-American life. He liked to go there, he found a strange feeling of relief there, he didn't know exactly why. Perhaps, he thought, it was because of Mary Tobias, she seemed to be so charitable in her understanding. Indeed, he liked her so much that he secretly bemoaned the fact that he had not married a woman like her. But then, who knows about such matters, he said to himself: he had thought that Miriam was exactly the sort of woman that Mary Tobias was, but she turned out to be something of a society woman, she enjoyed coming to the Tobias home, he thought, more because she liked to be in a spacious apartment, with beautiful furniture and tasteful service. She did sometimes mention the talk that went on there, but generally only in passing.

Four

When David became a member of the Tobias social-intellectual family he sensed that something new and wonderful had happened to him. He had at long last, so to speak, become mature as a Jew in the modern world. He had looked upon Judaism, hitherto, as more a religion than anything else, he had looked upon Jews as chiefly a people who believed in the Torah and in the 613 *mitzvahs* (commandments, rules, regulations), who adhered to the general ideas in the Talmud. Of course, he knew the Jews also produced a culture, a history, a literature, and much of this culture and literature was not connected immediately or even remotely with religious Judaism. David had read much of this literature, been in contact with much of this culture, but he knew this only on the superficial plane of his intellect; his innermost being somehow did not accept this knowledge as very significant.

David had had inklings of his new enlightenment in the past, far back in the past. He had an inkling of it when he first read Spinoza, shortly after his bar mitzvah. Spinoza was a Jew, but he was more than a Jew, he also belonged to the world scene, along with Aristotle and Plato and Kant, who were non-Jews. David had an inkling of it when he read articles by Louis D. Brandeis, a Jew but also a lawyer in the "outside" world. David had an inkling of it when he heard Mendelssohn music at Temple

Israel, the Reform temple in Boston. Mendelssohn was a Jew but he was not really a Jewish composer in the restrictive sense; he was a world composer. All this meant that a Jew was more than a Jew, he was a human being who happened to be a Jew and therefore had special traditions, special influences, but he didn't have to work within the boundaries of these influences, he could work outside them. How his traditions influenced the work he did outside the boundaries of these traditions was a fascinating question that David hoped to look into sometimes.

Now, at long last, at the Tobias home, David's emotions, so to speak, caught up with his mind, and he saw the whole stream of Jewish history in a new light. The revelation sent a glow through his whole being. It added a new and wonderful dimension to being a Jew. And to David personally it did something very special and equally wonderful, it gave the final confirmation and blessing to his desire to devote his major creative energies to the writing of all sorts of fictions about the Jews. It also gave a blessing to his continuing to write about non-Jewish subjects. When he wrote about these non-Jewish subjects, he would not be an interloper, he would be a human being, as all Jews were human beings.

One of the first things that David learned about at the Tobias home was the bulk of the periodical literature dealing with Anglo-Jewish affairs. Hitherto he had read such magazines as the *New Palestine* and the *Menorah Journal,* and while he sometimes found articles and stories and poems and reviews in them worth reading, he had also missed a certain editorial boldness, and the fiction above all disturbed him, it said so little, and the poetry was even feebler. The magazines were no worse than dozens of similar magazines in the general field, but they were not good enough for the Jewish field. Now he began to read several of the weekly Anglo-Jewish newspapers across the nation, and he was appalled at how bad they were as a group: so much society news, so few general cultural pieces. Some of these newspapers had no book columns at all, and those that did, printed reviews and news items that were little better than juvenile, praising some harmless and largely worthless novel or collection of short stories or poems by some local man or woman. Some newspapers devoted much space to praising the products of advertisers, which revealed how the advertisements were obtained. Yet David was not altogether depressed by this inferior type of journalism; he felt that such a press, by its mere existence, meant that there was a readership of considerable proportions that could be reached with a far better press. David had faith that this waiting public was superior to the newspapers and magazines that it was reading.

There was something else that David learned at the Tobias home, namely, that American Jewry was not confined to New York and Boston and Chicago and Philadelphia. There were centers of Jewish life in Cleveland and Cincinnati and Houston, and Los Angeles and Denver, Colorado and St. Louis and Kansas City. Dr. Nichtenhauser reported upon meetings of Zionists in Cleveland, where Rabbi Abba Hillel Silver was a dominant personality. Dr. Silver was the Middlewestern Rabbi Stephen S. Wise, Dr. Nichtenhauser had said. Dr. Silver was also a man of considerable learning. David learned more about the Reform seminary in Cincinnati. For a long time he had a strange idea of that institution, that it was hardly Jewish—David once heard an Orthodox Jew, who was veering toward Conservatism, say, "Reform I will never be, they're only Christians without a *tzaylom* (crucifix)"—David knew that this was an unkind exaggeration, and yet one side of him had been inclined to feel a little bit as did this man. But now he learned from the long sessions at the Tobias home that the Reform Seminary, the Hebrew Union College in Cincinnati, was the home of great scholars in Bible, the Talmud, Jewish traditions, Jewish history.

All American Jewry, all world Jewry, what was left of it after the Hitler murders, appeared to have a sense of destiny. Something mystical and prophetic was going to happen to the Jews, and this something was associated with what Dr. Herzl preached, that the Jews will get a home of their own, fifty years after his lifetime, and this year, 1946–1947, was the time. The very air seemed to be filled with the shadow of great things to come for the Jews. Lectures and articles proclaimed it: Whither World Jewry Now? . . . Will the Balfour Declaration Now Be Made A Reality? . . . Will Dr. Herzl's Prophecy Come True Now? . . . Has the Day of Glory Come for the Jews? . . . Will Jerusalem Be Ours Next Year?

There were other sides to David's new enlightenment. For the first time he fully realized how alive American Jewry was. It was not as rich as the Jewry of Eastern Europe at the beginning of the century. There were not so many *yeshivas,* in fact, very few, there wasn't the same intense Jewishness pervading the community, there were more "outside influences." American Jewry was an amalgam, a spiritual alloy, but it had vibrancy, more than David had ever recognized.

From this new realization there came to David a mystical feeling, almost a conviction, that the center of world Jewry, in culture, in literature, in other important respects, would for the next century, perhaps, be in America, no matter what wonderful things happened to Palestine, even if it once more became the Jewish national homeland. There were more Jews in the United States than anywhere else in the world, there was more Jewish activity. Destiny was working through them, giving Jewry and the rest of the world a preview of what was to happen to Jewish history, and one of these things would be the establishment of a center of Jewish culture right here in the United States. The United States would take the place of Eastern Europe as the center. This inner feeling made the future all the more exciting and added so much more meaning to David's own life.

His life continued to be lived on various levels. There was his writing in the general American field. There was his personal life, which now was sad and empty, devoid of the womanly sympathy and love that he had craved, that he hoped Sylvia would satisfy. This life of the heart he had hoped to achieve for so many years, first with Alice, then with Sylvia. And there was his increased involvement with Jewish life, which gave him deep satisfaction. He was now writing more on it, he already had several stories published in magazines, and he was hard at work on a novel of Jewish-American life.

The Tobias home was a sort of university of general culture and especially of Jewish culture. David was exhilarated by much of what he heard, and he was left in doubt by other things he heard, but altogether he was excited . . . and by hearing and seeing many things and many people. The Tobias home was now, to him, pretty much a second home, he was told to drop in whenever he wished to, without calling. "Be a foster son to us," Mary Tobias had said, and for a while David thought that this was only an exuberant, polite remark, but she repeated it so often that he took her seriously, and he did drop in whenever he wished, and always he was welcome. By being there often and listening to the talk, he felt himself becoming more perceptive, more mature not only as a Jew, but as a writer of fiction. People were becoming clearer to him, even in their complexity.

Two ideas that he had encountered in his past now had compelling meaning to him. One was Spinoza's concept of viewing all things and all people "under the aspect of eternity"—*sub specie aeternitatis*. He now really knew what that meant . . . it meant that one must never forget a thousand years before and a thousand years afterward when considering an event or a person. Time washes away so many things, both glorious and not so glorious. In the life of a star the petty act of a human being is nonexistent, and for that reason is to be viewed with compassion for the doer of the act, but the glorious act does have more endurance than the lesser act, it lives on in memory, it alone has beauty and strength, it alone has Godliness. The sublime act is akin to the stars at night, shining proudly. And the other remark that now had true and compelling meaning to him was a remark he had seen attributed to Anatole France: "The greatest tragedy and the greatest ecstasy of life, at the same time, is that we are all born alone, we live alone, and we die alone." This is the ultimate democracy of life. This is one of the stark and great truths of living. And Anatole France is reported to have added: "This every artist, literary and otherwise, must never forget. When he does, he is not an artist, but a merchant. When he remembers it he can at least hope to be an artist." This was now David's guide in his writing, it did away with all literary anger, it did away with jealousy, with all pettiness, and at the same time it added grandeur to human life in the entire scheme of things. The sense of eternity and the feeling of pity, these were the true watch words of the writer.

David's first feeling about Will Frimmer was that he was a rather shallow, if kindly, man, but slowly, as David came to know him better, he began to warm to him. Will was a lost man, who had done things he shouldn't have done and had not done things he should have done. He shouldn't have succumbed so easily to his own gift of "ghosting" autobiographies, he should have tried harder to write "real and true things," as he had wanted to do. He had not given himself a chance to find out whether he was a failure. Still, he only did and failed to do what so many other people did and failed to do. Much of life is determined by outside pressures, by certain aspects of our personalities that are alien to other aspects of our personalities. So many things that we do seem to be done by strangers to ourselves.

Will Frimmer was everyman. He knew his failures, he knew the trap that life had got him into, he probably felt that there was little now he could do about his failures. He was tired, his "successes" had sapped much of his real creative energies. He wasn't too happy with what had become of his married life, he wasn't too happy with what he had learned about Phyllis, and yet he was not too unhappy with her or with his married life. Phyllis's kisses and embraces, at times, were the kisses and embraces of the Phyllis of old, whom he loved, and perhaps that Phyllis was still the "real" Phyllis. There were times when he wasn't sure what was real and what wasn't real. His whole past life, with its sanguine hopes and dreams, seemed like the only reality and the future a mirage, but there were times when the opposite seemed to be the case. The present eluded him completely, it was the greatest mystery of all.

What drew Will to the Zionist movement, to Dr. Nichtenhauser, to all things Jewish, was not altogether clear to him. As he grew older his Jewish background appeared to get nearer to him. Phyllis had much to do with his reawakened interest in Jewishness, but he felt pretty sure that he would have come back even without Phyllis. His "failure" as a writer had something to do with his return: if he couldn't make a "success" of his own life, perhaps he could help his people become a success. As a matter of fact, there was something specially pleasant in the thought that in trying to help his people become a success he couldn't possibly fail. And there was something truly uplifting in his hitching his wagon, so to speak, to the star of the Jewish people; it just made sense in and of itself, it was good, it was glorious. Then again, as he often told David, "Being a Jew is not something smalltime, the way I used to think, it's bigtime thinking, bigtime living, and I sometimes think that the Jews may come out of all this mess, I mean the Second World War as the only winners. This sounds funny and tragic, you know what I mean, with six million or more Jews killed, but you know what I mean."

He liked working with and for Dr. Nichtenhauser, for Dr. Nichtenhauser was the kind of complex human being who appealed to Will. He was honest but "not fanatically so," as he told David. "His word is good, but he'll twist his word a little bit, if he's out to obtain a good end for the Jewish people. He's not a swindler, not at all, but he's a good trader, let's put it that way. He's like a woman, well, like the women I've written their autobiographies for, only he's not out to get a husband or a bank account or a contract with Hollywood or on Broadway, he has no interest in this kind of plus and minus, he wants to be the Machiavelli of and for the Jewish people, that's more of what I mean. And it's fun working for him. He smiles at you like a movie actress of the better sort, you know what I mean."

Will liked to ghost a speech for Dr. Nichtenhauser himself, and he liked to ghost speeches for United States Senators and Governors and Congressmen and college presidents. Dr. Nichtenhauser could write his own speeches, but he didn't have the time. He would tell Will, "I have to address a group of Reform rabbis in Philadelphia, a convention, they're coming back to Zionism, or they're just coming in, so write me something that makes them feel they've never been away, that the future of Zionism is so very much in their hands, somehow tie up Zionism with their old view that Judaism is dominantly a Messianic religion, not a form of what they called nationalism. You know, they had something in their Messiah idea, but they carried it too far, but you know what I mean, but don't you overdo it, understand?" Will understood.

Or Dr. Nichtenhauser would ask Will to write a speech for him for a group of very wealthy Jews who had given little to Zionist causes hitherto but who at the same time came from Zionist backgrounds—they've made money and forgotten where they came from. Dr. Nichtenhauser would tell Will just this and add, "Make them feel a little guilty, not too much so, if you make them feel too guilty, they'll rebel, they'll be too ashamed, but remind them of their parents and their grandparents, and of the dreams these forebears had about Zion, remind them of the prayer on Rosh Hashonoh and Yom Kippur and other holidays, 'Next Year in Jerusalem.' This has deep meaning for them, it comes from their childhood memories. And don't overdo. Just suggest. That's the best way of all. Suggest." And Will suggested.

Dr. Nichtenhauser now and then would appeal for help, financial or otherwise, to intellectuals, including college presidents. He was a soft-spoken and even a sentimental man, but there was a wide streak of cynicism in him, and Will liked that especially, for Will himself, through his "successes" with so many third-rate people, had become quite cynical himself. Dr. Nichtenhauser would say to Will, about a college president he would introduce at a certain meeting, where Dr. Nichtenhauser wanted to arouse an interest in, say, the Hebrew University (contributions of money, books, laboratories, and visiting professors), "Will, Dr. Langer, you know who he is, he's president of Middle-States University, he has a dozen or so honorary degrees. I believe he was once president of the American Philosophical Association, or maybe it was the American Psychological-Psychiatrical Association, or some other such group of high prestige, he's a name"—and a twinkle would come to his eyes—"well, he doesn't know quite as much as he thinks he does. Between you and me, he once told me that Maimonides lived at the time of the American Revolution, and he thought Ibn Gabirol was a Spanish painter. I didn't correct him. His vice-president, by the way, didn't know where Yemen was, he had a vague idea it was in Asia or Africa, somewhere in the middle of either. But Langer has a lot of influence, and the thing to do, when you write that speech for me is somehow to link up Einstein with him, with all the intellectuals in America, especially in his group, with Einstein and Morris Cohen, they have a lot of respect for Morris Cohen, though I imagine they understand very little of his philosophy, and you might bring in Henri Bergson somehow. In other words, point out to them that here, through the Hebrew University, they have a chance to help out their superiors. Intellectuals of that kind like that. Most of them are second-class, you understand, and want some first-classness to rub off on them, you understand?" Will understood. As Will said to David, "I tell you that man is a *Realpolitiker* in the grand tradition. I may be all off, but I think there'll be books about him in the future, the way he handles things, he's fantastic, you need a new language to explain him, even to describe him."

David was glad to be a friend of such people. He had never before met a Will or a Dr. Nichtenhauser. They were mystery men, manipulators, connivers, perhaps, very "practical," and yet there was a strange and appealing sense of dedication in them.

Dr. Nichtenhauser was dedicated to the future welfare of the Jewish people, especially to the re-establishment of Palestine as the Jewish national homeland, and Will was dedicated to the same thing for reasons of his own. Dr. Nichtenhauser was a Bismarck and a Metternich and a Machiavelli and a Moses and a King David and, perhaps, even a Mark Hanna, all in one. He and Will were acting out, in real life, a great adventure story, one of the greatest of our time.

David used to gasp with wonderment and bedazzlement when he read in the newspapers, the report of a speech by an influential United States Senator or a State Governor or the president of a huge industrial firm, and recognize in them Will's phrases and Will's logic—for Will by this time had made something of a confidante of David. The speeches were good for what they were aimed to do, and sometimes several of America's greatest newspapers would praise the Senator or the Governor or the business executive for his perspicacity and wisdom and "well-turned phrase." The speeches generally accomplished their purposes— a State legislature would pass a resolution calling upon the Congress to do all in its power and "to exert its high moral force to see to it that justice at long last is done the Jewish people," or a business executive would announce the formation of a committee of business men "to do all in our power to help set up in the Holy Land, under the guidance and sponsorship of the intellectual leadership of world Jewry, scientific and engineering institutions that will help lift the economic and general living level of the whole Middle East"—and along would come donations of considerable size.

There was one man, the head of one of the largest industrial empires in the United States, who had been born a Jew but who had become converted to one of the Protestant sects when he had married a Protestant girl. For more than three decades his name was in no way associated with Jewish affairs. Shortly after his conversion, in fact, he had politely rebuffed an appeal for help to the victims of persecutions of Jews in Eastern Europe. But Dr. Nichtenhauser had heard through mysterious sources of his own that this industrialist was greatly disturbed by what had been happening to the Jews during the Hitler massacres, that he had influenced his wife and grown children to be equally disturbed. Dr. Nichtenhauser formed a Christian-Jewish Committee for the Aid of the Victims of Nazism, got the industrialist appointed the chairman, and had Will write a speech for him at a large fund-raising meeting, at which were present a Methodist Episcopal Bishop, a Catholic Monsignor, a Baptist preacher of national renown, and a Lutheran pastor known in Eastern United States. The result of the meeting was the collection, in pledges, of nearly three-quarters of a million dollars—and, not long after the meeting, the chairman of the committee, the converted Jew, announced his personal donation of a million for the establishment of a center of engineering research in the names of his two parents, both of whom, of course, were Jewish. David was thrilled when he read this in the newspapers. Will made light of his own part in this affair: "It was a routine speech, only Dr. Nichtenhauser warned me not to say too much about the Jews as Jews but to stress the broadly human aspect of the Jewish catastrophe. Get the man's psychological insight." And Will added, "That man is truly one in a million. Pure genius."

David had thought that there were chiefly two forms of Zionism—General Zionism and *Poalay* Zionism, or Socialist Zionism. His own family, he assumed, were, in the main, with the General Zionists, though some of the aunts, especially Chashel, were *Poalay* Zionists. The *Poalay* Zionists were also, to some extent, inclined to be anti-religious or, to be more accurate, non-religious. To them Zionism was a form of re-establishing the Jewish nation in the image, so to speak, of Karl Marx. They were more or less in disagreement with Marx's dictum that religion was the opiate of the people. Still, there were Socialist Zionists who did think as Marx did, but they didn't advocate their ideas with belligerence. Apparently they still felt the pull of the Jewishness of their upbringing, or they didn't want to hurt the feelings of their religious parents. David knew about the Mizrachi, but only in a vague way. He knew that they were religious Zionists, people who looked upon Palestine as the Holy Land, as the land where the Jews will, in God's good time, bring about, or re-establish, a community where all life would be governed by the precepts of the Torah and the rules and regulations and suggestions of the great rabbis. They differed from other religious Jews in that they thought it proper to work with other Zionists, and thought it was not blasphemous not to put all their trust in the return of the Messiah.

88

At the Tobias home David learned that these three major parties had developed splinter parties. There were some two or three factions in the Mizrachi, and two or three factions in the General Zionists, and there was also a Communist Zionist party and several smaller parties. Then there was a party of Zionists who believed in the bi-national state, a state wherein both Arabs and Jews would play roughly co-equal parts in the running of the government and the general national life, on the theory that such a government would be only simple justice to the Arabs who, after all, had been on the land for generations. One of the proponents of this theory was Dr. Judah Magnes, rabbi of Temple Emmanuel in New York City.

This multiplicity of parties bewildered David—and also shamed him a little: he felt he should have known about them before. He didn't take sides, as he listened to the discussions in the Tobias home, because he didn't know enough, but also because his mind didn't run in the direction of party-Zionism. He was an involved, emotional Zionist and that was about all. This, David learned, was pretty much the way Rabbi Korngold felt.

The more he got to know him the more he liked Dr. Korngold. In his own eyes, when he thought about his life late at night and held confession with himself—and Dr. Korngold still did this at times, though the times were becoming more distant and of briefer duration—he probably considered his life a failure. Dr. Korngold's sense of values was being buried more and more by his "success" as an orator and a high-second-class Zionist politician, but it was still with him. Dr. Korngold's failure, to David, was of a higher degree than Will Frimmer's. There was more tragedy in it. Deep down in his soul Will Frimmer, thought David, knew that he would never be a really good novelist or poet, so his "success" as a ghost writer was only a partial failure. But Dr. Korngold, David had a hunch, could have become a scholar of considerable standing. He probably had the ability, but he merely didn't have the character to withstand the facility with which he could achieve temporary success. This made Dr. Korngold's sense of inner self-shame all the more bitter—he knew he could have become a more honorable man if only he had wanted to. David thought he saw this in Dr. Korngold's eyes, and in the occasional feeling of resignation that seemed to cover his face and overflow his whole being.

David also sensed in him the same lack of interest in inter-party politics that he himself had. Then, again, he liked his vast reservoir of general learning and Jewish learning. Dr. Korngold's learning was entirely selfless, he loved it for its own sake —he didn't make use of it the way Dr. Nichtenhauser made use of his: to raise funds, to get a man high in the American government or business to say or do something that was "good for the Jews." Dr. Korngold was more interested in learning for the sake of learning. He would tell wonderful tales about life in Medieval Europe, among the priest-intellectuals, and he would tell wonderful stories about the life of the Jews at that time. The Spanish Era in general European life and in Jewish life had a special interest to him. "That's one book I want to write, a whole set of books," he once said, "but I won't. I've become a speech-maker, not a maker of books."

"You're more than a speech-maker, though you're a very good one," said Dr. Nichtenhauser. "You're a builder of a nation."

Dr. Korngold was obviously pleased by this diplomatic re-mark, but right afterward—or so it seemed to David—he was also saddened, saddened that such flattery could please him.

"It was a really strange and wonderful Era," went on Dr. Korngold. "The Church was powerful, very powerful, but it was really not altogether Christian. It was mixed up with Moham-medanism, and God knows what else. For all of Spain was, in a way, the Marseilles of countries, religiously and philosophically speaking. All the religions came there, and all the philosophies, and they intermarried, so to speak, without benefit of clergy, lots of intellectual and philosophical miscegenation, and the re-sult was quite a hodge-podge: cruelty such as even the Catholic Church was embarrassed by, and paganism, too. There were Spanish bachannalias that would have made the Romans envious, and the number of illegitimate children who were born as the result of their pre-Lenten festivities was tremendous. The Church, of course, knew it, but winked at it. The Catholic Church is quite a winker when it comes to sin, though it al-ways wants to have its hand in the sinning, controlling it as it sees fit, and perhaps making some money out of it, by way of penalties meted out by the priests in the confessional, or by monsignori or bishops or even cardinals. The Church knows how to get money for religious purposes. Frankly, I like that aspect of the Church. It makes it human, aware of sin, inclined to forgive, for a price, of course."

Dr. Nichtenhauser, whose ears always seemed to be open when there was discussion of maneuvering and conniving, smiled and said, "Eh, I wouldn't blame the Church so much. Piety is a matter of how you look at it. Then, again, if I may be cynical, these bachannalias or other orgies may have been a way the Church had of converting Moslems and Protestants, and, who knows, maybe even Jews. I am sure that some Jews passed for *goyim* even in those days, I don't mean they wanted to pass as Christians, I don't believe there were many Jews who really wanted to pass, in their hearts, I mean, but a Jew has to make a living, he had to think of his wife and children, and if he can make some money selling candy and cakes and even little crosses, he'll do it, and if they ask him what he is, he says a Catholic, and business goes on, and to himself he says you know what. And, some of the Jews who did, maybe took advantage of a nice-looking *shikse,* you know, and he began to think, especially if he wasn't married. Some Jews are weak like some Christians are weak. I'd say the Church probably thought of all this. It's an old and ancient and very wise institution, it can be cruel, but it seldom makes the same mistake twice. So, that's all the mixed-up ideas I have to contribute to the subject of the Church."

"There may be a lot to what you say, Dr. Nichtenhauser," said Raphael Tobias, "more than you think, though I assume you were joking a little. The Church will borrow and steal and connive as long as it can get converts, save souls, as they say. Even their churches, architecturally speaking, there really is no set Catholic church design. People think that Gothic is the chief or only Catholic Church design. It is in Germany and France and some parts of Italy. But elsewhere the Church follows the design of whatever non-Christian church is dominant. It doesn't do it right away or slavishly, but it, let us say, borrows the design. Why? To make possible prospective converts feel at home. So in Spain and Portugal, there are many beautiful churches that look like mosques, Mohammedan mosques. The reason you can imagine. The Church, searching for souls to save, wants Mohammedans to feel at home in the Catholic churches, so they won't be lonesome for their old mosques. The Church is smart. It knows that once it converts anybody, a Mohammedan, a Jew, a pagan, it has won only half the battle. The second half of the battle is to keep him in the Church, keep him from backsliding."

"In Mexico they're always backsliding," interrupted Will, smiling. "The Catholic Indians go to mass, of course, but they also bring with them their old gods, they take no chances."

"And the Church winks at this," said Dr. Nichtenhauser.

"Sure," said Raphael Tobias. "I was in Mexico not long ago, and I talked to a Mexican priest, he was educated at Fordham University, a Jesuit, he was born in Minnesota, but he was interested in Spanish, Mexican, so after he was ordained he was sent on a mission to Latin America—Peru, Costa Rica, Chile— to missionize among the Indians, there are still quite a number who have resisted the missionaries, especially the Catholic ones, that's what burns the Catholics up, some of the Protestant sects, especially the Presbyterians, are having more luck than the Catholics. Anyway, so this priest and I got to be friendly, he was quite a well-read man, and he and I were once walking along a street in Cuernavaca, it was some feast day, and we saw a pile of Mexicans leave church, Catholic church, of course, and the priest, my friend, smiled and said, 'They're still only 20 per cent Catholics. I know that before the night is over they'll have one of their pagan religious services, and they might even tell their god or gods about the Catholic service they went to, because they like to tell their gods everything.' "

"So what did you say to him?" asked Dr. Nichtenhauser.

"Nothing, what could I say?" said Raphael.

"No, you can't say anything," said Dr. Nichtenhauser.

"Speaking of influences," said Dr. Korngold, "we Jews have also been influenced by the Christians, it's only human. Of course, our influence on the Christians is beyond description, I don't mean merely that we gave them their Lord and Redeemer and that we gave them their New Testament, which was written largely by Jews, and which is only a poor carbon copy of the Old Testament, and where it isn't even that, it's mostly foolishness and filled with a cold emotion. But we have influenced even their music."

"The Gregorian chant sounds just like the *davvening* in a synagogue," said Will.

"It doesn't just sound like it. It's exactly it, with some little frills added, and not such good frills, in my opinion," said Dr. Korngold, "though I suppose I'm prejudiced. Anyway, their Gregorian chants are Jewish through and through. Their church organization is also, to a large extent, Jewish. This is my personal theory. The Pope is sort of the *Kohen Godol,* the High Priest. And speaking of music, do you people know what Ernst Bloch says? He's the greatest Jewish musician we now have. You should hear his *Shlomo* and especially his *Sacred Service,* I think that's what it's called, the exact title escapes me now, but it's something like that, it takes in a whole service. He says that his music attempts to recapture the real Jewish music, that many of our *nigoonim* (tunes, melodies), even in Orthodox synagogues, are not Jewish at all, but Western, mixtures. He says that it's a disgrace that we should have allowed the Christians to take away from us the Gregorian chants, he thinks we should go back to this old and ancient and truly Jewish music, and he's in favor of rewriting nearly all of our ritualistic music, because what we have now is non-Jewish."

"That will be strange news to my father," said David.

"My father would be surprised, too, very surprised," said Will Frimmer.

"Is it really so?' asked Dr. Nichtenhauser. "I mean I believe what you've said, but I wonder . . . I'm just wondering."

"It's so. I read an article, or maybe it's an interview with him only a few months ago, and I was just as surprised as you. I asked one of the men at the Seminary about it, and he said it was true. Bloch was right."

Mary Tobias entered into the conversation, with apologies for presuming to discuss a subject that she confessed to knowing very little about. "I can't play a single instrument," she said. "Even the piano which I studied for so many years, maybe ten years. Mother was after me to practice and practice, you know, the usual Jewish mother with the usual problem child when it comes to music, and I didn't like the piano. Maybe I shouldn't say I didn't like it, I just wasn't crazy about it, it meant so little to me, I really liked the violin better, we called it the fiddle then, we've advanced from the fiddle to the violin, but I really just wasn't too interested in music. But I don't want to go into that. I'm not a musician, believe me. So I can't say too much about music with any authority. But I did hear some of Bloch, I think it was his *Shlomo*. I don't even remember whether it's called a symphony or a tone poem. Many of my musical friends told me I have to hear it. Well, all I can say is that I did hear it, and it meant nothing to me. I don't think it's Jewish at all. I don't even think it's very good music of any kind, just longdrawn-out dullness, well, maybe that's too strong a word for me to use, because I'm no expert, but it just didn't interest me. What I mean is that I think the old tunes and melodies I used to hear in the synagogue my father and mother went to, downtown in New York City and later in the Bronx, they were really Jewish. And I did once hear the Gregorian chants in St. Patrick's Cathedral, and they bored me."

"All that proves," said Dr. Korngold, "is that we can get accustomed to error and think it's truth. I said exactly the same thing you did, to that man at the Seminary, so he told me that he had felt the same way long before he had studied what Bloch had said, and this same man said that people who get accustomed to thinking that Irvin S. Cobb is a real American humorist, which he isn't, find it hard to get accustomed to seeing how much more truly American Mark Twain is. You get accustomed to error and you think it's truth."

"Like some people get accustomed to thinking that Swiss cheese comes from Switzerland," said Raphael Tobias. "Sorry."

"I just remembered what I started to say some time ago," said Dr. Korngold. "It's about how Jews have been influenced by Christians. Even in their synagogues, this will interest you, Raphael, but you probably know it anyway. But maybe the others don't. In Spain and Portugal and in some parts of Italy and France, and I understand it's also true in some parts of Germany, in the synagogues there is a stairway leading up to a pulpit, not far from the *Oren Kodesh* (Holy Ark), just like they have in the Catholic and even in the Protestant churches."

"I didn't know this, either," said David.

"Neither did I," said Will.

"You knew about it, didn't you, Raphael?" said Dr. Korngold.

"Yes," said Raphael. "I've seen several such churches in Spain. And if I may add something in this connection, this I saw myself and was surprised by it, in these synagogues, or some of them, at least, when Jews enter they do something with their hands, make some kinds of signs, a little bit like the way Christians cross themselves when they enter a church, I guess they do this only in a Catholic Church. What this signifies I don't know, I don't even know what they say when they do this, if they say anything."

"I've heard about this, too," said Dr. Korngold, "though I haven't seen it or heard it myself, I mean what they say. It's fascinating, the interplay of religious influences."

"But the influences the Christians have had on us have been outward things," said Dr. Nichtenhauser. "A pulpit here, a pulpit there, but it's still a *shul,* and not a church."

David liked the way Dr. Nichtenhauser came to the defense of Judaism. It was a little boyish on Dr. Nichtenhauser's part, but David liked it.

Will cleared his throat, and said, slowly, "I know very little of Jewish history or philosophy. For a long time I was hardly a Jew, I was like so many of us in the United States, a non-Jewish Jew, but now I am what I am. I have often thought about the essence of Judaism. I know the story about Hillel, the definition he gave on one leg, 'Love your neighbor as thyself,' or something like that. But it's too general a definition, frankly, this definition has seemed to me more dramatic than satisfactory, it just doesn't say enough. I've just been wondering if there isn't a better, more inclusive definition."

"All Jewish history is the definition," said Dr. Nichtenhauser.

"That's too easy an answer," hazarded David, "if I may say so. I imagine Will means that Jewish history, perhaps, can be condensed, reduced, summarized in a few sentences."

Mary Tobias smiled. "Maybe Judaism is like love and electricity, it can only be felt, sensed, not defined."

"It's a very good and interesting question," said Dr. Korngold. "I suppose I, as a rabbi, ought to be able to answer it, but I am not at all sure I can. Still, as I was listening to Will, certain ideas were running through my mind. It's silly to condense a way of life that is thousands of years old in a few sentences, real *choozpedich* (brassy), still, what I have to say may, in a way, answer Will's question, and it's a question. You'll have to bear with me for a while, because I have to make a *droshe* (sermon), a little *droshe,* and I'll be thinking out loud. It seems to me, and remember I am thinking aloud, condensing the whole Talmud

95

and the Tanach and all the big Jewish books by the great rabbis, in a few sentences, as I say, it's foolish in a way, still, maybe I can shed some light.

"It seems to me that the three principles of Judaism or Jewishnness, or whatever you wish to call it, that these principles are Mercy, Godliness, and Justice. Now, the Jewish God is a God of Mercy. All our important prayers somewhere or other speak of *El Molay Rachmim* (God of All Mercies). Jews forgive, they are taught to forgive. Perhaps I can best illustrate this with this beautiful *midrash* (parable, interpretation). A rabbi asked another why is it that Moses, our great lawgiver, the greatest Jewish lawgiver, one of the founding fathers of Judaism, maybe the chief, anyway, why was he given the name Moses, which in Egyptian means *found in the waters,* the name that Pharoah's daughter gave him when she found him floating in a basket in the Nile River three months after his birth. You will remember that her father had ordered that male children be destroyed in one way or another. But Pharoah's daughter saved the child we now call Moses, and she named him Moses. Now he had his real names, at least other names, we know some of them: Yard, Chaver, Abi Suchoo, Toovieh, Shoomieh, Abigdor, and other names. And yet it was the name Moses that has stuck to him. So the rabbis have held that the answer is very simple. Our great lawgiver has gone down in history with the name that Pharoah's daughter has given him in order to show the world in what high regard an act of mercy is held, and Pharoah's daughter's act was, of course, an act of the very greatest daring and especially of mercy. Pharoah's daughter ignored her father's orders, she followed, instead, the dictates of her heart, she put mercy above law, and that concept of Mercy is one of the cardinal principles of Judaism, of this I am sure."

"Very beautiful," said Will, David, Dr. Nichtenhauser, and Mary and Raphael Tobias.

"The *Midrash,* which contains this and numberless other parables," said Dr. Korngold, "is one of the great mines of Jewish lore. It comes, in the view of some, between the Torah and the Talmud, and some say it is an extension or an elaboration or a beautification of the Talmud. If the Talmud is like a great sea, the rabbis refer to the *Yam HaTalmud* (the Sea of the Talmud), then perhaps we can say that the *Midrash* is the endless Garden of Jewish Lore. This is not such an apt phrase, it occurred to me only now. But be that as it may, the *Midrash* is wonderful. We have the principle of Mercy. Now we come to the Principle of Godliness. I'm not so sure that this is the right word for what I have in mind. Maybe the right word is devotion, devotion to the law, to the commandments of God, to the commandments or rules of the rabbis, but devotion, and maybe devotion is a form of Godliness, I don't know. And this principle of Godliness or Devotion I also would like to illustrate with a *midrash*. And by the way, before I go on, I would like to say, or rather to remind you, because I'm sure you all know about it, that even in the concentration camps, on the way to the crematoriums, in the jails, in the caves, in Dachau or Auschwitz, in all the concentration camps, what did the Jews do to pass their bitter time? We know what they did. We have diaries, we have records. The Jews discussed Talmud and Torah and Midrash, the very things we are now talking about. Of course, as Jews, they also discussed Immanuel Kant and architecture and world history and astronomy, everything, but always, I should say, they came back to the *Tanach,* the Torah, the Prophets, the Writings, and many a Jew became a real Jew in the concentration camp, the concentration camps, in a way and for some, became and were *Talmud torahs*. Another thing for which we have Hitler to thank.

"But to continue. The Principle of Godliness or Devotion. It is told, I believe in the Midrash, that a pious Jew was walking along the road on Shabbes, contemplating holy things, as is fitting on Shabbes, when an ox runs into him, lifts him up on its horns and carries him forward in a wild run. So what did the Jew cry out? Does he cry out to be saved, to have his life saved? No, he cries out, 'Jews save me from riding on Shabbes!' It's a sin to ride on Shabbes, and disobeying one of God's commandments, to keep the Sabbath holy, it appears in the Ten Commandments, of course, this commandment, keeping it was more precious to him than his own life. This is a lesson of Godliness or Devotion."

"It's such a Jewish story," said Mary Tobias. "Somehow that tells me more about Jewishness than whole books. Really. It moves me so much, maybe even more than the parable about

Moses. I suppose because the first parable is a little abstract, but this one about the Jew and the ox and the Sabbath is so human."

"The rabbis knew how to tell stories," said Dr. Nichtenhauser.

Will looked at David and in their silence they too, said to each other how lovely this tale was.

"So now we come to the Principle of Justice," said Dr. Korngold. He hesitated, smiled, and said, "I must apologize again for my preaching. I didn't mean it to come out this way, but somehow I feel moved, and Will's question was a very interesting one."

"I wish all the sermons in temples and synagogues were like this one we're hearing," said Rapahel Tobias. "I have heard . . ."

"I know, I know," interrupted Dr. Korngold. "But if I may throw in a word for my fellow rabbis, writing a sermon every week, even when it's only twenty minutes long, and no sermon should be much longer, one lasting fifteen minutes, or twelve minutes, is better. But it should have something, and when a sermon has something, it represents a lot of study, reading, thinking, and a rabbi has little time for that. You all know that a rabbi is many things, I have already spoken of this many times, he has to be a real estate man, a job seeker for some of his congregation, he has to be a diplomat, smoothing out squabbles between Sisterhood ladies and Brotherhood men, and he has to be a little bit of a psychoanalyst, and he has to be rabbi, too —studying and reading and thinking, which is his main function, really. But that is all another matter.

"Anyway, we come to Justice. That is a very important element in Judaism, very important. I believe we Jews were the first to institute the concept of impartial justice for poor and rich alike, for citizens and strangers alike. Even in Babylonia and Egypt, especially Babylonia, which was supposed to have an advanced legal code, you know, the Code of Hammurabi, even in Babylonia, there was one kind of justice for the very rich, another kind for the not-so rich, a third kind for what we might call the lower middle class, and still another kind of justice for the poor, who, I suppose, had almost no justice at all. And then there was a special justice for foreigners, for those who were not citizens of Babylonia, and the justice the foreigners got, I imagine, was not as fine or good or just as the justice that citizens got. So, in a sense, there really was no justice, as we understand it in America. It was the Jews who instituted this modern concept of justice. In Leviticus and Deuteronomy, time and time again, it says that foreigners must have the same justice as Hebrews, Jews, and that the rich and the poor are subject to exactly the same laws of justice. The law is the same for all, under the law we are all equals. I believe a line saying something like this appears right across the new United States Supreme Court Building in Washington. Modern Justice is a Jewish idea.

"But this idea, too, I would illustrate with a story from the Talmud, or maybe it appears in the Midrash also, I don't remember at the moment. The story is told that a rabbi's wife had an altercation with her maid, and she decided to bring her to court. She told her husband, the rabbi, about it. He asked her when the trial would be held, and she told him. He said nothing. Came the morning when the wife and the maid were to go to court, so the rabbi said he is going, too. So the wife said, 'My dear husband, why should you want to go? You are not involved at all. It's an altercation only between me and the maid, and it's beneath your dignity as a rabbi to participate in such a trial.' So the rabbi said, 'In the first place, nothing is beneath the dignity of a rabbi that involves people and their problems. Besides, I am deeply involved in this altercation.' 'But how are you involved, my husband?' asked the wife. 'I will tell you,' said the rabbi. 'You are going to court, and the judges, the rabbis will know the law, the Jewish law, the whole Jewish tradition will stand for you, giving you real justice, of course, you will have invisible friends in court. Who will defend the maid? Must she appear with nobody speaking for her? I want to appear for her and plead her case.' The wife said nothing. She knew that her husband was right. That is Justice."

"These Jewish parables are so wonderful, so very beautiful," said Mary Tobias. "Why aren't we told these stories in temple? They tell so much more about Judaism, and so graphically."

"Some rabbis do, some don't," said Dr. Korngold, "but our Jewish people are not there to hear them, you know," he smiled.

"I'm afraid, dear," said Rapahel Tobias, "there is truth in what our rabbi has just very delicately hinted at."

99

"I suppose so," said Mary Tobias. "I'm as guilty as anybody else."

"But don't you all feel that there's something happening in America now, I mean, among Jews?" said Dr. Nichtenhauser.

"I think there is," said Rapahel Tobias. "I see it in my own field. Jews who seldom discussed Jewish matters in the open are now discussing them, at least a little."

"I notice it, too," said Mary Tobias.

"*Tsores* brings Jews together," said Dr. Korngold. "It's always been that way. It's good, and it's not so good. It would be better if Jews were together when there were no *tsores*."

"Always Jews have *tsores*," said Dr. Nichtenhauser, a sad smile spreading on his face. "And hope, too. The other day, Will knows what I'm talking about, I broached the subject of establishing a chair of chemistry at the Hebrew University in Jerusalem, which was founded, as you know, about the time of the Balfour Declaration, what am I saying, long before. Anyway, you know, some of us wanted to establish a chair of chemistry to honor Dr. Weizmann, and other chairs, too, in various sciences and the humanities. And I, or rather we, a group of us talked to some business men, some of them Jewish and some non-Jewish, and one of them, a non-Jew, I am glad to say, got up and said 'What makes you so sure you'll have a country, and that your university will last, that the Arabs won't wipe you out? Aren't you building on sand, on nothing, really? After all, you have to think about the future.' Well, he was right, but he was also wrong. The same objections were made when the university was first established and it's gone on and grown. I think it has a chance to grow even more now. Proof? I have no proof. I couldn't give any proof to the non-Jew who spoke or to the other non-Jews. Maybe even some of the Jews felt that way a little, but something held them back from speaking, at least, I think something held them back. Why? Because Jews have built on what looks like nothing for two thousand years now. Jews have built on *choorbons* (destructions, collapses) for two thousand years. They started planning for the re-establishment of their country right after the Romans took Jerusalem for the second time. This is all old and ancient stuff, and the children are taught it in Hebrew school, but it's still wonderful."

"Did you get any money for the university?" asked Mary Tobias.

100

Dr. Nichtenhauser smiled. "Yes. Pledges for ten thousand dollars, which wasn't so much, but still it was something, and I think I'll be able to get another five thousand from the group. And I think I'll collect every dollar of the pledges."

"Something is happening in America, in all Jewry everywhere, but in America especially," said Dr. Korngold. "I see new faces in my synagogue, other rabbis see new faces in their synagogues, and community centers are seeing new faces, Jews who had never come before. Jews are coming back, slowly, almost bashfully. They have learned something. What it is they have learned is hard to say, but whatever they have learned is bringing them back."

"They've learned what I've learned," said Will. "They've learned several things, the way I've learned several things. One is that Americanism and Judaism are not far apart. I really can't give you facts and figures, you know, but I sort of sense it. And another thing people have learned, and I have learned, is that America, wonderful as it is, still has some flyspecks as far as Jews are concerned, you know what I mean. An American Jew used to think that being a Jew was sort of incidental to being an American, but now, because of Hitler, they've become doubtful that being a Jew is so incidental. I'm not sure I'm saying what I want to say, but something is happening."

"I think I can tell you what American Jews are learning," said Dr. Nichtenhauser. "Dr. Shmaryahu Levin, the great Zionist, knew it years ago. He made a speech in Omaha, Nebraska. I was there. He was a great and wonderful orator. Of course, I don't remember his exact words, but he said something like this: 'You Jews think you're not in *Galut* (Exile). And I don't blame you for thinking so. After all, it really is wonderful here for Jews. You have jobs, you can vote, your children can go to college. Good, very good. But I say you're wrong. You, too, are in *Galut*. But there is a difference between you and European Jews. In Europe every Jew feels his *Galut* like a sack of one hundred pounds of iron. In America he feels it like a sack of one hundred pounds of sugar.' "

David was deeply impressed by this remark. He looked at Will, and he saw that he, too, was impressed. David looked at the Tobiases and saw that they were just as impressed.

"But wait," said. Dr. Nichtenhauser. "He said some other

things in that talk. I haven't thought of it for years, but it all comes back to me now. A very shrewd man he was. Ah, the very profound and humorous, and even, if you'll permit me, humorous-sexy remarks he used to make. He once addressed a group of a hundred very prettey young Jewish women. He was the only man present, he told this to me himself later, and the chairlady told me, too, and she laughed when she told me, she liked it so much, the humor of it. Dr. Levin, as I say, was the only man present, and he looked out upon the faces of the pretty, round, rosy, smiling Jewish faces of all these beautiful women, and said, 'I am overwhelmed with being in the presence of so many beautiful and desirable Jewish young women. With one beautiful young woman I would know what to do, but with a hundred I don't know!' The women burst out into laughter. He was the kind of man who could say such a thing to a hundred women and not offend them, and make them like what he said, find it humorous. But what I wanted to say is that, oh yes, another remark he made at that same Omaha, Nebraska talk. He told his audience that not long before he had been in Cincinnati, had met with a group of Christians, with whom German Jews and other Reform Jews had been fraternizing, you know, being social with, being 'thorough Americans' with. So Dr. Levin wanted to know how the Christians felt about the Jews who were trying to make friends with them. And one of them, apparently speaking for the group of Christians, said 'The Jewish people are fine folk, but we are a bit embarrassed by them because they speak such a perfect English, much better than we do.' And Dr. Levin added, this I remember especially, and I used to use it years ago when I would talk to Jews who were in favor of assimilation. Dr. Levin said, 'Some Jews think that the more they assimilate the more will the boundaries between them and the Christians disappear and do away with anti-Jewish prejudice. But in the end, it turns out, that the more Jews are assimilated the more anti-Jewish feeling they arouse.' "

The whole group gasped with the realization of the essential truth in Dr. Levin's remark.

There were a few moments of silence. Then Dr. Korngold said, "The truth is the truth."

David was startled by the realization of how deep anti-Jewish feeling was. He had known of this feeling before, of course, but

Dr. Shmaryahu Levin's remark dramatized it and exposed its long roots, so long that one could not see their ends, roots that seemed to wind around every aspect of living, roots that made their appearance on all levels of society, in business and in social life and in universities, everywhere. But now his heaviness of heart began to vanish, and a new hope and warmth came to David. He recalled what Dr. Nichtenhauser had said about the Hebrew University in Jerusalem. It had been established years before there was any Jewish settlement of any real size in Palestine. Jewish money and hopes and dreams were being poured into it all the time, and the university was growing and flourishing. David's heart lifted. A wonderful gladness spread through him.

Five

David's real life was lived at the Tobias home. He looked forward to going there. He recalled what he heard there long afterward and it was from that he had got his chief direction as to his future life. He wrote story after story about his Jewish background, and he planned novels about it, and also about Jewish life in general down the ages. He now began to fear something that he had never before feared, that he might not live long enough to conclude all the stories and novels that were burgeoning within him.

He had sent several of his stories and sketches to the Anglo-Jewish periodicals, but they had not accepted a single one. Then he sent the same stories and sketches to the general magazines, among them monthlies and weeklies of high respectability, and within a few months he had sold nearly ten stories to them. He was both satisfied and bewildered by this experience—satisfied because it was good to know that editors wanted his stories about Jewish life; and he was bewildered that the Anglo-Jewish magazines didn't print them, for he knew that they were good. He expressed his bewilderment to Mary Tobias, and she smiled and said, "I'm not surprised. Some of our Jewish intellectuals are filled with self-distrust, and they're what might be called intellectual climbers. You wait, any day you'll begin to get letters from the Anglo-Jewish editors, asking for stories from you, yes, the very same editors who had refused to take your material before."

This is exactly what happened. After two of David's stories had appeared in two quality national monthlies, three Anglo-Jewish editors asked him why he didn't send the stories to them —and each of these editors had rejected these same stories. One of the editors had even sent David a scolding letter for sending him so "thin and slight" a piece of fiction.

Meanwhile David was continuing his work on the *Globe*. He did his work more or less mechanically. He was perturbed by many aspects of the post-war *Globe*. One was the smaller amount of space that was being devoted to poems and literary criticism. Another was the belligerence of the political articles. A third—and most important to David—was the increasing influence of fellow travelers and even Communists. The magazine continued to pretend being "liberal" and non-Communist, the editor Bourne himself thought that he was running a "truly liberal" magazine, as he told his friends, but Edith Loring, who spoke for the Globe Associates, who had their ears, and therefore was, in some ways, the real editor, was wielding a mounting influence in the editorial direction of the magazine. Bourne had been trying to curb her for six or seven years, but he now realized that she was too strong for him. One day he would think that he was the editor in fact as well as in name, but then he saw that this was only an illusion—Edith had somehow managed to sneak in an article by this or that sympathizer with what was going on in Russia.

Bourne had been greatly disturbed by the Yalta and Teheran agreements that President Roosevelt had signed with Stalin. He thought that President Roosevelt had behaved most immorally, offering to Stalin parts of China and Japan and other "concessions" without consulting Chiang-Kai-Shek. He had written strong editorials against these "sell-outs to the man who only a short while ago had been blood-brother to Hitler and Hirohito. Our children and our grandchildren and our great-grandchildren will rue the day our President signed these shameful agreements. Stalin and his cohorts in the Kremlin are still our enemies. The expediency of war made us partners. Let us not allow the peace to make us traitors to our own principles." Edith had objected to these views, but he had insisted. Bourne thought that the *Globe* was once more "a truly independent and truly American organ, dedicated to the immemorial liberties of this country, ever ready to raise its lance in defense of the Bill of Rights and international morality."

But one morning, Bourne woke up and discovered that Edith Loring had been working behind his back and installed as foreign correspondents for the *Globe,* in Moscow and London, two men who were writing what he considered highly biased, pro-Russian, and anti-American dispatches. It was astonishing how she had done this. He now almost always called her Loring, and not Edith, for she seemed to be "a snake in the grass," as he told his wife Sophia. The distressing thing she had done was, on the surface, entirely "in order." She had managed to get his approval, and yet what finally came of it all was entirely opposed to his ideas, and he was sure that she knew what she was doing. "She is a female Machiavelli," he said to Sophia. One of the men, Lauren Pendelton had been writing for the New York *Dispatch,* a newspaper of considerable standing. He had been in Russia for two years, and his reports had seemed to Bourne to be dubious—he had almost never written anything unfavorable about events in Russia, but had often found fault with our State Department. He had not criticized Russia's lack of genuine democracy. But he had managed to win the approval of many "liberals" in American intellectual life, especially ministers and college professors. Bourne did not claim to be an authority on foreign affairs, so he, unconsciously, minimized his own doubts about the correspondent. Then Loring suggested that the correspondent represent the *Globe* in Russia and in the other Slavic countries. He had had some difficulties with the *Dispatch* and was now working for the New York *Observer,* which was not averse to his doing an occasional article for the *Globe.*

"It's a real break for us," Loring had said to Bourne. "And he'll do it for peanuts, a hundred dollars an article, and for us he'll do real background pieces. It will be good for circulation. Everybody is interested in developments in Russia now, Russia and the United States have come out of the war as the two leading Powers in the world, and everybody respects Pendelton."

Bourne hesitated, and Loring said, "If we don't sign him up, the *Eagle* (a rival weekly) will. So I'll tell him all right, it's a real break."

"Yes, I suppose so," said Bourne. "I assume he's reliable."

"Of course," said Loring, and she was off.

In his very first dispatch Pendleton said that "genuine Communism" was "in many respects, once you ignore the campaign shibboleths, what might very well be called Twentieth Century Americanism, and the conduct of the government in World War Two proved this." Bourne was appalled by this statement. He considered it a "brazen lie," as he told Sophia, "an unashamed lie."

Sophia reminded him, that the Rev. Dr. Jonathan Raphael Griswold, of the Allied Theological Seminary, and a writer on foreign affairs, had said this many times from the pulpit of the Midtown-Center Presbyterian Church. To which Bourne said, "This only confirms my opinion of Pendelton's statement, that it's a lie, a shocking lie, and I won't print it."

He was about to cut out the line from the dispatch, and make other cuts in it, but he dscovered that the dispatch was already in type and was on the way to press. In a rage he stalked into Loring's office. He ordered that the dispatch be killed. Loring calmly asked him to quiet down, and then said that it was too late. "The article is already locked up for the next issue, and we are late as it is. I kept the press open specially to get this first dispatch in, and you noticed I gave it a big plug, the first article in a series, Pendelton will write regularly for us, and so on. I may have forgotten to tell you that I promised him we wouldn't censor a line he wrote. Besides, you knew how he felt about Russia, he made no secret about it, and if you are in disagreement with him you can write a letter to the letters column. Don't worry, please. The article, Pendelton, all his articles, will do us a lot of good. I don't agree with everything he says either, but it's good for us."

"Good!" exclaimed Bourne. "He'll ruin our reputation. He's writing lies."

The article appeared exactly as Pendelton wrote it. His next three articles appeared to be factual, so Bourne could hardly complain. Then came the fourth article, which contained a mild criticism of Moscow's "foolish censorship," coupled with a hymn of praise to "Stalin's sterling qualities of leadership and courage," which annoyed Bourne, but Loring again reminded him that Pendelton agreed to write for the *Globe* only on condition that his material not be censored. "Besides, that is his personal opinion, and he's on the spot, whereas we're not. Further, we're getting some wonderful mail about the Pendelton pieces."

But Pendelton's next half dozen articles were so enthusiastically pro-Russian that Bourne was livid with rage. In one of them Pendelton claimed that "the dictatorship of the proletariat, as truly understood" was "as of now perhaps the ultimate in democratic government."

"How can any dictatorship be a democracy?" asked Bourne of Sophia. "A dictatorship is a dictatorship."

"I should think so," said Sophia, who had long before begun to hope that her husband would give up his connection with the *Globe*. He was now in his sixties, their children were grown, he was in comfortable financial circumstances, and his days at the *Globe* were only daily aggravations. She knew nothing about politics, she barely understood what was being written about Russia. She knew little about American politics, too, though in the past she had had a strange sense that her husband was being somewhat too moral in his views on politics, too hidebound, didn't realize the flow of political life, didn't appreciate the need for occasional confusion in political life, even the need for an occasional spree of what could perhaps be called political immorality. For herself, chiefly unconsciously, she had developed a vague philosophy of life that she also applied to the life of the state. She herself had been a passionate woman, far more so than she had at first thought, she had hoped for more sheer physical delight from her marriage, and the fact that Bourne had not given her that delight had been one of her great secret personal tragedies. Slowly she had learned to get some vague satisfaction from secretly dreaming of the passion that was absent in her bedroom. Those were her own periods of bacchanalia, and they made her life a little more tolerable than it otherwise would be. She thought that similar bacchanalias probably were also necessary in the lives of thousands and tens of thousands of other women and other men. From that thought she went to the thought that what was true of individual human beings was likely also true of societies. Then she decided that a student of politics should allow for these bacchanalias in public life, should not be so moral in his views.

108

Her husband did not allow for them, and this was another complaint she had against him: he was too "moral" towards her and he was too "moral" in his thinking about society. But as the years went on, she inclined to forget his "morality," she had less and less need for her periods of dream-passion. She did, however, admit that her "moral" husband was not without his very sizeable virtues as a political thinker: he was narrow-minded as a political philosopher, but he was also steadfast in his principles: he was for free speech and free assembly. As such he was pretty much of a lonely voice in the land. A new kind of political thinker was taking over, or, rather, a new type of philosophy was taking over and many old-fashioned "liberals" were succumbing to this philosophy.

"If anything I know is true," said Bourne again, "it is that a dictatorship is a dictatorship."

"Yes," said Sophia.

"But I don't know what to do," said Bourne.

"At least Matson is a little better," said Sophia, referring to the other correspondent whom Loring had "put over" on Bourne. "I mean a little better."

"A little, not much more, not much more. He writes light things about Russian women, Russian sports, he doesn't discuss politics, but, then again, maybe he's just as bad, because of his very simple-mindedness. From him people get the idea that life is just fine in Russia." Bourne stopped and looked off into space . . . a sadness came to his face, and Sophia wanted to go over and caress him and kiss this man who had been her husband all these years. He had brought her much disappointment, and yet there was something very solid and even admirable about this man, this hard, unyielding, rather cold and somewhat humorless man.

She wanted to kiss him out of admiration rather than out of passion. He seemed so helpless, and yet in his very helplessness there seemed to be a certain towering strength. She herself was now being filled with a gnawing fear that the day when the ideas of men like her husband prevailed or set the pace of thinking in America was coming to an end. A new type of man in the political realm and in the writing realm and in the whole cultural world seemed to be coming to the fore. This man believed in what some people were beginning to call "controlled democracy"—she didn't remember where she had read this phrase that appalled her, perhaps it was from some South American dictator—and in violence and in ugliness, and who looked upon beauty and love and honor as marks, not of the divine in man but of offensive softness. Sophia had been going to literary reviews at various clubs she belonged to (the Progressive Women's Association, the Midtown Cultural Women's Sodality, the New Women's Nook) and she had been hearing women talk about books and plays in a manner that made her unhappy.

So many of them looked like stouter or thinner editions of Thelma Tierney, who had spoken before one or another of these women's clubs. Miss Tierney was married to a celebrated novelist (it was her fourth marriage, and everybody knew that they were not living together, and that her husband despised her, said so in public on his numerous public drunken binges, and was openly living with a literary agent who was less than half his age), conducted a daily column that appeared in about 150 newspapers over the country. She was a tall, buxom woman, who seldom talked normally, as men and women talk when together in small groups, but always seemed to talk as if she were addressing an audience of several hundred people. She appeared constantly to be in a nervous state, running away from something or running to something, the nature of which, Sophia felt, Miss Tierney herself was not sure of. Miss Tierney's chief characteristics were hurry and the desire to appear omniscient. There didn't seem to be any desire in her to please a man, she preferred to please audiences, especially audiences of women. That fact arrested Sophia's attention, how few times Miss Tierney addressed men audiences. Men seemed to shun her, were offended by her manners, by her lack of womanhood.

Sophia wondered about her and her kind. Her kind was increasing in number among women. They talked as if they were carbon copies of her, some were a trifle softer in manner, a bit more belligerent or less obstinate, but they all seemed to be in such a hurry to prove something, and Sophia didn't know what that something was. She imagined it was a desire to prove that they were not "just women," but "mature people, irrespective of sex," as one of them had said. The same female orator had said: "I urge you women to fulfill yourselves in all ways, not merely in the accidental sexual manner. Do not let biology guide your whole life. Please do not misunderstand me, I am not telling you to ignore your biological duties. I am only asking you to go beyond them. Be first-class human beings, not just women of the three K's—*Kinder, Kuche, Kirche,* children, kitchen, church. And it is for this reason that I am so glad to speak to you today about the new books, the new novels and plays that are stirring the literary world. I am most eager to have you participate in this life."

As Sophia watched this woman and heard her, she was offended. She was not surprised that she was unmarried. Sophia was especially offended by the phrase "biological duty," it put the essence of womanhood on a lowly basis. Sophia wondered whether the New Emancipation of Woman, which undoubtedly had a good idea at its core at the time of its first enunciation, hadn't gone off in a wrong direction, bringing darkness and confusion and an especially dreadful form of enslavement to ideas that clashed with the deepest desires and dreams of woman-kind.

Sophia recalled several book reviews and play reviews that Miss Tierney and her disciples had given over the past four, five years. They praised ugly books and ugly plays and ragged and unintelligible poems. Sophia remembered especially a review that Miss Tierney had given of Hemingway's *Across the River and Into the Trees,* a book that Sophia had read and disliked very much as a novel, as sheer writing, and as a reflection of the type of fiction that seemed to dominate the literary world at the moment. Miss Tierney had begun by saying that this was not one of Hemingway's best, but quickly added, "Even as a second-class Hemingway novel, it is instinct with beauty and with heroism and with truth and with grace. Hemingway is not afraid to come to grips—and I say grips advisedly—with the secret emotions of man and woman. The love of the middle-age general for the young Italian girl is a love that many middle-aged men dream about, and it is a subject that should be treated by great artists, and Hemingway does just that in this novel."

That was one of the few times when Sophia Bourne had asked a question during the question period: "But, Miss Tierney, isn't Mr. Hemingway's treatment rather ludicrous,

111

even shabby, rather than pathetic? The book reads as if it were told in a Pullman smoking compartment, and haven't we a right to expect something better from our great writers?"

Miss Tierney looked at Sophia and said slowly, "I expected that question, and when I say that I do not mean to be condescending. I don't want to give that impression for the world. But, and I would like to emphasize this, don't you think it's high time that we looked at life straight in the face, and not flinched at it?"

"I believe we should look at life in the way you say, Miss Tierney," said Sophia Bourne, "and of course, you know so much more about books than I can ever hope to know, but, at the same time, it seems to me that Hemingway does not look at life straight in the face, he sentimentalizes it in the cheap way. Polyanna is sentimental, granted. I guess we women have been falsified a great deal, I mean several books, many books have presented pictures of us that are not real. But, at the same time, when they present us women, and men, too, merely as creatures who want nothing else than what a man like Mr. Hemingway says, or Mr. Faulkner, or even Mr. Dreiser, who is not heard of so much now as he used to be, but Sherwood Anderson is, well, these people, at least some of the time, but Hemingway and Faulkner and O'Hara, yes, John O'Hara, he seems to be the worst of the lot, I mean it doesn't necessarily mean that you are telling the truth about men and women when you make them all dirty-minded all the time, that is just as false as when you make them all angels. I don't think I'm a prude. I know I'm not, but truth and mud are two different things. And one more thing. I seem to be making a speech myself, and I didn't mean to, and I hope I'm saying what I wanted to say."

This all came back to Sophia. She was proud of her little speech, and she was angry with Miss Tierney for what she said immediately afterward: "First of all, madame, I'm sorry I don't know your name, I meet so many people during my lecture trips, I'm sure you all understand, I don't mean to be offensive. But to get back to your point, and, after all, that's what counts. I think we should meet this point head on. All of us, and we might as well face it, all of us, have a great deal of the Old Adam in us, or perhaps I should say the Old Eve. There is a great deal in all of us that is not quite so pure, I'm afraid a very great deal. And all these writers that you, madame, call dirty-minded, are really being truth-minded, if I may coin a phrase. I do believe that I am as sentimental as the next woman, after all, women are supposed to be sentimental, it's their birth-right. But, at the same time, truth is truth. And if I may speak truthfully, as one woman before another, every single woman among us has thoughts during the day as well as during the night, that we do not tell anybody else, not even our nearest and dearest friends. And that's where Dr. Freud comes in, he says, let's look at this truth, all these truths, in the face, and that's what the great writers do. Have I made myself clear, madame?"

Sophia Bourne did not think that Miss Tierney had answered her objections, but she didn't feel she knew enough about world literature to be able to answer her effectively, besides, she didn't want to continue the exchange, she didn't want to make a public spectacle of herself. However, she was sure that Miss Tierney was wrong, and she also wondered whether Miss Tierney was as sure of her position as she tried to make the audience believe.

In any case, Miss Tierney reflected something about the age that was disturbing. Sophia herself, as she looked back upon her disappointing life with her husband, a life of delights that were never entirely delights, except in prospect, began to wonder whether the times were not making a religion of their disappointments, whether they were not deifying the merely physical expression of delights, and ignoring the spiritual essences behind them and all around them. The pleasures of the body were really nothing, even offensive without something lovely and soft and profoundly spiritual accompanying them. And she began to look deeply into her own being without hesitations and fears, and she saw that while there was what Miss Tierney had called the Old Eve in her, there was also the Virgin Mary, the Eternal Mother of all mankind, and her own physical mother and her own father and her own whole family and all the wonderful and glorious traditions of tenderness and compassion and pity in the world, and these things were not lies, but they were as true as the ugly and the shabby in man. Man was an amalgam of good and bad, the ugly and

113

the glorious. It was wrong to say one was more real than the other but no, perhaps the good and the beautiful was more real and more true, because it was ever present in the human heart, it set the pace of human life, all its aspirations, one never had to apologize for it, it was a good in itself.

They who followed Miss Tierney's thinking, were living by a different set of standards, namely, that the ugly alone was real, the ugly in all forms, in personal relations, in communal life, in national life, and in international relations. Sophia feared that this new religion, for that was what it was, would be with us a long time, it seemed to attract so many people in their lowliest selves . . . the shabby movies and the shabbier books upon which so many of the movies were based—one blessing about the movies, it occurred to her, was that while so many of them were hollow and pointless and even suggestively pornographic, they were not quite as dreadful as the books which were their sources—and the shabby plays, too, even those by the better playwrights . . . Sophia loved the theatre, and she loved especially the plays of O'Neill, but something deep within her told her that O'Neill, great as he was, was succumbing to the new and ugly religion of the times . . . she remembered *Strange Interlude* and *Mourning Becomes Electra* . . . way back, in the early thirties, when she had first seen them, she had been greatly impressed, there seemed to be all this "Great Truth" in them, the very same "truth" that Miss Tierney had been talking about, and she had been annoyed with her husband because he had said that O'Neill was not telling the whole truth but only a part of it "and I don't think he's emphasizing the right part"—this last phrase Sophia now remembered with special clarity . . . and in that Sophia saw that her husband was right.

Indeed, she thought to herself, that was the trouble with that whole era she was living in. A certain animalism had come to the world, and along with it a certain moral vulgarity and spiritual lassitude. Men and women were gorging themselves with sex and with food and liquor, and pretending they were happy, and she was sure that they were not really happy, not in their deepest essences, their fraudulent happiness brought them sleepless nights and worrisome days, and they felt their

114

souls being spattered with the mud. The animal in man is important, but not when it runs rampant.

She was also troubled by the fanatical yearning for economic security at almost any price. The spirit of adventure seemed to have gone out of the world, and in its place had come a vast lack of spirit to do anything but to battle for the assurance of the bare necessities of life. On this she was very much confused. The bare necessities were important, perhaps they should be assured, the New Freedom was good, the New Deal was good, but people seemed to be wanting more and more security in economic affairs, and she didn't like it, though she didn't know exactly why she didn't like it or precisely what aspect she didn't like. The whole world seemed to be after economic security in a wild and irresponsible way. This was what she didn't like about all the fellow-travelers, not so to speak of the Communists: they were making a religion of security. She wondered, deep within her mind, whether all this didn't presage the coming collapse of Western civilization, for what she remembered of her study of ancient history, a similar state existed in Rome just before the fall of the Roman Empire. And when she put this thought together with the rise in animalism in virtually every aspect of culture, her sense of despair deepened and mounted.

Out of all these thoughts came a greater respect and admiration for her husband. He stood for things that had endurance and stature. He was everlastingly right in what he said about Russia and about the present state of morals and general culture, but she didn't know exactly what he could do to redirect the flow of events. He was too old to put up another fight such as he had been capable of ten, even five years before. Even if he had been able physically she wasn't sure that he would have had much success. The flow of vulgarity and animalism seemed too powerful, sweeping all before it. This flow was almost impersonal, like a moving glacier. Orson couldn't cope with what was going on in the world, probably nobody could. The tragedy was that Orson's magazine, on which he had put in so much work, and into which he had put so many of his deepest hopes, was allied with this alien and indifferent and depressing flow of the times.

Her Orson was alone now. This drew her to him, in spite of his failure as a husband. Life was so strange, so filled with inner contradictions. But this was all in the past now. He had been distant from her in the years gone by, now he was closer to her, getting closer every day, and she was both astonished and pleased—and a little bit frightened. How could she have changed so much? But she did change. There was something enduring about the Orson who was her husband. Now she had the feeling that her Orson was becoming a little bit like the Orson that she had yearned for. He was becoming more dependent upon her embraces at night, and his occasional love-making seemed to have more real desire in it—perhaps desire was not the right word. What Orson brought to the love-making was not eager, urgent, overwhelming possession. It was rather a need different from mere physical need. There was physical need in it, and she was grateful for that—it was very pleasant, very reassuring, very complimentary for a woman of her time of life, to be fondled by her husband, caressed all over, kissed, and whispered to. It was very lovely, indeed. And yet she sensed that her Orson did this not merely because he wanted her as a woman, as his wife, but because he needed the deep comfort of her being, her companionship, she was his life, she was his dreams, she was his whole past, she had been with him in his triumphs, she was now with him and would continue to be with him in his mounting and multiplying defeats.

Now she realized something else, and she was sad and she was happy. He needed her, but she also needed him, perhaps as much, and she hoped that it was as much, she was sure it was as much. She too was lonely in this new world all about them, she too belonged to a generation that seemed to be growing more and more distant from the contemporary world. Her Orson and she belonged to this old world, she liked this old world, she was not at home in the new world. Her Orson knew all this time what was going on. She hadn't known that he was right. Now she knew, and she was glad that Orson had been right, and she was glad that now he was getting comfort from her, and her ability to do so was part payment for her having been blind to what he knew and what he had told her, and it was part payment for having thought cold

116

and hard and sometimes worse things about him and how he had disappointed her. But this disappointment now seemed so far away, and not so important really, and yet she couldn't get rid of a certain feeling of guilt, of having failed her husband, this good and wise man. It was so good to cling to him now, for he brought her comfort, too. All day long, as she read the newspapers and the magazines and listened to the radio, she wondered what this world was that she was living in. She barely knew it. There were days, as she sat alone in the house, when she was afraid of what was going on outside her door, and she became impatient for her Orson to come back home, and as soon as he entered the door she was at peace again with herself, and the little world that he created by merely entering the door was a good and friendly world, and she would kiss him out of gratitude for bringing this good and friendly world into her home, and she would kiss him for himself, for having been her husband all these years, and she would kiss him for the comfort he had brought her the night before and the comfort that he would bring her tonight and all the other nights and the week-ends. She felt girlish and almost honeymoonish, and that was good, and she was glad she was a woman, and she was glad she was her husband's wife, and she was glad that Orson was her Orson.

But while they comforted each other, their joint problem with respect to the alien world outside remained. Orson's problem was a compounded one, for it included what to do about his position on the *Globe*. It was, in many respects, his paper, he was the editor, he was now, for long had been, the largest owner of "stock" in it—in other words, he had put a great deal of his own money into it, not as a business investment, of course, but as a contribution toward the perpetuation of a journal whose pristine principles were very dear to him. In a sense he could assume the control that his "investment" entitled him to, but the *Globe* was not a business, it was an idea, and it was understood that the control would be exercised by the Globe Associates, which included many subscribers of long standing, old men and women who had not only subscribed to the magazine over a longer period of time than had Orson Bourne, but whose families had subscribed to the magazine and otherwise supported it for decades. It was the

117

Globe Associates who had kept the magazine going, somehow, over the many crises that it had been through.

Further, these Globe Associates included some very distinguished people, among them professors, authors, clergymen, liberal members of Congress and of the state and municipal governments, social workers, and private "liberal" men and women. The Globe Associates controlled the editorial policy, in so far as there was "control" in the generally accepted sense of the term. Only on a very few occasions were they called upon to exercise "control"—and one of those times was when Edith Loring asked them to decide whether or not the *Globe* should be "liberal" with respect to Russia. Bourne lost that argument, and he remembered how hurt he was. He also remembered to what lengths he went to show the Globe Associates his side of the argument, what long quotations he had prepared from old editorials in the *Globe,* supporting his stand that the *Globe* had to criticise, and sharply too, the anti-democratic and dictatorial policies of the Soviet government. He had shown them that Russia was not a democracy but a sort of concentration camp, where no one had had genuine civil liberties, and that because of this alone the *Globe* was bound, by the very principles upon which it was founded, to denounce Communist Russia. But the Globe Associates voted in favor of the magazine being "friendly and sympathetic to our Russian friends in their present heroic struggles to free themselves from the Czarist yoke. The *Globe* can be more itself, more what its founders wanted it to be, by lending a helping hand to fellow human beings in a friendly country, which is trying to do what our own beloved country, after all, did in 1776."

Bourne thought of urging the *Globe* Associates to reconsider their decision. Then he got a letter from a professor of law, a man for whom he had the highest respect as a defender of civil liberties, who said that he was beginning to wonder, "in all candor, and I feel I can talk to you frankly, whether your wealthy upbringing and generally generous financial circumstances, are not influencing your views with regard to what is now going on in Russia. It may all be unconscious, but after all, our deepest views and convictions are often unconscious. But I suggest that you consider whether it is not possible that,

118

deep down, you are not afraid that what is happening in Russia may spread to the rest of the world, and in time endanger your inheritance. This may shock you, but I throw this idea out, in the friendliest of spirits, believe me."

This letter made him realize the futility of his position on the *Globe*. He continued to go to the office more out of habit than desire. He had nowhere else to go where he could keep in touch with world affairs. Unhappy as he was on the *Globe* he could read there magazines and newspapers from all over the world, and he could see many of the new books published. That was very important to him. It was his whole intellectual life. He had started several books, but he didn't make satisfactory progress. His mind was too distracted. Then he began to notice that his mind was too distracted in the office for him to be able to read there. He was getting lonelier and lonelier. He pleaded ill health, though he was in relatively fine physical shape, and stayed away from the office for days at a time. Sophia's heart ached for him, but she didn't know what to do.

He tried to find an answer to his problem in places where he had seldom been before—at the Harvard Club in New York City, at the Engineers Club, at the University Club, at the Century Club, at the Republican Club, at the Democratic Club, at the Lotus Club. He talked to men and women in these places. To his dismay a large number of them didn't realize what was happening to the country, especially to the intellectuals, and some of those who did were not very much disturbed. One man said, "Well, I guess the old days are over. Perhaps rugged individualism was a little too harsh, and maybe the Russians have something to teach us."

"But what about civil liberties?" asked Orson Bourne.

"Oh, I don't know," said the man. "We really don't know too much about what's going on there, there may be civil liberties, there may not. I don't know. But the people seem to be happy. Besides, civil liberties are all right, I guess, but eating regular is better, don't you think?"

Bourne was amazed. "People in prison eat regular, too," he said.

"Yes, but that's different," said the man, "much different. A little more control from the top isn't always bad."

This amazed Bourne even more, for the same man—he had known him for many years, though they seldom met—had criticised President Roosevelt and the New Deal for putting "too much emphasis on the authority of the Federal government. That's dictatorship."

One of the women he had seen at the Independent Democratic Club over a period of years—she seemed like a sensible, well-informed, calm person—joined him in conversation one afternoon. She admitted that her new literary interest was Ernest Hemingway: "I used to think that he was too harsh, you understand, much too harsh, and I didn't and still don't enjoy his prize fight stories, but his novels—they are different. There is something in them. They seem so clean and so honest. *A Farewell to Arms* is rather powerful fiction. I like the ending especially. And I've just got around to reading *For Whom the Bell Tolls,* and I must say I couldn't put it down, so interested was I."

"But aren't these books basically false?" pleaded Bourne. "How many Catherine Barclays have you known? And if you've known any did they behave the way she does in the book? And what do you think of the love scene in the sleeping bag in the Spanish novel, *For Whom the Bell Tolls?* Isn't that an adolescent point of view of love? There's something so childish about it? And is the writing good in it? In *A Farewell to Arms* the writing is a bit better, I admit, but even there it strikes me as rather, well, deafening rather than enlightening. Hemingway seems to think that all people speak in clipped sentences like prize fighters or his beloved bull fighters. People don't talk that way, and writers shouldn't make them talk that way."

"Yes, but . . . but he is exciting," said the woman. "I don't pretend to know how prize fighters talk, and maybe his writing is a little brittle, but it's still exciting. Anyway," she smiled, "it seems to be the new style, and maybe we're just too old fully to appreciate it. It could be that the younger folk are right, and we're wrong." She smiled again. "Frankly, I used to think the way you do, and maybe at bottom I still do, but my daughter and her daughter, my grand-daughter, she goes to Barnard, have been calling me an old fogey so long, a has-

120

been, because I like Edith Wharton and Willa Cather and David Graham Phillips and Sarah Orne Jewett, she has looked down upon me so much, especially the grand-daughter, her name is Ethelreda, and she has been praising the works of Faulkner and Firbank and Hemingway and Thornton Wilder and others, oh, yes, and poets like William Carlos Williams and Ezra Pound and Eliot, well, I decided to read some of them, or, rather, re-read them. Some of them I just couldn't understand at all, especially Pound and Williams. But . . . neither could I understand Faulkner, most of him. But Hemingway, at least, is simple."

"And simple-minded," said Bourne.

"Yes, that could be."

"He's not only an adolescent, he seems to be a belligerent adolescent."

"Yes, that could be, too." The woman sighed. "I get so confused sometimes. When my husband was alive he used to help me sort of unconfuse myself, if there is such a word. I often used that very word, *unconfuse*. He got furious with me. He said there was no such word, I should look up words I made up in the dictionary. Well, that seemed like such a bother." She looked off into the distance, smiled, faced Bourne, and continued. "It used to annoy him so much. But he did clear things up for me. Goodness, what was I about to say?"

"How your husband used to *unconfuse* you, how . . ."

"Oh, yes. What I wanted to say, he died four years ago, it will be four years a month from today, exactly a month. He used to hear our daughter talk about all these new writers, and he called them all trash, smart-alecks, that was his word, just little boys writing dirty words on fences and in toilets, that's another thing he used to say. He liked to upset our daughter, but I guess he did feel strong about these matters, the way he felt about so many of the new-fangled political ideas of Roosevelt's. He was simply furious with Roosevelt, he said Roosevelt was running the country, turning it into a Communist country, doing away with thrift and savings, and setting up the loafer as our ideal. This very minute I can see how livid his face used to turn when he talked about Roosevelt. Now what was it I began to talk about?"

121

"Writers . . ."

"Yes. My husband had no use whatever for Hemingway and those others, Odets, is there such a man?"

"Yes, I can't stand him myself. Shouts too much. I don't think he really understands people," said Bourne. "All his characters are the same, like he is, I imagine, sort of shallow philosophers tinged with shallow radicalism."

"I don't like Odets either. All those uncles in his plays are pretty much the same, aren't they?"

"Yes, the same and unreal."

The woman hesitated, then said, "I suppose it's like my husband said. I'm too tired to think anything through for myself. Now that I'm talking to you, I'm not sure about what I said about Hemingway and Faulkner and the others, especially about Hemingway. I guess I was just trying to take the easiest way out, by agreeing with my daughter and my granddaughter, and sort of finding something good in Hemingway, but I suppose I really feel as you do about him, them. I have been thinking." She stopped and looked off to the side. Then she said, "I have been thinking that it hardly makes any difference what you and I and my husband think, does it?"

"I don't understand," said Bourne, though he had a vague inkling of what she wanted to say.

"I really mean that it makes no difference what we, our generation, think about anything. We are all dead, living but dead. I sit by myself in my room, in my sitting room, in the Hotel Mansfield Park, on Park Avenue, I have an apartment right above my daughter's, I like to sit by myself sometimes, my apartment is on the twenty-first floor, and I can see the East River, and the big boats and the tug boats, I mean the big liners and the tug boats and the barges, it's just lovely and so peaceful watching them in the evening, in the morning, too, and especially late at night, like a fairyland. And I sit there sometimes, and I think to myself about that life outside, the life we have just been talking about, these writers and those politicians in Washington and in Albany, I get the feeling that all that has a life of its own, is shaping the world, no matter what you and I think. It's a great force, what is out there, doing its will. It's sort of an irresistible force, but you and I and our generation are not immovable bodies. We just don't

122

count. The force just keeps on moving. Don't you ever feel that way?"

"I'm afraid I do," said Bourne, who was thinking of his troubles at the *Globe* as the woman was talking. "But while I know little about books, I mean, about novels and short stories, I do think that we ought to discriminate in politics. What is going on in Russia is terrible, opposed to everything we stand for in this country. But, the New Deal, well, I think there are aspects of it that are good, and that Republicans as well as Democrats ought to admit are good, like the Federal Deposit Insurance Corporation, Social Security. I'm an Independent in politics, I've voted Republican and Democrat, and now I hardly know where I stand. I didn't like the idea of four terms or even three terms for Franklin Roosevelt, but I couldn't get myself too excited about Mr. Dewey."

The woman smiled. "My husband would have called you a damn spineless Democrat. He was violent. He used to get especially upset when Democrats would accuse the Republicans of wanting to push back the clock of American history to the days of President McKinley. He wanted to know what was wrong with the days of President McKinley. The country was prosperous, people were on their own, there was free enterprise. But I'm only repeating what he said. I hardly understand what all these things mean. I never was good in history. My husband read a great deal. I must say, though, he was very convincing when he spoke. Many of the people in this club think pretty much the way he used to think. He was president here for several terms. He was always a Herbert Hoover man, because he reminded him of Grover Cleveland, who was his hero, and he thought the New Deal mudslingers, as he called them, had done Mr. Hoover a great injustice in blaming the hard times of 1929 on him."

Bourne hardly knew what to think of what this woman had told him. In general what she said depressed him. It revealed that even so basically fine a person as she obviously was, was being influenced by the outside "alien" forces. Bourne was even more depressed by what the woman had revealed about her husband and about the general feeling in this Independent Democratic Club. The outside "alien" forces had penetrated here, too.

123

Later he learned something else, which also depressed him. There were people who felt as he did and as his wife did about literature, but several of these same people were totally opposed to some of the most important welfare measures that the New Deal had brought into American life, such as Social Security and Federal insurance for bank deposits, and the whole sense of responsibility that the government, on the Federal scale or on a more local scale, should take in the general well-being of the citizens, particularly in the areas of economics and health. Bourne thought that the government perhaps was going too far in more or less guaranteeing a minimum of economic security to its people, but this was a mode of extremism that was to be expected considering the grave injustices that workingmen had been subjected to over the years. In time this extremism would be righted. Surely some form of unemployment insurance was a good thing, and surely some form of help from the government in case of sickness in the lower income groups was also a good thing. Bourne knew that his wife Sophia was a bit stricter in this regard than he was, she thought the government was doing too much even in this respect, yet basically she agreed with him that the government never again could return to the days when industry and capital and finance and Big Business could, so to speak, rule the roost and let the devil take the hindmost. As a matter of fact, Bourne wasn't sure that even alcoholics and drug addicts and other such employable people who made themselves unemployable by such means shouldn't also be the concern of the government, for they were clearly mentally ill and needed professional attention.

Bourne was frightened by the large number of people who yearned for the days of the Robber Barons, who were opposed to all forms of progressive legislation, or who favored only a very small amount of such legislation. These same people looked upon those who thought otherwise, who subscribed to the funamental principles of the New Deal, as fellow-travelers, sympathizers with Communism. This kind of thinking, he thought, was madness. He was especially astonished that a man like Al Smith, whom he had respected profoundly as a genuine liberal, ever could think that way. Al Smith's "anti-progress" attitude influenced other "liberals," and this too depressed Bourne.

Bourne went from club to club—he belonged to several, chiefly out of sentimental reasons, in honor of his father's memory, his father had belonged to a large number, though he went to the meetings of few of them—and he became still more depressed. What he heard all around him seemed like lunacy: people were saying that the choice was between Bourbon capitalism and Communism. This was a bitter choice to him. It was also an unreal choice. For he saw that America was not a capitalist country in the classical sense. Now, in 1945–1946, there was a combination of capitalism and socialism and something that was peculiarly American, a sort of Judaeo-Christian capitalism that kept the individual constantly in mind, his needs and his sorrows and his hopes and his dignity.

The choice, then, was between this Judaeo-Christian capitalism and Communism, and Bourne was on the side of Judaeo-Christian capitalism. It was modern Americanism. It was, in his opinion, the form of society that would probably prevail for the next hundred years, for he was sure that Russian Communism would collapse from the weight of its own inhumanity. But few people seemed to agree with him. His friends were either for a return to the America of 1890, or they saw "something good" in what was happening in Russia. He felt like saying, "A plague on both your houses." However, he began to wonder how many there were besides his wife who agreed with him.

He now went to the office of the *Globe* three and sometimes only two days a week. The magazine continued to be sympathetic to Soviet Russia. Edith Loring didn't even bother to try to mollify him, though he was nominally the editor, and she knew how opposed he was to the direction the magazine was taking. Of course, she had the authority, in a way, to do what she was doing: the Globe Associates had, so to speak, given her a green light. Still, she was only the managing editor, and she had to get the approval of the editor, Bourne, for every line she put into the magazine. But so low had his authority sunk that such professional matters of procedure were ignored. He felt humiliated, but he didn't know what he could do. He found himself writing innocuous editorial paragraphs about the need for greater cleanliness on the New York streets, the need for a new city hospital. He would send these paragraphs in to Edith Loring, and she printed them word for word, but she almost never talked to him about them. She accepted more articles by Pendelton and Matson, who continued to see many virtues in Soviet Russia. Matson was now seeing "lovelier femininity in Soviet womanhood. The atmosphere of freedom has given a new charm to them. A new respect has come to them. They are no more chattels. They are now human beings. And that is a welcome change from the days of the Czar."

Bourne wanted to ask Matson what he had to say about Russian women cleaning streets and paving roads, what he had to say about the appalling rate of abortions and divorces. But he decided to say nothing. He was not the real editor any more. There were times when he would come into his office, dictate a few letters of no consequence, and wait around for Edith Loring to report to him, but she seldom came in, and when she did, she merely wished him the time of day, and told him that circulation was going up "not too much, but healthfully." She barely discussed editorial matters with him. Now and then, out of obvious politeness, she asked him if he would be at the next editorial meeting, and he would say yes or no, whatever came to his mind. But she didn't insist, and it was now weeks since he went to an editorial meeting, and no one said anything.

Bourne felt unwanted and unnecessary. At the beginning his secretary would call his house to find out if he was "well enough to come in today. The mail isn't really much, and if you don't wish to come in, it will be all right." Now his secretary hardly called, and when she did she merely said, "I thought I'd say hello. The mail is really not much." Edith Loring would call now and then and merely say, "Rest up all you wish, OWB, things are running smoothly. I'll have the boy bring over one of the very first copies of the new issue as soon as it comes from the press." Bourne felt that the magazine, New York City, the United States, the whole world were slipping through his fingers. He imagined this was the way people who knew they were going to die felt.

The *Globe,* his magazine, the magazine into which he had put so much of his life, which to him stood for so much of what was true Americanism, the magazine that he felt Thomas Jefferson and Abraham Lincoln and George Washington and Grover Cleveland and Horace Mann and Wendell Phillips and Nathaniel Hawthorne and all the other First Americans would have enjoyed reading . . . this magazine was slowly becoming strange to him, and then it began to become offensive. He noticed things in it that he never thought would have appeared in it, things, indeed, that he wondered whether any decent publication would care to publish. There was one "short story" by Erskine Caldwell, one of the new immortals, a man who, in his opinion, had virtually nothing to say, who appeared to glory in presenting the shabbiest and filthiest aspects of man, especially of woman. The "story" was entitled, "Mildred," and was about an unfortunate Georgia girl who somehow was pushed into prostitution, partly by economic circumstances and partly because, as Caldwell makes her say, "I like it." The story was done in a matter-of-fact fashion, there was no pity in it, no understanding, and the writing was undistinguished.

There was an article entitled, "In Defense of Divorce," by one Max Oncken Mauro, in which the author argued that there were not enough divorces, that many couples lived in "a state of mutual aggravation," and he thought that "all people should get married at least twice, for monogamy is against human nature, and not only men revolt against it, but women, too." Bourne wondered how even Edith Loring could have allowed this article to get into the *Globe.* It was cheap and smart-alecky.

There were some poems by "modern poets," and these Bourne didn't understand at all. They were so ragged, so pointless, and so offensive. One poem, entitled, "Third Avenue," by Ethel Kostac, read as follows, in part:

"Mighty mastodon
Mighty mountain of twisted steel
    Surrounded by broken corrugated dreams
Convoluted hopes that fly askew and
    Sneer at gravity,

Hello
And farewell
For through your interstices I see
Grass
And the horizon that never
Falters."

"What on earth does this mean, dear?" Bourne asked Sophia.
"I don't know," Sophia said. "This is another language."

And in the same other language were written other poems: "The Bowery—A Tone Poem," "The Weehawken Ferry," "Love in the Afternoon in Coney Island," "Kiss Me with Electrical Fury," "Rainy Nights Have Been in Wyoming."

The book reviews were also strange. There was one review that went out of its way to denounce F. Scott Fitzgerald for having written *Tender is the Night,* a novel, during the depression: "This," said the reviewer, "shows the bankruptcy of Mr. Fitzgerald. He never grew up emotionally, intellectually, spiritually, he never learned that the problems of the workers—who, after all, form the majority of human beings—are really worth writing about, that the wastrels he writes about form only a very small minority of the people."

Bourne was both annoyed and confused by this sort of literary criticism. He had thought that novels were good or bad depending upon their insight into human character, not upon the adherence of the authors to any particular system of sociology. Bourne had looked upon workers as people, and capitalists as people, both worthy subjects for novelists. Wastrels were people, too. Bourne liked the works of Thackeray and Dickens and Jane Austen and David Graham Phillips and Gustave Flaubert and Tolstoy and Dostoevsky—and it never occurred to him to ask whether their authors loved the workers and thought them the cream of existence on this planet or not. It never occurred to him to criticise Tolstoy because he so seldom wrote about peasants and workers in his novels. Again Bourne asked his wife what she thought about this sort of criticism.

"I'm afraid, dear, I have only one thing to say when you ask me about the *Globe* now. I just don't understand what is going on there. I don't understand their poetry, and I don't understand their reviews."

Sophia was about to add, "But, dear, aren't you the editor?"

But she thought better of it. Her intelligence told her that it was time for her husband to abandon the *Globe* and devote himself to writing books, and to writing articles for other magazines, and also to lecturing. She couldn't tell him so herself. She waited for him to suggest it, whereupon she would instantly agree with him.

The day came very soon. It was a Sunday afternoon. They had just finished dinner. In the morning they had gone to services at Grace Episcopal Church in downtown New York. Bourne's father had belonged to the church for many years, and Bourne himself had continued the membership, though he seldom went there. Sophia, who was brought up as a Congregationalist, had been accustomed to rather "plain" services in her father's church, but she rather liked Grace Church, despite its "sociableness and snobbishness," as Orson used to say. She was attracted by the beauty of the church and also by the colorfulness of the ritual. She agreed with Orson that it was rather "Popish," still, she felt at home in it. This Sunday they went to church at Orson's suggestion, which rather surprised Sophia, but she said nothing.

It was, happily, a perfect service to go to—for Orson, for Sophia, and for the times. The church was full of men and women and children. Virtually every seat was occupied. Orson was in good spirits. He turned to his wife and whispered, "It's good to see so many people here."

"It is," she said, and somehow she felt especially good. Her Orson was getting closer to her.

The preacher was a visitor from North Dakota. He delivered a blistering onslaught on "the complacent Christians of our time who were silent while that madman Hitler destroyed six million brothers and sisters of Our Lord Jesus Christ. We have much to answer for. We Christians will suffer psychological and ethical trauma for centuries to come on account of our silence. We could have saved many of these brothers and sisters of ours. We could have ransomed them. We could have given them haven when the Hitler government asked the nations of the world, if they objected so violently to his measures against the Jews, to take them off his hands. But there was not an answer from a single country in the world, not from England, the mother of parliaments and the mother of religious and racial tolerance. No answer from Italy, whose dictator, and I say it with embarrassment in a house of God, was living with a Jewish woman. There was no answer from France. Of course, there was no answer from Russia, which was almost as anti-Semitic as Germany itself, and still is anti-Semitic.

"But, worst shame of all, there was only silence from this country. Franklin Delano Roosevelt himself, the father of the New Deal, said nothing. From the American people there was silence. From the churches there was silence. It shames me that our own beloved church, as an organization, said nothing. Some of us did talk, but we were lonely voices. I say, for shame, for enduring shame to us Christians, to us, Episcopalians! Where was our sense of charity, where was our compassion, where was our feeling for the brothers and sisters of Jesus Christ? The monster Stalin will go the way of Hitler. But the Jews he persecutes this very moment are calling upon us for our help and mercy, just as did the Jews whom Hitler persecuted and destroyed. Are we going to be taken in by the spreading false 'sympathy and understanding' of what is going on in that huge concentration camp, Russia? I say, we still have a chance partially to repent for our sins in the days of Hitler. How? By denouncing Stalin and his fellow gangsters, and above all, by coming to the aid of the Jews, from whom Our Lord Christ sprang."

Orson was much shaken by this sermon. He repeated over and over again how much he liked it, as Sophia was preparing dinner. "That's Christianity, that's real Christianity," he said.

"I'm glad you liked it, dear, I did, too."

"That's Christianity in action. I wish that talk would be printed in some paper, and spread all over the nation. Ah, I wish it were printed *in toto* in the *Globe,* but I suppose Edith Loring and the Globe Associates would think I was old-fashioned, if I suggested this. Oh, well . . . "

Sophia said nothing.

Then he said, "I guess we have sinned gravely with regard to the Jews, I guess we have."

Sophia heard this, and a heavy burden began to lift slowly from her breast . . . she had long been unable to forgive her husband for his occasional anti-Jewish remarks—even when he spoke about Louis D. Brandeis, one of his heroes. He loved Brandeis, but he wasn't altogether too sure about the people he sprang from . . . and Sophia seemed to remember strange remarks that he made about Brandeis himself . . . these were very hard to forget . . . but what Orson has just said did make her view all these past remarks in a slightly different light.

"We probably have," said Sophia softly.

"That was a powerful sermon," said Bourne. "I had thought that so wealthy a church wouldn't permit any such liberal talk. I thought they were pretty cautious whom they invite."

"Preachers are preachers," said Sophia.

"Just what was his name?"

"I don't remember," said Sophia.

"Now isn't that terrible? We heard a fine sermon, and don't know the preacher's name." Bourne hesitated. "The Jews are truly a remarkable people. Their sheer vitality is astonishing. For two thousand years they have been wanderers, no country, spread far apart, yet they are a nation, in a sense. It's very difficult to describe exactly what they are. As I say, they are spread far and wide, speaking different languages, yet there is some form of community among them."

"It could be their Bible," said Sophia, daughter of a Congregational minister. "Father used to talk about the Jews, too, he marveled about them, the way you are, dear, and he thought it was their religion, especially the Bible, the Old Testament, of course, that holds them together. All of them everywhere, no matter what language they talk, they read a part of their Bible, the Old Testament, every week, and I think it's in Hebrew, or maybe, it's Aramaic. And that's what holds them together."

"Yes," said Bourne. "Strange, I've never been to a Jewish religious service. I understand the services are pretty much the same as they were in the days of Jesus. I don't know. I really should know. I don't even know if the Bible, the original Old Testament, is in Hebrew or in Aramaic. Shameful."

"I should be especially ashamed of myself," said Sophia. "Me, a minister's daughter. The preacher this morning made a very good point, it's not so new, of course, but we tend to forget it, the Jews are Jesus's brothers and sisters, and we owe them special consideration on that score alone, yet it's horrible what we've done to them. The Germans were, are Christians, too, yet they killed six million Jews."

"Almost incredible," said Bourne. "I suppose we are all in a way to blame. It may be the preacher is right when he said that it will be decades, perhaps centuries, before we'll be able to rid ourselves of the sense of guilt. Maybe we never really will be rid of the sense of guilt. But, then, we Christians have much to be ashamed of with respect to the Jews. We're all too easy, I mean we don't think when we say unkind things about them, they're like a dog among nations. I am frank to admit I am not without sin in this regard, I'm not without sin at all."

Sophia's burden of many years lifted and lifted, and she sighed with contentment. "I'm afraid that is so."

"I suppose we have a great deal to learn from them in the way of courage," said Bourne. "At this moment, I feel Horatio Algerish when I think of them. They don't seem to have the word *defeat* in their language. They just keep on going and going. I have come to like Rabbi Stephen S. Wise. I've never met him, but the reports about him are good, as they appear in the newspapers. He's a man of perception. Now that I think of it several of the friends of the *Globe* are Jewish, especially the Tobiases."

"Yes, I remember them," said Sophia. "They're nice people. He's an architect, isn't he, and she's a social worker or something."

"He's one of the most celebrated architects in the country, and she's a very pleasant woman," said Bourne.

"Then why haven't we had them over, dear?"

"I don't know. We should have. We're both to blame, I guess."

"And isn't your David Polonsky Jewish, too?"

"He is," said Bourne, "and a very conscientious man he is, too. I have the feeling that he's greatly disappointed with the way things are going on the *Globe,* but he doesn't say much. He used to talk a great deal, arguing about this and that, mostly about the general articles and about the book section, he thought both should be better, but then he stopped talking, he just attends to his business. I suppose he gave up the struggle, pretty much the way I have."

132

"Why haven't we had him over to the house, too?"

"I don't know. We should have. There's a strange, almost mystical look in his eyes. Did you know he used to be with Harry Brandt of the *World?*"

"I seem to remember you saying something about that."

There was a silence between them. Suddenly Bourne said, "Sophia, I have made up my mind. The preacher this morning helped me do it. I am going to leave the *Globe*. They don't want me, and I don't want them. Our relationship makes no sense any more. I admit it will be a wrench to do so; after all, it represents a great deal to me, but I might as well face the facts."

Sophia was delighted, but she made an effort not to show her delight too soon.

"Are you sure, dear?"

"I am. At this minute I can't think of anything I am more eager to do. I feel unclean by continuing to be on a magazine that doesn't speak for me, that seems to have run away from me. Besides, I am tired of editing. I'm too old for that. Nearly forty years in editing is enough for one lifetime, and whatever time is left for me I think I can make use of in more pleasant tasks. There are two books I still want to write, maybe three. Perhaps one of them will be a reinterpretation of Andrew Jackson, who looms very large in my eyes, the more I study him. He was a sort of Lincoln before Lincoln. Another book I am thinking of doing is on Horace Mann. He was, in many ways, our greatest revolutionary in the world of education. And other books. Perhaps also some lecturing. And we might do some traveling together. Oh, many things. Yes, the preacher this morning helped me make up my mind."

Sophia was so delighted that she couldn't say anything immediately. She hesitated, then she said, "Orson, I'm so thrilled I can hardly say a word. I have for a long time wanted you to say this. I worried whether I should say it, but always I said to myself that so important a decision as this you should make yourself. Darling, this is no place for you now, the *Globe*. I believe, and I say this not just because I am your wife, I believe that your work on the *Globe* will long be remembered. In the future people will talk about your *Globe,* not Loring's or anybody else's *Globe*. I know that I know little about magazining, but I can sense things, and I know that you did a wonderful job. The times have changed, and I think, as you do, they have changed for the worse. I think we are going through a mad stage in the world, in this country, everywhere. Goodness, I'm so excited, I'm talking too much."

"No, go on, Sophia," said Bourne, who was happy to hear what she was saying. He hadn't realized till now how important her opinion was to him. "Continue, Sophia."

She smiled. "That's really about all I wanted to say. How glad I am. I used to get so angry when I thought of what terrible times you were going through because of what those old Globe Associates had done to you, going over your head and agreeing with Edith Loring. There were other things that made me mad. But that's all water over the dam. You are now a free man. We can now be together more often, go places, travel, and you can do your books and your articles and your lectures whenever you please."

Bourne looked at his wife and saw a new loveliness in her. The memories of the wonderful nights they had lately had together welled up in his mind and in his heart, and he was very pleased. He went over to her and slowly kissed her and pressed her to him, and then kissed her again.

"Sit down right beside me, Orson," she said. "That's good, and give me your hand, darling." She kissed his hand, and continued holding it.

"I thought I might make some arrangement with Loring and the Globe Associates. I could, perhaps, have a column. I don't mean for every week, that would be too much. I want my columns to be important and weighty, you know what I mean, Sophia."

"Of course, dear."

"Perhaps two columns a month. That would be about right. Two weeks in which to do a column, maybe one thousand words, or a little over, that would be fine. I can't see how they could say no."

"They couldn't, and they won't. You know it. People for a long time read the *Globe* because of your writings."

"I like to think so."

"Of course, they did. But that's not so important. If the

Globe doesn't agree to your proposal, and I am sure they will, some other magazine will."

"I hope so."

"Let's not talk about it any more, I mean whether they'll give you the column on the *Globe* or not. They will. I'm just so happy about your decision. I feel like a girl again." She kissed his hand once more.

"I feel real good now, Sophia. Perhaps to celebrate we ought to have a little sherry. I feel like it. Perhaps a bit of brandy. Have we got some?"

Sophia kissed his hand again quickly, and stood up. "We have almost a whole bottle of brandy, have had it for years and years."

"Didn't somebody give it to us, Sophia?"

"Yes, the youngest son of one of your father's lawyers, was it Stanley Thompson or something like that?"

"Goodness, what a memory! It was Stanley Thompson. He came to this very room about eight, nine years ago. How time flies! Stanley Thompson. That reminds me." He stopped.

"What does it remind you of, Orson? You seem worried."

"Another shameful thing I've done or failed to do. Strange that I should remember it now. He sent us a letter soon after he was here, not just a thank you, bread-and-butter letter, but a letter that required an answer. Nothing terribly important, but it did require an answer, and I didn't answer him. All these years . . . "

"Oh, Orson, don't let that trouble you too much. You should have written, and I should have reminded you. After all . . . you just write to him, tell him you're sorry, and invite him over to the house, his wife and the children. It will be nice to have some young folks here again. Now I'll get the brandy, and I'll be back in a minute."

While she was gone, he picked up a Bible and read a passage here and there. Sophia was back now, and she put a tray down, with a brandy bottle and a sherry bottle, with the appropriate glasses. "That brandy smells awfully good, dear," she said. "I opened the bottle. I think I'll take a little sherry. Brandy is a little too strong for me. But you have your brandy. It has a lovely, heady bouquet."

Orson filled her glass and then his glass. "Sit on my lap, darling." He blushed. "I don't know what's gone over me."

"Darling, thank you. You're a darling."

She sat on his lap. They raised their glasses, and Bourne hesitated. So wonderful a feeling was flowing through him that he hardly knew what to say. "Sophia," he began, "here's to our second honeymoon. I love you so much."

They clinked glasses. "I love you, too, so very much, darling, so very, very much, Orson." she said.

They sipped their drinks. Then he buried his face in her breasts, and she held him close to her, and patted his head.

Suddenly he lifted his head. "Let's take another drink, you and me."

They did. They both smiled at each other. They were pleased with each other. She caressed his face. He patted her thigh.

"I feel like a college boy," he said.

"I feel like a college girl."

He picked up the Bible he had been looking at. It was on a nearby table. "Really a very great book. We should have read it more often. I was reading passages in the Old Testament. The prophets were great men—poets, seers, leaders. This passage from Isaiah sent a thrill through me: 'Comfort ye, comfort ye my people, saith your God. Prepare ye the way of the Lord, make straight in the desert a highway for our God. Every valley shall be exalted, and every mountain and hill shall be made low; and the crooked shall be made straight and the rough places plain. And the glory of the Lord shall be revealed and all flesh shall see it.' Isn't it wonderful, Sophia?"

"It is. This was one of my father's favorite verses. When I was a little girl I remember him crying softly when he read this. It was when Mother was so sick, the first time."

He looked at the passage again.

"I liked the way you read it, dear," Sophia said.

He patter her hand. "Those Hebrews, those Jews could say things so beautifully."

"Yes," she whispered.

There was a soft, quiet silence.

"I'm so glad we went to the service today," he said,

"I am, too, very glad."

136

"It's strange how things happen, suddenly, almost accidentally, it's very strange, Sophia."

"It is," she said softly, and was so filled with love for this man who was her husband that she could not go on . . . he looked like a little boy now, so helpless, so happy and so comforted in the arms of his mother.

"Things seem to be in their proper perspective now, so easy and simple and the way they should be."

"Yes, dear," she said. Slowly she took his face in her hands and kissed him slowly and fully and with a deep and quiet delirium. "I love, I love you, my darling," she whispered to him, and kissed him again.

Six

Bourne's resignation from the *Globe*—though he was granted the column that he asked for . . . the Globe Associates told him that he could run it as often as he wanted "and forever, if you so wish, as it certainly will be our pleasure" . . . Bourne was deeply touched, and the grant made his leaving a good deal less of an emotional wrench for him . . . he called the column "Free Inquiry"—set the magazine off on a more or less open pro-Soviet line. Edith Loring now called herself chairman of the Editorial Board, which is to say, she was the real, operating editor. Within less than six months after Bourne resigned there appeared in the *Globe* articles on the "Emancipation of Soviet Womanhood," "Russia, An Example of Industrial Democracy," "Soviet Youth Goes Free," "Soviet Technology Surges Forward," and "The Russian Church Goes Liberal." Bourne was appalled, and he made extensive notes to reply to every one of these articles after "a decent period of enforced politeness," as he angrily told Sophia. But then he changed his mind. He saw no sense in going into extended debates with the various authors; further it would perhaps be in bad taste for him openly to argue with his former colleagues. Nevertheless, he was embarrassed to be writing for a magazine that printed so many views to which he was violently opposed.

His wife Sophia came to his rescue. "Dear, why don't you

ignore these articles or the *Globe,* for that matter, and simply give your own views in your column, without any reference to what appears in the other pages of the magazine? It would be so dignified, and people would know exactly where you stand."

Bourne thought that was an excellent idea. Whereupon he plunged into a series of articles on the principles of free government, going back to John Locke and John Stuart Mill and Thomas Jefferson, and by very clear inference he showed that what was going on in Russia was in direct antithesis to what democracy has meant down the ages. To his great pleasure many letters of approval came to him and to the *Globe,* and to his surprise Loring printed several of them, without comment. Neither did she change a single word in his columns. Later he got warm letters of commendation from several members of the Globe Associates.

"Well, the *Globe,* thank God, still adheres to the principles of a free press," he said to his wife. "I must say I had had some doubts about this for a while, but what is true is true."

Bourne was now a happy man, that is, happier than he had been when he was nominal editor. Occasionally he would write his columns every week for a month or so, then he would skip a week now and then. He was also deep into his projected re-evaluation of Andrew Jackson, and he sensed a new warmth and loveliness in his home. He was so happy in his home life that one evening he burst out, "Sophia darling, you're a joy to my heart."

"And you are a joy to my heart, my love," she said, as she kissed him."

But what had brought happiness to him brought consternation to a considerable number of the readers of the *Globe.* Dozens of them cancelled their subscriptions as a protest against Bourne's resignation, which they sensed was, in a way, forced, and also as a protest against the blatantly pro-Soviet policy that Loring instituted. Bourne was pleased and puzzled. He hadn't known he had so many friends among the readers of the magazine, and at the same time he wondered why they hadn't given him moral support while he was struggling with Edith Loring. Why hadn't these same readers objected when the articles of Pendelton and Matson began to appear with regularity? Why hadn't they objected when editorial after editorial of pro-Soviet slant appeared? Now that his heart had been broken, and he had gone through months of agony as to what to do with his future life, his friends offered their sympathy. It didn't make sense. He came to the conclusion that intelligent readers were lazy folks, not too eager to make their likes and dislikes known, blowing off their indignation at home and letting it go at that. It was this same laziness, he thought, that accounted for so much poor government, poor public education, and injustice to the consumer on the part of large utility companies. The people grumbled at home but didn't let their displeasure be known by letters to their city councilmen and Congressmen and Governors and United States Senators.

The *Globe* lost many subscribers, and Bourne couldn't help feeling pleased, but then he became depressed when he learned that while the number of subscribers had declined the newsstand sales had increased to such an extent that they more than made up for the loss in subscribers. Obviously the *Globe* was now appealing more to "the common reader," who sympathised with Russia but couldn't afford a full-year's subscription. This clearly was the case, as became apparent soon enough, when two of the leading avowed Communist publications began to praise "the new vigorous direction that the *Globe* is now taking, a direction that is in line with the thinking of the Founding Fathers, who were friends of the proletariat as against the moneyed classes." This was a wholly original interpretation of American history, and Bourne couldn't help smiling to himself. It saddened him, and for a while he thought of leaving the *Globe* completely, as a protest. But Sophia argued him out of this notion. "If you go, the readers will be deprived of one voice of sanity. You owe it to them to stay. Besides, there are still many of your kind of readers, who take the *Globe,* even if only out of long habit."

All the time David was finding life on the *Globe* more and more unbearable. He was just as opposed to the pro-Soviet line as was Bourne, but he was also offended by the mounting self-righteousness and general dullness of the magazine. He found the company and the conversation and the thinking of Loring unappetizing. Now that Bourne had given up the editorship of the magazine she became more pretentious and talked in round, pompous phrases: "We should insist, I believe, that

140

government is a public trust, and I think, further, that we should insist that journalism truly is the fourth estate of the realm, and that it is a semi-public profession, and that the journalism that isn't courageous and pioneering and challenging is an unethical journalism. Always we should keep in mind the long view. History has its own laws of evolution, and I do not claim to know all these laws. Indeed, I am only an amateur historian, and know far less than many a professional historian, much less, very much less. But one thing seems clear to me. One must always try to view things in perspective. One must also not be too eager to judge an event outside its context, don't you think that is so? I refer, of course, to Russia. There are things going on there now that we in this country, from the vantage point of our own security and our own fine economic status and our own political development, might view with some misgivings. Take civil liberties. I don't see how we can deny that civil liberties are to a large extent absent in the Soviet Union. And yet, have we a right to insist on them in so primitive a land, especially now, in a time of crisis? All in all, I should say that what is happening in Russia is of a liberating nature, and what liberates makes for greater freedom in every realm in the long run, don't you think?"

When David first heard Loring say this, he could barely control himself from laughing. He repeated it to Dryfus, who smiled and said, "I wouldn't call that a great contribution to philosophy, not on a plane with, let us say, Spinoza's system of thought, and yet I don't see how you can deny the basic truth of it."

"Well," began David, who was beside himself as to what to do about his future.

"My boy," said Dryfus, "the *Globe* is even more dead than the *World*. There's only one difference between them. The *World* got rid of its deadwood, which is to say, it got rid of Brandt, but Slack ruined it then when he made what's-his-name editor, now what is his name?"

"Morton Jackson."

"Yes. What a lousy name for an editor. Anyway, that only assured the magazine a double death. Insurance companies should pay double indemnities for double deaths. All right, all right, that's not so funny, even I can see that. But the *Globe* is something else. They fired their good editor, Bourne, I know, I know, I spoke against him, he's a fussy, smelly, moralistic Prohibitionist, and that I don't like. He's not my man, that's all, I don't know if he's really a Prohibitionist actually, but he might as well be. For Christ's sake don't give me that helpless look, that questioning look, you look like a professor who was going to ask me to spell some hard word like *obloquy*."

"Spell it," said David, who now became a little more light-hearted. He wondered why he hadn't seen Dryfus more often lately.

Dryfus became serious again. "David, there's only one thing to do, and that is to quit. You're not planning your life, you're putting the wrong things first, you're not keeping your eye on the ball. The *Globe* is just a job now, and a bad one, they're not paying you enough, and every day is agony. I would rather work in a circus than be associated with Loring, she's not a woman, she's a caricature of a woman. And she's not an American. I mean that. I mean it seriously. She's not a Russian either, she's only a fashion-follower. It's fashionable now in certain quarters to be a fellow-traveler, it makes these cheap people, especially the cheap women, feel superior. Hell, Loring is not for Russia, she's for Loring with the new intellectual dress on. She has few principles, just a horrible female. Bourne stood for something. He really did. He was an American. He was for freedom, civil rights, free speech, free press, things of that sort, and that's important. He saw through that Russian swindle a damn sight earlier than I did, he sees through it now better than anyone of us. Of course, he has his blind spots. One thing he doesn't understand is that bad as things are in Russia, and I believe they're even worse than you and I will ever know, the Russian politicians are damn liars and swindlers, lying and swindling is part of their religion, Lenin said so, right in the open. Well, what was I going to say?"

"Bourne . . . "

"Yes, Bourne. I've made plenty fun of him. I still wouldn't like to go on a picnic with him, and whenever I think of him in bed with his wife I shudder. But yes, what he doesn't see is that the Russian business is significant. It is showing us, in a horrible way, that the time has come for the world to get more civilized in plain economic and financial matters. It took mankind a million years, well, a few thousand years, maybe less, maybe more, I'm no statistician, it took the human race a long time for when a man gets sick in the middle of the street, for an ambulance to pick him up, rush him to the hospital, and forget the money. The same if his family is down and out, there are organizations that help. The same with parks and schools. People are now getting things as their birthright what the lords and barons and the statesmen used to say, if they haven't got them that's that, they can drop dead. Well, things have changed, and Russia has shown up the change in the feeling of world history. Russia is like a fever of the human race, it indicates something, it indicates an illness, an economic and social and religious and all that kind of illness. The time has come for the community, all right, the state, to take over everything that has to do with economic and financial security, take all that worry off people, and let people be human beings. That's what Bourne doesn't see. History is a funny thing. You can pass a moral judgment on it as it passes you by, and that is important, if there's garbage on the stream, you should say so, but you also have to see the meaning, the deep meaning of the stream, and it's the deep, underlying meaning that Bourne doesn't see. But Bourne is calling the shots as he sees them, he sees garbage in Russia now, and he calls it garbage, which is very important. It's really a wonderful thing to have a man on the job reminding us of the Declaration of Independence and the Constitution, it's really wonderful, and that's one thing that this country needs badly now." He stopped and smiled.

"What's funny?" asked David.

"I was just trying to picture to myself Bourne in bed with his wife. What a slow motion picture that would make!"

David didn't think that was funny.

"Why do you look so glum, my boy?" asked Dryfus.

"Am I looking glum?"

"You look like you had athlete's foot. Well, I forget now and then your horrible Boston upbringing. But Bourne is good, was good. A damn good editor. The *Globe* is nothing. Leave it. You can get a job. Plenty of jobs. Meantime write your fiction and your poems and your essays. How are you making out with your stories? Those last two you had published are fine. You must have had a dozen published now, eh?"

"Just about. And I'm working on a novel and some poems."

"That's the best news of all. The rest is nothing. There's only one thing you lack now, my boy, only one thing." He stopped, apparently not sure whether he wanted to go on.

"What's that?"

"Love. A girl."

A sudden stab went through David.

"What happened to Sylvia was dreadful. I'm sorry I never met her."

"Yes," said David. "We talked about it often. I don't really know what happened. One thing and another. Then she got sick, and went South, and . . . "

"Yes."

"I don't know what to say. I guess I don't know what to do," said David.

"I know," said Dryfus.

David wondered just what Dryfus meant.

"No love, no real joy," said Dryfus. "I suppose it's true, though not very new, that where there's no love there's only existing, no real living, life is then only a job, sometimes a good job, sometimes, more often, I suppose, just a job. I don't want to tell you what to do. In such matters, every man to his own salvation. I suppose if I were in your shoes, I'd have a pile of girls, a different one every night, you know what I mean, and I really wouldn't find any comfort, but you're not that kind. You're more decent than I am. So I don't know what to say. These things right themselves, or they don't right themselves. I know that's a pompous, crummy way of talking, I'm really not saying anything, and I wish I could help, you know that. I gather you get some pleasure out of seeing the Tobiases, especially Mary Tobias, I mean the smell of woman, a certain softness, like out of a teacher in a grammar school, the kind of love a little boy has for such a teacher. It's all right. But it's not enough, not for a grown man. Every man needs a woman who takes her girdle off, not only around her fanny, but around her heart and soul. So it will happen or it won't happen."

144

"Well . . . "

"But quit your job. I hear the old manipulator Simmons, is that his name?"

"Lester Simmons."

"But you know about that as well as I do," said Dryfus. "He bought out Slack and Jackson and everybody, and now the *World* is his, lock, stock, and barrel. Perfectly legal, of course, a guy like that never does anything, not a damn thing, that's really illegal, he has good lawyers. But I suppose you also know who his new editor will be?"

"No. Who?"

"I don't know myself, but I'll bet you a million dollars it will be Lester Simmons himself."

"No!"

"That shows how naïve you are, my boy."

"But he's so ignorant," said David.

"Naturally, and stupid, mealy-mouthed, and with few real ideas and he has dandruff and cavities in all his teeth, including his false ones, and he has hangnails, and he's allergic to reading. All these things, sir, are prime qualifications for the editorship of a general, cultural magazine nowadays. The old days are gone, my boy. In the old days you had Dr. Charles W. Eliot as President of Harvard, he could read a little, and he could write a little, and there was Dr. Andrew White at Cornell, and Dr. Gilman at Johns Hopkins, but now there are public relations men in the top posts at colleges and universities, and politicians. Not at Harvard, I know. And one or two other places, but Harvard and the one or two other places are a little backward. I predict that any day you people will get some admiral or general or politician or some other numbskull for President. Anyway, Simmons will be editor of the *World*. Maybe he is already."

"It's hard to believe," said David.

"No, I don't think so. Nothing is hard to believe. Think of all the people who believe Jesus was killed and then rose from the grave. Think of all the people who are sure that if they behave themselves they'll get four or five or whatever-the-hell number it is of wives they will sleep with in heaven. Think of all the people who think a cow is a divine animal. The old Egyptians, and they weren't wholly dumb, though their descendants are plenty dumb, well, in the great days of Egypt, their learned men believed that the cat was not just a cat, but a very holy animal. And wasn't Cleopatra herself proud that her mother or father or somebody in her ancestry was a cat?"

"I think so."

"So don't talk to me about not being able to believe anything about human beings. Now that I've spoken, I am sure Simmons is editor, and I am sure of another thing, he'll get in touch with you and offer you a job back on the *World.* And you know what my advice is? Take the job. And you know why? Because the *World* will last longer than the *Globe,* and speaking microscopically, I think it's also more honorable. How do you like that?"

Dryfus was partly right. Lester Simmons had taken over the *World* in a complicated legal maneuver, by which he put in virtually no money whatever, but used the monies of two other people: Morton Jackson, who was editor for a short time, and Betty Garde. Morton Jackson had married a wealthy Jewish girl, who was eager to have her husband involved with "something cultural." He had worked on newspapers but that wasn't cultural enough for her, and since she was paying the bills for their two homes—his own income was barely sufficient to pay for part of the bills of one home—he could easily be persuaded by her to do as she wished. That was how he became interested in "molding public opinion in the direction of the eternal verities and the foundation spirit of the American people," a phrase he liked to use when called upon to talk on quality journalism before various clubs and women's associations, the invitations to which were largely inspired by his wife. The *World* did poorly, despite all of Jackson's ideas of "livening it up," and Slack was eager to sell. Simmons discussed the sale with him at length and finally got his price down to a very modest figure—$15,000. Whereupon Simmons went to Jackson and got him to put up $7,500, for which he got 30 per cent of the stock. The understanding was that Jackson would serve as editor and get a salary "if the business warranted it."

Simmons needed another $7,500. His wife Clarice recalled that a college friend of hers, Betty Garde, whose parents were wealthy, was eager to go into "some sort of journalism." Mrs.

Garde was married to an architect who had a large office but virtually no business. He did considerable drinking, and Betty suspected that he also went out with other women, and from his conversation she also suspected that Negro girls of "the lower sort" were his favorites. They had two children, both girls, she wasn't too happy with the children either, one was clearly below normal intellectually, and the other was below normal in her physical development, she was very short, she was very thin, and she had a nervous tick that baffled the doctors. As Betty said to Clarice, "I am slowly going crazy, my dear, and if I don't get out and do something, I don't know what I'll do. What I would really like is to be on some magazine."

She was associate editor of the *World* not long after Simmons heard about her desires. She put in the other $7,500, and for this she got 30 per cent of the stock. Like Jackson she was told that she would be paid a salary "if the business warranted it." Simmons took 40 per cent of the stock for himself on the ground that it was all his idea, and he would supply the business management to the magazine—and by that he meant running the office, taking care of the circulation, and obtaining the advertising. On the surface it looked like a just deal. But the magazine went down steadily in circulation and in advertising, and Simmons began to complain to Jackson about his editing.

"But I thought you liked all my ideas," said Jackson.

"I did," said Simmons, "but the ideas haven't worked out. Or maybe you didn't work them out well enough. All I know is that people aren't buying the magazine."

"Maybe it needs more and better promotion," ventured Jackson.

"Maybe. But you know as well as I know that the best promotion is an interesting magazine. And it looks like our magazine isn't interesting enough. It's really your job, you're the editor."

Jackson did all he could to "liven up" the magazine with "intellectual crossword puzzles," with a "sophisticated" motion picture department, and with a dance column—his wife was interested in modern, interpretive dancing, and she thought that "thousands of people" would read such a column. Nothing

147

seemed to help. The thousands of dance lovers did not buy the *World*, indeed, it was not at all clear that a dozen of them bought it. Three women sent in subscriptions to the *World,* solely, as they made it abundantly clear, because of the dance column. Simmons suspected that all three were friends of Jackson's wife, and a bit later he told him so. Jackson told his wife, and she was so infuriated that she said she would not stand "such insulting insinuations from that cheap man." A few weeks later Jackson offered to get out of the magazine, and he was willing to sell his share of the stock for half the money he put in. Simmons at once borrowed the money from his father-in-law and now he owned 70 per cent of the stock. Now he had a magazine which he controlled, and an associate editor who had money but was hardly an editor. Simmons decided to try editing himself. Clarice was delighted. Secretly she always had wanted her husband to be something more than a mere businessman, though she didn't object too much to his being a mere business man. A combination business man and editor was ideal. She encouraged him.

"Maybe I can help," she said gleefully. "I don't know the technical aspects, but I'm the public, aren't I?"

Thus Simmons became the editor in fact, though not in name. He was afraid to take the responsibility in case anything happened that would reflect upon him as an editor. But it was impossible to have a magazine that had no editor's name on the masthead, so he put his wife's maiden name on the masthead as managing editor; there were a number of magazines that had on their mastheads the names only of their managing editors. Luck was with him from the very beginning. Clarice went to a party that was given by an old college girl friend of hers, and there she met a man whose name she had heard of vaguely: Dagobert M. Prunye. He was a writer of mystery stories, and the literary critic of the *New Slant,* which was on the order of the *New Yorker,* had praised him as a writer of great talent: "He is more than a writer of murder mysteries, he has a sharp eye for the murderous streak in all of us. I would be doing him an injustice to mention the name of Dostoevsky along with his, and yet, there are some aspects of Dostoevsky's genius that I detect in Mr. Prunye's work."

148

The motion picture companies were interested in his work, though not one of them had as yet bought any.

He was a presentable young man, in his middle thirties. Clarice liked him on sight. He told her that he had a short novel that he didn't quite know what to do with. The *New Slant* had kept it a long time, and then returned it with regret, because "it doesn't quite seem right for us." But the literary critic of the magazine was enthused over it. Luckily, the critic was also at the party, and he spoke of the manuscript with excitement. Clarice asked whether she might read it for possible publication in the *World*. Prunye agreed readily. Clarice read the whole script that night, and she liked it very much. The script seemed to have everything: sex, love, excitement, mystery, and good, swift writing. Lester read it the next night, and he liked it, too. But, with his usual caution, he did not wholly trust his or his wife's judgment. He got a written statement from the literary critic of the *New Slant* in which he said how much he liked the script. Lester got another good statement from a friend of the literary critic. Lester now felt secure.

He took a chance and printed the whole book in one enlarged issue of the *World,* and on the day of publication he took a small advertisement in The New York *Times* and in the *Herald Tribune.* The issue did amazingly well on the newsstands, not only of New York but of Philadelphia, Boston, Chicago, and several of the Pacific Coast cities. There were several hundred new subscriptions. But Lester was shrewd enough to know that he could not repeat this stroke of luck. Besides, he was shrewd enough to know that he shouldn't even try to repeat it, because then he would have a wholly different magazine from the *World* as it was in Brandt's heyday—and he very much wanted to be identified with that *World,* and so did his wife. But the experience gave him various ideas— there was clearly a market for mystery magazines and other such magazines. He didn't know the field very well, but he would keep his eyes open.

Simmons—who was something of a bewildered merchant —for a while didn't know exactly what type of magazine he wanted. He wanted a magazine that paid for itself, but he also wanted a magazine that had some prestige. But he wasn't quite sure what kind of prestige he wanted. There was the prestige that a magazine such as *Foreign Affairs* enjoyed—it was read carefully by all the important people in the foreign offices of virtually every nation in the world. But it had a relatively small circulation. That meant it was exclusive, which was a good thing, in a way, but in another way it wasn't exactly what Simmons wanted. He liked to be talked about by many people. He wanted to be popular. He wanted to be popular in a social-intellectual way. Also, he wanted to be newsy, somehow implicated with public affairs. It was thus natural that his ideal magazine was a sort of combination of the *New Yorker* and *Time* and the *Reader's Digest*. He knew what a difficult time these magazines had in getting started, how much money they had lost at the beginning. That aspect of their history didn't please him. He not only didn't like to lose money, he didn't like to take any chances with things that might lose money. He wanted to have the reputation of a courageous editor, but he wanted to get that reputation by doing relatively safe things.

As this ideal magazine came to the forefront of his mind, he realized how unfit he was to be the editor of such a magazine—or, indeed, of any magazine that aimed for the highest quality. At the same time he liked the idea of being called editor. By reading the table of contents page of *Life* carefully he learned for the first time that there was such a thing as executive editor. A solution for his dilemma immediately came to his mind. He would get a man who had worked on some of the better popular magazines, preferably the *New Yorker,* and make him executive editor, and at the same time announce himself as editor. He now had the "loophole" that he always liked to have in a complicated situation. If the executive editor worked out, and the *World* came back to life, he, Simmons, could still get the major credit, for then people would say that it was really the editor who had originated the ideas that were successful. Simmons was sufficiently cynical about the world to know that it was the nominal heads who nearly always got the credit for the good ideas of their subordinates. And if the magazine didn't succeed, Simmons could blame it on his executive editor. He had morals, but he was "realistic."

Once Simmons was wholly clear in his mind as to the sort

of executive editor he wanted, he had the feeling that luck would be with him, as it had so often been with him in the past: that he would meet his executive editor soon. That is exactly what happened. Betty Garde's husband had recently obtained one of his rare commissions to design a house in the country for a celebrated ex-opera singer, who happened to have a son, who was working on the *Reader's Digest*. He liked the magazine very much—which immediately put him into the good graces of Simmons, who also liked the magazine very much, indeed, he envied it its basic idea . . . Simmons saw no sense in the criticism made in certain intellectual circles that the *Digest* generally supported a conservative point of view in politics and literature and culture in general, that it usually emasculated the articles it digested, that many of its "digested" articles were really "planted" by the *Digest* in "original" magazines . . . in short, that the *Digest* was basically an anti-culture "brain-shrinker," as one of the critics called it. Simmons thought this was all nonsense, so he liked this man's devotion to the *Digest*.

But he—Thomas Bly was his name—wanted to have "a greater say in a periodical of somewhat higher scope, that at the same time kept the common touch, a magazine that appealed to intelligent people, rather than to the intelligentsia, that also participated openly in public life, for the times call for a positive return to American political fundamentals." Simmons felt pretty much the same way. When Thomas Bly said that he thought President Truman was "too much the common man, that it was high time that the country were in the hands of a middle-of-the-road, truly liberal yet genuinely conservative Republican," Simmons knew that Thomas Bly was his executive editor.

And yet he did not entirely trust Bly either. Simmons was a super-cautious man. He sensed that Bly would give the *World* the "liveliness" that it needed, but he wasn't sure whether he would give it the "quality" that he wanted the *World* to retain. He didn't want to lose the old readers of the magazine; they still numbered over twenty thousand, and he imagined that many of them continued to read the magazine out of loyalty to what it had been, but that they would leave it if the magazine strayed too far from what it had been. And it occurred

151

to him that the one man who really knew the old *World* was David. Whereupon he offered David a job as associate editor or managing editor ("I can get my wife out, if you insist, that's easy, only I want you on the magazine, and you'll have plenty of leeway. Don't worry about Bly, he'll be executive editor, but I'll handle him, I'm still the publisher"), and promised him "plenty of freedom to get really good pieces in. Bly will look out for the light stuff, I want you to look out for the better things, you know perfectly well what I mean."

David saw in Simmons the same old "manipulator," he didn't trust him, he was sure that Simmons would compromise "intelligently, of course," on quality if there was a question of sales involved, but Simmons did offer a much better salary than the *Globe* did, and there was something strangely clean—at least relatively speaking—about Simmons's manipulating as compared to the pretentious morality of the *Globe,* and David was sure that Simmons was not a fellow-traveler. The blindness to facts and the total naïvete represented by fellow-travelers were especially obnoxious to David. Then there was another reason why David was attracted to the *World*. He had become cynical about so-called quality journalism, and the *World* job was simply a better job than was the *Globe*. Not only was the money better, the working conditions also were. David never felt that he was free to come in and out of the *Globe* office, he always felt he had to put in eight hours a day, whether it made sense or not. He also felt that he could not take more than the usual two weeks of vacation, even after five years of working on the magazine. And there was something about the atmosphere of the *Globe* that was depressing: there was little humor there, there was too much self-righteousness, too much pomposity, too much of the social workers' atmosphere. David accepted the job of managing editor, determined to get good articles and stories for the magazine but at the same time resolved not to become too perturbed if some or even many of his choices were rejected. He was also determined to take as much time off as he could, for his writing, chiefly to finish the novel he was working on.

"I am proud of you," said Dryfuss when David told him about his decision. "Do not disappoint me. Simmons is a cheap and shabby man who'll go far in the world. Pay as little attention to him and the job as possible. Try to print as many good things as you can. But don't let your heart be broken if you have little success on the magazine. Your heart now, my boy, is in the highlands, writing. From now on I want to hear as little as possible about the *World*. Just talk to me about your stories and poems and especially about your novel. These are the only things that matter. There's only one thing missing in your life now. A woman with an apron and with big breasts, outside and inside. A woman with a heart. A Jewish woman with a heart."

Seven

Davidavid felt very much at home back on the *World* and also very much not at home. It was a more lively office, there was more humor in the air, there was little pretentiousness of the sort that prevailed on the *Globe*. There was an open-faced cynicism. And yet, in one sense, the people on the *Globe* were more his sort of people than were the people on the *World*. They were more concerned with underlying problems in the social and literary realm. There was an offensive spirit of "do-goodness" about them, there was also much naïveté, so much of it, indeed, that some of the editors were trapped into seeing much good in what was going on in Russia. Yet, now that David was away from the office, he began to wonder whether this very naïveté wasn't, in some way, also a virtue.

As usual with David, he was in a conflict of emotions about his decision to leave the *Globe*. From a practical standpoint, it was obviously a good move. For a while he was quite cynical about what he had done, and there was some sort of relief in being cynical, but that relief didn't last very long. After a while he began to feel ashamed of his cynicism, and then he knew that cynicism was an emotion that made him uncomfortable, it was an alien emotion. He was now in a turmoil. He had to admit to himself that he occasionally yearned for the sort of life he lived on the *Globe,* with all its dullness and

154

pretentiousness. At the same time he found much pleasantness and freshness of spirit on the *World*. There was more grand hilarity on the order of Dryfus's—not as high or as perceptive but belonging to the same general class. There was also a greater latitude of literary styles, and that pleased David especially. One of the things about the *Globe* that had irritated David was the uniform dullness of the articles and the general sameness of the phraseology. The poor were often referred to as "the underprivileged," the wealthy were often called "capitalist overlords" or "Bourbons" or—in certain cases—"robber barons." Now and then there would appear the phrase, "It behooves us to say," a phrase that was especially annoying to David. He had heard this phrase so often from public platforms and read it in so many speeches by dubious people that he found it hard to associate it with entirely honest people.

On the *World* no such phrases were used. Bly, the executive editor, wrote simple, clear, if undistinguished English, he let others write as they pleased, provided it was good English, and he did not pretend to having any profound convictions. He claimed to be only a journalist with a yen to be associated with something that was quality in his eyes, and he was not too fanatical about the quality. He didn't want to be associated with a magazine such as the *Elks Magazine* or the *Rotarian Magazine,* though he respected both ("They perform their honorable function well"), simply because he wanted to print articles with "somewhat more thought content." Neither did he want to be associated with any of the mass-circulation women's magazines, because "they appeal to a special audience, women, and, of course, I have nothing against such an audience, but a magazine catering to women alone of necessity has to be a service magazine, which is all right, too, but I envisage a larger, more cosmopolitan audience, made up of opinion molders." The last two words—opinion molders—were frequently on his lips.

David found him human, even humble, and without any desire to missionize any of his opinions—first, because he had no strong convictions, and second, because, even if he had any, he would not have wanted to impose them upon anybody. Ideas just weren't quite that important to him. He was for ideas, of course, and he could spot outrageously hollow ones, and he was for free speech and free press, but he wasn't fanatical even about this point of view, and certainly there was nothing moralistic in his personality. He was not without principle. Perhaps it would be more accurate to say that he was for the immemorial virtues of honesty and decency and moral integrity. There was little trickiness in him, almost none, in fact. There was almost no cheapness in him, personal or journalistic. He was not a Morton Jackson, the former editor of the *World*. Bly might not object too violently to the idea (Jackson's) of having a department called The Mother of the Month or The Bride of the Month. But that would be chiefly because he couldn't readily think of a logical reason for his objections. But his instincts would be offended by such ideas. He was a good father. He was a good husband. He was a good citizen. He wasn't too bright. He wasn't stupid, far from it. In the long run he could be depended on to vote "right."

He was a Republican in his politics, but about that, too, he was not fanatical. He disliked Truman not chiefly for political reasons, but because he sensed in him something "not quite on the square," as he once said. At the same time, if anybody proved to him conclusively that he, Bly, was wrong, he would admit it and might even become something of a missionary for President Truman's ideas. He called himself "a Jeffersonian Republican," which just about describes his political ideas. He read the two leading news weeklies, he read the *Globe,* he read the *Christian Science Monitor,* he read the *National Geographic,* ("I always did like geography, even in high school, even in grammar school, matter of fact, I have a great big globe in my den, I love it"), he admired Walter Lippman ("He's a thinking man, he clears things up for me"), and his favorite playwright was Philip Barry, whose *The Philadelphia Story* and *Holiday* were almost ideal plays to him. But he was not without humor. His humor would barely be noticeable for days, then he would burst out in an imitation of a smalltown preacher or a village atheist or a smalltown businessman that would be truly hilarious. He was a superb mimic, and he had an astonishing ear for nuances of speech. While he himself was to a large extent the typical citizen of Middletown, he was not blind to the pomposities of the leading citizens of

Middletown, its politicians, its men of affairs, its clubwomen, its lecturers, its grammar school principal, its high school principal, the president of the local business college.

Not long after David returned to the staff of the *World* there was a special afternoon meeting at the office "to discuss plans for the future and how to restore leadership to the *World* in the realms of culture and public affairs," said Bly's note. Simmons and his wife, Clarice were there, so was Betty Garde, and David, of course, and three other people whom David had seen at the office now and then. David didn't quite know what they were doing, they went in and out of Simmons's office, they seemed to know Betty and Clarice, they sometimes sat in on editorial meetings, though they seldom said anything, they seemed to be "studying the situation." David had been introduced to them, they were polite to him, but almost never talked to him at any length. He had not gone out to lunch with any one of them, though each had said several times, "We must have lunch together one of these days very soon, a real, long lunch, to talk things over." David slowly got the general idea that one of them, James O. Dawson, was a sort of assistant to Simmons on the business side of the magazine, that another, Kermit Stern, who generally talked in epigrams and had a penchant for describing, criticising, and pontificating about statesmen and labor leaders, was a sort of silent co-editor, or at least an editorial consultant to Simmons, and a third, apparently the most carefree of them all, Peter Goldstein, would be in the circulation department, a sort of absentee circulation manager.

On this afternoon the talk turned, at the beginning, to a certain Christian clergyman, who at the moment was in the headlines because three of his books were simultaneously on the bestseller lists: *Everybody Can Be a Success, You, Too, Can Win,* and *Love Is Infinite.* All agreed that the three books were pretty shabby "psychological aspirin," as Kermit Stern said, "just what the Russians have always said religion is, and in that respect they were pretty much right." Stern had been to Russia as a correspondent, for a time was quite partial to Russian Communism, and then became disillusioned and wrote a book about his disillusionment, entitled, *Farewell to Myopia.* David had read the book and had not liked it, despite the very favorable reviews it had received. He sensed something

157

of the charlatan in Stern, though he agreed with what he said about Russia.

"Yes," Stern repeated, "Harold Hinton McTavish is a circus barber. And listen to this. Bernard Erickson"—David had heard of him, too, he was something of a pundit whose "brilliance" was the talk of New York, who wrote very little, who had no private income, and yet who somehow managed to live fairly comfortably—"Bernard Erickson pointed something out the other day, and it's really true. He said that Harold Hinton McTavish is the only writer in all literary history who wrote one book, if you can call it a book, and if you can call it writing, and put three different titles on it, and made the world think he had written three books."

The others agreed.

"Matter of fact," said Bly, who had been silent till now, "matter of fact, his books have something else remarkable about them. Turn them upside down, and they read just as well. I mean if you read them backwards, you'll get just as much out of them. After all, he says the same thing all the time: faith conquers all, read the Bible and you'll be saved, no matter whether you suffer from toothache or stomach sourness or whether you are pessimistic."

"Let's get down to business," said Simmons, who found little diversion in this sort of discussion.

"I don't see how we can do much business without some liquid refreshment," said Peter Goldstein, who immediately produced a pint of whiskey. "Help yourselves."

"None for me or Clarice," said Simmons, who was annoyed, but who realized that he could do little at the moment to get to the point of the meeting. He knew that Peter rather liked his whiskey, and he thought he might as well let him have his way. Besides, he had considerable respect for Peter's knowledge of the newsstands over the city that were patronized by the better class of readers, the sort of readers who, in his opinion, set the pace or rather stamped the kind of public a magazine would appeal to. Somewhere, he didn't remember where, Simmons had heard that Peter had much to do with the circulation success of the *New Yorker* in its struggling days, and Simmons wanted to make use of Peter's talents.

Bly took a small drink, examined his glass carefully and

meditatively took another drink, began to smile, and then said, still smiling, "Harold Hinton McTavish. There are a great many McTavishes in this world of ours, a great many, I might even say a large number." A blush spread all over his face, but it was a special sort of blush. It was the blush of a little boy about to do something that his parents told him not to, but that he knew they enjoyed seeing him do . . . it was a lovable smile, and David was very pleased with him, and David sensed that the others, too, were pleased, all except Simmons who couldn't make up his mind whether he should be pleased or annoyed, but he kept quiet. Apparently he was beholding an aspect of his new editor that he had not known of before.

"Yes," repeated Bly, "there are many McTavishes in this world. Some of them, so to speak, write books, as does Dr. Harold Hinton McTavish. But there are others who do not write books. They speak. They lecture. They hold forth. They run for public office. They run for private office, that is, they campaign, within their own limited bailiwicks, for what might be called local honors, and these local honors are very important to them. It's life and death to them. It really is. Many a life is ruined by not being elected to the presidency of the local Kiwanis or Eagles or Beavers or Red Men or the American Legion Sisterhood. I mentioned Sisterhood. Well, my friends"— he stood up now, and took the pompous stand of a preacher in a popular pulpit, one foot forward, back straight, his right arm extended forward and the forefinger pointed upward—"I should say, my very good friends, for that is what you are, the McTavishes of this world are not merely male, they are also female, they are, indeed, sexless, neither male nor female, but McTavish, they are born out of blather, live lives of blather and bluster, and die in clouds of blather and bluster. They are truly a new species in this world, perhaps that is one of America's contributions to civilization. But it's hard for me to believe this, there must be McTavishes all over the world. I should say they are a part of humanity. In America and in the other Western countries, there is a special breed of them, I guess, and that is one of the prices we pay for democracy. It's small enough a price."

A smile spread across his face. He continued. "It behooves me, fellow citizens, fellow Americans, fellow human beings to

159

bring to you good tidings on this great holiday, a national holiday, the newspapers tell us, and so it is, ah, yes, so it is, but I say to you, from the very bottom of my heart, that it is more than a purely historical, political holiday. It is also a religious holiday, and that, indeed, is why we are here in this House of God. For what brings us together is good resolve, no matter what it is, and it is inspired of Him on High. All that is true, all that is good, all that is beautiful, all in this glorious mansion of God, is of God.

"In the words of our great poet, Henry Wadsworth Longfellow, life is good and the grave is not its goal. Heaven is its goal. Heaven is its only goal. Yes, my friends, life is earnest, life is noble, but do you know what the greatest aspect of life is? Its godliness, its divinity, its sheer beauty, its sheer wonder. I say to you, and I say it unequivocally, life is vital. Life is dynamic. One might even say life is vitally dynamic. Life is thrilling."

Bly stopped, wiped his brow with a flourish of his handkerchief, obviously mocking the composite spell-binding preacher-politician-lodge official he was mimicking. David was smiling. What he was hearing was delicious to his ears. He was both puzzled and delighted by this strange facet of Bly's character, he never would have imagined that Bly had this quality in him, that he was capable of this sort of perception.

Bly went on, "Fellow Americans, the future lies before us! Let us not forget this, never, never! The future is unknown, for who is there among us who would be so rash as to say he knows the future? Yes, the future lies before us. And do I hear criticisms of the youth of today? Methinks I do. As I travel along the highways and the byways, and the highroads and, if you will permit me to say so, the lowroads, too, of this great and God-fearing nation, I do see evidences among our youth that would lead one to think that all is not as it should be. Some of our young folk have taken too much of the reins of life into their own hands. They look down upon their parents, their teachers, their ministers. What hurts me personally even more is that our young women, only a few of them, I am glad to say, yes, very glad, have become a little brash, shall I say, a little loud? I note a bit of harshness in their faces. Ah, that is the most painful tragedy of all, for womanhood, even young womanhood, perhaps I should say, especially young womanhood, is the very flower of creation, the very crown and glory of God's firmament, the song and the melody and the wonder of this world. Woman is our model. Woman is our paragon. Woman is our ideal. And when even one woman sullies her heritage, her God-given heritage, I am ready to weep for what has befallen us. And I have wept at the sight of one such tragic sight, as my good wife, will testify. I am not ashamed to say I have wept.

"But"—Bly almost shrieked this word, and he stamped his foot, as he turned his eyes toward the ceiling, and also pointed his index finger in the same direction—"as God, the Ever-Loving, Ever-Merciful God is my witness, I do wish to say to you, by way of fact and by way of reassurance—that these straying young men and young women form a microscopic, a minuscule minority. I say to you, and I say it with all the moral suasion and persuasion at my command, that the vast majority of our young people, both young men and young women, are sound and true-blue and good and decent and God-loving and God-fearing, the flower of our country, and we need have no fear on that score, oh, no, we need have no fear on that score at all. I have told you that I have seen things over the land, among the young, that have made me hesitate and blush and shed a tear or two. But I must also tell you that, by and large, and from the broad point of view, our youth is looking upward, looking for guidance from Heaven, expressing devotion and loyalty, too, to Eternal Things and Eternal Values and Abiding Truths, which is God. That, my friends, is the Good Tidings I bear you."

Again Bly wiped his forehead, and now he spoke in a more resonant voice. "I am here, frankly, and I do want to be frank with you, I owe it to you as fellow citizens, I would expect the same frankness and honesty and truth-telling from you, and I know full well, I am sure, that I would get it from you, so I say frankly to you that I am now addressing you, with your kindness, for the purpose of seeking your franchise for the honorable office of your representative to the State Legislature. And what have I to offer for the trust I ask you to put in me? Nothing less, my friends, than my whole-hearted dedication to your service, to your welfare, to your well-being, to the progress of this flourishing and wonderful com-

161

munity, the finest little community in all this great land of ours, a community where my great-grandfather and my great-grandmother were born, where my grandfather and my grandmother were born, where I was born, where my good wife was born, where my children were born, and where, in God's good time, my wife and I hope to be put to our eternal rest. I have a stake here, my family has a stake here. My heart is here. Here is my home, my all. And I want to give back to this community the all that it has given me, and by the all I mean service, without reservation, without qualification, without favor to anybody, be he wealthy, be he less fortunate, be he friend, be he mere acquaintance, all are alike as citizens of this wonderful community, there will be no favorites, or perhaps I should say, there will be only one favorite, this community, Grasshopper Corners."

David and the others burst out laughing. Bly wiped his face again. He was serious. He continued: "Thank you, thank you for your confidence in me. Your applause is sweet music indeed to my ears. The approbation of one's friends and peers is the sweetest music. And in closing I wish to say a few more words, for I know you good people want to go back home to attend to your duties. The young married women must pick up their sweet little burdens at school, and they must prepare supper for the breadwinner of the family. What I wish to say is that I am so glad to see so many young ones here today, young ones in their early and middle teens. I say bravo for you! And again bravo! How much more glorious is it to be in the forum of public discussion than to be engaged in something less worthy! It is good, indeed, to see young people informing themselves about the public weal. For never let us forget that the children of today are the citizens of tomorrow. And so I bid you a pleasant day and a pleasant evening, and blessings to you all, to you and yours. I thank you from the very bottom of my heart!"

Bly sat down, and the bouquet of his speech seemed to evaporate as if by a magical spell. He was now his "old" self. A quiet smile spread across his face, he looked at Simmons and at the others, apparently more out of politeness than out of anything else.

Peter Goldstein said, "I'm no editor, but I think that what

Bly has just said ought to be printed. I mean it. It's funny as hell. Print it as is. It would be the best commentary on Harold Hinton McTavish."

"You're not serious, Pete?" asked Simmons, who seemed to be frightened. His eyes narrowed as if in bewilderment at what had been going on at what was to be an important conference to deal with basic plans for "the new *World.*"

"I am serious," said Peter. "I don't mean Bly should sign his name to it. No. Put some penname to it. That's all. You don't have to say anything else, what is there to say?"

"I don't see it," said Simmons, who gave David the impression that he wasn't sure he could fight Peter Goldstein's suggestion.

Bly came to Simmons's rescue. "No, that's out," said Bly. "That was just a stunt of mine. I pull it at a party now and then. An article like that would cheapen the magazine. We don't want that. It was only a stunt. Forget it."

The others said nothing. A dullness slowly spread through the room. David felt as did Peter Goldstein, but he kept silent; he didn't feel like beginning his return to the *World* with an argument about basic policy with both the chief editor and the publisher.

"Well, what's our policy?" asked Simmons. "We've had meetings and meetings, and we still haven't decided about policy. At one meeting we decided to be interesting, but that's no policy, not to me, anyway. Then we decided to be readable. Well, I don't see that as a policy. We decided to 'expose' Russia. That's more like it. But how? Get interesting articles? But what kind? We decided to print more human interest things, but what kind? Well, maybe what I'm about to say would be all right, I don't know. Anyway, see what you think of it. It has to do with medicine and psychiatry. Clarice knows what I'm going to say. It might make a series." He stopped and suddenly David sensed a new aspect to Simmons: the man appeared to have secret fears and worries and strange bewilderments.

Simmons continued, this time a bit hesitantly, almost as if he began to doubt whether he should say what he had wanted to say.

"You mean about Aunt Marilyn?" asked Clarice.

"Yes," said Simmons. "This Aunt, it's on my side of the family," he smiled, "not Clarice's, so it's all on me. She had headaches. She went from doctor to doctor. Some said migraine, some said sinuses, some said some kind of allergy. They all gave her medicines, pills, injections, even special exercises. Nothing helped. Her headaches got worse. Really splitting headaches. It was really pathetic to see her suffer, wasn't it, Clarice?"

"Simply terrible."

"So then her daughter, her older daughter, the one who went to Smith or was it Wellesley?" He turned to Clarice again.

She smiled. "It was Barnard."

"Of course. Barnard. This girl studied psychology, maybe took a course in abnormal psychology, maybe more. Anyway, she took psychology courses."

"It was her major," said Clarice.

Simmons looked at her, then continued. "So this girl said her mother should see a psychiatrist. So her mother saw a psychiatrist, and he said there was nothing physically wrong with her. She was nervous, had some neurotic syndrome. He suggested that she start analysis treatments at once. She did. She got better for a while, but she used to get better now and then before, without these psychiatrical treatments. Ordinary aspirin would sometimes make her feel better. But then she got real bad, very much worse. She got so bad, with the psychiatrical treatments and all, that she could barely sit up. Then she had pain even when she lay down. Then she was so weak, she could hardly go to the bathroom. The funny thing is that she ate like a horse, but she was dizzy. If she stood up for a minute, she said everything swam around her. Then she stopped eating, she felt full and nauseous, she said. Then she couldn't go at all to the psychiatrist, not even twice a week, he made her go every day, at first, isn't that right, Clarice?"

"Six days a week, Sunday off."

"Well, the time came when they had to do something drastic, you could see the woman was passing out. So they took her to a brain surgeon, or maybe it was a neurologist."

"He was both," said Clarice. "Dr. Malcolm B. Minton."

"Dr. Minton, that's right. He took X-rays of her head, and he found a tumor as big as an orange, he said she'd had it for months, maybe years. So all the time she was seeing this psychiatrist, she had a tumor, and the dumb psychiatrist probably killed her by not telling her to go to a brain man. Anyway, she died on the table, the tumor was malignant, and maybe it was just as well she died. What I say is this, a hell of a lot of people are going to these psychiatrists and people like that . . . "

Bly interrupted Simmons. "Maybe this man was a psychoanalyst, not a psychiatrist. There's a big difference. A psychiatrist is an M.D. A psychoanalyst doesn't necessarily have to be an M.D. Many of them, perhaps most, are only Ph.D.'s. So maybe this psychoanalyst who saw your aunt, I mean, maybe he was a psychoanalyst, not a psychiatrist. But no matter who he was, I should think he'd first ask for a medical examination."

"I don't remember at the moment what he was," said Clarice.

"I don't exactly remember myself," said Simmons. "But what difference does it make? Here was a man who virtually killed a woman by keeping her from going to a doctor, a real medical doctor. That burns me up. Now, I understand there are a lot of psychologists in New York City, all over the country, who are fakes, telling poor innocent people to get married or get divorced, or change their jobs, or God knows what, and they don't know a thing. The state ought to do something about these fakes."

"But these fake psychologists have been exposed several times," said Bly, with a bluntness that surprised David and all the others, including, thought David, Simmons and Clarice.

"I've seen these exposés myself," said Betty Garde, who spoke for the first time. David thought he detected a certain mild displeasure in her manner of speaking. She seemed to be saying, in effect, that Simmons's idea for a series of articles on psychologists and psychoanalysts and psychiatrists was not so good. "And these articles I read pointed out the differences between all three branches, all three people, plain psychologists, psychiatrists, and psychoanalysts. It pointed out that plain psychologists don't know too much. Some do, those

165

who have been trained in proper places, and I think I read somewhere Freud himself said that he himself would say that a Ph.D., not an M.D., generally makes a better analyst, because the M.D. is inclined to look for some physical cause for what is mostly a disease of mental origin. But a lot of psychologists just don't have a Ph.D. Many don't even have an A.B., I think, they just put out a shingle, and poor people, fools, come to them. Well, anyway, that's how it is. Like in every other profession, there are swindlers in psychology, too. But it's all been said before. Of course, Lester, if you have a new angle, that's different."

"This is all dangerous stuff, I think," said Peter Goldstein, "and I'm not sure it's for the *World*. The war is over, we licked Germany and Japan, and people want to know what's going to become of the world. They want to know about what the A-bomb is going to do to civilization, they want to know about Russia, I smell a lot of trouble with Russia. I'm not afraid of Russia, but I am afraid of Stalin, he's a gangster. What I mean is that this is no time for psychology. I'm sorry, Lester."

Lester Simmons for a while seemed defeated, then he turned to James Dawson. "What do you think, Jim?"

"Oh, I don't know," said Dawson. "I don't know. I think it's sort of interesting, psychology. I know lots of people who go to analysts, and I have the same feeling you do, Lester, that they're being swindled. They want to kill their grand-mothers, or they want to kill their wives, or something. It's all daffy to me."

"But suppose you have no wife?" asked Kermit Stern. "I have one, but I know several people who don't. Whom do *they* kill? Seriously, though, a series on psychology might make a good secondary feature. Of course, it depends on how it's done, but I agree with Pete, that Russia, world affairs, that's our best bet."

David was worried that Simmons would ask him what he thought. If he were asked, David would have to hem and haw . . . he saw little sense in the psychology series, he wasn't too sure that Bly and Simmons would publish the sort of solid yet readable analysis of the Russian situation that a magazine like the *World* should have. Simmons was out chiefly to sell copies of the magazine, and Bly didn't seem to be interested in scholarship, even in the second-class kind of scholarship that the *World* used to print in the better days of Brandt's editorship. David had begun to think, as the result of listening to Bly over the past few weeks, that Bly wanted to make a sort of superior kind of newspaper Sunday supplement out of the *World*. That notion depressed David, and he would have argued against it, and vigorously, two years ago, even, perhaps a year ago, but now he was resigned to merely earning his living on the *World*. As magazines went, the *World* wasn't too bad, it was rather shabby intellectually, the writing was journalese, Bly was hardly a strong enough personality to run a really good magazine, but still it wasn't too disgraceful. And occasionally it did and probably would continue to print a fairly interesting and adult article. David, of course, couldn't say this in an open meeting.

"Well," said Simmons, "I still think my idea is a good one. At least it's something definite, something concrete, and there may be a hell of a lot more people interested in what's wrong with themselves emotionally than are interested in Russia and world affairs, and there are a hell of a lot of more people who'd like to know who are the swindlers in this psychology racket than would be interested in foreign trade and even the A-bomb." He seemed to be angry. He hesitated. "All right, I might as well tell you straight from the shoulder, I think Freud was a good deal of a swindler himself. He's just one big fraud."

"Why, Lester," began Betty Garde. "Why, that's just . . . well, it's just not so. Freud was a very great man."

"Of course he was," said Peter.

"Sometimes I think he was a great man, sometimes I think he was a fool," said Kermit.

David had to say something. "Whatever mistakes he made, he was a pioneer. I don't see how you can deny that."

"He was a pioneer all right," said Simmons, who appeared to be getting angrier. He looked at his wife Clarice, but she said nothing. David wondered whether she agreed with her husband or whether she agreed with the others.

"But what kind of pioneer was he?" continued Simmons. "What he said was all magic, just plain foolishness." He

167

stopped and looked around. The room was thick with silent skepticism. And it became more apparent to David that there was much disturbance in Simmons . . . things that had been bothering him, in his unconscious, for a long time, were now, it seemed, coming to the fore. David had known that Simmons was a maneuverer, but now it was becoming clear that his hardness covered up a great deal of uneasiness.

"Let me tell you about myself," went on Simmons. "After all, I . . . "

"Oh, Lester, don't go into that," said Clarice, who was obviously troubled by what her husband was about to say. "It was nothing, something personal, and you make a to-do about it."

"I have nothing to be ashamed of," said Lester, somewhat annoyed with his wife.

"Do as you wish," said Clarice.

"I will," said Simmons. "I had a stomach upset, have had it for years. I had a little of it in college, maybe before, but I paid no attention to it. I'd have aches and pains all over, in the strangest places. I doused myself with pills and all kinds of medicines, and I went from doctor to doctor, and they examined me plenty. Then somebody suggested I go to Battle Creek, Michigan, where they treat you with diet, it's a perfectly fine, legitimate place, regular doctors, and everything."

Clarice interrupted him. "Oh, Lester, do you really have to go into all that? It's gone and past, and what's the point, you're so hipped on these medical things. If you'd stop thinking about these things, besides, after all . . . "

"Let me go on," said Simmons sharply. "Yes, Battle Creek. I was there for three months, or maybe it was six weeks, I don't exactly remember, no, it was ten weeks, yes, ten weeks, and they tested me with all sorts of things, had me on diets of all kinds, bland diets, and fruit diets, and combination diets, and various forms of therapy. It was a nice place, it's a high-class place really, nice for a general rest, and the doctors, I guess, are fine. They said there was nothing wrong with me. But I still had aches and pains. They said I shouldn't have them, but I had them. So I left the place, after it cost me plenty of money. I came back to New York, and I suffered. Then I met this man, and he said he had the same thing, and he suggested I see his psychiatrist. This man said maybe I had psychosomatic aches and pains. I was so discouraged I was ready to try anything. So I went to see this psychiatrist. He lived in Newark, New Jersey. I didn't like him on sight. A big, fat, laughing man, who looked like a football player for Notre Dame. He asked me to talk, and I talked, and I talked, that first time I must have talked for more than an hour and a half. Then he said he'd be glad to take me on, but he warned me I might have to see him for a long time, maybe two, three years, at least three times a week, and the charge would be $25 an hour. That was too much for me, so he reduced it to $55 a week, which was still pretty steep. But I was glad to try it. His name was Dr. Melville P. Thornton, wasn't it, Clarice?"

"Yes, it was, but what difference does it make?" she said. "Besides . . . "

He ignored her. "So I went to Dr. Thornton for three months, think of it, three months, three times a week, and I almost went crazy. He did nothing. I was on that couch, and I talked my head off. Finally, I got plenty mad and angry, and I asked him why he doesn't say something, and he said he wasn't ready. So I said it was about time he was ready, at $55 a week. Besides, I didn't like some of the questions he asked me. All about my mother, how much I was attached to her, and he kept on asking and asking, and he kept on asking how I felt about being a Jew, did the word Jew make me feel funny inside when I said it, he asked me these questions now and then, but I got angry. So I kept at him, and then he said, 'Well, it could be you have a mother fixation, I really am not sure, I have to hear more from you, but so it seems to me, that you have a mother fixation.' So I said to him, 'You're crazy. I love my mother, but I don't see what that has to do with my aches and pains that travel all over my body.' So he said, 'That we'll see later,' and he shuts up. I was going to ask him about the Jewish business, but I decided to stop seeing him, so that's what I did. How do you like that? I have a mother fixation he said. How do you like that?"

169

There was a tense and embarrassing silence, lasting a few moments. Finally Betty Garde said, "I don't see that that proves anything."

Simmons's face became red. "What it proves," he said, "it seems clear enough to me, is that the psychiatrist, this Dr. Thornton, was a fool. Assuming that I do have a mother fixation, whatever that is, what has that got to do with my aches and pains, in my head, in my feet, in my stomach, in my fingers, all over, the aches and pains run all over, day and night. These are physical aches and pains, besides, my mother has been sick for a long time, and just because I am concerned about her health, doesn't mean I have any fixation, it's plain silly, don't you see?"

Peter Goldstein asked, "Are you still going to him?"

"No, I dropped him long ago, but I was thinking about him and his kind, not him personally, though I don't like him. I mean the whole field of psychology and psychoanalysis."

"That would be foolish," said Betty Garde. "It's a perfectly honest science, a little young, as the psychoanalysts and psychiatrists, the good ones, are themselves ready to admit. But they're learning all the time. And they've done lots of good. I could name you lots of people they've saved from all sorts of troubles, family troubles, sex troubles. I could name you lots of homes they've saved, just a little psychological counselling has saved many marriages I could name you. Sometimes I think," she smiled, "we could all use a little psychoanalysis or mental hygiene of some sort, I don't see how anybody can denounce the whole science of psychology and all its branches. Might just as well denounce medicine, which has made lots of mistakes, and is still learning. You have to view these things from a balanced point of view. I don't know much about it myself, but I think it would label the *World* as a sort of crackpot if we went at psychoanalysts hammer and tongs."

"But isn't the *World* supposed to be a trail-blazer?" asked Simmons.

"Yes," said Betty Garde, "but only if we get our facts straight. Just attacking a whole science, because somebody is dissatisfied with one practitioner is, well, I don't see the point of it."

"But people are always interested in problems of health,"

said Simmons. "That's why there are so many health columns in the newspapers, people read them, they write to the doctors who run them. Health, that's what hits everybody. Without health there is nothing, everybody knows that. And while I'm at it, I want to say this, there's a lot of charlatanry in medicine, too, they're not always right, the regular doctors. If they were, people wouldn't go around shopping for all kinds of cures. The regular doctors don't always help them, so they go elsewhere. I don't mind telling you myself, even Clarice doesn't know this, but I've gone to chiropractors and osteopaths and naturopaths, and some of them have done me some good, not much, but a little, and that counts."

"Lester," began Clarice, deeply troubled.

"What?"

"Have you been seeing that chiropractor again, or was it . . . ?"

"It was an osteopath," said Simmons. "But I'm not ashamed to tell you that I've seen chiropractors, too."

"But, Lester, you promised you wouldn't see any of these people again," said Clarice pleadingly.

"I know I promised, but that was some months ago, and I felt well for a long time, but then the aches and pains came back, and I didn't want to worry you and . . . "

"But you're worrying me more now," said Clarice.

"Oh, I'll be all right. I got a very good manipulation from this osteopath last Monday, and it really did me lots of good. There's something to their theory, and the osteopaths and chiropractors agree on that, that a person's health depends a great deal on the condition of the spine. If there are misplacements of vertebrae and kinks in the muscles around it, then you're bound to have ill health, because all the important nerves start in the spine, or maybe all of them do, anyway, their theory makes a lot of sense."

"My God, what's this, a psychopathic clinic?" burst out Peter Goldstein.

This remark cleared the air a bit. A cloud of depression of spirit, mixed with embarrassment and bewilderment at what Simmons was revealing about himself, had hovered over the room.

Bly said, "All I can say is that I don't trust any of these

irregular practitioners, they all seem like charlatans to me. But there may be something in Lester's idea for an article on occasion dealing with health."

"Not just an occasional article," said Simmons. "I have in mind a whole series."

"I don't know about that," said Bly. "What do you think, David?"

"I don't know," began David, who was against any series on health, and certainly was against giving a hearing to chiropractors and other such dubious healers, but he didn't feel like offending Simmons too much. "Well, we might begin with, say, an article by a regular M.D., a really good and prominent one, in which he openly confesses what medicine doesn't know, and then he might comment upon the other major healing cults. And if they want to answer, we might give them space, with the M.D. answering their comments. Something like that. We don't have to commit ourselves in advance. Sort of slide into it, and go on, if we get any decent reader response, and then drop it, if we feel that there isn't enough in it as far as our readership is concerned."

"Fair enough," said Simmons.

The others agreed, but it was clear to David that nobody was really enthusiastic about Simmons's idea. David was looked upon as something of a hero since he had saved Simmons's face, and at the same time had given Bly and the other editors an out. David was not elated about his coup, so to speak, but he was pleased that for a while at least he would have some status in the office—and he could devote more time to his writing, which was now his main interest.

This was the end of the editorial conference, as it had been the end of previous editorial conferences, and as it was to be the end of many editorial conferences that followed. David learned slowly that most editors had no real policies, they had only vague notions of the sort of public they wished to appeal to, and their "policies" were shaped by what they thought their audiences wanted. It would be inaccurate to say that they had no journalistic principles whatever. They did, but these principles were flexible. If an editor personally did not like the fiction of Edna Ferber and, on assuming his editorial duties, was resolved to print superior fiction, his resolve would become less and less firm as he became convinced that his readers did like the fiction of Edna Ferber. He would at first be embarrassed, but then he would rationalize what he knew he was going to do: "Well, our audience isn't quite as advanced as I had thought and hoped, too bad, too bad. I really did think they would take to Jessamyn West and Marjorie Keenan Rawlings, but they're gobbling up Frank Yerby and Temple Bailey that our competitors print. But then, again, come to look at it, West is only a little better than Edna Ferber, at least as compared to Willa Cather, besides Ferber has done things that are not so poor, her early things, for instance, so I'll pick and choose from her things." And that's how inferior work is reasoned into, so to speak, a magazine that the editor had resolved never to print.

This was pretty much what happened on "the new *World*." Simmons didn't quite know what he wanted in the way of a magazine, except that it should have some "quality" and should sell. Bly was pretty much of the same opinion. Slowly they convinced each other what they would try to do, which was to attract the readers of *Time* and the *New Yorker* who wanted, on occasion, once a month, say, to read a longer piece on a topic of general interest, a piece that was excitingly but not too cheaply written.

At the beginning the magazine floundered somewhat, but then it began to assume a character of sorts at the same time that it was without character: it was largely a department store of periodical literature, specializing in nothing, but appealing to the type of reader who could spend fifty cents for a magazine, that is, the reader who was as bewildered as the editor and publisher of the *World* . . . the reader who was superior to a steady fare of the tabloids or the news magazines or the *Reader's Digest,* but who didn't know exactly what kind of better reading he wanted. This reader wanted to know about the world of Broadway and the world of Hollywood and the world of local and national and international politics, but he didn't want the articles to be so scholarly and so soberly written that he would be confused by them. He wanted the articles to be light but not frothy, informative but not too heavily laden with facts, and in general of a calibre that he could discuss them with some intelligence at home and with his friends. He also wanted to be "in on the know" about certain affairs in all walks of life, he wanted "behind the scenes" gossip, yet he didn't want the gossip, so to speak, to be too gossipy.

The *World* soon was printing articles about the "inner workings" of the United States Justice Department and of the Treasury Department, especially of "T" men, who apparently were a special secret police concerned with smuggling; there were articles about the several career men "who, in an important sense, really run the State Department;" there were articles about the complicated workings of the Post Office Department, with special reference to the adjustments that have to be made in the field of mail to foreign countries. Then there were sketches of the Chief of the Secret Service at the White House and about the operations of the men under him. Indeed, there were three articles on this subject, one of them devoted to the minute and complicated arrangements generally made with local police authorities when the President goes out of Washington for any reason. There were two articles on the Coast Guard and the useful work it does in tracking down icebergs. There were sketches of women high up in the Civil Service. There were articles about "What Has Happened to the Children of Our Presidents?" Following these articles was a series about "What Happens to the Widow of a President?"

One afternoon Simmons walked into Bly's office, all eager to present to him a new idea: "I was on the way to Philadelphia to see the Supreme Oatmeal people for a series of advertisements, and in the train I picked up a small book of little essays, nature essays. I didn't think I'd be interested, but I began to read it, and it was fascinating. Here it is. Little pieces about deer and chipmunks and snakes and birds and all kinds of dogs, I never knew how interesting dogs could be, some of them, poodles, are very intelligent, and bull dogs are really not wild, some of them, that is, and there were articles about plants and about the night life of nature, and I found myself reading and rereading the pieces, so much I almost didn't get off the train in Philadelphia. Why can't we get this author to write for us? I think our readers would be interested, don't you?"

Bly wasn't too happy about the idea, and neither was Betty Garde. David was non-commital. He liked to read an occasional article on animals, but he wasn't too sure about a series. Again he made a compromise proposal. "Why not try a few pieces by this man, and let's see. If they go over, fine. If not, nothing lost." The suggestion was agreed to, and once more David achieved respect as a mediator. He smiled at his new distinction, but he was genuinely glad. Now he could coast on his reputation, and concentrate on his writing.

The nature articles proved to be enormously successful. The first one was on squirrels. It was a very short piece, yet it contained considerable information, apparently, that was fresh to most of the readers of the *World*. Squirrels, said the author, Oren P. Lovejoy, were highly intelligent animals, kindly, and friendly to human beings. They also had a relatively advanced social order. Then he wrote an equally interesting article on bats, then one on field mice. The response from readers was large and highly favorable. Whereupon Lovejoy was given a monthly column, which was called *The Friendly Outdoors*. Pretty soon the *Reader's Digest* reprinted one of Lovejoy's articles, and that was the highest praise for his editorial acumen that Simmons could have asked. Now there was no holding him back on his idea for a series on the medical and psychological healing arts. Bly had asked an osteopath to present the arguments for his profession, and the osteopath had promised to have the article ready in a month, but three months had gone by without an article from him, and Bly had deliberately let the matter slide. But now Simmons came back to his idea, and Bly wrote to another osteopath, who, very much to Bly's and Betty Garde's displeasure, agreed to have the article ready in two weeks—and, most unfortunate of all, in their view, he had it ready on time, and it was well written.

"Now we're really stuck," said Betty Garde, who now was even more opposed to the idea of a healing arts series than she had been before. "We'll get thousands of letters from crackpots, and the regular M.D.'s will laugh at us. The worst of it is that these osteopaths have a little bit of the truth on their side, and my private doctor admits it. The spine is important, as the osteopaths say, and some manipulation does do some good. Then again, the more advanced osteopaths are not much different from regular M.D.'s, except that they give you a little massage, and I hear some good osteopaths are really good surgeons. But the die-hard osteopaths are against all medicines, and they claim that most diseases can be healed by rubbing the back or manipulating the spine, and that's plain quackery, and what I want to know is why we should get mixed up with this sort of stuff. This osteopath who did the article for us is one of the advanced ones, it seems, but as soon as we print his article we'll have to print pieces or letters by the orthodox osteopaths, and we'll have to get a regular M.D. to answer every one of them, because we can't let this sort of stuff get printed unanswered, so we'll become a screwball magazine, read by neurotics and hypochondriacs, and you can't tell me that's good for circulation, in the long run. And most of these medical crackpots have no money and don't buy quality magazines."

Bly agreed, but he didn't see how he could drop the project right now. "Lester is fanatical about this," he said. "I just don't understand him. But he has us, with the success we've had with the nature series."

"Frankly, I don't like that either," said Betty Garde. "I mean it's all right, but who the hell wants squirrel lovers for readers? I mean they're all right, but there aren't too many of them, for one thing, and for another I don't like them. They're all queer, getting up early in the morning watching birds and snakes and worms and all that sort of stuff. This is not the stuff that will build up the magazine. And now with all the other queers, osteopaths and chiropractors and all that, we'll be in a hell of a fix. Speaking from an advertising point of view, I can see why an advertiser won't want to buy space with us. After all, what kind of readers will we have? These people don't buy anything except carrots and peas, pictures of birds and bird seed, and all that."

She agreed, however, that they had to go ahead with the healing arts series. Bly got an M.D. to answer the osteopath, and printed both articles in the same issue. There was an avalanche of letters from what looked like every osteopath in the country, objecting to this or that "interpretation" of "basic" osteopathic philosophy. Some of the letter writers, with a D.O. after their names, complained that the author of the article was an ignoramus, a heretic, an enemy of the "whole philosophy of osteopathy." "In the name of fair play" they demanded equal space to present "the true story about osteopathy." There were also complaints from the medical profession. They argued that "the *World* had vulgarized its pages by printing such quackery as that by your 'scientist,' who is preaching the ignorance of the Middle Ages. What he says has been disproven time and again, and it is a crime that such people have been able to win over the editor and publisher of a magazine that I used to think stood for intelligence and real scientific progress." There were some correspondents, with M.D.'s after their names, who agreed with the osteopath but asked the editor not to reveal their names: "The medical profession is a huge trust, run by a gang of racketeers, who don't want to let any new light in. They don't want the osteopaths to have a chance for fear that they'd lose business, the medical men would. God bless you."

Then there were letters from chiropractors and naturopaths and physical-therapists who denounced both the osteopath and medical men for "daring to present to the American people so much ignorance." They all wanted "equal space" to present "the true picture of healing," and they all brought up the argument of "fair play." Bly was worried. "I have never got so many illiterate and squawking letters in all my editorial life. And they have me over a barrel. We are more or less bound to give them some space, and if they insist we do have to give them, at least some of them, equal space. I only hope we are getting some increase in circulation out of all this mess. I only hope so."

It was impossible to know for sure what the first two of the healing articles were doing in the way of circulation. The magazine had been on the stands only two weeks. Simmons went from stand to stand, asking how well the magazine was selling. Without telling Bly or Betty Garde, he had increased the print order of that one issue by ten thousand, making the total print order 70,000. Thus he had a considerable stake in his own editorial idea. He was told by the newsdealers over New York City, the first week, that there wasn't much of a pickup in the sales. This depressed Simmons, but he said

177

nothing about this in the office. He now went from stand to stand in the two major terminals, the Grand Central and Pennsylvania Station. There, too, the reports were far from encouraging. He bribed some of the newsstand vendors (he gave each $5) to display this issue of the *World* prominently. This, too, didn't help. Then he sent anonymous letters to *The New York Times,* the *Herald Tribune,* and the *Post,* calling the attention of their editors to the articles on healing in the *World*. Again nothing happened. The editors completely ignored his letters. He thought he would have better luck with the editors of the tabloids. Once more nothing happened.

He discussed the matter with Clarice. He suspected that she had not been too sold on his healing articles idea in the first place, but he was sure of her loyalty and he also respected her judgment on some things. He told her everything about the state of the sales in New York City. "It's a failure," he said, "in New York City. It's three weeks now that this issue has been on the stands, and it's a dud."

"Well," said Clarice. "Maybe that was to be expected. The people here are too sophisticated. Maybe the sales out of town will be better."

This gave Simmons a thought: he would send out 250 posters over the country, especially in the smaller cities, such as Toledo, Akron, Evanston, Seattle, and Corpus Christi, Texas. The posters would feature the two first healing articles, and there would also be a line indicating that these articles would run regularly for an indefinite time. This sort of poster, he hoped, would arouse interest in the current issue of the *World* and in subsequent issues, so that if the present issue didn't do so well, future ones probably would do better. Further, he inquired whether this issue of the *World* couldn't be allowed to stay on the stands in these smaller cities for three or four days longer than usual, and he was told it could.

He got to work at once, and invested another $500 to pay for posters and postage and long-distance telephone calls. He would show the skeptics in the office, he would make them ashamed of themselves. But the first reports from the smaller cities were not very encouraging. The issue was moving very slowly, in fact, in some of the smaller cities, a bit slower than usual. Simmons couldn't understand it.

The issue with the first two healing articles was off the stands, and Bly was working on a similar set of articles on chiropractic. Meanwhile he was also wondering what to do with all the mail that had been aroused by the osteopathy article and the medical man's answer to it. Whenever he went through this mail, he felt as if his hands were being soiled, there was something quackish about it all.

What his wife said embarrassed him especially. When she read the mail that the first two articles aroused she became very unhappy. "Darling," she said, "I was all for you when you said you wanted to leave the *Digest* because you wanted to be associated with something better, something that appealed to a better kind of audience, an audience that did some thinking of its own. And now see where you are. I know you didn't like the idea in the first place, and I appreciate the position you were in . . . you were on the job only a few weeks, and you didn't want to antagonize Simmons too much at the beginning, but you may have a real battle on your hands. These people all are crazy, they all ought to be in institutions."

Bly agreed. His wife went on, "It really boils me up, darling, when I stop to think that you gave up a big-paying position on *Physical Happiness,* the cheap health sheet that Thornton McGuire or McGittrick or whatever his name is ran, because you didn't want to be associated with such a publication. Remember the kind of ads they ran? Goodness gracious! Pills to increase sex desire in frigid women, pills for men who were losing their manhood, powders to do away with eczema and psoriasis, ordinary doctors say very little, if anything, can be done with eczema and psoriasis, but these men, they have the strangest doctor degrees, they can cure everything with a little powder. I'm surprised the federal government doesn't get after them, but, then, I suppose they have shyster lawyers who know just how far they can go. And there were ads about eyeglasses, write to Chicago or some place in Georgia or Nevada or whatever it was, and they'll send you a pair of glasses for $1.67 or $2.01, no examinations, nothing. It was horrible."

"I know," said Bly sadly.

"What worries me, darling, is that pretty soon these same

advertisers will swoop down upon the *World,* and you'll be ashamed of yourself, and rightly so. This man Simmons, I begin to think, is very strange. I know, he took me in, too. I thought he meant it when he told you you would have a free hand, how did he put it, 'a reasonably free hand, you'll have every opportunity to show what you can do, can you ask for more,' and we both fell for it. Now that I think of it, I don't like the look in his eyes, and I don't like his smile, it's the smile of some sort of dubious person. I may be wrong."

"Oh, now, darling," said Bly, "you're overdoing it. He's no shyster, he's just a business man, and I can still talk him out of it."

"You can, eh? Well, what you told me he said at that meeting, he's sick, too, mentally sick, he has more ailments than any normal man I've known. He probably steals stamps from his own office, and blames his secretary for the loss. He's a very sick man."

Bly knew his wife was right. He had been thinking the same thoughts. He wished he were back on the *Digest.* The *Digest* had its own problems, at least in Bly's eyes . . . there were too many articles praising the virtues of faith and not enough calling upon ordinary men and women to develop their characters and minds and assume more responsibility for their own lives and the welfare of their communities . . . the whole atmosphere of the *Digest* was so damn goody-goody. But there was little of the sort of quackery that was now beginning to fill the pages of the *World,* and medical quackery seemed to Bly to be particularly offensive and perhaps even criminal. He admitted to himself that he knew almost nothing about medicine and really was in no position to judge the virtues of osteopathy and chiropractic and other irregular healing arts. Perhaps they had hold of some part of the truth, but Bly sensed that in the main they were shabby cults, and he felt embarrassed for Simmons, who had, so to speak, forced all this on the magazine. He wished that David and Betty Garde would help him, but he didn't blame them for not doing any more than they already had. Betty actually had come out vigorously against the whole series, and David had offered a compromise plan, and it was pretty obvious that David had no more use for the series than did Betty or Bly himself.

"Well, we'll see," said Bly.

And what he saw and learned wasn't too good. The reports from New York City newsstands and from newsstands outside the city were not very encouraging. The two articles on osteopathy had very likely not gone over. The two articles on chiropractic were now in, one from a chiropractor and an answer from a medical man, and Bly felt even worse about them than about the osteopathy pieces. On the face of it chiropractic seemed to be a good deal of a swindle. The chiropractor claimed that chiropractic manipulations had cured cancer and leukemia and arthritis and curvature of the spine and colds and rashes and pimples and indigestion, and he offered "testimonials." Bly discounted the "testimonials," as an old newspaper and magazine man he knew that it was possible to get "testimonials" for almost any form of charlatanry. He had often laughed at them in the past, but he couldn't laugh at them now.

The two articles on chiropractic were in the magazine, and so were four whole pages of letters about the osteopathic pair of articles. By this time it was clear that the last two articles didn't do well at all. Simmons admitted he was wrong, but he predicted that the two chiropractic articles would be "a sell-out. Out West most people, well, a lot of them, go to chiropractors, and they'll want to know what we say about them, and what regular doctors have to say about chiropractic. Besides, I have ordered five thousand posters all over the West and Middle West to advertise these articles. You may have a surprise coming to you."

"I hope so," said Bly. "This stuff really has me biffed. I spend so much time answering letters I hardly have time left for anything else. Is this a health magazine, or is it a general magazine?"

"It's a general magazine," said Simmons. "First, let's build up the circulation, and then you can do whatever you want."

Bly wanted to say that the circulation hadn't gone up much even with the nature series, but he thought he better not talk about that series. Besides, he had another worry. Simmons had told him, gleefully, that several osteopaths and chiropractors had bought advertising space in the *World,* "one of them asked for two full pages right away, and then a half page for nine months straight, this man is a sort of combination osteopath-chiropractor, maybe I have it wrong, but he's paying cold cash, and that's all that matters, isn't that wonderful? And I think I'll give the osteopaths and chiropractors, I mean the people who go to them, I can get the lists somewhere, I'll give them a special rate on the *World*, eight months for a dollar, I think I can get away with that with the Audit Bureau of Circulation, maybe I can't, the drop from four dollars to one dollar is kind of steep, but then maybe I can shave it down to a dollar and a half or maybe two dollars."

Bly was depressed. He wanted to object to the advertisements, but it didn't seem right for him to object to advertisements in a magazine that was having financial difficulties. Besides how could he object to them? In most of the nation chiropractic and osteopathy were recognized healing arts, their advertisements appeared in newspapers and magazines, and to refuse to run their advertisements would be tantamount to censorship. Still, Bly felt very uncomfortable with the notion of chiropractic and osteopathic advertisements in the *World*.

His worries soon multiplied. Simmons told him with unconcealed glee, one day, that lately he had been getting "feelers" from a large advertising agency, "well, not so large, but fairly important, Horowitz & McGovern, they handle smaller accounts, but they're solid, they've been feeling me out about a series of ads for handwriting people and astrology people and something called extra-sensory-perception, they have a foundation of some sort, some screwball woman runs it, but the money behind her is all right, and her backer is all right, too."

Bly's stomach sank . . . his mind returned to the word *handwriting* . . . one of his aunts was a fanatic about this, she claimed that from handwriting you can learn a great deal about one's physical and mental health and that you can even predict a good deal of one's future. Aunt Honor May Lou Becton, who had been a widow for some thirty years, had gone to what she called "a really scientific school of handwriting interpretation," had obtained a diploma and some sort of degree from the school, and she even practiced "handwriting reading." Strange elderly men and women, and sometimes younger girls, used to come to her to have their handwriting read, and they paid for her "professional" service. Bly knew nothing about the scientific basis for her work, but he had a hunch that it was largely quackery, and he often wondered whether the Federal Trade Commission or the United States Post Office couldn't get after her. In any case, she was one of the jokes of the family.

"But, Lester," he said with controlled politeness to Simmons, "are you serious about taking any of those handwriting ads? Aren't they like tea-leaf readers and head-bumps readers, and all those queer ones?"

"Well," said Simmons, "they are and they aren't." He stopped and looked off into the distance, and suddenly Bly saw what a manipulating man he was . . . he could almost see him thinking up arguments (which he himself didn't entirely believe) for taking advertisements from handwriting-readers and the others. "Some of these handwriting people are fakes, no doubt about it, but then many doctors also are fakes, and a hell of a lot of psychologists are fakes, too. But this hand-writing-reading can be a science, and the man from Horowitz & McGovern showed me letters from real M.D.'s and others who claim that handwriting does show something. After all, it stands to reason. If you're nervous, your writing is nervous, right?"

"Well, yes . . ."

"So when you're sick inside, physically, it affects the nerves of the body somehow, it has to, doesn't it, it's only logical, isn't it?"

"Well," began Bly, who felt he was somehow being trapped into admitting something he was not at all sure about. Simmons's talk was too fast for Bly to follow, he wanted to ask him to show him these testimonials, he wanted to know something about these M.D.'s he was talking about: where did they get their degrees, what was their standing in the profession . . . perhaps some of them had been expelled from the profession. Bly continued, "Well, I was just wondering . . ."

"Wondering about what?" asked Simmons, suddenly become somewhat stern.

Bly couldn't control himself any longer. "I was wondering whether this kind of advertising would do us any good in the long run."

"Why not?"

"Because, to be perfectly frank, it's a little shabby."

Simmons's face became red. "Shabby? What's shabby about perfectly good United States money? This sort of stuff is advertised in respectable newspapers out West and in the East, there are schools of handwriting, I mean reading handwriting. And let me tell you something else. I had a man up the office tell me about extra sensory perception. It's not all crazy stuff. I used to think it was, but he explained things to me. Spiritualism has fakes in it, sure, but there's something to it. You can't tell me that a man like Conan Doyle was a complete fake. Well, he believed in it. And there's something to telepathy, too."

Bly was getting angrier, but he tried to controll himself . . . at the moment he was ashamed of himself . . . he was sorry that he had ever become associated with Simmons . . . he had heard of the experiments of a Dr. Rhein at Duke University, he had read about extra sensory perception. There was no doubt that legitimate scientific investigation was going on in the field, but he suspected that Simmons would have taken the advertising whether it was respectable or not. He suspected that Simmons would take almost any advertising, unless it was outright fraudulent. Bly was afraid that some of the advertising, perhaps all of it, that was being offered to Simmons was from shady people who conducted spiritualistic seances in rundown, dubious parts of the city. He doubted very much that respectable scientific investigators had any interest in advertising extra-sensory perception in the *World* or in any other magazine or newspaper.

Bly still wasn't ready for a showdown battle with Simmons. He asked, "But what about the astrology advertising?"

"Well, there you may have some real ground for objecting," said Simmons. "I kind of don't like it myself. I was thinking maybe Horowitz & McGovern could rewrite the stuff, not make it so loud, maybe they could print it in smaller type, I don't know."

Bly smiled to himself. This man Simmons was out to get every possible dollar for the *World,* he would compromise and "adjust" to "make things look right." Bly wondered just how many things there were in this world "successful" business men wouldn't do to make a dollar.

184

"I don't know what to say," said Bly hopelessly.

"Leave it to me," said Simmons. "Believe me, I don't want to hurt the *World*. I have its interest at heart just as much as you. But we got to make it pay. Is there anything wrong in that, is there, tell me?"

"Well, frankly, I don't know," said Bly, who knew very well, but he didn't feel ready to say so directly to Simmons.

The second in the series on the healing arts sold even more poorly than did the first one. The readers in the big metropolitan centers were not interested, and neither were many of the people in the smaller communities in the Midwest, the South, or the Far West, where Simmons had predicted there would be a pick-up in sales. In only two respects was the series a success: the mail was tremendous, and the number of advertisements from all sorts of irregular healers and sellers of "health foods" was also tremendous. Meanwhile Bly was working on the third pair of articles in the series, on Christian Science. Simmons worked himself into a considerable excitement over these two articles. "That will do it," he said, "that will do it. A hell of a lot of people all over are Christian Scientists, and a lot more believe in it though they don't belong to any of the Christian Science churches. And they're all over, in big cities and in little cities. And, to be perfectly frank, I sort of incline that way a little bit myself. I mean that the mind has a lot to do with health, not the way the psychoanalysts and the psychiatrists say, but in a common sense way. I don't go for all the Christian Scientists say, after all, if you have a cavity in a tooth, you can pray your head off and read all of Mary Baker Eddy's *Science and Health,* and the cavity will remain there and get bigger, if you don't go to a dentist. And the same with other things, like ulcers, bad eyes, and things like that, if your eyes are not so good, you have to get glasses, that's all there's to it, but in a lot of things, it's the way you look at things that decides pretty much how you're going to feel. Anyway, we'll see."

Bly found a great deal of difficulty in getting an article from an official of the Christian Science Church to defend his faith as a healing art. The Scientists gave Bly the feeling that they didn't think their faith needed any defense. Slowly, he got them around to seeing the value of an article done by one

185

of them, but once they agreed to that, they insisted that the article appear by itself and that no medical man be allowed to reply to it. To this Bly objected vigorously on the ground that it was unfair in itself and it also was an invasion of his rights as an editor. Suddenly the Christian Science official with whom he was dealing changed his mind. The two articles appeared and the whole office, more or less alerted by Simmons, who had spent several hundred dollars publicising the articles, waited to see what would happen on the newsstands in New York City, in Philadelphia, in Boston, and in other major urban centers in the East, where the magazine went on sale first. Usually, when an issue of a magazine has a strong appeal to the public, it leaps up in circulation sometime during the first week, often during the first three days. But after a week, even after ten days there was no indication anywhere that the Christian Science pair of articles had any unusual circulation value.

Bly was now ready to talk to Simmons. The series was a failure, and he refused to proceed with it. He said so to Simmons in an open editorial meeting. Simmons agreed to put an end to the series. He also said that he wasn't too sure about the advertisements that Horowitz & McGovern had promised: "We got some, we'll get some more, but I don't know how much longer they'll run. Horowitz & McGovern, I learned, make all sorts of promises but they seldom come through. I know when I'm licked." He stopped, then raised his voice. "At least I had an idea. What have you people got?"

Kermit Stern immediately suggested that the *World* start a new series. "The magazine might even devote a whole year, even longer," he said, "to a realistic consideration of the real truth about Russia, nobody is really doing it, and we could make capital out of it. God, I ought to know."

Kermit had been a correspondent in Russia, and for a while had been sympathetic to Communism, but lately had changed his mind completely. He was now, at least, in the opinions of some of his old friends, an arch reactionary, who looked upon the late President Roosevelt as pretty much of a fellow-traveler.

Simmons was cool toward the idea, and yet it was plain that he was a bit attracted. Bly liked the idea very much. He was for it, and he was also for another series, on air power.

186

Kermit Stern immediately agreed with Bly: "I was going to suggest the air power idea, too, but I thought that one idea a day was enough."

Peter Goldstein was also attracted by these two ideas. "They sound good," he said. "Let's talk about it some more."

Thus began a major revolution on the *World*. New ideas and new people began to appear in the magazine, which seemed to be tapping a new market of readers. David was not at all happy with the revolution. He was more and more uncomfortable in the world of political ideas, and the pros and cons of air power had no urgent meaning to him—and neither did the world of labor, which very soon also made itself felt in the pages of *World*. Quickly he learned how to appear interested, and he made sure that he did his fair share of the writing and editing but no more. Thus his mind was clear a good deal of the time for his own writing.

Eight

Kermit Stern had been born in Russia in the last decade of the nineteenth century, the youngest of twelve children and the only son. Thus he was much the favorite, not only of his parents but also of his sisters, to whom he was a delightful oddity. He was of delicate health as a child, which meant that his sisters fought over the privilege of feeding him and playing with him, and this naturally spoiled him still more. He went to Hebrew school, and for a while his father thought of sending him to the yeshiva to study for the rabbinate, but Kermit— his name then was Kalman Stein—didn't like the idea of being a rabbi, and his wishes were almost commands to his father. He remained at home, doing very little till he was fifteen. This was unusual in a home of the modest financial circumstances of his father, who barely made a living for his large family in his little shop where he made and repaired shoes. But the family, and the neighbors, too, understood. After all, Kalman was an only son in a family of twelve children.

Kalman then began to walk about the little town where he lived, talking to other young boys, both Jewish and non-Jewish, and through them he learned something that he could not learn in his house, which was the usual Orthodox home: and what he learned outside his home was that there was a whole world of learning that had little or no relationship to the

Jews. He began to read non-Jewish books and magazines and newspapers. He did not tell his father, for fear of a severe reprimand from him. In many Orthodox Jewish families in those days "worldly" learning was frowned upon as the doorway to atheism and assimilationism. But Kalman reassessed his powers in the family, and he told his father that he wanted to go to the gymnasium, a sort of high school. The father was not pleased at all, for he had heard of young Jewish boys who had gone to the gymnasium and had stopped praying and observing the Sabbath—and he remembered one young man who had married a non-Jewish girl. He also remembered that some of the Jewish young men who had gone to the gymnasium had gone on to study medicine in Berlin and in England, and that was something else.

Kalman's father agreed to his son's going to the gymnasium. But that was easier said than done. There was a quota on Jewish boys admitted to the gymnasium, one had to bribe officials, and there was no guaranty that the bribed officials would stay bribed for long, which meant that most of them would have to be bribed regularly. But, said Kalman's father, "If Kalman wants it, he will have it, no matter what privations I and the rest of my family have to suffer." The rest of the family felt the same way. Kalman went to the gymnasium. He was thrilled. He took to the "worldly" learning like the proverbial duck to water. His father was pleased that he did not become a skeptic: Kalman still prayed daily and he still observed the Sabbath and he still fasted on Yom Kippur, and he promised his father that he would never marry a non-Jewish girl. All this was easy for Kalman to do and to promise. He had no convictions for or against religion. A polite boy, he decided, more or less instinctively, not to hurt his father by ceasing to do what he had been doing in his father's house. And as for not marrying a non-Jewish girl, that, too, Kalman could promise without any strain on his philosophical convictions: he almost never thought in a romantic way about non-Jewish girls, though he had gone out with some of them, not telling his parents, of course. He didn't like these girls. He didn't quite know why, but he didn't like them. He preferred Jewish girls, and he knew that when the time came for him to marry he would marry a Jewish girl.

But something did happen to Kalman that would have shocked his parents, and Kalman was shrewd enough to know not to tell them. He was rapidly becoming a socialist, almost an anarchist. He was especially drawn to the teachings of Peter Kropotkim, the Russian philosophical anarchist, but at the same time he saw wisdom in the somewhat more practical ideas of the Kautsky-Bernstein school of socialists. He joined the underground socialist society in his gymnasium, wrote for its underground newspaper, under a nom-de-plume, of course, and promised to work for the cause in some big city as soon as he was graduated from the gymnasium. He got in touch with a socialist leader in Kiev, who promised him a job as a journalist and added, "We will see to it that you do not get in trouble. We want our agitators and workers to stay out of jail and away from Siberia. In jail and in Siberia they are of little good to our cause." Kalman didn't have too much trouble in getting his father to agree to let him go to Kiev. Kalman told his father that he would probably work in a lawyer's office there and see if the law interested him. The father was pleased.

Kalman never saw his father or mother again. He proved himself a capable agitator and organizer, and the socialist underground sent him to various localities to propagandize and to collect funds. He was still, in part, an anarchist, and by this time he began to see sense in occasional violence against the authorities. He participated in the burning of some soldiers' barracks and arsenals and municipal buildings, and he also had a hand in the assassination of a local judge who was especially cruel to poor people in general and to poor Jews in particular. He fell in love with a Jewish girl who worked with him in the socialist movement. Her parents had gone to America a few years before, and she had remained in Russia, because, as she said, the movement needed her. She was willing to do whatever was best for the movement, but she wanted very much to see her father and mother at least once more, and she asked Kalman to take her to America for just a few months. Kalman agreed, and the party functionaries gave their permission. By this time Kalman and his wife, Teibel, were the parents of two children, a boy and a girl, and taking them along somehow made the projected trip more exciting. "Our two children will at least be a little bit Amerikaner," said Kalman.

What happened was that Kalman and Teibel became so entranced with America (they landed in New York) that they decided to stay. In a short while Kalman Stein became Kermit Stern, though many of his friends still called him Kalman, and Teibel became Toby Stern. The little boy had been named Avrohom, after Teibel's dead father; here he became Allan; and the little girl, who had been named Yente, after Kalman's dead grandmother, here became Janice. Kalman immediately went to work for the Yiddish press, which at the time was sympathetic to socialism. He finally found a comfortable niche for himself on the editorial staff of *The True Voice*. Not that he was entirely happy with the policy of the paper. He especially didn't like its attitude toward Palestine and Zionism. The paper was non-Zionist, while Kalman was inclined to be pro-Zionist. Then there was the matter of religion. *The True Voice* was non-religious and sometimes it made fun of Jewish religious customs and of rabbis in general. Kalman himself was not overly religious—he had long ago given up praying the traditional three times a day, and now and then he mixed *milchig* with *flaishig* when he ate in restaurants. But his home was *kosher,* and he was glad that his wife lit candles on Friday night. Of course, he did not work on the High Holy Days and he fasted on Yom Kippur. Kalman was unhappy about the attitude of *The True Voice* toward these matters. But all in all, it was the best of the Yiddish newspapers that had an opening for him.

In the meantime he went to night high school, he attended lectures at Cooper Union, and he read English books and magazines and newspapers. Pretty soon he was one of the best informed men on *The True Voice* about American history and American literature and especially about American labor movements. He was amazed how advanced the United States was in its labor philosophy—that it, in the labor philosophies held by such men as Eugene V. Debs and Samuel Gompers and Daniel de Leon and Thorstein Veblen. He learned that the United States labor movement had agitated for the eight-hour day long before the labor movement in any other country, and he learned that its concept of suitable labor conditions was more enlightened than similar concepts anywhere else. Further, the union movement here was vigorous and courageous. When he had been a socialist agitator in Russia he somehow had got the idea that the Russian revolutionaries were the most advanced in almost all realms, but now he realized that the Russian revolutionaries had much to learn from the American labor leaders. The latter couldn't quote Marx as readily, some even sneered at Marx, and more than a few didn't read him at all, but they knew what labor wanted and needed, and they had clear ideas as to how labor's needs could best be met. The government on nearly all levels was far from friendly toward unions, in many places strikes were forbidden and picket lines were outlawed, yet Kalman himself had seen picket lines, and witnessed battles between police and pickets. He read in the newspapers how, in certain places in the West, pickets were actually mowed down by gunfire, yet there were always other pickets to take the places of those who had fallen.

The First World War broke out shortly after Kalman and his wife came to America. Along with other journalists he didn't know where his sympathies should lie. Of course, he was for England and France, but he didn't see how he could be for Czarist Russia, which was now on the side of the democracies. But before he knew it he was saying pleasant things about the Russians—and when General von Hindenburg began to pound at Russia, Kalman became more and more pro-Russian. And when the Kerensky Revolution came he was violently pro-Russian. He begged the editor of *The True Voice* to send him to Russia as a correspondent. Kalman reported the last days of the Kerensky Revolution, and his enthusiasm hardly knew any bounds, as he indicated in his reports to *The True Voice*.

Just about the time of the Bolshevik Revolution he returned to the United States, because his wife was ill. He remained here for several years, for his wife became a chronic invalid. But he kept in close touch with what was happening in Russia by reading the Russian periodicals and newspapers, and by interviewing many American correspondents who came back here on visits. At first, Kalman was dubious about what the Bolsheviks were doing. He had been a devout Socialist, which is to say, he had belonged to the same party as Kerensky had belonged, and so he was inclined to look unfavorably upon what the party of Lenin and Trotsky had done. But then he be-

192

gan to veer in their direction, first for ideological reasons, and then for other reasons. Perhaps, he said to himself, the Bolsheviks were right in their contention that "sometimes history makes a sharp turn, and only the weaklings jump off the train of history." Kalman didn't like the restrictions on personal liberty, but there was some truth in what Trotsky and Lenin were saying about the grave dangers surrounding Russia. England certainly wasn't friendly, neither was France, neither was the United States. The Cordon Sanitaire that her former Allies had thrown around Russia was plenty of reason for the Russians to feel that a good deal of the world was violently against them. Then there was the matter of the status of the Jews in Russia; the Bolsheviks had definitely improved it. True, Kerensky had also been friendly to the Jews, but the Bolsheviks certainly did not reveal any animosity to the Jews, the Bolsheviks at least spoke as if they were the best of friends to the Jews. Trotsky himself was Jewish in origin, so was Karl Radek, so was Maxim Litvinoff, so was Kaganovitch. There seemed to be more Jews in the Bolshevik government than in the Kerensky government. But to come back to the matter of civil liberties, perhaps one should take Lenin and Trotsky at their word, namely, that as soon as conditions were settled civil liberties would be restored.

Much to Kalman's dismay the editors of *The True Voice* thought that the Bolsheviks were enemies of freedom, and one of them said, in private, that as far as he was concerned, even the Czarist tyranny was to be preferred to what was now going on in Russia, and he was sure that "the future will be even worse, we are here dealing with hooligans, they are the worst enemies of the working class." Kalman felt so out of sympathy with the views of *The True Voice* that he looked for a new job. Fortunately, there was founded about this time in New York City, under the auspices of the Communist Party in the United States, in association with dissident elements of the Socialist Party and the Trotskyite party—by this time Trotsky was exiled by Stalin, and the world Communist movement was divided into two camps: Stalinists and Trotskyites—a new publication, called *The Friend of the People*. It claimed to be "politically independent, subservient to no party, except the party of the people." Cynics said that the new paper would be the mouthpiece of the Stalinists, but the editors of the paper called such people "slanderers, lackies of the capitalist class."

Kalman went to work for the new paper. He was given a signed column, and this pleased his ego. He became a power in the New York pro-Russian world. Some of his old friends of *The True Voice* days criticised him as a Communist party member. He told them that he was still a socialist, that he did not receive any orders from anybody as to what he should write. "You will receive your orders when the time is right," he was told. And the time came soon. Kalman had written a column in praise of Trotsky's "heroic work for the Revolution. His place in history is secure no matter how wrong his present attitude may be. He helped build the new nation ideologically. He led the people's army to victory." Kalman looked for the column in its usual place in *The Friend of the People,* but it wasn't there. He was surprised. Before he could decide what to do he was called in by the chief editor. The editor was all smiles. "I knew how you would feel, Kalman, when you didn't see your column in the old place, so I called you as soon as I came in. Mind you, I don't want you to think that we were censoring your column. We've never done it before, have we?"

"No," said Kalman, who was vaguely annoyed by the editor's manner.

"And we're not censoring you now," continued the editor. "We just held it out for you to think over. I don't know how close in touch you've kept with the evidence against Trotsky. He really was a criminal."

"No!" exclaimed Kalman.

"I knew you'd be surprised when you heard this. I was, too. After all, you say to yourself, Trotsky, who fought side by side with Lenin, how could he be a criminal? Well, he was. He was in touch with the Allies, he was all ready to sell out Russia. Tonight, maybe tomorrow, they're busy tonight, I want you to meet some people who know a great deal about what's going on in Russia now, they'll tell you about Trotsky. They'll give you proof, evidence, everything. You'll be shocked."

"But he did lead the Army, didn't he?"

"Kalman, calm yourself. He was the nominal leader, that is true. The real leader was Stalin, no, it was Stalin and Lenin.

Trotsky was a figurehead, a mere figurehead. Anyway, in view of this, you see why I thought you'd want to think this column of yours over. And while you're here I want to tell you how wonderful your columns have been. All of us have liked them, and you've seen some of the letters in the Correspondence Column. And there's something else I want to tell you. I didn't plan to tell you this till sometime next week. How would you like to go to Russia as a correspondent for *The Friend of the People?*"

"Really?"

"Yes, really. I'm glad you like the idea. But we'll talk about this is a day or two," said the editor, as he handed Kalman the manuscript of his column that was not printed.

Kalman went home with mixed feelings. He was thrilled that he was going to Russia as a correspondent, but he was troubled about that column he wrote. He still felt as he said in the article, namely, that Trotsky had earned the gratitude of the Russian people. He had heard all sorts of rumors about Trotsky since Stalin had expelled him from the country—Kalman didn't know exactly where Trotsky was now; in Turkey or in Persia or in Mexico or, perhaps, somewhere in the United States. Kalman had not believed a single one of the rumors, they were just ridiculous to him. The man he did doubt was Stalin, and he thought several times of expressing his doubt in *The Friend of the People.* He didn't, just because he had not yet come around to it. Now he didn't quite know what to think about this. In a way, it was lucky that he had not written about Stalin, for then the editor would surely have reprimanded him, and would not have allowed the articles to be printed. But there was little satisfaction in this feeling for Kalman, for he still felt the same way about Stalin. Stalin, to him, was a vulgarian, a criminal, a man who had merely bested Trotsky as a political maneuverer. Besides, Kalman had heard rumors (they were more than rumors to him) that Lenin had grave doubts about Stalin as the proper man to be a leader in Revolutionary Russia, since he was a boor and an ignoramus. Now that Kalman thought of it, he had never heard this point discussed in the offices of *The Friend of the People.* He recalled, with a strange feeling of fear, that once he himself had brought it up, but that those around him greeted him with stony silence. At the time he had wondered about this silence, now he saw more meaning in it. He felt more and more hemmed in.

Then there was the purely personal matter of his wife's ability to go with him to Russia. He asked a doctor, who gave his permission, saying, "You might get a place for her in the warm Crimea and this would do her good, and I understand they have good schools there for your children. Your wife's ailment is not very serious, it's only a form of rheumatism, well, we call it osteo-arthritis, the progressive form, but the rate of progress can be slowed down, and often a warm climate and rest and freedom from worry is just the thing for it. You might try it for a year or two."

His wife was pleased and not so pleased. "It would be nice to go back. Russia is Russia," she said. "But I wonder about several things."

"About what?" asked Kalman.

"Well, dear, about what's going on . . . and other things. You and I are socialists, and it seems to me that the gulf between what you and I think and what is going on in Russia now is getting wider with the years. But, then, I don't know. I agree with the Communist press, with your own paper, that you can't believe what you read in the American newspapers, not everything, at least. So, from that angle, it might be nice to find out for ourselves. I agree that the people there are doing wonders. But the government . . . well, I don't know, I just don't know. And I'm a little surprised that your editor wants to send you as a correspondent. After all, you're not a Communist, and they must know you have some doubts."

"Yes, they know, but I begin to think that they're more clever than you and I imagine. Maybe it's because I'm not a Communist that they're sending me. They may be wanting to convert me, and through me to convert others like me."

"They may," said his wife, "they may, but I wonder . . . "

"I'm wondering myself," said Kalman.

"I'm almost afraid to say what's running through my mind," said his wife.

"Tell me."

"Well, I'm wondering why they keep you on, or, rather, why they have kept you on. It's all a puzzle to me. A big puzzle, dear. You've had several of the staff here, and I don't remember anybody else who's not a member of the party, all of them except you. Well, maybe Tomaso, the one who runs the column of Italian news and editorial comments."

"I've wondered about him, too. Sometimes I think he's a socialist like I am, sometimes I just don't know. As a matter of fact, I've discussed Trotsky with him several times, and I told him what I wrote in the column, the one they didn't want to print. And all Tomaso did is shake his head this way and that way, and I didn't know what he meant, if he was with me or against me, I mean. I still don't know what he thought about Trotsky. He just wouldn't talk. And once, I just remembered it, I wanted to talk to him about Norman Thomas, but Tomaso just smiled. He called him a clergyman, a priest, and he said he wasn't realistic, but he did say he was sincere, but when I tried to find out from him if he agreed with Norman Thomas in what he said about Russia, the lack of free speech and things of that sort, he wouldn't talk, just shut up. But there's something I don't understand, I mean something else I don't understand. They don't call me in to editorial meetings. Well, they do call me in sometimes, but only for small matters, where to place this or that news item, suggesting I write a short column for this or that day, because of the pressure of news, but never on policy, on really important matters. And yet they want to send me to Russia now."

"Well," said his wife, "there's the United Front to consider. I always did believe in that. And Leon Blum seems to believe in it."

The United Front was an idea, apparently initiated by the Communists of the world, the burden of which was that the "progressive labor and political forces of the world" should unite in "the fight against war and fascism," on the theory that defeating this enemy was more important than for the "progressive forces" to fight among themselves. The idea seemed to electrify the liberal forces in all Western countries, and socialist and communist groups did join hands in England and in France and in Italy and in the United States. Leon Blum, the socialist leader in France, was taken with the idea for a while. There were thinkers who were violently opposed to the United Front on the ground that it was a trick on the part of the Communists to demoralize all the liberal forces who had fought them because of their anti-democratic practices: a one-party ballot in Russia, the absence of real free speech and a real free press, the absence of real freedom of worship, a general atmosphere of intellectual oppression that was permeating all levels of the artistic and even the scientific worlds. The same skeptics insisted that the Communists, by one trick or another, would dominate every United Front organization.

It wasn't long before they had much evidence for their point of view. They pointed to the United Front as it existed in the Newspaper Guild and in the Fur Workers' Union. There, according to the skeptics, the Communists had maneuvered various important meetings in such a manner that at a particular time enough members would be present to form a quorum but the vast majority of those present would be Communists, in other words, the meeting would be "packed," and definitely pro-Communist resolutions would be passed. Some of the resolutions had nothing whatever to do with the specific problems of the Newspaper Guild or of the Fur Workers' Union, but the Communists could point to the resolutions as representing "the point of view of militant American labor." Among these resolutions were those denouncing the United States government for its "imperialistic" policy in Latin America, and for "interfering" with the "Peoples' wishes" in China, particularly when the "Peoples' wishes" happened to coincide with the wishes of Moscow in China, which were entirely inimical to whatever Chiang-Kai-Shek had in mind for China—and what he had in mind was the routing of every vestige of Communism from his country.

"Yes, the United Front," said Kalman. "I still think it's a good idea. Some people say the Communists are using an old trick, and will try to run things. I suppose they will. But then there is also the chance that some of the Communists, talking to socialists and other liberals, will see how wrong some of their own ideas are. It works both ways. So maybe their wanting to send me to Russia is a part of the United Front idea. So it can't be all bad," said Kalman, who felt a burden lift from his heart.

"No, it can't be all bad," said his wife, who still wasn't too sure.

"I was thinking, I'm probably the only non-Communist working on *The Friend of the People,* so maybe the Communists have right along believed in the United Front and have practiced it. It could be, couldn't it?"

"It could."

"Well," said Kalman, who now felt vaguely reassured about many things, "what harm could it do for us to go to Russia? We could see things at first hand, and if things are really good there, then that's that. If not, I'll say so in my dispatches. And if they stop my dispatches, then . . . well, we'll see when we come to that. It would be an experience. Besides, I would like to see some of the old places, wouldn't you?"

"Very much, Kalman, very much." This consideration, indeed, was what finally won over Kalman's wife and Kalman himself to the advisability of going to Russia.

In his enthusiasm Kalman forgot about his column on Trotsky. Instead, he wrote general pieces about labor meetings in various parts of New York City, about early Russian history, about the cities and towns he knew as a young boy, and now he found himself writing about "the glory of the Russian soul, which is more profound than that of any other country," about the "wisdom and the goodness and the kindness" of the Russian peasant, and about "the cruelty of the Russian capitalist class that kept the Russian people oppressed for so many centuries." Kalman found it very easy and pleasant to write these columns, and when the chief editor said to him, "Kalman, those last few columns of yours were just wonderful, we're all talking about them, and if you send us dispatches like them from Russia, we'll just be tickled pink. Keep it up!", Kalman was not only delighted, he was a bit ashamed that he had ever had any doubts about the editor and about *The Friend of the People.*

In Russia Kalman and his wife and children were greeted most enthusiastically. He was pleased but somewhat surprised, for he was only a correspondent, and he couldn't understand the motive behind his reception. He discussed it with his wife, but she was also in the dark. "Who knows?" she said. "Maybe we're wrong in being so skeptical."

"Maybe."

When they asked to be permitted to go to their home towns they found only a desire to make their trip comfortable—no troubles whatsoever. Kalman cabled his home office if it was all right with them, and they immediately cabled back it was perfectly all right. All they wanted was "fine, good articles about the people, about what the government is doing for them, about how happy they are, all written in the way you know so well."

Kalman was happy and so was his wife. "Maybe we were wrong," he said to her again and again. "After all, we were in America, five, six thousand miles away, and unfriendly propaganda was all around us . . . the people here are very friendly, nobody has stopped me anywhere, nobody has censored anything I've written . . . "

His wife had vague doubts about all sorts of things . . . she still couldn't get out of her mind that her husband's column in praise of Trotsky was censored, no, thrown out . . . she had been somewhat upset that he had not "re-written" it . . . it would have been interesting to see how the "rewrite" would have fared . . . altogether she wondered about many things . . . the reception was just too enthusiastic, people were just too friendly, things were just too easy for them . . . but she didn't want to disillusion her husband, he seemed to be so happy, and she, too, was very happy to be back in Russia.

They finally settled in Moscow. Kalman was free to roam wherever he pleased. At the beginning he sent "human interest" stories: about the state of women (how much better it was than it had been in Czarist days), about the status of education (how high the literacy rate was), how fine the hospitals were (there were not enough, but there were more than ever before, and they were increasing in number constantly), how many new parks there were, how many more opportunities there were for bright young boys and girls in the professions and in the trades and in the military services. These articles went through the censorship untouched. He got to know the censors intimately, and one of them said, "If all the correspondents were like you, we'd have no trouble." When Kalman inquired what the nature of the trouble was, the censor answered, "Some of the capitalist reporters just tell the seamy side of things, and they harp upon one thing, that we have a one-party system, that we're not a democracy."

"Yes?" said Kalman, who was eager to hear how the censor answered these correspondents.

"Yes, that's what they harp upon. I point out to them that if the people weren't satisfied, they'd complain, and they don't complain. That should be proof enough, don't you think?"

"It certainly is proof," said Kalman . . . and immediately he was ashamed of himself . . . he had told a lie . . . there was some pressure that made him tell a lie . . . he didn't quite know what the pressure was . . . he was disturbed . . . but he didn't tell his wife . . . he didn't want to upset her, she seemed to be improving in health since they came to Russia.

Kalman then decided to write a series of articles on the condition of workingmen as compared to their condition in the United States and with special reference to the place of unions in the two countries. He discovered quickly what he had suspected when he was in New York, that Russian unions were little better than what in the United States would be called company unions: they had no authority beyond that granted to them by the Communist party, they were virtually forbidden to strike—there wasn't a record of a single strike since the Communists came to power, the leaders were not really chosen by the workers themselves but by Communist party functionaries, that the discussion at union meetings was dull, since there was seldom any controversy—a functionary would let it be known what "the party line" was and the others seemed to know at once that it was safest not to go against the line. Kalman also learned that the general pay scale was far below that of the United States, that the hours were far longer than those in the United States. But above all Kalman noticed that there was an atmosphere of fear at all the union meetings he went to. At American union meetings the members looked to their union not only for help and guidance in their working problems but also for social entertainment . . . The American union member was a free man, who looked up to nobody, who joked with the highest officials in his local union and also in the national offices. The union members in the United States talked freely, they recognized no such thing as a party line, and when they felt like it they denounced their officials openly and even violently.

Kalman was astonished and yet he wasn't astonished. He had expected that there would be a difference in the general labor situation in Russia. After all, Russian labor was young, and the Revolution was young. Russian industry also was young, for the country had been a predominantly agricultural land for centuries. Kalman was willing to allow for all this, he was also willing to excuse a somewhat lower pay scale and even somewhat longer hours, but what he saw was too much: the pay scale was outrageously low, the hours were equally outrageous—but worst of all, the workers didn't dare to talk, they were not free agents, they were the slaves of their Communist Party leaders . . . they had no more to say than the workers in the "kept" towns of certain sections of the Pennsylvania coal regions and the New York State shoe and business machine regions.

His instinct told him to wait before writing the labor series he had been so eager to do. Instead, he continued to write "human interest" pieces . . . about a farmer, nearly sixty, who had been illiterate till he was fifty-five, but was taught to read and write at a local Communist party center . . . he was getting a small pension because he had been injured at a nearby collective farm . . . he also obtained whatever medical attention he needed without expense . . . one of his sons was a captain in the army . . . two of his grand-children were about to enter a university . . . he was happy: "If the cursed Czar had still been with us, we, my family, all of us, would still be slaves, perhaps dead. I don't have to worry. My worries are over. I vote. This is something I've never done before, and I see the people I vote for. And so many people are talking about my problems. So it's good."

Kalman interviewed a common laborer, who used to drive a wagon before the First World War. He was now working in a munitions factory, it was dangerous work, it kept him indoors, whereas he used to work out of doors, and he liked the out-of-doors, but he was content: "Now I work for some-thing, for a country that is really mine. I don't grumble. I am happy. Things could be better, of course. But I think of the miracle that has happened in so short a time, and pretty soon we will beat the capitalistic countries, only they shouldn't want to destroy us, like our leader Stalin says they are trying to do. We have freedom and liberty, real freedom and liberty, not like in America. Here, everything is for the workers."

Then Kalman saw a group of Jewish men and women. It was not long after the purge of 1927, when several Jewish intellectuals suddenly disappeared from the scene. Kalman had heard from some American correspondents that Stalin was anti-Semitic, and that this was to a large extent the cause of his battle with Trotsky: Stalin wanted to get rid of him for reasons of power, but he also hated him for being a Jew. Kalman didn't believe this rumor wholly, but he was uncomfortable about it. He wondered whether he should ask the Jews what they thought about the rumors of Stalin's anti-Semitism. They told him how good their general conditions were, more or less using the same words that the farmer and the common laborer had used. They also pointed to the provisions in the Soviet Constitution that promised complete tolerance to all races and religions and that guaranteed freedom of worship as well as freedom of speech and of the press. Kalman couldn't control himself any longer, and he asked one of the Jews why it was that so many distinguished Jews, like Trotsky and Kameneff were no more in positions of high authority, and why it was that the synagogues were so empty and why so many of the young people were so hesitant in going to synagogue, and why the state made it so difficult to print Yiddish and Hebrew newspapers and books.

The Jew looked at him for several seconds, rather puzzled. Kalman got the notion that the Jew was trying to make up his mind what he should say and whether he should say anything. Finally, he did say: "The Soviet Constitution is very clear about freedom of worship. Nobody bothers any Jews who want to go to synagogue, and about newspapers and books in Yiddish and in Hebrew, there are several around."

"But why aren't there as many as there used to be?" asked Kalman.

"Well, I guess for the same reason that there are not so

many other religious newspapers. The Soviets are not friendly to religion, but they don't bother anybody who wants to go to any church or synagogue."

"What I'm talking about is not just religious books and newspapers," said Kalman. "I mean novels and stories and essays."

"You must be mistaken," said the Jew, and it was clear he didn't want to continue the discussion.

Kalman went to some synagogues, and he tried to talk to various people in them about the state of Judaism in Russia. Not one answered him freely or honestly. He felt that they were holding back something. They all hesitated before answering him. The general tenor of their replies was, "We're not complaining, you see we have a synagogue."

When he inquired if there were any obstacles put in the way of their children going to synagogue or Hebrew school, they hesitated again and then merely said, "Where did you get the idea there were obstacles?"

As Kalman traveled from city to city searching for "human interest" material, he heard disturbing tales . . . a man was asked to come out to see somebody late at night, and was never heard from again . . . inquiry was made at the police station, but the police were not interested . . . Kalman inquired about the man . . . with much difficulty he found out that the man had made critical remarks about Stalin . . . there was another man who went to work in the morning (he worked in a cotton factory), and he too has not been heard of since . . . there were rumors that he was in Siberia . . . again Kalman inquired, and again after much difficulty he learned that this man's nephew had been a partisan of Trotsky's . . . the man himself was not a Trotskyite, he had little interest in the Stalin-Trotsky battle, but it seemed that he and his nephew were good friends . . . Kalman also learned that the man's wife and children were in deadly fear that soon or late some punishment would be meted out to them, not because they were Trotskyites or were critical of Stalin, but simply because the head of their family was suspected of being unfriendly to Stalin.

Kalmon was puzzled what to do: should he try to write about these things or not—and if he wrote should he try to camouflage his findings, or come right out with a clear report of what he saw and heard? The mere question annoyed him. He felt humiliated. He put the whole subject out of his mind, or he tried to. He would continue to talk to people, travel about, and somehow find things worth writing about for *The Friend of the People*. He found a great deal that he could write about and with a clear conscience. The literacy rate really was rising phenomenally, the schools were filled with eager students, high schools were multiplying at an astonishing rate, so were colleges and universities. The status of women was most admirable. There were women in colleges of all sorts, especially medical schools. No man or woman, young or old, with high intelligence need have any worries about his or her education, the state was genuinely interested in making full use of brains wherever found. The medical services were free and quite good, and were improving constantly. There were newspapers and magazines everywhere. The libraries were fairly well stocked with books and magazines, and new libraries were being built everywhere. There were also fine concerts and operatic performances, and everybody could go to them. It was really inspiring to see a whole local union—of subway workers or street cleaners or shoemakers or bakers—fill a hall to see a performance of *Eugin Onegin* or Tchaikovsky's Symphony Pathetique—or to see one of the many ballet companies perform *Swan Lake* or *The Nutcracker Suite* or *Sylphide*.

He also liked the nurseries for young children: they were huge, bright, and extremely well run. When he compared the plight of the young American mother with several young children, who had to work, with the opportunities open to her in Russia he was forced to say to himself that it was no wonder that the Russian people were inclined to be friendly to the government. He also liked the new homes for the aged and infirm that were rising in several cities.

So impressed was he with all he saw in the way of the general social relation of the government with the individual men and women that he began to wonder whether he wasn't wrong in entertaining any doubts about Russia as a whole. As he said to his wife, "Things are not perfect, that is true, but there are so many things that are so good, that perhaps we ought to have patience, and isn't that exactly what spokesmen for the government are saying?"

"You may be right," said his wife, who still had doubts, but now she wasn't so sure about these doubts.

"About liberty and freedom, well," continued her husband, "maybe there is something, too, here in what officials are saying. The country really is surrounded by enemies, and there's no telling when these enemies will spring on her. Capitalists can be very cruel."

Kalman continued to travel over the country in search of human interest material. He made a special trip to Birobidjan, where a Jewish "autonomous" community had been established. The Communist press had made a great deal of this expression of friendship for the Jews, hailing it as a model of "what a country with true friendship for minorities does to make them feel at home, in peace and in security." Kalman had heard about this community when he was still in New York, and he had also heard several people express doubt about it. He recalled that on *The Friend of the People* he had not heard a single doubt expressed about Birobidjan. At the time he was disturbed by this unanimity, but he knew nothing about Birobidjan beyond what he read in *The New York Times* and in *The Friend of the People,* so he kept quiet.

What impressed him first as he arrived was the strange apathy of the Jews there. He had expected to find them in exuberant spirits, but they seemed to be troubled. He inquired how they liked their "autonomous" community, and all he got out of them was, "We're not complaining." He had come to think that when Soviet citizens said this, they were, in effect, saying that they were not happy. Slowly he learned why they were unhappy. Birobidjan was not an autonomous Jewish community any more than was White Russia or the Ukraine or Georgia or Outer Mongolia.

There were a few more Jews active in community affairs, and he heard more Yiddish spoken on the streets, but there was very little genuine spirit in the community. He sensed that while Yiddish was spoken here and there, it was not encouraged as a speaking or as a reading language. There was one Yiddish newspaper in the whole community, and he gathered, from various hints, that the management had difficulty in getting newsprint or in getting the newspaper properly distributed. The newsprint authorities claimed that there was a shortage, but apparently there was no such shortage for any newspapers printed in Russian. Kalman also noticed that the study of Jewish history and literature was not encouraged. There were few Jewish books in the libraries and few magazines, in Yiddish or in Russian or in Hebrew. The study of Hebrew, in fact, was openly frowned upon. Zionism was denounced by government officials as "a despicable form of cosmopolitanism," a phrase that meant everything and nothing to Kalman. He asked some of the Birobidjan Jews what it meant, and they said, "It's clear enough." He persisted in asking what it meant, and then one of the Jews took him out for a long walk and told him in a hush-hush voice, "Don't you understand? Russia, Soviet Russia comes first all the time. There is only one loyalty here, only one. That loyalty is Russia. One cannot be loyal to another country, even another dream of another country. If Palestine becomes another country, as Zionism hopes it will, then Jews will have two loyalties, that is, Zionist Jews. Soviet Russia cannot permit that."

"But why? Zionism is permitted in the United States, in England, in France," said Kalman.

"I know," said the man, who was beginning to be annoyed— and Kalman had the feeling that the man was sorry he had talked at all—"but those are capitalist countries."

"But if they're not afraid of it, why should Russia?"

"Look, I'm only a loyal Soviet citizen," said the man.

"But you're also a Jew."

"Yes, but first I'm a Soviet citizen, and I don't see what else there is to say."

Kalman asked questions: Why were there so few people at services in the only synagogue in the whole community, why was there only one synagogue, why were there no meetings of organizations dedicated to the study of Hebrew or Jewish culture, why was there no Zionist organization, why was there virtually no contact between the Jews of Birobidjan and the Jews of the outside world, why were non-Jews in positions of higher authority to Jews, in the various departments?

Kalman was outraged. He wrote an article about the synagogue for *The Friend of the People,* but he was ashamed of it. What he was told was true, but there was much he didn't tell, especially the lack of a true Jewish atmosphere. This was no real *shul,* it was cold and riddled with silent fear. When he got his copy of *The Friend of the People* with this article he noticed that the two paragraphs in which he deplored the absence of youth in the synagogue was deleted. He showed this to his wife, she said nothing, and he said nothing. Then he wrote an article pointing out the total absence of Zionist feeling in Birobidjan, and he deplored this, too, and again the paragraphs of criticism were deleted. Then he wrote an article in which he said, as diplomatically as he could, that Birodijan was hardly the haven for Jews that he had imagined. This article was not printed at all.

He got a letter from his editor in New York, saying: "We know perfectly well how you feel about Birobidjan. It is not perfect. But you have to view these things in broad perspective. You know the old saying, Rome wasn't built in a day. In time Birobidjan will be a real haven for Jews, within the framework of the Soviet Union, of course. We must look ahead with optimism. Little is gained by pointing out deficiencies now; that only discourages people. The proper thing to do is to point out good things in Birobidjan, and I am sure you can find many good things. For example, is there anti-Semitism in Birobidjan? There isn't. Then it would interest our readers to know it, not merely theoretically but by example. And you can give human interest angles as nobody else can. Think it over, Kalman. And keep up the good work."

Kalman was infuriated by the letter. It didn't really answer anything. Besides, the editor did not explain why he had deleted paragraphs from other columns. Kalman did not answer the editor. He didn't discuss the situation with his wife either, except that he told her about the editor's letter, and let it go at that. Her arthritis had become aggravated, and she didn't seem to be in the mood to talk things over, and he wasn't in the mood to talk them over with her. He decided to bide his time. He traveled far and wide (no one interfered with him; he could go wherever he wished) and he wrote human interest stories about coal miners and stone masons and street car conductors and railroad employees and postal employees and doctors and dentists and lawyers and school teachers and college professors.

He got to know one college professor rather well. At least, the professor made him feel more at ease than did any of the others. He asked many questions about the academic life in America, and all that Kalman could give him was second-hand information, for Kalman had not gone to college. The professor also asked about newspapers, about the freedom of editors to criticize the government. He asked about the Jews. Kalman didn't think he was Jewish, he gave no inkling what his religious faith had been, but he did look non-Jewish, his face was quite Slavic in appearance. There came times when Kalman felt that the professor had sought him out. He wondered why the professor had not invited him to his house, to meet his family, but Kalman said nothing. It then occurred to Kalman that he might do a human interest story about the professor's university, and the professor helped him out, answering whatever questions Kalman asked him. Kalman wrote his article, showed it to the professor, and the professor said, "If you were in one of my classes, I am a specialist in history, as you know, in contemporary events, why, then, I would give you the highest grade." Kalman was pleased, and yet he had the strange feeling that the professor didn't quite tell him everything—about the university or about himself.

One afternoon the professor and Kalman were walking in a park not far from the university. They had come upon a clearing. The professor looked around and in back of him, as if he were trying to make sure the two were alone, and then he said, "I'm Jewish."

Kalman was astonished. "You don't look it."

"I know. But I am. I wish you would keep this a secret. It's not very safe to be known as a Jew in Russia now. The officials know, but if I don't talk about it, it's in my favor."

"What do you mean?"

"It's simple, my friend. The Russians are just as anti-Semitic now as they ever were. Stalin is a violent anti-Semite, and you will notice that there are almost no high army officers or navy officers who are Jews, and there are no chairmen of departments in universities who are Jews. Jews are the only people who have to state in their police identification papers their religion. But that is not all . . . "

"But . . . ," began Kalman.

"Please, my friend, let me finish. I want to say whatever I have to say, I want to do it quickly. It's dangerous, but I feel I can tell you. So let me finish. Some other time, or even a little later now, I may change my mind and again go into silence, and I may even be sorry later now . . . "

"Oh, no . . . "

"Let me go on. We professors are slaves to the political commissars, we teach what we are told to teach, especially in my subject, history, and I am forced to teach lies, about Trotsky and about Stalin and about Bolshevik history, just lies and lies. And there are spies in our classes, to make sure we actually teach the lies. Our own pupils are spies. Let me tell you an instance."

"Children spying on teachers!"

"Yes, but please let me go on. I am rushed for time." He looked in back of himself and to the right and to the left. "Children spy on teachers, they do. They are told to by the political commissars. How do they do it? It sounds barbaric. But they do it. A commissar tells them that the safety of the state is paramount. Without the state there is nothing. The Soviet state is the finest in the world, it is surrounded by enemies, and you know the rest. And the children are told to be little soldiers for the state, to report everything they hear that is inimical to the state, to report what they hear in the home and in school. I can tell you of many instances. I'll tell you one. One of my colleagues in the history department, he was a professor from way back, a very distinguished man, he was very much in love with his wife, they were students together, they had no children for years and years, and then, when they already did not expect any children, she became pregnant, and you can imagine how happy they were. A little boy. He grew up and went to school. He was in the gymnasium, what you call in your country junior college. A fine boy. The professor was not very happy. He didn't want to teach lies. And he said so at home, thinking that it would remain there. He told his wife he hoped he could get a position in some university outside the country, outside Russia. And he spoke about Stalin, what an ignorant man he was. My friend was not Jewish, but he was friendly to the Jews, and he told his wife how anti-Semitic the administration of the university was. Then one day he was called by the local branch of the Party, and he was questioned there for hours and hours, and they told him everything that he had said at home, and he was sure that his own son had told on him, and he asked his son and his son turned red in the face and cried. Well, you know. And this is a civilized country, it is claimed!"

"What happened to the professor?"

"There is no more professor, there is no more Mrs. Professor, and there is no more son."

"Killed?"

"We don't know. The professor was called another time by the political commissar, and he never returned home. That was two years ago, and his wife did not get as much as a card from him. She asked the authorities, but they kept quiet. Then they told her not to ask them any more. A little later they told her that they would take her son and put him in a school in another city, 'for his own good,' since, they told her very plainly, his home atmosphere was not healthy. The mother pleaded with the authorities to let her go along, she told them he was her only child, but they didn't listen. She got sick, melancholy, and one day the authorities came and took her away, and that's all we've ever heard about her or about her son, or about her husband. The police later came to her apartment and took all the furniture away, and that was the end. Another horrible thing is that we at the university are afraid to talk about the professor. If we talk they might think we are sympathetic with his opinions. Then there is another thing. Not one of us really knows who among the professors isn't himself a spy. Yes, that's how bad it is. Well, I just thought you ought to know about this. We are living in a prison, and Jews are living in a double prison. Perhaps you can tell the people in America the truth."

Kalman was profoundly shaken. He knew he could not stay on in Russia and continue to write what he had been writing. He was ashamed of himself. At the same time he fully realized for the first time that *The Friend of the People* was completely under Communist control, that he had been duped when he was told he could write whatever he wished. He also saw the falseness of the United Front idea. The Russian Communists were tyrants, in some respects, far worse than the Czar was. He was at a loss what to do immediately. There was no question of his sending truthful stories to *The Friend of the People*. He could not discuss his problem with his wife, who was now almost bedridden. Then there was the problem of his children who had got to like their school and their schoolmates and Russian life in general. He spent sleepless nights struggling with his problem. Sometimes his wife would ask him how things were in general, and he said fine, but he knew that she knew that he was not telling the whole truth.

Finally, he made his decision. He would continue to send human interest stories, and he would make them exactly what the editor of *The Friend of the People* wanted them to be. Suddenly one afternoon he was informed that the professor who had spilled out his heart to him had disappeared after being awakened late one night by the police. Kalman's heart sank. He was now more determined than ever to carry through his plan: to continue to please his editor, and then ask him to transfer him to some other country, or perhaps have him return to the United States because of his wife's worsening health. After six months he did make the request and much to his delight his wish was granted: he could return to the United States.

Kalman could hardly believe his good fortune. His wife was equally delighted, though neither said anything openly till they were on the American ship that took them from Bremen to New York. For the first time they talked openly. His wife told him that she sensed almost from the beginning that Russia was a despotism, that Stalin was a gangster, that they were trapped and she was hoping that he, Kalman, would somehow manage to get the family out. Kalman also determined to leave *The Friend of the People* at once, and to tell the editor exactly why.

"Nothing pleases me more," said his wife. "You will have no trouble in getting work."

"I don't think so either. I can write up my experiences in English newspapers, and maybe I can do a book. It's shocking what is going on in Russia."

He had no difficulty in getting a job on the New York *Observer-Chronicle*. At first he helped write editorials on foreign affairs, then he wrote some articles for the Sunday edition, then he was asked to write a regular series of articles on his experiences in Russia. When the editor told him that his copy would not be edited ("You tell the truth, and we'll print it") he believed him at once. He knew he was dealing with a far more honest man than the editor of *The Friend of the People*. It was on the *Observer-Chronicle* that Kalman Stein assumed the name of Kermit Stern for good. His friends called him that, his associates called him that. Only his wife called him Kalman, and he liked that . . . there was something deliciously secret and personal about her doing that . . . and he liked especially to hear her calling him Kalman when they made love.

The more he wrote about Russia the angrier he got about his own blindness to what was going on there before he had actually seen and heard with his own eyes and ears. He was ashamed of himself, he should have known better, and he should never have been taken in by *The Friend of the People*. As his series continued, his old friends and colleagues on *The Friend of the People* began to denounce him as a capitalist, one "who had sold out to the oppressors of labor." Then *The Friend of the People* denounced him editorially for five days straight as "an ingrate, a renegade, a turncoat, a lickspittle, a social-fascist, a slave of the Robber Barons, a snake in the grass, a disgrace to all Jews and to all honest men and women. We deplore the time that we trusted him, we deplore the time that we looked upon him as a man of integrity, we deplore the time he worked with us here on *The Friend of the People*. We predict that his end will be the end of all traitors."

Kermit was somewhat troubled by the last sentence, for by this time he had learned of the long arm of the Soviet Secret Police. They never forgot "enemies," whom they hunted down and "liquidated." He wondered whether he was important enough to be "liquidated." He came to the conclusion that he wasn't—but there were times when he had

213

his doubts. After all, he was becoming more important, his articles were being syndicated over the country, and he had just signed a contract with a publisher to bring them together into a book—plus some additional material. But his wife reassured him: "Darling, they won't touch you. It would be too dangerous. You are a national figure now. But I think they will vilify you, and God knows what they will say about you."

His wife was right. When his book, *Farewell to Myopia,* came out, the Communist press, especially *The Friend of the People,* made wild accusations against him: that he had had, years before, a colored mistress, that he was on the secret payroll of the National Association of Manufacturers, that he was in constant touch with the Federal Bureau of Investigation to whom he betrayed "countless honest men and women," that he had "a mysterious past record, involving illegal acts that are now being investigated," and that the White Russians of Paris and of New York were paying his apartment rent and the medical bills of his ailing wife. The last accusation annoyed him especially and he threatened to sue *The Friend of the People,* but his wife prevailed upon him to ignore the Communists. "What will you gain, dear? Only aggravation. And if you win, you will get nothing, except more insults and God knows what else. Besides, it will take years and years. I don't mind, please forget about it, that's the only way to deal with such people."

Kermit forgot—and he didn't forget. It rankled in his heart. He began to doubt his own powers of perception about people. He began to wonder about various New Dealers . . . who knows, maybe they were disguised Communists? He read in the Hearst press and in various other newspapers that Communists had infiltrated deep into the government, even into the State Department and the Department of Commerce and possibly also into the Defense Department. Years before he had smiled at these charges, but now he wasn't so sure . . . he began to look for Communists in many places . . . and now he became suspicious of the New Deal and later of President Truman's Fair Deal, especially of the first. He had been a vigorous defender of President Roosevelt and his New Deal, and he had voted for him three times, but when

Roosevelt ran against Dewey Kermit was for Dewey. Kermit's wife was surprised.

"How can you, dear?" she asked.

"Well," he said, "I just don't feel comfortable about the New Deal people, they're too friendly to Russia, and I don't like that."

He was not happy about the alliance with Russia during the Second World War, and he predicted that no good would come out of this. "The Russians will use us as long as they have to," he said, "then they will knife us."

He was especially vigorous in his opposition to the concept of One World, which Wendell Willkie had enunciated, and which the country seemed to have accepted for a time. Kermit insisted that the world couldn't be One World so long as Soviet Russia was a major power. "Russia is the deadly enemy of the free world," he insisted. "They cannot live at peace with the democracies, and the democracies cannot live at peace with Russia. No tyranny, whether fascist or communistic, can live at peace with the democracies. Sooner or later, the tyranny must go to war with the democracies."

Kermit's book, *Farewell to Myopia,* was well received and sold nearly 40,000 copies. It gave Kermit much prestige and he had many lecture engagements and requests for articles. He made a good living, but he was ill at ease. He wanted some steady connection with a periodical, and when Lester Simmons was introduced to him at a party, he cultivated Simmons's friendship, and when Simmons asked him whether he wouldn't like to work "in a sort of advisory capacity . . . maybe we'll find something definite later," Kermit was pleased. He tried to sell Simmons on the idea of turning *The American World* "into the only truth-telling organ in America about Russia, and especially into an organ that tries to ferret out all Communist and other subversive elements in the Federal and state governments." There was something about this idea that appealed to Simmons very much, but he wanted to see what Bly would do. Not having many enduring, solid convictions of his own, Simmons was ready to adhere to almost any convictions that were good for the magazine. Besides, he had a notion that sometime somehow Bly and Kermit could work together. He checked on Kermit with Bly, and he checked on Bly with Kermit. Both Bly and Kermit suspected that Simmons was doing this, and thus they naturally got to distrust each other, which made for a considerable tension at editorial meetings, and Simmons obviously knew about the tension and its cause and equally obviously he enjoyed what he had done, and his enjoyment, in turn, intensified the tension.

Bly was by nature kindly and inclined to see good in everybody until somebody proved him wrong by some outrageous act of cruelty or dishonesty. His center of interest also was the United States. He admitted the existence of other countries, and he admitted the necessity of America's involvement in world affairs, but emotionally, deep within him, he did not feel at home in this outside world: it was strange and inclined to be inimical to the welfare of this country. Like so many other Americans he was, in his innermost soul, a good deal of an isolationist, which is why his real and abiding hero in national politics was Senator Robert Taft. And he wanted to make of *The American World* a wholly American magazine. This is why, regardless of other considerations, he did not feel too comfortable with Kermit Stern, since Stern stood for "the other world," "the outside world." He was also a little afraid of him, for Kermit plainly knew much more about that outside world than Bly did.

There was something else that Bly felt, namely, that Kermit was a constant reminder to him that isolationist editing, so to speak, was probably at an end for a general magazine, but, at the same time, he wanted to give his kind of magazine another try. He was having difficulties with Simmons, he was especially annoyed with the health series, he was ashamed of the crackpot advertising that had crept into the magazine. Bly was sure that Kermit felt exactly as he did about the health series and about the advertising, and he wondered whether he couldn't enlist his aid in the silent battle with Simmons. Bly sensed that Simmons had much respect for Kermit's judgment, but Bly was afraid: an alliance with Kermit might mean a surrender to his kind of magazine, one devoted almost exclusively to foreign affairs. Bly knew that Kermit was eager to take an active part in the running of the magazine. Bly needed him and he was afraid of him.

216

Nine

Bly was worried by Kermit Stern, but Peter Goldstein
puzzled him completely. He had never met anybody quite
like him. Bly liked him on sight, and he also disliked him on
sight. There was a streak of cynicism in Peter, and that Bly
liked, for he had a streak of cynicism himself. But he acknowl-
edged it, so to speak, only now and then—when he wanted
to be a little wild by himself or in his home or among friends.
These periods seldom lasted very long. Bly knew that the
main business of the world was very serious, and one had
to deal with it in a serious vein. Only the young and the
irresponsible dealt with it in any other way. Peter wasn't
young, and one could not say that he was always irresponsible:
he knew the magazine business, he had sensible ideas about
politics and literature and people. He was well spoken, he
had good manners. And yet Bly had the feeling that under-
neath it all Peter believed in nothing except man's depravity,
his abiding immorality, the complete worthlessness of life
and most of the dominant values in it. Peter was Jewish, but
all that Bly could see in him that was Jewish were his sharp
sense of humor and his uninhibited derision of all things
Christian, especially Catholic. Sometimes Peter would burst
out in an editorial conference, "Well, my friends, it's time
for Holy Mass. I'm hungry and I feel like eating a piece of

the Lord." This offended Bly deeply, though he was not a Catholic. He thought that no one should talk that way about a major tenet of another's religion. He once said so to Peter, in a friendly way.

Peter apologized and said, "From now on I'll talk only about the Virgin Mary and whether she wore girdles or not. Would you be offended by that?"

Bly said he would. Peter said he wouldn't mention the Virgin or the Mass again, but a few days later he brought up the matter of holy relics. He asked Bly, "Do you happen to have a piece of dandruff from the sacred cranium of St. Peter or some other saint, I'm not particular? You see, I have a cold, and I want to get rid of it quickly, and I hear that if I put some holy dandruff on my throat, the cold will vanish."

Bly, of course, objected to this, too. Once Lester Simmons was present when Peter indulged in some of his anti-Catholic humor, and Simmons quietly told him that it might be wise to control one's self in this regard. Peter said he would behave himself for several months, but he wondered whether he couldn't talk a bit about rabbis. Simmons asked him to desist from talking about all religious leaders. Again Peter promised that he would desist for a few months, but he quickly added, "Ah, what a wonderful job it is to be a man of the cloth! You're immune to all criticism, no matter what damn nonsense you preach. Not even the President of the United States has that kind of luck. Lincoln was lambasted all over the lot, so was Washington, so was Jefferson, so was Wilson, but a crummy little ignoramus, holding forth about the hereafter in some flea-bitten town can go on talking his nonsense without fear of anybody saying anything against him. God bless free speech for the few!"

Nobody knew exactly what Peter did. He seemed to have no set occupation, yet he seemed to be involved in many occupations. He lived downtown, in the Village, in a basement apartment. There were two huge rooms. One was the studio of his wife, a painter, and the other was the combination living room, kitchen, bedroom. His wife, Sally, was non-Jewish, and one of the persistent forms of humor between them was his remark that he had married down when he married her: "Such a dumb *shikse* I had to get tied up with, but then all *shikses* are dumb. I did her a favor by marrying her, but I thought I could reform her, get some sense into her, but it's no-go. But she's aggressive, the Christians in New York are getting much too aggressive, and we'll have to put them in their place." Another joke between them was the Christmas "present" that Peter gave to Sally every year. He made a considerable event out of it and told everybody about it: "Well, I've decided what to give Sally for Christmas. I can't give her *Chanukah gelt* (literally, Chanukah money, which parents and relatives give to young children on that festival). It would make her money conscious. So I'll give her the only thing she'll appreciate, and it will be useful. I'll give her a mop. Keep her busy."

Sally wasn't Peter's legal wife. Both were legally married to others, but neither took the trouble to get a divorce (their legal mates were involved in similar attachments to persons of the opposite sex), and yet they referred to each other as husband and wife. Peter was born in St. Louis of Orthodox Jewish parents. He had gone to Hebrew school for two years after his *bar mitzvah,* and for a while seriously thought of becoming an Orthodox rabbi. Suddenly, almost overnight, he became a non-believer. He told David about it shortly after they met at the office of *The American World.*

"I know exactly how it happened, David," he said. "I got up one morning, and I felt differently. I asked how I knew God was listening to my prayers three times a day, I asked how he could possibly listen to every Jew. We were living in the St. Louis slums, and I asked myself why God allowed that. Whom was he trying to punish? And why should God want to punish anybody? If He was that kind, then He was no better than any ordinary human being, who punishes people, who gets angry, shouts, and things of that sort. It all hit me like a thunderbolt. I stood there all alone near my bed, and I didn't know what to do. I sat down on the bed. I must have sat there a long time, because Mother came in and told me it was late, to hurry to synagogue. In those days I was very pious, of course, and I prayed before I ate. I said yes to Mother. I didn't want to go to synagogue, but I didn't want to hurt my mother, so I went, but I was a different man then."

He was fifteen years old at the time, and he began to read

avidly almost everything he could put his hands on. He read only non-Jewish books, books of history and philosophy and science, and he read novels and essays and short stories. He deliberately kept away from Jewish books and newspapers and magazines. He got to dislike them, he got to feel about them as if they had been his prison. In the meantime he got a job in a local department store, as a shipping boy. His parents and brothers and sisters pleaded with him to "make something" of himself. But he didn't listen. He felt he was making something of himself, he was reading and he was going to concerts and lectures. By this time he came out openly against the Jewish religion, and his parents were outraged, for they had hoped that at least one of their sons—they had four—would become a rabbi, and they had been sure that Peter would. He did not argue with his parents, for he had too much respect for them. He merely repeated, "Please, listen to me, I don't want to argue. I know, I may be wrong. I know that. But I just can't believe any of those things anymore, I just can't. If I change my mind, I'll believe again, I will."

His father said, "No, you won't change, that's what hurts so much. When a Jewish boy leaves his religion, he doesn't come back, he stays away. Nobody ever goes away and then comes back, nobody." But his father did get one promise out of Peter, namely, that he would not marry a Gentile girl. Peter had no qualms about making this promise, for at the moment girls were far away from his mind. When he was twenty he decided to go to college, and he enrolled at a local college, in the night division. He wanted to get a bachelor's degree. He was told that by going nights he could get such a degree in about seven years, but only if he also took some summer courses. He said that he would be willing to go that long and to work hard.

His first year at college he enjoyed immensely: he took courses in English composition and American literature and American history and elementary science and something that was called Contemporary Affairs, which was a combination of current events and going to the theatre and to concerts. Peter felt that now he was doing exactly what he wanted. He was happy—in the main. He was still an employee in the shipping department, though now he was in charge of a special section that was concerned with shipping to Canada. But he didn't like the men he had to associate with, they were ignorant and all they thought about were liquor and women. Peter then got a job, more or less by accident, in the circulation department of a local newspaper, and that he liked at once and immensely. At least he was doing something related to literature, and the men he associated with were of somewhat higher calibre than his former associates. It was in this department that he met his first wife, Dora. She was about his age, and was working as a secretary in the editorial department. She already had her college degree, and now, as she said, she was trying to find herself. "I want to write, I think," she said, "not just ordinary things, but things that matter, but I don't know exactly what." He learned that she liked to go to lectures and concerts, and he wanted to take her out. But he was worried that she would refuse him since he was working only in the circulation department, and he was going to night college.

To his great surprise and pleasure she said she would be glad to go out with him, the first time he asked her. "I tell you frankly," she said, "I could go out with Ph.D.'s, but many of them are just stupid and ignorant, and all they know is their specialty, physics or science or political theory, and I like a broad man, one with wide interests." Peter didn't know just how to take this. He didn't like the condescension in her little speech, but he did like what she said about Ph.D.'s who were narrow in their interests. He enjoyed her company. She was pretty and she dressed neatly, he liked her smile and her conversation. She really was well-read, and she did know her way around the various lecture halls and concert halls.

Then she did something that puzzled him. She said to him one afternoon, as they were going to a concert, "Peter, why should you pay for me? I only mean that it's expensive, and I'm not your child, you understand, and it would make me feel so much freer if I paid my way. Do you mind?" He didn't know whether to mind or not. He was afraid that if he agreed she would cease being his girl. She would become little more than a friend, and he was slowly falling in love with her. He began to hem and haw, and she interrupted him, "Oh, you men, you're so silly about such things. Really, please, let's do as I say." He agreed, but he was uncomfortable.

Then he learned that she was somewhat radical in her political ideas, and once she blurted out, "If I had the courage I'd join the Communist Party, it's the only decent thing to do." She went to several Communist or Communist-inspired meetings, and she castigated people who left the Communist Party at the time of the Hitler-Stalin Pact: "They're stupid, they don't understand that Russia had to sign the pact for self-preservation. In politics you have to be tough." Peter said very little, because he knew so little about politics, but the little that he did know made him dubious of much of what Dora said to him. Peter thought that it was disgraceful for Russia to have made any alliance with Nazi Germany for whatever reason. But he did not tell Dora, for fear she would squelch him with facts and figures, and probably leave him, too. He did, however, pray that she would not join the Communist Party officially. He once asked her point blank if she was a party member, and she answered, "To you I will tell the truth. I am not a member, but I'm ashamed of myself. I'm afraid to join because I might lose my job. The paper you and I are working on is death on Communists." Peter was pleased, but he said nothing.

Now and then the Jewish question would arise, and Dora made light of it. "It's only superstition, plain superstition. My people, as I told you, are Orthodox, like yours, and I don't do anything to hurt them, but I'll never run a kosher house, you can be sure of that." Peter was disappointed in what she said. He felt as she did about Orthodoxy, but he hoped that she would mention some other things about Judaism that he still liked, such as the tender songs of Friday evening in synagogue, the lovely melodies of Rosh Hashonoh, and the atmosphere of an Orthodox Jewish home on Passover. Peter merely smiled. By this time he began to resent certain things about her: she seemed to be doing all the talking when they were together, she seemed to be deciding what plays and concerts and lectures they should go to. When they met friends of hers, she did not often introduce him at once, but waited till the friends were about to depart to do so . . . as if he were an afterthought. He wanted to say something about this, diplomatically, of course, but he was afraid, and the more he was afraid the angrier he became with her, and just as he was about to decide to talk to her, he became afraid again, and so it went round and round in circles.

222

Then when they'd meet again, he would be so drawn to her that he forgot his anger, and was content just to be with her. At first, he was also afraid to touch her, but slowly he did embrace her and kiss her, and now and then he played with her breasts. One afternoon they were in a local park. They had a picnic lunch. Dora had prepared the sandwiches and the coffee, and throughout the afternoon she didn't say a word about politics or work. She was quiet and she was very lovely in Peter's eyes. They lay on the ground, in a distant secluded spot, and kept silent. The evening came upon them, it became a little chilly, and slowly Dora moved closer to Peter. "Warm me up, dear," she said to him. He embraced her, and they kissed each other and explored each other's bodies with their hands.

Suddenly Dora said to Peter, "Don't you like me?"

Peter was startled. "Like you? What do you mean?"

"You haven't asked me to sleep with you, that's why."

Peter was even more startled now. He didn't expect this remark. He barely knew what to say.

"Well . . . ," he began.

"Don't you want to?" she asked, as she moved her finger across his lips, and slowly began to move her hand in his shirt, caressing his chest, and moving her hand farther and farther down.

"Well," he began again.

"I like you," she said, and almost before he knew it, he was making love to her.

Peter was disappointed, though he didn't know what he was disappointed about. Strange feelings were going through him. An overwhelming sense of duty was engulfing him, and he suddenly turned to Dora and said, "Let's get married, right away, Dora, right away."

She threw her arms around him, and then kissed him, and then whispered in his ear, "That's what I have wanted to hear from you all these months."

"But I didn't know," said the surprised Peter.

"I know you didn't know," she said.

Two weeks later they were married in an Orthodox synagogue. Peter's parents were delighted that he had married "a nice Jewish girl" and Dora's parents were delighted that she had married "a nice Jewish boy." Peter heard both sets of parents congratulate one another, and he felt strange. He didn't quite know what the parents were happy about. He couldn't get rid of the feeling that had Dora been non-Jewish he would have married her just the same. At the same time, even on his wedding night, as the rabbi was performing the ceremony, he was sorry that Dora wasn't more Jewish-conscious.

At first their marriage was one continuous delight. Dora was all he had imagined she would be as a wife. One thing, however, troubled him, namely, that she clearly was not a virgin when he married her, or when he first slept with her in the park. He tried hard to conquer this feeling, but he couldn't. Even in the midst of his greatest delight in her, he couldn't forget that some other man, or perhaps it was many men, had been with her. He wished he knew what thoughts were going through her mind, as she smiled at him and kissed him and embraced him: he wondered whether she was comparing him with other men, and he wondered how he was measuring up, and he was sick of the thoughts that were running through his mind. But he said nothing. He was glad that she had almost lost her interest in politics and in economics.

Slowly, however, she began to talk again about the Party . . . and then she began to ask him why he didn't join . . . he refused, and she persisted that he join . . . he still refused, then she stopped asking him to join, but now she spent more and more time at meetings of this or that labor organization . . . this annoyed him . . . he asked her to stay home more, but she made light of his request . . . then, with deliberate intent to hurt her, he said to her, "What has become of your desire to write? If you'd stay home more, you'd write more." She figuratively stopped in her tracks and looked at him in a surprised manner. Then she said, "That's rotten of you to say. Here I am active in various public matters, meetings, you're doing nothing, and yet you criticise me. I know I'm not writing. That is the sacrifice I am making for something I consider important, and if you don't think it's important, with your bourgeois mind, then it's too bad."

Dora left the house in a state of anger and he did not see her again till very late that night. He imagined that she had gone to a meeting. He waited up for her. When she came in she merely said hello, undressed and went to bed. Having her near him excited him and he touched her, but she repulsed him. The following morning she was up early, ate her breakfast, said to him, "Your breakfast is ready, you can make your own coffee," and she was off. She did not come home for dinner. Again she came home late at night. So it went on for almost two weeks. Peter was getting lonely. He went to one of the meetings where he knew she was. She was holding forth on some intricate union matter at a meeting of the Office Workers Union. There was a hard determination in her speech, and he didn't like it, and neither did he like the way she clenched her fists when she wanted to emphasize a point. Apparently she did not see him. Dora stepped down from the platform, and sat down on a seat next to a tall man. The tall man took hold of Dora's hand and kissed it. Then the same man kissed her on the cheek, and they held hands while somebody else was talking. Peter was furious. He asked the man near him who the man was who was sitting near Dora. "Oh, he," said the man, "he's Solovey, from Washington, from the national office."

"He's rather romantic with Dora, isn't he?" said Peter.

The man smiled. "Yes, I guess so. They say they're sweet on each other, and things like that. I don't know, but it makes no difference. They're both good union people."

Peter went home. He waited for Dora. She came in at three in the morning. Again she said hello, and started going to bed. Peter stopped her. "I want to talk to you."

"Not now. I'm tired," she said.

"No. I want to talk to you now. What are you tired from?" She stared at him. "What do you mean?"

"Exactly what I said. The meeting couldn't have lasted longer than eleven, twelve at the latest. It's three in the morning now. Where were you?"

"I don't understand," she said slowly.

"I asked you a question, and I expect an answer."

"I was busy."

"Doing what?"

"Listen, Peter, this is not a third-degree, and I won't have you talk this way to me. I was busy at a meeting."

"No you weren't."

"Have it your way. I'm tired."

"Who is Solovey?"

Dora looked at him intently. "Solovey?"

"Yes, Solovey, the man who kissed your hand and then kissed your cheek, and then you two held hands, like adolescent love birds."

"He's from Washington, he . . . "

"Was he sent down here to kiss you?"

"Are you insane?"

"I was once, about you. But no more. Are you and Solovey having an affair?"

She looked straight at Peter, breathed deeply, then said, "Isn't that an insulting question?"

"Answer it. Are you or are you not?"

"You're too ridiculous," Dora said, and started walking off.

"Answer me," insisted Peter.

Dora didn't answer.

"Answer me!"

"I will answer you, if that's what you want, Peter Goldstein. I didn't mean to say this, because it didn't matter to me as much as it seems to matter to you. But you insist, so I'll tell you. I have been to bed with Solovey, because, like all you men, it seemed to mean so much to him. But it wasn't because I love him. It was just, well, he was so insistent, and besides, . . ."

"Besides, what?"

"Besides, I was angry with you."

"Is that a reason for going to bed with a man who's not your husband?"

Dora burst out laughing, but Peter had the feeling that her laughter was forced. "My God, you talk like somebody from the Victorian era."

"And I suppose you went to bed with somebody before you married me."

"Yes," said Dora sharply. "I did. And it's none of your business. I wasn't your slave before I met you. I'm not accountable for my whole life to you before meeting you. I resent the implication."

"That's all I wanted to know," said Peter, and left the house.

He was away for a week, living in a hotel not far away. He didn't tell Dora where he was. Then he returned home. Dora was waiting for him. She said nothing, he said nothing.

She asked him if he wanted something to eat, "No," he said. She didn't answer. Then she said, "Well . . ."

He looked at her. She seemed determined to talk. "What do you want me to say?" he asked.

"Whatever you wish."

"I don't like it," he said.

"What?"

"Everything. I suspected you slept with somebody before you met me, and I didn't like it. Now I know, and it hurts plenty, I don't mind my telling you. And now you tell me you slept with Solovey, and you make light of it."

Dora got up and walked around the room. "You make a mountain out of a molehill," she said. "It didn't mean anything before, it didn't mean anything now."

"It meant something to me, and it means something to me now. I might as well be honest. And there are other things. I don't like your activity in party affairs, all these meetings. I'm liberal, I guess, but I don't like all your Communist connections. All right, I might as well say it, I want a home."

She hesitated a moment, then she said, "I might have known."

He wanted to ask her what she meant by this remark, but he suddenly realized that he really didn't care what she meant. He said, "Well, I'm going to sleep. I'm tired."

She didn't answer.

They came home every day for the next two weeks, and she prepared food. They spoke to each other coldly, between long silences. Then he decided to skip dinner at home. He ate in a restaurant. He didn't tell Dora beforehand, he didn't call her. He came home late that night, and didn't find her home. He didn't care very much. Thus, after a while, their home became a sort of post-office and nothing more. So it went on for almost three months, then, one evening he came home and found a note from Dora, which read: "I'm going away. Good-bye." At first he was surprised, but not bitter. Then he felt relieved. Two weeks later he moved out of the apartment to a small hotel not far away. Dora meant almost nothing to him now.

He took a course in literature at St. Louis University. He became friendly with a girl, Sally Winters, non-Jewish. She appeared wholesome, clean, honest, different, he thought, from

227

what Dora had been. He told her about Dora, and she told him about her own unsuccessful marriage, and they discovered that they were both separated from their spouses but not divorced. They became lovers, and Peter found her enormously comforting. She seemed to know what to say and when to say it, and she seemed to know when and for how long to be silent. There was something utterly good and decent and natural about her love making. He found that it was easy to talk to her about anything that was on his mind, and suddenly he discovered that there was a great deal on his mind. He recalled with a shudder that he barely could talk to Dora. Sally listened to him intently and with love in her eyes. "Oh, darling," she would say, "I love your anarchistic strain, I love your wildness. You say just what I wish I had said or could say. I think I'm more like you than anybody I have ever known. You bring out the best in me, sweetheart. The best which is the wildest. A lot of people, darling, my father and mother, too, they think I'm a dowdy old maid, happy all by myself and with my knitting, home in my little telephone booth room. But I never was, and I'm not, you know that, sweetheart."

He kissed her long and passionately. "Of course, not."

"And you've brought it all out in me. And I just love to hear you talk, all your wildness, I love it."

Again he kissed her, and he said, "Talk is a verbal essence. It is mere words, trailing clouds of loving glory. Talk is song without music. It is what binds and unbinds and winds and unwinds. But, then again, all life is a form of material that clergymen can turn into non-material by merely calling it spiritual. And speaking of spiritual, a Christian is an undeveloped Jew, a half-baked Arab, a half a man."

Sally smiled and kept silent in admiration.

Peter continued, "But if talk is good, kissing is better, and loving is best of all. But loving is also talk. Sally, what would the world be like without talk and its other forms, kissing and loving? Terrible."

"Terrible, darling."

"And the printed word is the holiest kind of talk, because it is silent talk, and what is silent is always better than what is heard, but what is silent must also be talk. Now does that make sense, Sally?"

"It does," she said, and threw her arms around him.

Peter found, much to his surprise and pleasure, that he could talk freely to Sally about Judaism. He told her what he learned at Hebrew school, and about his *bar mitzvah* . . . and he told her about the Talmud, the little that he knew, and he told her about his parents, how pious they were . . . and he said he wondered what they would say if they knew he was living in sin with a non-Jew, and a Methodist, too.

Peter was happy with Sally, and he was happy that Sally was happy with him. He felt himself being himself for the first time in his life. He talked freely and openly and lovingly, and as he talked to Sally the more did he have to say, and the more he said the more he learned about himself, and the more he learned about himself the more he liked himself.

"Darling, what you hear me say is mere words, but they are words tinged with glorious agony, which is another word, or brace of words, for delight . . . John said he wasn't well, but I told him that that was only physical, and that didn't matter. Well, adultery, it all depends: adultery is usually physical, I dare say, but sometimes it is a form of forgetfulness, not a form of completion, and often it is only physical, and yet always we infuse it with spiritual, so much importance do we put upon a man and woman getting as close as nature and physiology will allow them, and that is a sadness, and that is a glory. Well, Jews and Christians, I can never ever be anything but a Jew, it is the only form of decency, Christianity is Judaism plus superstition, Christianity doesn't laugh, Christianity has no jokes, and I think that God is a great humorist, that's what makes him God, and that I love, I mean, God is love, God is humor, God is bewildered, and that is why I am a Jew . . . Christianity is for unimaginative people . . . but, Sally, I love you, you're a lost Jew, you're in the wrong club, you belong in my club, all decent people belong in my club. Hell, do I believe in God? Of course, I do. I have to. Otherwise, if there were no God, this world would have been destroyed long ago. How do I know? That's easy. There is so much malice, so much damn meanness in the human heart that people would have destroyed one another millions of years ago, if God didn't somehow keep people from murdering one another. God dulls the hatred in human beings, so there just must be a God.

"And, I believe in God for another reason. He not only

dulls the hatred in human beings, he occasionally instills divinity in them, especially in women, and that's when I say hallelujah. Oh, there are bitch women, I don't want to get personal in mentioning names, as there are bitch men, God is very impartial that way, he hands out bitchiness rather evenly. But, then, I don't know. Sometimes I get the idea, that he hands out a little less bitchiness among women than among men, anyway, He seems to hand out more of His divinity among women, of that I'm pretty sure, pretty sure, I say, though not altogether sure, I'm still waiting for all the returns to come in. Well, now, where was I, Sally?"

"I love you, Peter, I love you, I love you."

"Oh, yes, divinity. When God kisses a woman and gives her a lot of divinity, then we got something, then we really got something, and that is why I love you, Sally, that is why."

She rushed to him, and whispered to him: "Kiss me, love me, oh, love me darling to your heart's content, love me, love me right now and forever."

After a while Peter did not discuss Jewishness with Sally as much as he used to . . . he didn't feel he had to . . . he felt at home with her as far as Jewishness went . . . he felt at home with her in other ways . . . yet he didn't feel entirely at home with her, and he didn't know why . . . always there was a cool breeze between them . . . perhaps, he thought, it was because he had not yet told his parents about her . . . they asked where he lived, and he told them in a place not far from where he used to live with Dora . . . he said he wanted to be by himself, and he didn't want to tell anybody, he felt cheap for saying this, but he didn't see how he could tell his parents that he was living with a non-Jew . . . at the same time, he felt that he couldn't keep this information from them much longer . . . and he felt it wasn't fair to Sally, either . . . their secrecy made their relationship seem cheap, and it wasn't cheap, and he wanted to keep it not-cheap. . . .

He decided to tell his parents and the rest of his family . . . but there was the matter of the irregularity of his relationship with Sally that had to be considered: he wasn't divorced, and she wasn't divorced. Perhaps there should be divorces, but that would take time, perhaps months, and it would cost money, and neither he nor Sally had any money. He had left the university, and she was a secretary in an office. He was working now on a local magazine that wanted to become the St. Louis version of the *New Yorker*. He liked the work, but he didn't make enough money to support both of them. A vague uneasiness was entering his heart; he tried to hide it, all the more so since he noticed how happy Sally was, how little she cared about the irregularity of their relationship. Yet he wondered whether she really didn't care.

One evening Sally told Peter something that clarified and at the same time complicated their situation. She said that at her office a memorandum had been sent around, asking all the employees to give salient facts about their private lives, including marital status, and "I, dear, put down that I was Mrs. Peter Goldstein, and that I lived here, with you, of course." Peter couldn't help smiling at Sally's innocence, and he couldn't help feeling warm with gladness all over. He wanted her to have said what she said, he was glad she did it instinctively, but he wondered about the complications: now there were two Mrs. Peter Goldsteins, and now there were also two husbands of Sally, as far as the law went, and now, too, he felt he had to tell his parents. He dreaded the prospect. He asked Sally how he should tell them.

"Oh, that's nothing to worry about, dear," she said readily. "I was thinking of telling my own parents. I imagine my folks will be even more outraged. A Methodist living with a Jew! You don't know my parents. They claim they're liberals and almost free-thinkers, but I always did think that they disliked Jews. I'll just tell them that I can't find Malcolm, that's my husband, in case you've forgotten, and you and I love each other, and we want to be happy with each other, and we can't wait for divorces, and we haven't the money, and anyway, we're living together, and we want to be friends with them. That's all, I guess. I won't say it, of course, in just these words, but I'll let them know that if they don't approve of our arrangement, then it's too bad, and we hope in time they will approve. And I guess that that's probably the way you should tell your parents. I'm dying to meet them. I know I'll like them, and I hope they'll like me. I'll try to make them like me."

It all sounded very simple, as Sally said it, and he wondered whether she was as assured as she sounded. He came to the conclusion that she probably was. He was learning several new and wonderful things about her: that she was profoundly loyal, that she was possessed of much common sense, and that she had great courage. As a woman she was in a more embarrassing position than he was, yet she didn't even mention that fact.

"Well, darling," he said, "I don't mind telling you that I'm afraid to face my parents, especially my father. One of his great joys was that I didn't marry a Christian."

"Oh, maybe he won't mind so much, Peter. He may say something, but deep down he may not mind, after a while, anyway. People get a little more tolerant as they get older."

"I wish that were true," said Peter.

Sally smiled, but said nothing.

"Why are you smiling?" asked Peter.

"Oh, I just was thinking, I'm not sure myself about what I said. I guess I was just wishful thinking, or thinking wishfully, or whichever is the way you say it."

"You're wonderful," he said, and threw his arms around her and kissed her.

"I wish the world didn't bother us," she said.

"Yes, but . . . "

"I know."

Sally offered to tell her parents first. She had told them a fantastic story about living with a group of girls in some vague cooperative apartment, and thus managed to keep them from knowing about her and Peter. They had asked her now and then what would be the outcome of her separation from Malcolm, but she had evaded answering them.

To the surprise of both Sally and Peter, all the parents concerned accepted their relationship without too much open objection, though not one of them was happy about it. Sally's father said, "I think you're letting yourself in for a peck of trouble. You're old enough to know what you're doing. Call me narrow-minded, but I think that Peter's being a Jew and you're being a Methodist will cause trouble, and you should see about a divorce, and he should, too. I'll try to help out financially. All I can say is that I hope you really know what you're doing. I wish you had asked me before, but now that it's, in a manner of speaking, done, there isn't much we can do. You really should see about the divorce." Sally's mother only listened to her husband, and kept silent most of the time. About all she said was, "I didn't think a daughter of mine would be in such a situation. I do hope you will get the divorce soon, so that a little decency will remain. I must say Peter is rather a nice man. He should get his divorce, too. And after that, you two should get married. But what will I tell the relatives till then?"

While her parents were talking, Sally, for the first time, wasn't so sure that she should have entered into the relationship with Peter. For the first time, she felt a bit besmirched. Her parents didn't object violently, they seemed to accept, as graciously as was possible for people of their background, the fact of the irregularity of the relationship between herself and Peter. But she couldn't get out of her mind the picture of her mother crying after they left, and she couldn't get out of her mind the picture of her father, all dressed, sitting up alone in the living room, late into the night, and sighing.

When they left her parents' home, Peter said, "Sally, I like your father and mother. I wonder whether we shouldn't have told them before."

"They're wonderful," said Sally, as she pressed Peter's arm to her body. "They're hurt, but they took it beautifully."

"Yes. I wish my folks take it the same way," said Peter.

The faces of Peter's father and mother became pale when he told them he and Sally were living together, and that neither had gotten a divorce, but that they hoped to get them soon.

"So this is what you came to tell me," said his father, after a while.

Peter's mother put her hand to her mouth, and looked at her husband for guidance.

The father got up, walked about the room a minute, then sat down again. He sighed, and said, "I don't know what to say. When a thing happens, it happens. I don't know what else to say. Happy I am not, but you two seem to be happy. I know I speak for your mother, Peter, when I say that you two should get your divorces, and then get married. I know too much money you haven't got, but maybe I can help a little for the divorce. After you are married, then we shall see about other matters."

Peter knew what he meant by the last remark, and he was fairly sure that Sally also knew. He believed that Sally wouldn't object to being converted to Judaism. Peter wished that Sally would become Jewish. But as he looked at his father and mother, in their deep silences, Sally somehow became less important. His parents were far more "reasonable" than he had expected them to be, but he knew that he had hurt them profoundly. He knew that as soon as he and Sally left they would burst into tears, that they would be ashamed, that his brothers and sisters and relatives would know everything before the week was over.

In six months Peter did get a divorce from Dora, and Sally got a divorce from Malcolm. While the divorces were going through the usual steps, Sally and Peter had moved to New York, where Sally got a job as a copywriter in an advertising agency (she had submitted some ideas which the agency liked, much to her surprise, because she had not done advertising copy writing before), and Peter got a job as an assistant circulation manager on a literary weekly. Both liked their jobs, and both were even happier in New York than in St. Louis: being away from their respective families seemed to have intensified their love for each other, and their love-making reached new heights of delight. The parents of both wrote to them in New York, asking when they were getting married, and also suggesting that an event be made of it. The latter suggestion was made only by Sally's parents. Peter's parents were interested only in his getting married. Peter's mother was also interested in having Sally converted. She appeared to be more interested than was her husband. She talked more often about it. At one time she gently chided her husband for not showing as much interest in Sally's possible conversion.

"Ah," he said, "this, I sometimes think, is all *narishkeiten* (foolishness). At first, as you know, I wanted her very much to convert, but now, well, I don't know. A *shikse* is a *shikse,* always remains one, no matter how much converting she does. That kind of Jew we can get along without. I know the rabbis admonish us to treat converts as we do all other Jews, with kindness and consideration, and, so of course, it should be. But I sometimes wonder, I sometimes wonder very much."

"So you want our son to be married to a *shikse?*"

"No, I don't, of course, I don't. What he has done I can't forget. Still, I keep on thinking about Sally. The only time I saw her, you know when that was."

"She was over here another time, just before they went to New York, they had dinner here, don't you remember?"

"Ah, yes, of course, my memory is getting bad. We saw her two times. She helped you wash dishes the last time. I do remember."

"Yes."

"What was I going to say? When my heart is heavy I hardly remember anything. I've eaten my heart out so much about all this, I hardly know where I am. But, we have to admit that Sally is a fine girl, Christian or not. Very fine. I think she is good to Peter, and after Dora he needs someone to look after him. What worries me is Peter himself."

"What do you mean?"

"I mean what has happened to his Jewishness. In his own quiet way he has become an *apikores* (non-believer). I can't understand it. I don't know what to think. When he was young, as you know, I thought he might become interested in Jewish matters, I even thought of him as becoming a rabbi. But out of all this dreaming has come nothing, plain nothing. Only one good thought do I have out of this that has happened to us, one only."

"What is it?" asked his wife.

"That our son is with Sally not because she's a *shikse,* to hurt us, he is with her because he likes her, he wants her. Nu, so it is."

"Yes," whispered his wife. "Even so, I hope that Sally becomes Jewish."

"So she'll become Jewish, will that make her Jewish? Let's not fool ourselves, a convert is a Christian who wants to marry a Jewish girl or a Jewish boy. A big *simche* (festive occasion) it isn't. Would I object if Sally becomes Jewish?

No. I would not. It would please me very much, you know that. But very much happiness from it I wouldn't get. More happiness I would get if our own son would become more Jewish. But that's America." He sighed. "A wonderful country, a *goldene medine*. But it's also full of *tsores* for us of the older generation. We pay the price. We see our children slowly going away from Jewishness, becoming *goyim,* it's really worse than that, they become nothing, plain nothing, believing in nothing, like dogs, like cows. How much longer can this go on?"

"Even so I wish Sally becomes Jewish," said his wife again.

"She probably will," her husband said. "She probably will."

"I hope so."

"She will. To me she looks like a girl who will do what her husband wants her to do. That I must say for her. I'm sure of it. They will get married, and she will become Jewish."

"Don't you think she should become Jewish before they get married?"

"I do," said her husband, "of course I do, but what makes you think it will do any good if we tell them what we want? In America children don't ask their parents for advice, what they should do. First, they do, and then, if the parents are lucky, the children tell them. All parents can do in America is wait for their children to tell them or not to tell them."

"Maybe we ought to write?"

"No. Besides, they probably are already married. What I think, and I have thought about it many times, what I think is that when they write to us they are married, then it will be easier for us to suggest to them that she become Jewish. It's easier to write such things to married young people, when they're married, they listen a little more. I hope they do. So let's wait a day or two, when we hear from them they are married we will write to them, or maybe we can wait till they visit us."

"Maybe you're right, I don't know. It eats me that Sally is not seeing a rabbi and he is preparing her to become Jewish. But you may be right, you may be."

"Let us wait. Something tells me it will all be all right."

But it didn't turn out all right. Peter and Sally, after getting their respective divorces, spoke about marrying only sporadically and without much interest. She called herself Mrs. Goldstein, her stationery said she was Mrs. Peter Goldstein, and Peter introduced her as his wife, and she introduced him as her husband, and without saying so, they saw little sense in going through a marriage ceremony. One evening Sally told Peter, in passing, "I've written my parents that we are married, they've been bothering me so much, as I told you. So this will stop their writing any more about the matter. Maybe you ought to say the same to your parents."

He was a bit startled by her statement and by her suggestion with respect to his parents, though he wasn't sure why he was startled. "I suppose I should," he said. "I suppose it's the thing to do."

He felt vaguely uncomfortable about it all, but not sufficiently unhappy to make an issue of it with Sally. He wondered why Sally wasn't interested in going through a marriage ceremony, even a brief civil one, but just as he would be about to talk to her, he would look at her and his whole being would melt for the want of her, and whatever need he had to talk to her vanished. Soon he began to wonder whether there was any sense in their going through a marriage ceremony. He wrote to his parents that they had been married in city hall, his parents replied they were glad. A month later he got a letter from his mother suggesting that he try to have Sally converted to Judaism. He kept the letter for more than a week before discussing it with Sally. She listened carefully as he read the letter to her, then she said, "You really should have told me about this letter from your parents as soon as you got it."

He was filled with shame and remorse. "I should have," he said, and threw his arms around her. "Forgive me, darling. I don't know why I did it."

She kissed him in return, and with fervor, and said, "I'm not chiding you, darling. I understand."

He wanted to ask what she understood, but he refrained, and this too filled him with shame. He realized that marrying a non-Jewish girl—or rather, living with her—was not a simple matter, especially for one with his wholly Jewish background. He was paying a price: he had to hold back things in his mind, he had to lie, his home was not wholly a home, it was not a place to feel completely easy in, a place

237

to say what was on one's mind and in one's heart. His home with Sally was a place to be cautious in. A sharp pain went through his being as he thought these thoughts. He wondered whether Sally had similar thoughts and a similar pain, but this, too, he did not dare to ask her. He felt himself being ensnared more and more. A despair was creeping over him, a despair mingled with love, yet riddled with remorse and bewilderment. He pressed her close and hard to himself and he kissed her long. "I love you, I love you, Sally."

Suddenly she asked him, "Peter, tell me, honestly now, do you want me to become Jewish?"

Peter wanted to say yes, but something held him back. He felt she was trying to shame him into not saying what he wanted to say. He said, "No, not especially. You do what you want."

Sally looked at him intently, and Peter shuddered inwardly with the suspicion of what was going through her mind.

"Well," she said, "I don't especially want to. I'm not asking you to become Methodist. It really doesn't matter to me, one way or another, any more than it matters to you."

He felt she was unfair, for he sensed that she knew that it did matter to him. Her whole attitude was making him uncomfortable. He wished she had said instantly that she wanted to become Jewish, because she felt that he wanted her to. He wanted her to do this for him out of love for him. This would have welded her to him forever, but she didn't. She was being "reasonable" and "rational," and that, to him, was a form of disloyalty. Of course, he couldn't say this to her. This was another form of lying to her, lying by failing to say what he wanted to say. His heart sank lower and lower. Now he breathed in her sweet and warm and lovely aroma, and he said, "Oh, Sally, forget it. I'll just write my parents that you and I are discussing it, I'll tell them something. The way you put it makes me think, you're not asking me to become Methodist, and your parents aren't asking me, so my parents really shouldn't be asking you to become Jewish."

She kissed him hurriedly, and said, "Let's forget about it. You write your parents whatever you please."

Peter was even more deeply hurt. Now Sally seemed to be treating the letter from his parents as a matter that concerned only him, and he didn't like it. It was another act of disloyalty on her part. Sally, who, he had thought, had such marvelous intuitive powers, was proving herself obtuse in matters that meant much to him.

Peter wrote his parents that Sally wasn't feeling very well ("Some strange infection has set in her stomach, the doctor doesn't know exactly where, and she's running a high fever, she's been in bed for days now. But it's nothing serious, so don't worry, and as soon as she's better, I'll talk to her. I'm sure there will be no difficulty, because she likes Jewish customs, and she's very fond of both of you"). As soon as he mailed the letter he felt ashamed. He was lying again, and, just as bad, he didn't tell Sally about the lie he had told about her. He tried to comfort himself by saying that it was a white lie, but he wasn't at all sure that it was white: it seemed black to him. He was sure that he would tell more lies about this conversion matter, for he knew that his parents, especially his mother, would continue to ask about the conversion.

Slowly he began to wonder, at first in his deep unconscious, whether his love for Sally was worth all this deception. This thought caused him much misery, for he still was deeply in love with Sally, she was even more desirable to him now than before, and living with her was a delight. He liked what she had made out of their home physically and socially. She had made out of it, what one of their new friends in New York, had called "a real music box." The furniture was tasteful, arranged with a fine regard for the requirements of the different rooms—they had only three, but Peter always had the feeling that they really had more—and Sally knew how to make even of the breakfast meal a festive occasion. She seemed to know how to make of almost everything a time of holiday happiness and lovely carefreeness.

And yet Peter never could forget how she had spoken to him about his parents' letter with regard to her conversion, and he was still hurt that she had, in fact, if not in so many words, refused to become Jewish. The whole problem bothered him in other ways. He had long ago given up believing in many of the tenets of Judaism as his father had taught them to him. He didn't think it was necessary to abstain from eat-

239

ing pork and shell fish in order to be a good Jew, he didn't think it was necessary to refrain from mixing dairy and meat products when eating. For a long time he thought these were no longer tenable regulations.

Peter almost never went to synagogue now. He would drop in occasionally into an old little *shul* in the poorer Jewish sections of his home town, just to sit and take in the atmosphere, and also to listen to the praying, but chiefly just to sit. There was something about the atmosphere of a *shul* that gave him comfort. He used to go to *shul* all by himself often in the lonely, miserable days with his first wife, Dora. He did not tell his parents, though he knew that the knowledge would make them happy, it would prove to them that he was still, at heart, a Jew. But he was ashamed to tell them why he went; it was, at the time, chiefly, to find comfortable oblivion. He didn't tell Dora, because he was afraid that she would laugh at his "superstition." Now that he was in New York with Sally, he had not yet gone to a *shul,* though on many occasions he had wanted to. She probably would not have called him superstitious, she was more polite than Dora, but he knew that she would give him one of her significant silent looks, as if she were saying to him, "Now, really, darling, do you really mean it that you went to synagogue? But why? Do you really and truly need it?" He would not answer her, but he was sure what he would say if he did answer her, it would be, "Yes, Sally, I do need to go to synagogue, though I don't exactly know why. And I think I ought to tell you that I am very much Jewish, yes, very much so, even though I am not an observant Jew. It's hard for me to explain. There are thousands and hundreds of thousands of Jews like me, Sally. In the eyes of their parents they are *goyim,* but their parents are wrong. We are very much Jewish, it's in our blood. And what hurts me, darling, is that you, because of your upbringing, it's not your fault, of course, it's nobody's fault, you had no more to do with your Christian upbringing than I had with my Jewish upbringing. Anyway, it's impossible for you to understand what I mean when I say that, even though I am for all intents and purposes married to you, and I do love you dearly, I cannot possibly say to you why I want to go to *shul.* Only a Jew can understand it, only a Jew who does not observe, yet is a Jew. I'm afraid, darling, there will always be this gulf between us, and I say this, even though, as you know, I love you with all my heart."

That he didn't say this to Sally only emphasized again the spiral of lies, both of omission and commission, that he had got himself into as the result of marrying her—by this time he had got to thinking of their relationship almost as she looked upon it, as a marriage in everything but in law. But only almost. He was in a confusion of feeling about his "marriage." It was a marriage, of course, yet it wasn't. And the mere absence of a marriage certificate wasn't quite the only thing that made of their relationship not quite a marriage. Deep within his heart, his marriage to Dora was more of a marriage, even though Dora was not the lovely person and lovely woman that Sally was, even though she was, perhaps, even anti-Jewish, possibly even a member of the Communist Party, which to Peter represented an anti-civilization group. He wasn't at all sure he could put into words what there was about his relationship with Dora that made it a real marriage, for a while at least.

As he looked back upon his brief life with her, he had to admit that he was more relaxed with her; he said, for a while, pretty much what he wanted to say . . . when he felt like talking Yiddish, he talked Yiddish and she answered him in Yiddish, and they both enjoyed talking Yiddish now and then, and they smiled at each other lovingly when they did so, and there was an ease, a warm and comforting and pervading ease, between them. When Dora spoke Yiddish and, on occasion, made him dishes that were common in her mother's house and in his mother's house, he felt that, in a way of speaking, something more than their love for each other was holding them together, it was also their common heritage that went back hundreds and thousands of years . . . unconscious memories that included miseries and joys and lovely aromas from the kitchen and from the *yeshivas* and from the *Talmud Torahs* (Hebrew schools) and the synagogues, not only those that their parents went to, but the synagogues in Russia where their grandparents had gone to, and the synagogues long before in time, even the Temple of Solomon . . . memories that included the sovereign culture that was the glory of Eastern European Jewry at the turn of the century . . . memories of Jewry in the ancient lands, and memories of Jewry in England and France and Spain and Portugal . . . memories of Jewry in Germany and in the rest of Europe during the Hitler era.

What prevailed in their kitchen, those early Sunday mornings, early in their marriage, when he and Dora had breakfast together and were suffused with the loveliness of the night before and sang and hummed snatches of song and religious melodies first heard in their homes and in Jewish centers and in Hebrew school and in synagogue . . . what prevailed was something that was in his blood now and in his heart and in his soul: it was Jewishness, it was what bound all Jews together down the eons of time, Jews of all and of no denominations . . . perhaps this was what makes Judaism Judaism . . . all Jews are really religious whether they observe or not, observance was only a certain degree of Jewishness . . . Jews were all bound together by what Peter felt then, and by what Dora felt then, by what was over and above them, and by what trailed them, in their innermost essences, all their days. One sensed it, one was suffused with it, one knew that it was an integral part of one's being.

Suddenly he became angry that history and traditions were in the way of his happiness with Sally, the mere thought of whom gave him a deep delight. In his anger, he said to himself that there was something barbaric in refusing to marry someone of another faith because of a difference in religious and emotional traditions—it was cowardly to allow traditions to stand in the way of one's happiness . . . he would try hard to make his marriage to Sally endure. But even as he said this to himself the chill of contrary thoughts began to creep through him. He began to see that what had been between him and Dora, on those few, wonderful Sunday mornings would probably never be between Sally and him, that all of Sally's loveliness would have within it an island of strangeness, an island that would separate them rather than emphasize their union: their love could go so far and no farther, beyond that they would be living in different worlds and speaking different languages.

What surprised Peter was that as his doubts were mounting,

his love for Sally was intensifying. She seemed to be flowering in New York—and also changing. He wondered what her parents thought about her not really being married. He wished she had asked him how he was dealing with his parents' desire that she be converted. Now and then she would speak of herself playfully as a *shikse,* and Peter was so taken with her cuteness when she said this that he didn't bother to pursue the subject of conversion with her. There were also times when she would say impulsively, "I wonder what it would be like to be a Jewish girl," but then she would drop the matter, and Peter just didn't have the courage to insist they discuss it. His parents continued to ask him about Sally's conversion, and he continued to evade them. Finally he got a letter from his mother in which she said, "Nu, my son, I won't trouble you any more about your wife's becoming a Jewish girl. You're a grown man now, and you know what you're doing. How I feel and how your father feels you know. Stay healthy."

Peter's heart sank as he read the letter. He read it over and over again. He noticed that Sally's name was not mentioned in it. For this and other reasons he didn't show her the letter. He was ashamed. He was sinking deeper and deeper into a morass of lies. Worse, he didn't tell these lies of his own volition, so to speak; he was being forced into telling them by Sally, whose whole attitude toward him was becoming that of a grand lady of Greenwich Village. She still loved him, he was sure of that, but he was no more sure that her present love was the love he wanted. It seemed so impersonal.

Peter didn't get another letter from his mother or father for weeks, and when he finally did Sally's name wasn't mentioned again. When he didn't get any mail he would call up long distance, and his parents were cordial enough, though on the telephone, too, they didn't ask about Sally. He himself would volunteer the information that she was fine, and they would say, that's good, and that was all about Sally. At first Peter was annoyed by this omission of Sally's name, but then he didn't mind so much. Somehow he felt that Sally had earned this. Now and then she would ask how his "people" were, and he would answer they were all right, and her interest went no further. He had been in the habit of asking about her parents; now, in anger, he stopped asking, hoping that she would take the hint and show some more interest in his parents. But she didn't seem to mind. She volunteered the information that she had heard from her mother or father, had got a card or a letter, and then she would drop the subject. Peter was becoming more and more bewildered. He still did not dare to ask her to sit down with him and discuss the situation with him. But whatever anger he would have would disappear at night when she would snuggle close to him and love him passionately.

They were now in New York for two years. Sally's job was paying her a good salary. Peter had several jobs, with various magazines in the circulation departments, and he also did some selling for the smaller publishing houses, and altogether he made only a fair living. Sally suggested that he get himself a steady, full-time job with some magazine or book publisher, but he always said that he liked what he was doing, he didn't want to get tied down to any one employer, besides, he had dreams of becoming his own publisher. Sally said nothing more. For this silence he was grateful to her. A good deal of his eagerness about things in general had left him. A good deal of his day-time eagerness with respect to Sally had also left him. Her attraction to him was now almost wholly of the night.

Then, on their third Christmas Eve together in New York, Peter came home rather late and in a somewhat intoxicated condition. He had been going through the day from publisher to publisher and taking drinks at the various Christmas parties. He had been drinking more and more lately, but he had not been drunk before. Now, he had apparently drunk more than he could easily tolerate, and he lost his sense of time—and he came home when it was almost eleven o'clock. What he saw when he entered his apartment shocked him: he saw wreaths and holly and Christmas candles and in the middle of the kitchen-living-room table was a small Christmas tree all lit up. Sally was dressed up, sitting in a chair by the table. She had not gotten up to greet him.

"Well," he said, "this certainly is a surprise. What in hell is all this?" The boldness of his question startled him, even in his drunken state.

244

"I thought I'd surprise you," Sally said softly. "Don't you like the house in a holiday mood?"

"No, I don't. Christmas is no holiday by me."

"Oh."

"Yes, and you know it. I thought you were all over such things. Are you a Christian or are you a woman?" he asked, and suddenly he pushed the tree off the table, and then he kicked it on the floor. He walked about the room and tore down the wreaths. "I thought you were all through with such things. What made you do all this? Tell me. I've had some drinks, I have, but I'm cold sober, sober enough to talk to you and to want you to talk to me. But before you talk to me, you take off your holiday fineries. This is no holiday for me."

She looked at him, saying nothing. Then she got up slowly, walked into the bedroom, quickly changed her dress to an everyday one, and returned, and sat down where she had sat before. Peter pulled a chair over near her, and sat down. "Now tell me," he demanded.

"Tell you what?"

"Why you did all this. Are you so dumb that you don't know I don't like it, I don't want it, this Christmas and everything that goes with it?" He felt good he was now talking the way he had wanted to talk to her for almost three years. At the same time he was deeply attracted by the helplessness all over her face. He knew she was holding back tears, and this made her seem all the lovelier, but even as these thoughts and emotions were going through him, he sensed that something had ended between them, and he was glad and he was sorry . . . and he also learned that Sally was not the free-thinker or non-religious person that she had boasted to him she was, but, then, he thought, neither was he.

"Tell me why you did all this?" he asked again.

"I just thought it would be nice, Peter," she said softly, almost in a whisper. "It's not the religious angle, honest." Tears were beginning to come down her cheeks. "It isn't."

"But you knew I don't like it, didn't you?"

"Yes, but I didn't think you'd mind, Peter. I only thought we'd make it a sort of holiday evening, for the first time. It happened to be Christmas, everything is holidayish, and I

245

only wanted to give you a surprise. I even baked some things myself. I got the recipe for *strudel,* with raisins and apple slices, and I was worried where you were, so late, and not calling, I was frightened, and . . . " She hid her face in her hands. Then she said, her face still in her hands, "I thought we were going to have such a good time tonight, a sort of holiday supper . . . I even got some of that Passover wine you said you liked."

He couldn't help smiling to himself—Christmas and wreaths and Passover wine . . . and suddenly a wave of pity for her and regret for the manner he talked to her came over him, and he went over to her and embraced her and kissed her. They had the holiday supper she had prepared, and Peter said that he was sorry . . . and they both had Passover wine, with seltzer (she had also got seltzer) . . . and that night they loved each other with special delight. The incident seemed to have drawn them together closer for a while, but Peter continued to feel that a cool wind had come between them. What had happened, he felt, was more than a passing quarrel.

Then Sally began to ail. She had many colds, she had trouble with her menstruation, then she began to bleed. She went from doctor to doctor, one gave her pills, one suggested cauterization, another suggested she take injections of Vitamin K. She went for a thorough check-up at a hospital, and the doctors there suggested immediate cauterization: "If this doesn't work, and we hope it does, then we'll have to try something else." Sally became frightened. "Do you think I'll have to have a hysterectomy?" The doctors assured her that this was far from their minds at the moment: "A hysterectomy is only a last resort, there are some other things we can try. We hope and believe cauterization will do the trick. Such fibroids, fibroid tumors as you have are quite common, generally respond to cauterization."

Unfortunately, Sally's condition did not respond to cauterization, and both she and the doctors became despondent. The doctors tried several kinds of medications that were in the experimental stages—compounds of sulphur, heavy doses of Vitamins A and D in various combinations (some local doctors had achieved at least temporary success with one or another of these combinations), and ray treatments: X-ray and infra-red, especially. For a period of time every one of these attempts at a cure would relieve Sally, and she would be happy, but then her old difficulties would return. Then, one night, she suffered a severe hemorrhage in her female organs, and the following morning the doctors decided to perform a hysterectomy.

For a time she seemed to be her old self again. Her doctor told her that her sex life need not suffer, and for the first few weeks she and Peter were very happy—or so it seemed to Sally. He went through all the motions of eager love-making, feigning all the old excitements, but inwardly he had many hesitations. Sally's extended difficulties with her female organs had somehow infused him with a distaste for her. At first, the distaste was vague in his mind, but then it came more and more to the fore. He was astonished, he was frightened. It seemed to reveal something inhuman and cruel in him. Married or not, converted or not, Sally was still his wife in every important respect, she had comforted him throughout the years of their association, she had given herself to him joyously. He began to think of excuses for going to bed late, so as not to have to submit to her embraces. At first, she pleaded with him to "come to sleep, you're tired," then she merely went to bed by herself. His conscience bothered him and now and then he would follow her to bed, and she would express her gratitude to him by kissing him passionately, and she would cry on his breast, and she would hold on to him desperately. Then came a night, when she burst into tears, while they were in bed, and she said, through her sobs, "Don't ever leave me, darling, I couldn't stand it, I don't know what I'd do." Then on a Sunday afternoon, just after dinner, she again burst into tears and said, "I have to talk to you, I have to talk to somebody. I'm afraid to hold it to myself any longer. I'm not a woman anymore, I'm nothing, just nothing, ever since that operation."

"That's silly. It's an operation that many women have."

"I know. But it's terrible just the same. And I can't have any children. I was hoping maybe we could have a child, a little girl, but now . . . "

"Oh, well, such things happen. I mean I haven't thought

247

about it myself. I suppose women think about these things more, but that's no serious trouble. I thought you had some terrible thing to tell me."

"You're very understanding," Sally said, wiping her eyes.

Peter felt that Sally knew he was lying at least a little bit, and he was sure that Sally would be troubled about her sterility for a long time, but he didn't care very much, and as time went on he cared less. He went to bed with girls and middle-aged women who appeared to be rather free in their sex lives, some he liked more than others, with some he had an affair that lasted days or weeks, and then he would break away . . . some he would have liked to have had a permanent relation with . . . legally he was free to leave Sally whenever he wished . . . now he was glad that they had not married legally . . . but he was sure that he never would leave Sally, solely out of pity for her. She was now getting rather cranky, her face was getting lined, there were long hairs on it here and there, which offended him, she was becoming stout and careless about her dress. Coming home was no longer the joy it used to be to Peter. He drank more. Sally objected for a while, then she saw her objecting wasn't doing any good. Both knew what was happening to their love: it was seeping out of their lives, and now their home was no more a place of joy but a place of convenience: it was an address, they knew each other's tastes in food, they knew each other's habits, they knew when to talk and when to keep silent, one had to have a home, and they were used to this one . . . they made love once a month, sometimes only once every two months, and then it was only out of a strange sense of moral obligation to each other, some justification for sleeping in the same bed together, otherwise living together would make no sense at all.

Life to him became a matter of unpleasant routine. It was her person that offended him most. In the past the mere sight of her, the mere aroma of her would excite him, and he could hardly wait to embrace her and kiss her and pinch her and caress her and run his fingers through her hair and kiss her neck and her fingers. Now she was only an object of spreading offense. Years before when she would bend down to pick up something, her hips would appear so tantalizing that he had to control himself from rushing over and hugging them. Now seeing her bend down to pick up something filled him with revulsion.

He wondered what he should do. He couldn't leave her and at the same time have any respect for himself. He couldn't get rid of the feeling that somehow he was to blame for her hysterectomy. He had to be with her for the rest of her life. He slept more and more with other women, but there was only temporary pleasure in that, and, as he reviewed the women he had slept with, he was sure that if he had entered into any permanent or semi-permanent relationship with them they would probably end up as Sally had.

As time went on he developed a technique of making love to Sally once a month. A short while before the date he had set for making love to Sally he would drink consistently throughout the day, and as he drank on and on he would try to think of Sally as she had been years before. Sometimes it was difficult, and then he discovered that if he called her endearing names and if he talked about the wonderful times they had had together years before in St. Louis, she would begin to appear less and less unappetising, and then he would make a heroic effort to keep the image of her years before firmly in his mind. This would help his love-making. Otherwise he would be virtually impotent.

He did become impotent, or very much so, in other ways. He became more interested in ideas and in knowledge, and for the first time he realized what the philosophers meant when they spoke of the great joy in intellectual exercise, but he didn't have the patience to read for more than a half hour at one stretch: his mind would wander off, and he would sink into a morass of pessimism. He began to find more and more pleasure in classical music, but he couldn't listen to it for very long either. Then he began to wonder whether there was something psychologically wrong with him, whether he was abnormal. He really didn't care whether he was abnormal or not. As he now often said to himself, life was one huge cruel joke, and about all one could do with it is make one's passage through life as tolerable as possible, and the more oases of oblivion one managed to create for one's self throughout one's life the more fortunate was one. Then he learned that many, possibly most, people were in his predicament, and they were not all relative wastrels and time-servers, as he pictured himself to be: some were as he was, unhappy wanderers who just manage to stay alive and away from the wolf of hunger and the octopus of despair, many were professional men, doctors and lawyers and professors, who had established positions in life and had achieved some social dignity. He met many of them in saloons and at literary parties . . . the men were virtually all unhappily married or unhappily involved with some woman . . . apparently there were no happy marriages, at least Peter had not encountered any so far, and he was becoming more and more convinced that monogamy was a silly and impossible institution, not just for men but also for women, for he learned that women were often as unhappy as men were in the married state.

He learned that in very many human relationships little tyrannies and little cruelties creep in, and that marriage is distinguished by the fact that it somehow engenders more such tyrannies and cruelties than do other human relationships . . . marriage often seems to be an area where each partner seems to feel legally and morally free to hurt and insult the other partner . . . but Peter learned that there was a deeper unhappiness in people: they seemed to be dissatisfied with the whole scheme of things.

He got new jobs. He was an assistant circulation manager on a liberal weekly, and raised the Manhattan circulation considerably, but he gave up the job, because, he told Sally, he didn't like the circulation manager, but the real reason probably was that he was afraid he would be too successful at the job and would eventually supplant the circulation manager, and Peter didn't want the responsibility that went with it: he wanted to be completely free. He met a celebrated popular novelist, who liked him on sight, and made a confidant out of him. Peter learned that the novelist despised his wife ("She's the damndest snob and social climber in creation, and how in hell I missed seeing it when I pined to sleep with her is beyond me. But I guess a man in heat is not a perceptive animal"), that he was heartbroken because one of his sons was studying for the Protestant ministry

("That really hurts, I never knew I would sire a son idiotic enough to believe in all that hogwash"), and that he was depressed that his last novel was not only poorly received by the critics but also did poorly in the bookstores. Peter at once offered to try to sell some copies in and around New York—and he did sell almost 10,000. The publisher was astonished and wanted to make him sales manager for the New York area, but Peter refused the job: "I don't want to be tied down," he told the novelist, "and please don't tell Sally, she won't understand." The novelist smiled and said, "You're crazy, but I'm glad you are, and don't worry about my telling Sally. I never discuss anything important or unimportant with any woman. If you're not married to the woman, she keeps silent because she has nothing to say; if you're married she talks and says things so silly and vulgar that you feel like killing her. So the best policy is not to talk when a woman is in the room."

Peter also became associated with a new book club that specialized in scientific books, he offered to sell subscriptions on a commission basis, and in six months he had earned such large commissions that the director of the club offered him a position as subscription manager, but Peter refused it: "No, thanks, I'll keep on selling some subscriptions now and then, if I'm broke. Don't worry, I won't sell too many to break you, but I don't want a steady job. That's for other people." Then Peter became associated with a new liberal monthly that lasted only nine months. The magazine had no policy of any wide appeal, it was poorly edited, and there were few advertisements, but it had a fantastic circulation for so feeble a job: 25,000, most of them full-time. And Peter did it all, only on a part-time basis; here, too, he refused a full-time job, though he actually put in full-time. He worked strictly on a commission basis, and in about six months he earned $5,000, which was more than anybody else on the magazine made.

It was on this liberal monthly that he came in contact with Lester Simmons. Lester was having worries about the *American World,* circulation was going down, advertising was going down, the magazine didn't seem to make much sense editorially . . . he had faith in his new editor, Thomas

Bly, but he also had doubts . . . and in his usual fashion he tried to surround himself with protections against his doubts: He got Kermit Stern and he got James Dawson. The first was for general ideas, and the second for general business, chiefly advertising and circulation . . . Lester hired Dawson before he met Goldstein . . . if he hadn't he probably would have offered the job to Peter Goldstein, though at the time he had no idea what sort of person Peter was. Lester was offended by his streak of cynicism and carefreeness, but he was also impressed by his abilities as a builder of circulation. Peter had contempt for Lester on sight. He knew that the *World* was in difficulties, and deep down he was glad. He had liked Brandt's *World* in the early days, but he despised it in Brandt's later days. As he told his friends, "No man has a right to be that stupid. That bastard says there's no depression, and he's for the Nazis, well, not in those words, but there's very little in what he says that Hitler could take objections to." Peter also didn't like what Brandt said about President Roosevelt: "All right, FDR is a politician, as Brandt says, but so was Lincoln. The big point about FDR is that, as a politician, he has his ears to the ground, and he may turn out to be the greatest President we've had since Lincoln, even greater than Wilson. There's something uncanny, almost mystical about FDR. Anybody who doesn't see that is a plain dope."

Peter didn't like the *American World* under Morton Jackson: "He's just a dumb *goy,*" he said. "He doesn't know the difference between steak and cherries, I mean he's just a dumb *goy*. Even my *goy* wife Sally knows more than he did." He also had no respect for the old publisher Slack: "He's just lucky, he has no brains, but he knows enough to keep quiet when in the presence of brains. And he knows enough to do what they tell him to do." Peter didn't like Lester even before he saw him: "A publisher who signs his name to that kind of magazine [Peter had seen two copies before he met Lester] is just out for pennies and nickels, and the *American World* needs an idealist. Only an idealist publisher can make a go of it." Yet, when Lester asked him to come on in an advisory capacity, Peter agreed, but only after he got Lester to agree to give him a "retainer's fee" of $50 a week—and Peter insisted that this agreement hold only for a year, "and you have the right to break it any time you want to, and I have no such right." Lester was surprised by such conditions, but he accepted.

For a long time Peter merely listened and roamed about the office, examining reports, asking questions, reading letters from readers, looking at manuscripts as they came in, looking over Bly's letters when Bly was out of the office. (Peter had asked Lester if he could do this, and Lester said, "Sure. It's office business." Peter knew he would agree to this suggestion, for he believed that Lester was highly "realistic." Peter despised him for this, but he was glad that Lester agreed). Peter knew that Bly had no ideas big enough for a magazine like the *American World*. Peter was pleased that Bly objected to the healing series that Lester had suggested, but he was deeply disappointed that Bly did not object vigorously enough. Bly, in Peter's opinion, should have threatened to resign. Peter was sure that if Bly had made that threat, Lester would have backed down. Peter also had almost no respect for James Dawson, who impressed him as a humdrum, unimaginative circulation man. And yet there was something appealing about being on such a magazine as the *American World,* run by people who seemed to Peter to be little better than shysters. He decided to use them for his own ends. He would build up the circulation of the magazine by means of combination offers with the *Atlantic,* the *American Legion Monthly,* and two or three mass women's magazines. The income to the *World* would be little, and Peter was sure that this circulation wouldn't stick, but the figures would be accepted, in part, by the Audit Bureau of Circulation, and Lester would be pleased—and then Peter would leave, his $2,600 well and honestly earned, as such things go.

The *American World* was just another pointless experience to Peter, to be relished and discarded. And since this experience was so fraught with deceit and incompetence and immorality Peter was all the more attracted by it. He had hoped that Bly conceivably might turn the magazine into something worthwhile, but as soon as he spent five minutes with him he knew that Bly was, for all his relative honesty, only a good-natured, stupid man, without principles but filled with the clichés of life and of journalism—a dull, harmless, worthless man, fit to be the husband of a dull, harmless, worthless woman and the father of humdrum children. He thought of him as *a goyishe kopf* (literally, a Christian head), and it would have pleased him to use the expression to his wife, but she was a *goyishe kopf,* too, and a female mess besides.

He was a homeless man, without roots, without attachments, with little faith in principles. The world made little sense to him, he looked with contempt upon people high in the professions, for he had seen and talked to too many of them to have much respect for them. The heads of medical foundations knew little medicine and lorded it over men who were their superiors in knowledge and morals. The big-name preachers were little better than floor-walkers. Peter met two bishops at a literary tea and he was appalled by their smugness and ignorance—and even more so by their unctuous manners, probably the very same manners that got them their high posts.

Peter's attachment to Judaism continued. He would go downtown to the East Side—which was slowly becoming more and more Americanized, so that one now saw more Buicks and Cadillacs and Pontiacs than beards and *sheitels* (wigs worn by pious Jewish women over their cropped own hair). Still there were restaurants where one could sit down for a meal and for leisurely talk. He would go to these places alone. He had hardly any friends, his wife was not even a friend any more, she was barely an acquaintance. At these Jewish restaurants he would talk to the waiters and he would talk to people at neighboring tables, and at times he would join other tables. He liked what he heard: a certain glorious resigned acceptance of whatever life offered, together with a cynicism about nearly everything and everybody, mixed with an occasional recognition of true goodness and beauty and courage and loveliness. There was also mixed with this cynicism a combined appreciation and contempt for the people as a whole . . . *der aileom iz a golem* (the public is a lummox) and *der ailom iz klug* (the public is wise) . . . the same people who saw the greatness of Moses also worshipped the golden calf . . . the same people who saw the greatness of Maimonides also sat by in silence as certain elements of the rabbinate in his day burned his books.

And Peter also heard true and sharp things said about women and about men and about Russia and about America and about Franklin Delano Roosevelt and about Truman and about Churchill . . . he heard one Jew say. "About England

and Churchill, all I can say is that we must always watch them, when it comes to Jewish matters or other matters, but I also think that there is no country in the world that one has to watch less. A crazy country, and a wonderful one, very tricky and full of principles." . . . and Peter heard another Jew say about Truman. "Listen, men, I loved Roosevelt, that you know, but listen to me, this Mister Truman, he is a bigger man. He has dealt with Jews on the grocery store level, so he can be trusted about Jews. If, God willing, we should get some foothold in Palestine this time, Truman will be there to help us to the limit, of that I am sure. If Roosevelt were alive, well, I don't know. He would first think if it's politically smart to do it, not for his party or for himself, I mean politically for the United States in the world. Truman wouldn't think that way. He would and he will do the good and the right thing for the Jews just because it is the good thing and the right thing. So wait and see." . . . And Peter heard a third man say. "About Russia I know what will be. It will die of being choked with too much success won by swindling, and I prophecy that we will get more anti-Semitism from Russia than before, as much, maybe, as under Hitler. Germans and Russians are alike. They're afraid of Jews, and the only way they know to deal with them is to kill them."

Peter liked this sort of talk . . . it brought him back to his mother's kitchen and his father's synagogue, it brought him back to Moses and to Maimonides, and he knew that he would always be Jewish. He was not wholly at home in the world outside his Jewish background, though he didn't know precisely why. He looked upon himself as a failure as a human being, a failure as a Jew, a failure as an American, a failure as a man —and Sally represented to him the sum and substance of all his failures, and she also represented his entrapment by his failures . . . he could do nothing about himself, as he could do nothing about Sally—he had to live with them, as he had to live with Sally . . . he was a cauldron of failure and confusion and misery and a vague yearning for some way out of his misery. He knew he would find no way out, except temporarily in liquor and in bed with women who were overly willing . . . he was astonished whenever people looked upon him as a carefree, happy, optimistic man, but he did not take the trouble to disillusion them.

255

Ten

Peter Goldstein offered no opinions about the health series that was proving to be a total dud, neither did he offer any opinions about Kermit Stern's notion that there should be more articles about Russia, "showing up its slavery," and also articles about the supremacy of air in the coming war—Kermit had become greatly interested in air power through ghosting several articles for an Italian airman who insisted that the Navy and the Army, as major combat forces, were finished, and that henceforth they would be auxiliary to the Air Force. This notion shocked both the United States Army and Navy officials, but former Army and Navy officers secretly were inclined to agree with the Italian airman. Kermit was also of the opinion that a Third World War was inevitable, on the theory that no dictatorship in history could possibly exist without a war: a dictatorship, by its very nature, was bound to run down a nation's economy and then was faced with dissatisfaction at home, which it could deal with only by raising up the spectre of an outside enemy and then plunging the nation into a war, which kept the country quiet for a while.

Lester Simmons, the publisher, was becoming more and more depressed about the *American World*. Circulation was declining, the health series brought in virtually no new readers, some osteopathic and chiropractic zealots sent in enthusiastic letters

("You are to be congratulated for daring to fight the Medical Trust that is ruining the health of the country"), and they subscribed for six months, if they subscribed at all, then they disappeared . . . the advertisements by chiropractors and osteopaths and other irregular healers did look rather shabby in the pages of the *American World,* and the advertisements by astrologers and handwriting experts and spiritualists, for all the editing that Lester and Bly did on them, also looked very much out of place. Lester discouraged new advertisements.

Lester felt he could discuss his problems only with Peter, who was increasing the subscription list phenomenally, even while the newsstand sales were declining. The new subscriptions were parts of combination subscriptions, with the *American World* being only one of four or five of a package subscription deal, and the income to the *World* was about one-third or even one-fourth of the usual three-dollar annual subscription. This was little enough income, but the Audit Bureau of Circulation did give credit for such subscriptions. Besides, one always had the hope that a certain percentage of such subscribers would end by subscribing for a whole year at the regular rate. Peter doubted that many of them would subscribe, but he said nothing. He had little respect for Lester or for his magazine or for any of the people on it. He was out to make some money in a relatively honorable manner, and that's all. He disliked Lester, but Lester respected him. One day Lester suggested to Peter that he worm his way into James Dawson's job, which was chiefly advertising: "You look around and sort of take over, without telling him that you're doing it. He's not much anyway." Peter was outraged by this treachery. He didn't want the job anyway: "No, Lester, I have my hands full with circulation."

"Well, what can we do, Peter? Things aren't getting better? Should we go in for airplanes and Russia?"

"I don't know Lester, I don't know. Let's see what Bly has in mind. Give him a chance. I'm having no trouble in getting subscriptions. Of course, we ought to increase our newsstand sales, but maybe Jim Dawson will do something about that. Give him a chance." Peter knew that Jim Dawson would not be able to increase the circulation of the *World;* the magazine was going in all directions, it was a raffle-barrel.

257

Lester asked Peter if he knew anybody who could save the *World,* "somebody with ideas, real, live ideas."

"I still think you should give Bly a chance. Building up a magazine that has virtually died, is no easy job."

"He should have shown some results by now," said Lester.

"I still think you haven't given him a real chance. You made him go through with one of your ideas, the health series, and I din't think he was hot for it, and the idea didn't succeed, nobody's fault, some ideas work out, some don't, it was an idea, but it wasn't his idea, so you have to give him a chance. An editor needs time." Peter didn't know why he went to such lengths to defend Bly, for whom he had little respect. Was it because he wanted to hurt Lester by showing up his idea for the failure it was?

"Well, I still think Bly should have done more than he has," said Lester.

At once he began looking around for another man to give him advice. "He's looking for another Jesus," said Peter to himself. "That kind of manipulator is never happy unless he has a stableful of Jesuses, and he makes them show what they can do. He creates enmities among them, he tears down one in front of another, delicately, or indelicately, all in the name of honesty."

At a party that a publisher gave, Lester met a man, Bernard Erickson, obviously Jewish of face and from the type of humor and satire he was expressing. He seemed to hold everybody's attention with his witticisms: "Emma Goldman? She's a spiritual hemophiliac. . . . American democracy was stillborn with Washington. It was born with Jackson . . . Philosophy is a form of day-dreaming that only philosophers take seriously. Women look upon it as a form of the male menopause. . . . Women, who know themselves, naturally assume that all women are frauds. . . . The only women who are honest are those who are still in the foetus stage or those who are over eighty-five, and I'm not sure about the latter or about the former . . . A Jew naturally looks upon a bright Christian as an exception, and a Christian can never really be truly tolerant to a Jew, because he, the Christian, knows that all of Christianity is hoked-up Judaism, and it took a Jew, St. Paul, to do the hoking. Jesus himself was not a Christian. Everybody knows that . . . Rabbis nowadays are not rabbis at all, they're program directors. I know very few of them I can take seriously, they look like polite football players, most of those I have met, yet I have very great respect for the rabbinate as a class. I feel that if it weren't for rabbis many American Jews would be even more vulgar than they are. Imagine an American Jewry with a half million Jesse Strauses of Macy's or Arthur Hays Sulzbergers of *The New York Times!* It would be horrible, all decent Jews would have to move into the little Orthodox *shulen* down the East Side."

Lester wasn't sure he liked these remarks. They were "extreme and unreasonable," and he didn't see any point in making fun of Jesse Straus and Arthur Hays Sulzberger, for both of whom he had much respect. He wished he were in either man's shoes, preferably Mr. Sulzberger's, for Lester still liked to be known as a respectable publisher, but he would certainly not turn down an offer to be the president of Macy's. There was something else about Bernard Erickson that Lester didn't like: his smirky attitude toward many of the values that Lester held dear. He had heard him sneer at Babbitts and "publishers who are really paper merchants, with no more interest in ideas than cats have," and at "short people who don't have to bend to reach the ground"—Lester himself was short. Still, Lester was impressed by what he heard about Bernard Erickson: "Brilliant . . . enormously well informed . . . nobody knows more about the labor movement than he does . . . I hear he's consulted by the Truman administration, as he was by the Roosevelt administration . . . did you know Erickson wrote the NRA regulations? . . . What he wrote about the New Deal and the Fair Deal is the best anybody has written. Did you know that the Communists are more afraid of his pen and his tongue than of anybody else? . . . Too bad he's lazy, he writes like a house on fire, and he has more ideas per minute than all the editors in America. What an editor he would make, if he liked to work!"

Lester was impressed by the last comment far more than he was by Bernard Erickson's own remarks. Ordinarily he would not have talked to him at any length or invited him to his house, but business is business, and he was willing to swallow his pride and try to make use of him. Who knows, perhaps he could save the *American World*. Lester would appoint him as consultant, pay him, say, fifty dollars a week, for a period of a few months, pay him extra for his articles, and all the time pump him for ideas. Besides, he probably knew a great many people of importance in the labor and political worlds, and they might write for the *American World* if Bernard Erickson asked them, whereas they might not do so if Bly or Lester himself asked them.

Lester asked him to lunch, and found Erickson to be pretty much as he had found him at the party. Before the lunch he had inquired about him around town and learned many things that disturbed him. Erickson had a reputation of signing contracts with book publishers, taking advances, and not delivering the manuscripts he had contracted for. One publisher's editor said that Erickson was "in hock to almost ten publishers for about $6,000 altogether. Some say that's how he lives, for he doesn't seem to have any regular job." Another publisher's editor said that people thought that Erickson was "being kept by various women. He's almost fifty, some say fifty-three, but the women love him." Lester learned that Erickson lived in a spacious apartment in mid-Manhattan, the hotel where he had his apartment was old and modestly priced, still, his apartment must have cost him about $150 a month, and it was a mystery how Bernard Erickson could possibly pay for it from his meagre earnings. The only source of income he had, it seemed, was from occasional articles and reviews that he did for newspapers and magazines. But these contributions were very occasional, indeed, since Erickson was a slow worker. He did not write more than about two articles and perhaps five reviews a year, and his income from these writings was limited.

Few people knew very much about him, and apparently he told different stories about his origins and doings to various people. He told some that he was born in Poland, others he told that he was born in Germany, and still others he told that he was born in "Southern Denmark, just where the two countries meet, the town was so small it appeared on no maps that I can recall. I barely remember its name. Lilje I think it was called, or maybe it was Kildam, it was the latter more likely, I'm pretty sure it ended in *dam*." His year of birth was also mysterious: he gave it as 1890, 1897, and 1899. He was equally vague about the month and the date. It was April 25, May 7, August 19, and sometimes he would say it was December 24. "I missed out by one day from giving Jesus competition." He spoke fine Yiddish, and he obviously knew about Jewish customs and holidays and foods, but he hinted that he was "not wholly Jewish, just how much I don't know. You see, my parents died when I was very young, maybe five, and I was pushed around from relative to relative. Some told me that my father was part Jewish and my mother was Lutheran, others told me it was the other way around. Then some told me that both parents were Gentiles, but that I was adopted by a Jewish couple who had no children of their own, and brought me up as a Jew, they had me circumcised, thank God for that, so I really can't say."

Erickson's marital status was also problematical. He claimed to be legally married to a non-Jewish woman, by whom he had a son, who according to him, was seventeen (or eighteen or nineteen) and who lived in Minneapolis (or St. Louis or Cleveland) and who was going to college, but nobody ever saw the son, and nobody knew who his mother was. Several women of the radical-political and labor worlds would share his apartment from time to time, more or less openly, but not one of them made any pretense of being his wife. He was often invited out to lunch, by publishers and editors and journalists, but nobody recalled when Erickson invited anybody to lunch. Nobody recalled when he picked up the check at a restaurant.

He claimed that he had studied at Harvard and at Columbia and he spoke about John Dewey and Charles A. Beard and Thorstein Veblen and Harry Thurston Peck as if he knew them well, and he hinted that every one of them had consulted him about this or that book, yet people who were on intimate terms with these men did not recall the name of Bernard Erickson ever being mentioned by them.

He traveled about a good deal. He went to Washington often, and had no trouble getting free accommodations. He also seemed to have little difficulty in getting into Presidential press conferences or press conferences of Cabinet members. He also knew Washington correspondents of several leading national dailies and magazines, and he was seen in various bars and restaurants with them, and some even quoted him, occasionally,

261

in their columns. What he was quoted as saying was epigrammatic, but it didn't stay long in the mind. He said of President Truman that he was "Everyman on a binge," but nobody quite knew what that meant, though it did look profound on first sight. He said that Jesse Jones, head of the Reconstruction Finance Corporation, "had the big heart of a Texan and the little soul of a Tennessean," and that seemed very smart, too, but when one began to think the phrase through, one realized how untrue it was. Jesse Jones was an able man, who had a good head and a kindly heart, he was cultured, well mannered, and at home in several of the arts.

Erickson was friendly with various Negro leaders, and he posed as something of an authority on the Negro question. He was a guest in the homes of distinguished Negroes in New York and Washington and Baltimore and Philadelphia, and he argued with them on a basis of equality of information and insight, but these same Negroes, behind his back, spoke slightingly of his knowledge and his ideas. Why, then, did they see him at all? Skeptics said that it was merely to raise their social standing by having a white man of Erickson's reputation in their homes. Erickson was especially violent about Booker T. Washington and William E. DuBois. He claimed that both were "really white Negroes. I mean, they aped the ways of the whites, and were ignorant of the Negroes' genuine problems. Booker T. Washington had the soul of a Pullman porter and DuBois has the soul of a Baptist preacher, who would like to be an Episcopalian." Some of the Negroes who heard Erickson say this were outraged. One said to him, "You just don't understand us. You just don't understand Booker T. or DuBois. Booker T. was no St. Paul to the Negroes, but he came at the right time for them. He was history's true child. DuBois is no St. Paul either, but he reflects the impatience of a large element of the Negro population of America with the rate of progress of social welfare for them. They are very important, and they will hold high rank in the history of the American Negro."

Erickson dismissed this talk with the phrase "racial chauvinism." He continued. "The Negro is the American's consciousness of guilt. The Negro is the reflex of his enduring frustration of spirit and sex. The whole problem of segregation is basically a desire on the part of the white man to steer clear of that which he wants most. The Negro is the mystery of the white man become visible."

"But what does all this mean?" asked one Negro, who was a professor of economics at Howard University in Washington.

Erickson replied, "It's clear enough. The white American is grateful to the Negro for being what he, the Negro, is. Without the Negro to relieve him of his guilts and self-deprecation, he would find his trauma unbearable."

"Again I ask what does all this mean? The Negro wants the right to vote, the right to send his children to good schools, the right to travel wherever he pleases, like every other citizen. Guilt and deprecations and the rest of it have no meaning to him."

This happened often in Negro homes that Erickson visited, yet he continued to be invited to these same homes.

It was in the realm of labor relations that he boasted he knew more than anybody else. There seemed to be some foundation to this claim. The evidence seemed to be good that he had been a student of Professor John R. Commons, of the University of Wisconsin, one of the country's leading economists. Erickson also had studied with Professor Thomas Nixon Carver of Harvard, whose economic ideas were on the opposite side of Professor Commons's. Thus Erickson had reason to say that he knew both the liberal and the conservative attitudes toward labor, and that he also had heard the major aruguments in support of both points of view. Then, it was true that, at various times, Erickson had written for several labor papers, that he had attended many labor conventions, both international and craft. Erickson also said that he had interviewed Samuel Gompers once, and he even quoted several remarks that Gompers had made to him. Erickson couldn't prove that he had interviewed Gompers, but nobody could disprove it. It was strange, however, that Erickson did not publish his interview with Gompers, especially since at the time, according to his own accounts, he was an important editor of or contributor to important union and general labor periodicals. Erickson wasn't embarrassed. He said, "It just didn't occur to me. It is true that not too many people interviewed Gompers, he was along in years, but he was already a figurehead rather than a leader, so it just didn't occur to me."

Erickson spoke familiarly of William Green, successor to Gompers as head of the American Federation of Labor, and of John L. Lewis, head of the United Mine Workers of America and the founder of the Congress of Industrial Organizations (CIO). He didn't dare to say that he was on intimate terms with either, apparently because there were too many people among his friends and acquaintances who really were, but he often spoke of them as if he had been present at their press conferences. He undoubtedly was at several such conferences; almost anybody at all involved in labor matters could go to them.

Apparently Erickson did do some reading in labor union literature, but not as much as he tried to impress people he did. He got much of his information by careful listening to well-informed labor reporters on newspapers, and he got himself invited to social affairs where labor and union leaders were also invited, and to these people he also listened carefully. He would, so to speak, wherever possible and without too much work on his part, spot check what these people said by consulting some labor reports and running through books and articles in general and specialized magazines. His ideas were the result of the workings of his sharp, intuitive mind upon the information that he thus got. In short, he was a gifted dilettante in the realm of labor philosophy—but so gifted that he deceived many into thinking that he was a man of profound and original ideas. He also had an uncanny gift of knowing which way the trend of the "best thinking was going, and how to be both with the trend yet critical enough of it to appear superior to it in a manner that reflected credit upon his independence and intellectual integrity and sheer knowledge. He was, therefore, always "in the swing" and also always "above the battle." He never was sharply in opposition to any line of thinking that was popular among the "elite."

His gifts led him into strange places, and made his record rather spotty. Fortunately for him, not too many people knew his record, and the few who did were men and women who had already achieved reputations of being "trouble-makers." Years before he had been a sharp critic of Samuel Gompers, calling him "an antediluvian, simple-minded, ignorant of the American scene, really one of the worst enemies of American labor." He especially derided Gompers's insistence that American labor remain independent politically, that it choose from among the candidates of both major parties, depending entirely upon their labor records and ideas. Erickson especially sneered at Gompers's unfavorable views of the British Labor Party. "Gompers doesn't think too highly of the British Labor Party," said Erickson. "I trust the British Labor Party will not be too offended. But I wonder how the American workers feel about Gompers's attitude. They read that the British Labor Party has obtained for the British workers social legislation far in advance of that which obtains here. The British Labor Party got a labor man into the Prime Minister's residence, and British history has not been the same since. There will be other labor prime ministers. Ramsay MacDonald did not reach his high post by a miracle. He got it through the aid of the Labor Party, which has been an active part of British political life for a half century. Pure and simple trade unionism such as is advocated by Mr. Gompers will never get the American workers a labor man in the White House. So long as the philosophy of Gompers prevails so long will American labor go after and get the crumbs from the table of American industry, so long will American labor be a beggar."

Erickson thought little better of William Green at the beginning: "In Gompers we had a poor cigar maker. In Green we have a retired Baptist preacher. And between them we have American labor flat on its back." Erickson at first, gingerly, and then quite openly, espoused the Communist attitude toward the two chief labor unions: the AFL and the CIO. The Communists called for Unity, and Erickson called for Unity. John L. Lewis appeared to be in favor of Unity, but on his terms, which is to say he was for a unified labor movement organized not on a craft basis, as was the AFL, but on an industrial basis, as was the CIO. The Communists were for labor organization on an industrial basis, so they supported John L. Lewis, and it seemed that he welcomed their support. Erickson was for John L. Lewis, hailing him as "a labor statesman of world stature, the first such statesman that American labor has produced. He is the very personification of realism in labor-capital relations. He knows what Gompers never knew and couldn't possibly know, and he knows what William Green will never learn, for a Baptist preacher's entire mentality is impervious to teaching, that labor cannot be divorced from politics, and that the life of politics is labor. The majority of voters are workers, therefore what workers want can be made felt in the halls of Congress. For labor to be politically non-committal in a democracy is a form of treachery to the workers themselves and to their wives and children."

At the time Erickson was also sharply critical of Norman Thomas, leader of the American Socialist Party. Erickson disliked Thomas's "gradualism," calling upon him to reveal more "dynamism." Some thought that he meant that Thomas should get closer to the Communist position, which called for a banding of all workers to "gain control" of American society. Thomas was for greater participation by labor and other people in the running of the government, but he was opposed to the use of force of any kind: he was entirely for the use of the ballot. Erickson also criticised Thomas for his "unrealistic world view, especially his attitude toward Russia." Thomas was against the Communist government because it was undemocratic, autocratic, and oblivious to the welfare of the people. He was for helping the Russian people in their attempt to free themselves from their centuries' old yoke, but he thought that part of that yoke was Communism. Erickson therefore was, in effect, for the present-day Russia, otherwise his charge of lack of realism on the part of Thomas made no sense. When somebody would ask him if that wasn't his view, he would say that, while he had much to question in the Communist position, he could see "much sense in their present realistic conduct of affairs. After all, international life is not run on the same principles as a sewing circle."

Erickson's closeness to the Communist point of view was even more clearly revealed in what he said about President Franklin D. Roosevelt. While the Hitler-Stalin alliance was in force he looked upon Roosevelt as but a tool in the hands of the "English-French-Polish bunglers, whose hands are as dirty as Hitler's, and Stalin's, if you please, but who are unctuous about it. Hitler is no angel, but he only did what the great democratic leaders of England and France and Poland tried to do, but couldn't, namely, make a deal with Stalin. And who in his right senses can call the Poles democrats? The piety which is issuing from London and Paris and the Polish Government in Exile is nauseating."

But right after Hitler invaded Russia, Erickson changed his views. When people questioned him about his about-face, he said, "New conditions call for new philosophies. Only dreamers stick to their theories without regard to the realities." And Erickson was very much taken with Wendell Willkie's concept of "One World," which fitted in nicely with the Communist line. Many intellectuals, especially among writers and editors, during the war were, at least, sympathetic to what was going on in Russia, but then the trend began to change . . . Stalin violated his word about the self-determination of the liberated peoples . . . he gobbled up Poland and Czechoslovakia and Bulgaria and Rumania and Hungary . . . he made vassal states out of Esthonia and Latvia and Lithuania . . . people in America began to question his integrity as a leader, and they began to wonder whether the "reactionaries," after all, had not been right about him, namely, that Stalin was a gangster, whose word was worthless, whose sole aim was to rule with an iron hand, who had no conception of the meaning of civil liberties, who answered critics with the firing squad, who was, in short, a tyrant, perhaps even more so than were the Czars. Intellectuals who had "cooperated" with Communists left the various "front" organizations, and began to talk against the Stalin regime and against Communism as a whole.

Erickson sensed all this, and began to change his ideas gradually. He began on a high philosophical level, by reminding people what Lord Acton had said, "Power corrupts, absolute power corrupts absolutely." Some of Erickson's listeners pointed out that power had corrupted Stalin and his fellow Communist leaders long before 1941–1945. To which he answered, "But that corruption was in reply to the Cordon Sanitaire that prevailed till the day Hitler invaded Russia." Erickson referred to the days right after World War One, when many of Russia's former allies were dubious of the Lenin-Trotsky regime and were hesitant in helping it. What relationship that Cordon Sanitaire had with the corruption of the Stalinist regime was hard to see.

Then Erickson announced—that was the way he was now talking—that "the logic of history is on the side of the Western Powers. The center of civilization is now clearly in America, with England and France serving as handmaidens." He immediately began to denounce Russia in every area of life. He also denounced every individual who had been sympathetic to Russia and whom he had defended, and he also began to praise the very same persons whom he had hitherto criticised because of their lack of "dynamism" or "realism." But first of all he "reappraised" Wendell Willkie's concept of One World. "One World," he now said, "is a naïve concept. It is a laudable dream, but for the time millennia away. As a description of real life it is an untruth. As a policy it is a vapid sigh, unfit for diplomats who have to deal with realities."

He then found many things to praise in Norman Thomas. "Thomas's gradualism may well be the gradualism of nature itself," he said. "And he may well be right in his devotion to civil liberties at all costs. There is no time in history, no time whatsoever, when it is safe to abrogate civil liberties. They are the very life blood of the body politic."

Perhaps most surprising of all, Erickson began to see many virtues in Samuel Gompers, in the American Federation of Labor, in the whole American union movement. He discovered —what American labor historians had known for decades— that the American labor movement was far in advance of the European labor movement: that it was the American labor movement that was the first to agitate for the eight-hour day and for special legislation in favor of women workers, and that was opposed to child labor. It was the American labor movement that had made of Labor Day a national holiday, something that no other nation had.

Erickson also discovered how great a man Samuel Gompers was, how honest, how dedicated, how well he understood the American worker, how well he understood the American worker's dedication to free speech. Erickson also saw for the first time how well Gompers understood the peculiar nature of American capitalism, that it was like no other capitalism on earth, certainly not like the capitalism that Karl Marx described in *Das Kapital.*

"American capitalism," said Erickson, "is not a capitalist's capitalism. It is a people's capitalism, the offspring of industrialism and democracy, the first such offspring in all history. It is a capitalism that has its door always open to the worker, and hence the labor movement in the United States can never be like the labor movement in any other country."

This led Erickson to praise Gompers's concept of "pure and simple unionism" unaffiliated with any party and in no way involved in politics, except to support friends of labor and to combat enemies. Said Erickson, "This revealed a great shrewdness on the part of Mr. Gompers. He realized that the American worker was an American first and a worker second, that he was a Republican or a Democrat, before he was a miner or a teamster or a textile worker. Gompers also realized the tremendous part played by geography in American labor. In the South, American labor is narrow-minded, segregationist, racist, easily corrupted, while in the North and in the West it is more progressive. Gompers could have cracked down on Southern labor, insisted on the abolition of segregation in the unions, to which, of course, he was opposed. He had to make a choice: to abandon Southern labor to the exploiters there, and thus turn the unions down there into company-unions, which are slave unions, or try to keep the Southern unions in the American Federation of Labor and try to educate them. Gompers picked the second road, and he was, of course, right, eternally right."

Erickson now saw little to praise in John L. Lewis. He was shocked by Lewis's long-time devotion to the Republican Party. Everybody had known about this devotion and wondered about it, but Erickson had somehow forgotten it, or it didn't mean too much to him. Now he saw an enemy of the people in Lewis, and he denounced him further for having "revealed a strange affinity for the methods of the Communists in the days when it was fashionable to follow the party line and appear patriotic at the same time." Of course, Erickson now saw great virtues in Franklin D. Roosevelt and Harry Truman.

Toward the end of Truman's first administration some of the intellectuals began to wonder whether Truman wasn't only "a common man," who had been catapulted into office by fate, and they began to talk about the need "for more vigor in the central government, more leadership, more intellectuality." The candidate of the Republican Party, Thomas E. Dewey, didn't seem to be the man to them, so they were in a quandary. They were for Truman but without too much enthusiasm—and yet they saw some virtues in Dewey because he appeared to be more forthright in his attacks on the Soviets. Which is about the way Erickson spoke and wrote. He was for Truman but he wasn't too opposed to Dewey. This position he liked, for it gave him the opportunity to be epigrammatic and profound about both without losing caste among the people he visited. He called Truman "a *shnook* of the Baptist variety, who has had his wits sharpened somewhat by his Jewish business partner," a reference to Eddie Jacobson, Truman's partner in the haberdashery business in Kansas City. And Erickson called Dewey "an undersized Machiavelli, who would be still shorter without his mustache. He will finally die from auto-conflagration, so much venom is there in his system."

David had met Erickson several times at the home of Mary Tobias, and had looked upon him as an intellectual vaudevillian, without much principle and something of a high-grade scavenger intellectually and socially. Mary Tobias didn't like him very much, her husband didn't like him, yet he kept on visiting them, and they didn't quite know how to stop him. Many years before, a college classmate of Mary's had brought Erickson to the house. The classmate had ceased seeing him long before, but Erickson apparently liked the food and the drinks at the Tobias home and he would invite himself. Some people thought that occasionally he also "borrowed" money from them, money which he and they knew he would never return. Erickson mystified the Tobiases as much as he mystified nearly everybody else. They didn't know how he lived, how he paid his bills, what he did with his time. They were puzzled by his attitude toward Judaism. When he was first at their home he was something of an assimilationist, and Jews to him were "just people, like you and me, only they cook better food and tell better stories." He was anti-Zionist when pushed to the wall to give his views about Zionism. Actually, the whole Jewish problem didn't interest him. The Tobiases were sure that he was completely Jewish, that he had gone to *cheder* (Hebrew school), that at one time, surely, he could speak Yiddish, but in his adult years he had moved away from Judaism to "humanity."

When Erickson saw that the Tobiases were ardent Zionists and were interested in Judaism in other ways, he began to soft-peddle his anti- or non-Zionism, and after a while, especially when some of the Tobias's Zionist and rabbinical friends were at the Tobias home, he began to reveal a new sympathy for the Zionist idea. At first, this pleased the Tobiases: they were making a convert, but then they, especially Mr. Tobias, began to wonder whether Erickson was being converted or was merely being diplomatic.

Sometimes Erickson and David walked for a while after they left the Tobias home. On a few occasions they stopped off at cafeteria for a coffee and pastry, and after a while David noticed that not once did Erickson pick up the check. At the very beginning Erickson spoke slightingly about the Tobiases. It was the period when Erickson was not enthusiastic about Zionism, and in general gave the impression that Judaism was an archeological subject to him. He would then say about the Tobiases, "Narrow-minded Babbitts, Jewish Babbitts, too. Still interested in all that ancient stuff—Palestine, this and that Jewish Fund. Times have changed."

David said that he was also interested in Zionism, "not to the extent that the Tobiases are, or, rather, I should say, I'm as much interested, though I can't do as much financially and in other ways. If I could, I think I would."

"Well," smiled Erickson, "it's your emotional attachment, your parents were Zionists. It makes no sense in this day and age. Another nation only means more nationalism in the world."

But when Erickson began to feel more at home with the Tobiases, he began to talk differently, not only in front of the Tobiases but also before other people, including David.

"It could be," said Erickson, "that Dr. Weizmann is one of the really great figures of our time. Nationalism is not the end-all of social living, but the world being what it is, it is necessary, especially for the Jews. Palestine is needed not only as a haven or refuge for the remaining Jews in Europe but as a sort of symbol for the Jews the world over. A psychological necessity."

"That's what many Jews have felt for more than fifty years," said David, who had an impulse to expose Erickson for the ignoramus he was with respect to Jewish matters. "Dr. Herzl was not the first Zionist, though he did a great deal to spread it among the Jewish people. Did you ever hear of a man called Moses Hess?"

"No, I don't believe I have."

"Well, he was a Zionist about fifty years before Dr. Herzl was. I think he died in 1875 or thereabout. He was one of the teachers of Karl Marx. Some people think he was a bigger man than Marx, he knew more, he was less flamboyant, and stuck closer to the facts, and he was against class warfare. Personally he was a great deal finer and kindlier."

"Moses Hess, I better look into him. Was he the founder of Zionism?"

"No," said David. "At least I don't think he was the first man to come up with the idea of Palestine as a Jewish homeland. But he was one of the very first German assimilationist Jews to see how wrong he was."

"I'll read him," said Erickson.

"Read his *Rome and Jerusalem*," said David. "It is a bit crude in its writing, somewhat rhetorical here and there, but it shines with honesty and dedication. The man was not only a great Jew, he was a great human being, with plenty of faults, but his virtues were greater, far greater."

"I'll read him," repeated Erickson.

Erickson was naturally delighted when Lester Simmons asked him to lunch. His instinct told him that he had made an impression on Simmons. He knew that Simmons was in difficulties with his *American World,* and he smelled money around the man. He wasn't at all sure that he could fool Simmons long, for Simmons was a practical man, and such men want results in terms of "returns": more readers, more advertising, and the only "returns" that Erickson could promise were vague ones. Still, Simmons was in a position to pay

Erickson with money for some reason or other, and Erickson was sure that he, Erickson, could think of some plausible reason.

Erickson saw at once what Simmons wanted. He wanted nothing less than salvation for his magazine, and Erickson knew, as Peter Goldstein knew, that so long as Simmons was publisher the magazine couldn't possibly be a success, for he was cheap and too eager for quick money, he had virtually no philosophy, he had poor taste, he only wanted to be known as a friend of culture, but on condition that such friendship "paid off." Simmons told his problems openly to Erickson, and he humbly asked him, "Can you do something?"

"Well, I'm not an editor, Mr. Simmons," Erickson said, in a sombre voice, "but the magazine still has a good reputation or tradition, or whatever you wish to call it, and the people you have are able, I know them all, but it could be, in the labor and related fields, and these are important, and politics, too. . . . "

"They are very important," said Simmons. "We are living in a political age."

Erickson caught his breath at this Elk-like remark, but he could still smell money in the man facing him, so he said, "Yes, of course. I might be able to advise, attend editorial meetings, but, of course, this would take time, and . . . "

"That's all I wanted to hear," said Simmons quickly. He offered him $50 a week. "Let's see how it works out."

Erickson attended the editorial meetings regularly at first. He kept quiet, and he felt that his silence was making a good impression on Simmons, but he also knew that soon he would have to make some concrete suggestions. His instinct told him that he better make the suggestions broad, so that he would later, if necessary, be able to defend himself by pointing out that no attempt had been made fully to realize his suggestions, and, of course, he would say this without actually criticising Bly or anybody else. His first suggestion was for "a realistic, critical, and objective re-appraisal of the philosophy of current dynamic labor leadership." When Simmons asked him (with a puzzled look on his face, that troubled Erickson) what this meant, Erickson said, "Well, perhaps

273

I can best explain this by suggesting that one real dynamic leader of labor is David Dubinsky of the International Ladies' Garment Workers' Union."

Betty Garde, who didn't like Erickson for a reason that wasn't entirely clear to her, said, "That's strange. I thought you once said that Dubinsky was a leader of the blind leading the blind, or something like that. When did he become dynamic?"

Erickson was stunned. It was true that he had criticised Dubinsky severely, but lately he had met him and he rather liked him personally. Erickson had a sudden inspiration. He said, "Yes, I did criticise him when he did things that, in my opinion, merited criticism. Since then he has changed, and now he is, again in my opinion, worth commendation."

"I don't see how he has changed," said Betty Garde, who relished watching Erickson's discomfort. "He was against the Communists then, and he's against them now. As far as I can make out, he has no new ideas about his union and things of that sort. Maybe it's you who have changed."

"Oh, come on," interrupted Simmons who was annoyed with Betty Garde for her "obstructionism"—she had vigorously objected to Simmons's series on health, and while the series was a failure (it wasn't even completed), he did not like remembering that she had predicted it would be a failure. "What's all this got to do with what Bernard is suggesting? I think it's a very good idea. Let's discuss his idea. I'm all for an article on Dubinsky, on Hillman, on Lewis, on all of them. Maybe that would give us a shot in the arm. God, we need something! Why don't you start off with an article on Dubinsky, Bernard?"

Erickson was startled. That was more than he had bargained for. Actually he knew very little about Dubinsky. To do an article on him he would have to do research, have a personal interview (or rather, a series of interviews) with him, and then he would have to write the article—and there was also the question of whether Simmons would pay him extra for the article. Apparently Simmons knew what was going through his mind, and said, "Of course, there will be special remuneration for the article."

Erickson was trapped. "Well," he said, "I'll see what I

can do. It will take some time, and I'm a little tied up right now, but I'll see."

Erickson did nothing on the article for the next three weeks, though he told Simmons, Bly and the others that he was "digging into it." When Simmons asked him if he had already arranged an interview with Dubinsky, Erickson said that Dubinsky's secretary was hard at work on it: "Dubinsky is a busy man, and he's always traveling." Then, by sheer luck, Erickson was at a press conference that Dubinsky gave just before leaving for a labor conference in Europe, and Erickson told Dubinsky that he was doing an article on him and would like some information. Dubinsky told him to ask the public relations director for material, and he expressed his regret that he couldn't give him any time personally. This was an ideal out for Erickson, he could now tell Simmons and the others that he saw Dubinsky, and soon would have the article finished. Already he had "worked" on the article for almost four months, and Simmons and Bly were getting impatient.

Actually Erickson did not have a single page of manuscript ready. He had to do something, he had to say something. He told Bly and Simmons that he had changed his mind completely about the nature of the article. He saw no point in doing an "orthodox" article. "Anybody can do that. What I wish to do is a psychograph."

"What's that?" asked Simmons.

"That's a portrait of a man's soul. It bears the same relation to an orthodox article that a painting bears to a photograph. You wait till you read the piece. It won't be long, but it will be worth a hundred ordinary articles, if I say so myself."

Simmons was disturbed. He had already paid out to Erickson about a thousand dollars for "advice," and all he got out of him was promises—Erickson now seldom came to editorial meetings, his excuse being that he had to work on his Dubinsky article. At long last, the Dubinsky psychograph arrived, and Simmons read it before Bly, then Betty Garde read it, then David, then Clarice, Simmons's wife. The only one who offered an opinion immediately after reading it was Betty Garde: "I think this stinks. It's all wisecracks. And gags. Erickson says that Dubinsky is, listen to this, 'the obverse of the legend of Americanism. He's a go-getter tinged with altruism conditioned by the Higher Selfishness.' I don't think this means a thing. And listen to this, 'American labor embodies the perpendicular dream of the Founding Fathers. And yet, on the other hand, Dubinsky might be called the supreme *kibitzer* of the democratic process.' What does this mean?" She turned to Simmons and said, "And this will cost you plenty of money, in addition to what you're paying him for advice, of which I've seen very little that's worth much. You wait, he'll ask for at least $750 for this, think of it, $750 for a piece that's less than 3,000 words long. You wait."

Betty was right. Erickson asked for $750 shortly after he had submitted his article. By that time Simmons and Bly and the others agreed with Betty. Nobody liked the article. All were convinced that it was what they called a "quickie," something that Erickson had written in a hurry from the top of his head. Bly was so incensed with what Erickson had tried to put over that he told Simmons that he couldn't print it. Simmons saw he was wrong about Erickson. At the same time he wasn't sure that firing him would be quite right, for he was still under the impression that Erickson had strange powers in the New York literary world. Simmons therefore thought he would merely tell Erickson that the article wasn't just right, that it needed more work, that Bly felt this way, that everybody felt this way, that he, Erickson should spend more time on it.

But when Erickson heard this from Simmons he was outraged for many reasons, first, that Bly, the editor, hadn't talked to him about it, second, that all his scheming had got him nowhere, and third, that Simmons didn't say anything about payment.

"But I'm going to be paid?" said Erickson.

"Why?" asked Simmons as coolly as he could.

"I put all this work on the piece."

"But it isn't right. Listen, Bernard," said Simmons, who was embarrassed to be talking this way to a man who spouted epigrams, many of which he didn't understand. "It sounds strange for me to say this, and I'm probably not saying it right. But it really will not do you good for us to print this as it is. Bly thinks so, and the others think so. I think so myself, in all honesty. I really do. It's for your own good."

"Who the hell are you to tell me what you think about my articles?" blurted out Erickson.

"Now that's no way to talk," said Simmons.

"But it is. I resent what you are saying. That's one of the best pieces I have ever done, and $750 is cheap for it, and you will pay it to me."

"I won't."

"You will. I will take you to court."

"Now, Bernard . . . "

"Don't Bernard me," said Erickson.

Simmons was astonished by the childishness of the man before him, a man for whom he had had some respect until now. "Now, listen, act mature. You don't want to take this to court. It will make you look foolish, really, think about it."

"But I want my money."

"If you write an article that we like, we will pay you. Otherwise we will not pay. It's as simple as that."

"You will pay," said Erickson, as he walked out.

Bly assured Simmons that Erickson will do nothing "drastic," and he was right. Erickson never again showed up at an editorial meeting. Simmons sent him a check for two additional weeks of "advice," and expressed his regrets at "the severance of our relationship."

This trying experience made Simmons only more conscious of the plight of the *American World,* for by this time he realized the relative valuelessness of the subscriptions that Goldstein was getting, and he also realized what more and more were telling him, that the magazine had no purpose, that there was little in it worth reading, and yet all seemed to think that the *American World* was still "an important property." Simmons didn't know what that meant, though he also thought it was "an important property."

Eleven

David was not much disturbed by what was happening at the *American World*. The magazine had ceased meaning anything to him, save as a job. There was a danger that it would die and David would have to get another job, which would be a nuisance, but David was sure he could get another job, and quickly, too. To his surprise the editor of a mass circulation magazine had sent him a note that Brandt had sent to him, in which he had said: "David Polonsky is, next to me, the best editor now practicing his foul profession in America. If he'd learn to drink straight whiskey, instead of that horrible concoction, Passover wine and seltzer, he would be even better as an editor that I am." The mass circulation magazine editor enclosed a personal to David: "You can have a job with me any time you want one, but I imagine you don't want to work for the likes of me. But I can always find something for you here, that will earn you three times what you're getting on the *American World,* or what I imagine you're getting on the *World.*"

Yet David was annoyed by all the commotion on the magazine. It interfered with his work on his stories and poems, and especially on his novel. He said the diplomatic things at editorial conferences, now and then he suggested an article idea (for example, he suggested a series of articles on the dormant Nazi parties in America, that even the defeat of Hitler did not kill entirely . . . they were hardly parties but associations of mentally disturbed men and women who were guided by the editor of one magazine, *The Horrible Truth,* openly published in New Jersey, a magazine that preached anti Semitism, anti-Catholicism and anti-Negroism, but which specialized in disseminating anti-Semitism). The article was finally done and was the subject of editorials in many parts of the country. David was delighted that his idea proved so fruitful, but he was even more delighted that now he could coast for a while and devote his energies to his "real" work.

Still, being in the office was uncomfortable. Besides, he was lonely. He was barely seeing anyone. He had not gone out with any girl since the death of Sylvia. Then there was the really disturbing news from his father's home in Boston. Father was having troubles with his digestion, and David at once began to wonder whether there wasn't some cancerous condition. His father had long complained about constipation and vague pains. Naturally, the fact that these complaints had been of long duration was fair evidence that the condition was probably benign, still, there was always the other possibility. But even more worrisome was the news that his older sister had been sending him about mother: there was a recurrence of her dizziness and of shooting pains on the left side of her chest and in the left arm: was this sheer nervousness, or was it a symptom of a serious and persistent heart condition? Adele wrote to David that the family doctor had made light of mother's complaints, but David was still worried.

The only place David had to go to for sociability and for forgetfulness was the Tobias home, and now he went there even more often than hitherto. Mary Tobias made him entirely comfortable, and so did Raphael Tobias. Both, especially Mary, sensed that he was troubled, and Mary offered to give him a key to the house, and she even told him that he could sleep there whenever he wished, (they had a guest room). He refused with thanks, but he did go there often, sometimes as often as three times a week. Generally he would sit all night and say very little. He liked to hear what the others were saying, and nearly always there was somebody who had something interesting to talk about. If only the Tobiases were home, they would talk a bit, and then spend the rest of the evening chiefly listening to classical records.

One evening David walked in and found one other person there. She seemed to be in her middle or late thirties, with strangely piercing eyes, a bit full of bosom, and she was dressed entirely in black, but he had the feeling that she was not in mourning, she apparently liked the color black. As the evening wore on he was sure that that was the reason for her completely black outfit. The same evening he also learned that she was formerly attached to the Baruch Haba Theatre, a celebrated troupe of Jewish actors, dedicated to the dissemination of Hebrew drama. Her husband was one of the founders, and he was also a director and a choreographer. She had been introduced as Mrs. Helen Davidson, but David found himself calling her Helen less than fifteen minutes later, and he wondered why, for ordinarily he was shy about calling people by their first names even weeks after meeting them. Helen called him David in return. Towards the middle of the evening Helen seemed to become a new woman, her eyes shone, she became talkative, she walked about the room, and once delivered a longish speech in Hebrew from a Hebrew play whose title and author had no meaning to David.

As she delivered the speech David was impressed by her warm and full womanhood. She seemed to be possessed of so many of the things that come to mind when one thinks of motherhood, and yet there was also something girlish about her, the way she walked, the way she turned her head, the way she smiled. There was something lovingly beckoning, even coquettish in her manner, and yet there was an innocence in this coquetry. David noticed that she was looking and smiling at him much of the time, and he began to wonder whether this was in response to this absorption in her, and he felt embarrassed. Then something was served by Mrs. Tobias, and David liked the way Helen went at her food, with eagerness, yet also with gentility. To her, apparently, eating was more than just eating, it was a delightful pastime, almost a form of love, for as she ate, her eyes seemed to dance with a pleasure that was more than merely physical. Suddenly she stopped eating, and said excitedly, "Ah, Mary, when will you do what I tell you! When, when! Coffee is the best when you make it in all-milk. Put the milk in a pot, let the milk boil, then put a lot of coffee in the pot, and let it boil some more, and stir, and then you will have coffee like you never had before in all your life. Didn't you like the coffee I made when you were in my house a week ago?"

"Yes," said Mrs. Tobias. "But it was so rich."

"And so good, too," added Helen.

"And fattening," said Mrs. Tobias.

"Ah, fat, fat, that's all American women think about, fat, and they forget that men like a little fat on their women, a thin woman is not a loving woman." She smiled as she said this, and her smile slowly became a laugh. David was very much taken with this bit of dialogue, especially Helen's part . . . her remarks were deliciously physical, and vague notions about her rushed through his mind. Suddenly he heard Helen saying, "David, where is your mind?"

"Oh, I'm sorry."

"It's not very polite," said Helen, "for a man to think of other things when women are in a room. 'When a woman is in a room, a room shouldn't think of anything else,' said Chekhov."

"Maybe when a man is in a room, a woman shouldn't think of anybody else, either," said David, and he was astonished at what came from his mouth.

Helen patted his knee and then his hand. "That is very good, what you just said, very good, I like it." She said this as if she were praising a good piece of bread and butter or a good piece of steak that she had just eaten.

"David," said Mary, "Helen is one of the few women I know who not only cooks well, but also loves to cook. She just loves it."

"I do love it so very much, so very, very much," said Helen.

David liked her speech . . . one moment it was perfect English, another moment it had overtones of some other languages. Her accent also was a bit Russian. No matter what she said or how she said it, David was pleased.

"How is the rehearsal coming along?" asked Raphael Tobias.

"Oh, good, bad, very good, very bad," said Helen. "A rehearsal is a rehearsal. Today was not so good. So tomorrow it will be better."

She explained to David that she had just translated a longish one-act play by Maxim Gorki that had never before been performed in English or in Russian anywhere outside of Russia—and even in Russia it had been performed only rarely. "But it is just wonderful, so humorous, so deep, so dramatic. I won't tell you the story. You must come to the opening, as my guest. I think you will love it as much as I love it."

"How do you know I will?" asked David.

"Eh," said Helen, smiling, "I know you, I know you very well. It is just the sort of play that I know you will adore. Wait and see. I know I will be right."

"When Helen says she is sure, she is very sure," said Mary. "A woman of very positive ideas, and she sticks to them. It's one of the reasons we love her so much. There's never any doubt what she thinks."

David naturally offered to take Helen home. When they were outside it occurred to him to ask where she lived. She smiled and said, "Don't worry, David. I don't live in Long Island, or even in Brooklyn. I live only a few blocks away from here. If you feel up to it, we can walk, only fifteen, twenty minutes walk from here, but if you wish we can take a Third Avenue bus."

They walked. They said nothing to each other for two blocks. Then she said softly, "You're unhappy."

David was startled. "Well, no, not exactly."

She put her arm in his, as they crossed a street, and she kept it there. "I'm sorry," she said. "I didn't mean to pry."

"That's all right."

They walked on in silence. Then she said, "I really would like to have you come to the opening of the Gorki play."

"I want to come very much."

"It worries me. I like it, I like it very much, but I don't know if the American people will like it. We're putting it on in a small theatre off Broadway, but it's still an investment." She hesitated, then she said, with a strange gaiety, "Well, it doesn't matter. It will go, or it won't go. Before you came Mary was telling me about you, what a wonderful writer you are, how many hopes she has for you, and so many more things. I was dying to see you. Mary is seldom so enthusiastic."

"Are you disappointed?"

"The opposite."

"What do you mean?"

"You want to know too much."

David was silent. Then Helen said, "I know many things about you, David, even though Mary didn't tell me."

"Such as . . ."

"You have a wonderful mother and a wonderful father, and lots and lots of brothers and sisters."

"Yes, and both my father and mother are not well, and I'm worried."

"I'm very sorry, David. I hope it's nothing serious."

"I hope so."

"They'll get all better." She pressed his arm to her body.

"I hope so. I know so."

David felt relieved. There seemed to be such deep reassurance in what Helen had said.

They were at the door of a brownstone building. "I live here. Do you wish to come in for a while?"

"Yes."

The house was old, brownstone, in the past it probably was the residence of a fine family that occupied all of it, but the family had long since moved, and now the house was divided into several small apartments. In short, it was a somewhat superior rooming house. They walked along a narrow hall, covered with once red and now frayed red carpeting, and there was a smell of genteel decay. Suddenly David felt closer to Helen, he now knew a great deal about her. They had the same or similar backgrounds. She opened a door, and they were in a huge room, with couches against two of the walls, a table against another, and off in the corner there was a door that was partly open. Helen walked over on her tip toes, and gently closed it. "Yossi is sleeping."

David looked at her.

"My son," she whispered. "I don't want to wake him."

"Oh."

"He's thirteen, and he feels like an old man." She smiled. "I was worried all the time we were at the Tobiases. This was the second time I had left him alone. But he insisted I go out. He wants to be the man of the house. He says he's afraid of nobody."

She rolled up the sleeves of her dress, and something specially warm seemed to come from out of them. Her arms were firm, plump, but not too plump, and there was a lovely roundness to them. He noticed that she had a bit of a second chin, or so it seemed in the dim light, and he rather liked that.

"I'd like to make you some of that coffee I was talking about. Shall I, David?"

"It's late . . . "

"Please, it will take only a minute. I feel like it."

"All right."

When the coffee was ready she filled two cups on a little table, and then brought a bag of oatmeal cookies. "Try these," she said. "Azriel, my son, is just crazy about them, and I've begun to like them, too." She laughed softly. "You look like him."

"Really?"

"Yes. Your hair, your face, your cheekbones. When I first saw you, when you came into the room, at the Tobiases, I gasped. Azriel doesn't look at all like his father."

David wanted to ask where Helen's husband was, whether he was coming in soon. David began to worry: if Helen's husband came in now, and saw them drinking coffee, there would be considerable embarrassment. David had never before been in such a situation.

"This is a big room," he said, hoping that somehow this would elicit from her more information about her husband.

"Yes, it is. I have this room, the little kitchen over there, and Azriel has his room. It's enough for both of us. I sleep on the couch over there."

David was relieved.

Suddenly she said, "I wish you would let me sometimes wash your hair. I like its thickness and its richness. Will you?"

David immediately wanted to say yes, but something kept him back.

"I want to smell your hair right now. I think it smells just like Azriel's." She walked over to him, put her face to his hair, sighed, said, "Just like Azriel's," and kissed his hair. She did not go away, she remained, standing close to David, and wove her finger through his hair. Her aroma was spreading through his being, and he put his arm around her waist, whereupon she sat down on his lap. Suddenly she got up. "I'm too heavy for you," she said, and walked back to her chair. "I'll make some more coffee, it will take only a minute."

He hardly knew what to think. He had never before met such a woman. He imagined that she could be a bulwark of strength in almost any situation. He had never before encountered so much confidence in a human being. Not that Helen actually said anything that would lead him to think so; confidence radiated from her. He was conscious of a strong desire for her, and he had the feeling that she also had a strong desire for him.

Helen was back with more coffee. "Like it? I meant to ask you before."

"Yes, very much, but it is rather fattening," said David.

"But it's good," she said. She took a sip and David liked the way she put her lips to the cup. Then she said, "The Tobiases think the world of you."

"I like them, too."

"You make me feel very good," she said, smiling at him the fullest and most beckoning smile he had ever before seen on a woman.

"I'm glad," he said softly. He wanted to say more, but he didn't know what.

"Do I make you feel good?" she asked.

"Yes."

Suddenly a cloud of sorrow spread across her face, and he wanted to ask her what was wrong, but he didn't.

"Do you believe in things happening suddenly?" she asked, as a smile came back to her face.

"I suppose so . . . some things, I imagine," he answered, and a strange feeling went through him, both happy and uncomfortable . . . what was happening this very moment could almost be in a pulp novel . . . the words were a trifle shabby, the whole surrounding was equally so . . . a married woman, her husband away, her son sleeping in a room nearby . . .

an unmarried man with a married woman, obviously separated from her husband, drinking coffee together . . . only a minute or so ago she had been sitting on his lap . . . she had just said that he made her feel good, and he had said that she made him feel good . . . and yet, despite all this, there was something wonderful and lovely between them. David was very glad. A thought suddenly came to his mind, namely, that the innermost essences of pulp stories do reflect something true in the secret yearning of all of us. What makes pulp stories pulp is that their authors do not realize the sanctity of these secret yearnings and treat them as if they were shameful things, perhaps they don't even realize how sacred and how secret these yearnings are, how tenderly they are to be dealt with, that they can best be suggested rather than exposed to the glaring light of print . . . perhaps all that can honestly and properly be done with them in print is merely to use words to hint at them, anything beyond that tarnishes them a bit.

"Let's sit on the couch," she said. "It's more comfortable there, and I don't like to sit nearby when dishes aren't washed, and I don't want to wash them now, besides, it would make noise, and Azriel might wake up."

They were sitting on the couch. "You look like somebody one can talk to, because you probably talk a great deal to yourself," she said.

David was startled by her insight: he did talk a great deal to himself. "Well," he began . . .

"I knew it the first minute I saw you. But you have troubles, important troubles about your life and your future, I mean worries, really, not troubles. And I like that. I mean I don't like people who are normal, who have no worries. You look so uncomfortable. Move way back. Here, take this little pillow, and put it behind you, it will be more comfortable." She was close to him now. "Isn't that better?"

"Yes," he said. He was glad that she was so close to him, but he was also a bit uneasy.

"Do you want me to massage your neck? My Azriel likes it."

"Yes. Thank you."

She began to massage his neck gently, and a soft ease went through him, and this ease combined with the warmth and sweetness that came from Helen, and the whole world began to seem more friendly. Suddenly she kissed him tenderly on his cheek, and he was so thrilled with the kiss and the warmth of her breath and the softness of her lips that he didn't know what to do or what to say.

"I hope I didn't embarrass you," she said, and while he wasn't looking at her he knew that she was smiling, and he was glad.

"What you're doing to my neck is very relaxing," said David, who was grateful that something occurred to him to say.

"Actors always have this done to them, and dancers, too," said Helen, as she continued to massage his neck, and now and then her hand wandered up to his cheek. "All the tensions, well, many of them, are centered in the neck, they become like knots, the cartilages or something in the neck, and when these knots are unwound relief comes at once. It's wonderful. Everybody should have a massage at least once a week, all over the body, and every night one should have a massage in the neck, and down the spine. Do you want me to do it to you a little now?"

"Yes, thanks."

"Then take off your jacket, and put your face in my lap and I will do it gently first, because if it wasn't done to you before, it may seem strange and even hurt a little bit. Most people's spines are brittle, and you have to massage them easily at first. Is this all right?"

"Yes, it's wonderful."

"It will get better. Do you feel as if tiredness is going out of you, like rays, almost?"

"Yes, that's exactly how it feels, like all my tiredness is oozing out of me. How do you know so much about all this?"

"My husband taught me. He has wonderful hands for massaging. He learned it from a Swedish masseur. He met him when we were in Stockholm with the Baruch Haba company. This Swedish masseur was a great Hebrew scholar and a Zionist, and this was his profession, he was a medical doctor, too, and he said that many of the sicknesses could be cured, not by medicine but just by resting, fasting, and massaging. And he was right."

The mention of Helen's husband sent a discomfiting stab

through David, who still had his head on her lap . . . he was without his jacket, and he was tantalized by the soft-hardness of her thighs, and by the gentle warmth that was coming from them.

"Tell me about your husband," said David suddenly.

She said nothing, continuing to massage David's spine and neck, more and more gently. She stopped, her hands resting on David's back, and now she once more began to massage him, and now she played with his hair. Slowly David began to sense a great embarrassment come into the room and twine itself about him and about Helen and about both of them . . . but still David wanted to know about her husband. "Tell me," he said.

He felt Helen draw in her stomach, which became hard against David's head, and for a few moments David felt that Helen's whole personality had changed, he could almost see the silent laughter disappear from her face, and a tightness come to her mouth, and he could also see some wrinkles form on her forehead.

"Mordecai means well," she began. "Mary Tobias, who likes him, says he's the best-meaning man she's ever known. But we shouldn't have got married." She stopped, but she kept on massaging David, who felt she was doing it mechanically now, hardly knowing what she was doing.

"Why?" asked David.

"Oh, many reasons."

"Maybe I shouldn't have asked in the first place. I'm sorry."

"No. I'm glad you asked. I wanted to tell you later, but I might as well do it now. You're very sensitive and you want to know." She hesitated.

She continued, "Mordecai is almost twenty years older than I am. When we met, at the Baruch Haba company, I was a foolish girl, dying to act and dance, you know, we met in Odessa, and he was so handsome and so worldly, and when he smiled at me I thought I'd die. He knew a little French and German and that made him seem even more worldly. In the European theatrical world men and women are always kissing, even more than here, it sounds funny, but you know what I mean. So it meant nothing, but when he kissed me I would shudder with delight all over inside, and, of course, he knew it, and when he came close to me, very close, and stroked my hair, I had very long, black hair then, I could almost faint." She sighed. "Life is strange, everything is strange."

David felt her lift her breasts . . . her stomach seemed to cave in almost suddenly, and now it began to fill up again against his head . . . she kissed his hair quickly, again began to massage his neck and his spine, and continued, "He had, he has a brother, Melech. He was so *frum* (pious) it was painful. He prayed three times a day, he wore *tstises* (a small prayer shawl worn over one's undershirt), and he never ate *trafe* (non-kosher) food, and waited exactly six hours, usually more, between meat dishes and dairy dishes. He almost never looked at a woman, we all thought he would never get married. But he was a wonderful dancer, but even as a dancer he wasn't interested in women. That's strange, isn't it?"

"Yes."

"So then we learned he's become interested in a Russian prostitute, a young and very pretty girl, but a prostitute. He brought her books and magazines and newspapers, Hebrew and Russian and Yiddish books, and it all seemed so silly, because she could hardly read Russian, and she was so foolishly religious, ran to her church all the time. He must have had some ideas in his mind, to make her get converted, maybe, but to this day we don't know why he brought her all those books, she certainly wasn't interested. Anyway, she stopped being a prostitute, and all the credit belonged to him. Of course, he brought her to all our meetings, and she was pretty as a picture. Then one day he told us that they had got married, and that she promised she would become Jewish. Well, five months later she gave birth to a baby. Isn't life strange?"

"Yes."

"She never became Jewish. She took some lessons from him, and then she stopped. She just told him she couldn't be bothered."

"Is he still *frum?*"

"Worse than ever. I guess he now feels that he has to pray for her, too."

"Do they have other children?"

"No, but they're still married, and they fight like cats and dogs, and we're all sorry for her and for him. I don't think she really cares for him, but he's still in love with her, and she's still pretty. Well, this happened about the time that I met Mordecai. Oh, I forgot to say something. Melech was not Zionist, he said that the Jews should wait for *Moshiach* (the Messiah), and he said the Zionists were *apikorsim* (non-believers), you know. But Mordecai and the others in the Baruch Haba company were ardent Zionists, especially Mordecai, and I liked that very much in Mordecai. I was very idealistic, naturally, for Palestine, I still am, I guess, in a way, Zionism is the only thing I really and truly believe in. Anyway, Mordecai was very upset by what Melech had done, but I think he was most upset by the fact that Melech and the Gentile girl had lived together before they were married." David sensed that she smiled.

"Why are you smiling?" he asked.

"Oh, life, the funny little jokes that God plays with people. As I told you, I was very much in love with Mordecai, and I would have done anything for him, and he knew it. And I mean anything. One night he was in my room, it was raining, it sounds almost like a popular novel, doesn't it?"

"Go on, Helen."

"He had a little cold, so I told him to stay over, I made a bed for him with chairs. But, well, during the night, he came over to my bed and made love to me. Would you believe it, I was so simple, of course, I knew what was happening, but in another way I didn't, I really didn't. So we became lovers. The rest of the company knew it, there are very few secrets among actors, and that was that. He asked me to marry him right away, but something told me to wait, so we were just lovers. But then, one month, I was two weeks late, and I told him. I was worried myself, and he pleaded with me to marry him. The funny thing is by then I wasn't so sure I really loved him, but I was worried, and we were married. And a day after we were married, I got my period again."

She stopped, sighed, and continued. "In about a year and a half Azriel came, and he was a joy, a perfect joy. I thought I'd learn to love Mordecai because of Azriel, but it was the opposite." Again she stopped, mussed up David's hair hurriedly, and said, "Oh, darling, must I go on? It's so unpleasant. Besides, I can't tell everything."

"I'm sorry," said David. "Do as you wish." Impulsively, he took hold of her hand and kissed it. She said, "Thank you, darling. I wanted you to kiss me. The memory is painful to me, but in a special sense. I don't really know what that sense is, but I think you know."

"I do, Helen, I do," David said, and again kissed her hand. She caressed his lips with the same hand, as he continued to kiss it.

"I think I will go on," she said. "I just couldn't love him, and then came the time I couldn't respect him. We had some difficulties on Baruch Haba, some failures, we lost money, and he became angry. He insulted actors and actresses that he had known for years, he called me all sorts of names, vile names. He insulted me terribly and shamed me, but I kept quiet. Because to myself I felt that he had a good reason; he was married to a woman who, he knew, didn't love him, and that must be a terrible humiliation to a man. And I imagine I insulted him, too, the way a woman can insult a man. It got so that I would dread his coming home at night. Then he suddenly collapsed, I mean, mentally. Have you ever seen that happen to a man, and a big man, Mordecai is a big man, have you ever?"

"No, I don't think so," said David.

"It's terrible. He just stopped talking to anybody, he refused even to get out of the house. He would just sit and read the English newspaper and the Yiddish newspaper and Hebrew magazines and Zionist books, books that he had read many years before. He would just sit there sprawled out, sometimes just in his slippers, unshaven, and Azriel, his son, maybe four, five, we were then already in America, would ask him why he didn't go to work, you know how children are, and Mordecai would shout at him, it was simply terrible. I told him to stop shouting at our child, and he didn't answer. I used to have a terrible time sending him out to get something in the grocery, he was ashamed to go out, or something, I didn't know the reason. You can imagine what happened then. There was no money. I had bought things at the grocery store and at the dairy on credit, and then they refused to give me any more credit. So I got a part-time job at Macy's, it was Christmas time, and one wonderful man there let me stay on after Christmas, I told him my troubles: If it weren't for that I just don't know how we would have managed. I fill up so when I think of those days."

She stopped. Then she said, "Finally, I couldn't stand it any more. I mean I had to talk to somebody. I talked to Melech and his wife. And what do you think the pious Melech said? He said that I didn't understand Mordecai, that he had suffered a great defeat, in the trouble that the Baruch Haba company was having, as a matter of fact, there was talk that they would have to disband, that was terrible, I know, it was the only company of its kind, and Mordecai loved the Hebrew language, and so do I, and I did sympathise, but a married man has responsibilities. I said this to Melech, but he said nothing to that. All he said was that Mordecai would come out of it, that Mordecai always was moody, which was something I hadn't known before. So I didn't get much help there. I got all kinds of other jobs. I wanted to get acting parts, of course, but it was difficult to find anything that would suit me. Then there was my slight accent. I addressed envelopes at all sorts of places, for a while I got a job as a clerk in a large linoleum store." She laughed. "I remember that especially, because the owner found out my troubles home, that I had a child, and he let me bring Azriel to the shop, and Azriel just loved it, he would slide down the inclined rolls of linoleum, and he loved the smell of linoleum, and he made me bring home small pieces of linoleum, so that he could smell it all the time. He brought home bigger and bigger pieces, and Mordecai got angry."

"Why?"

"Oh, he became jealous. He said that I was having an affair with the man who owned the linoleum store. He said it right in front of Azriel, and Azriel must have understood. I laughed at Mordecai. I said that was the farthest removed from my mind. He was angry, and I couldn't blame him. By then I had made up my mind not to live with him anymore as husband and wife. I just couldn't. I sometimes think I never really liked it with him, but I was only a young girl when I married him, I just didn't realize what I was doing. Then he accused me of going to bed with other men, some actor friends who would kiss me when they came to visit us, and others. Then one evening I came home from work—I was then a house maid for a woman way up on Riverside Drive—and I found Mordecai drunk, plain drunk, and I could smell the whiskey as soon as I entered. I had left Azriel with him, and the poor child was crying, and dirty, and his father was slobbering all over. I don't know where he got the money for the whiskey, and I just don't know why, because he had never before drunk much whiskey. Well, to make a long story short, I left him the next morning. I took Azriel with me. It was very difficult at first, terribly difficult. You'd be surprised the kind of work I did. In the end I started a little acting school, and that's what saved me. I was surprised how many pupils I got."

"Where's your husband now?" asked David.

"He lives in Brooklyn, with Melech. He's a little better now, I mean he gets a job sometimes, mainly teaching Hebrew in *talmud torahs,* he's probably a very good teacher, he speaks perfect Hebrew, and he translates from Hebrew into Yiddish, for the Yiddish newspapers. I've asked him for a divorce, because I've told him I'll never live with him again, but he refuses, he says I'll come back to him. So that's how things stand. I've told Azriel about us, I mean, about Mordecai and myself, and Azriel wants to be with me. So now you know everything," she concluded, and David could feel a sigh of relief go through her body.

He snuggled up close to her, put his head close to her stomach and kissed it. She caressed his head and said, "Thank you. Why don't you sit up now? I haven't seen your face for ages."

He sat up, and saw tears on her face. He had not expected to see them. In the dim light the tears made her face astonishingly lovely. She reminded him of his mother, when he was still only a boy. It was a Saturday evening, his mother was alone in the front room, she was looking out of the window, it was raining outside, and he came in and she turned to face him, and she then looked so marvelously beautiful, and she looked at him, and he had forgotten what he wanted to say, and he came over to her, and put his hand to her face, and he said, "You look nice," and she caressed him and said, "You're my wonderful son." He wanted to say more, but he didn't know what to say . . . but he had never forgotten that look on his mother's face that Saturday evening. Now Helen's face looked like his mother's then.

"You look wonderful," David said to Helen, and he threw his arms around her, and rested his head on her shoulder. She disentangled herself, took his face in her hands and kissed him slowly on the lips. "I love you," she said, and smiled.

David was surprised that he didn't feel perturbed by this declaration . . . neither did he feel any strong compulsion to say anything . . . Helen took his hand in hers, held up his hand to her eyes: "What lovely fingers you have," she said. "I've never seen anything like them in a grown man. Almost like a young girl's, so delicate, so gentle. Why aren't you married?"

"How did you know I wasn't?"

"I knew. Tell me."

"Oh, I don't know."

"Tell me, please, David. I told you."

David proceeded to tell her about Alice and then about Sylvia, "and that's all there is to say, I guess. I want to get married very much, I want children very much, but things turned out differently, so far, anyway."

"You should have married Sylvia right after you met her. A quick marriage like that, darling, can bring lots of misery or lots of happiness. To you it would have brought lots of happiness, for a short time, but it would have been wonderful. You really loved Sylvia, didn't you?"

"With all my heart. I think you would have liked her, too. I don't think I'll ever get over her death."

"Don't say that, David, don't. God is kind. Please don't say that, David." She kissed him softly on his lips. "Promise you'll never say that again."

"I promise," said David, who was profoundly moved by her gentle, soft kiss and by what he sensed she was going to say.

"My father, David, was a very learned man. You would have loved him, darling. I know you would have, I'm sure. He was a *Chassid,* but he was so wonderful a man. I mean he was very pious, he was not a Zionist, he was angry with me for being a Zionist. Oh, it was all sort of complicated, he really was a Zionist, but he didn't like some of the Zionists in our little village, they were not *frum* (pious), you know; they shaved, didn't pray three times a day. He often talked about God, even when we were very little, and I like that, don't you darling?"

"I do, my father also does sometimes, but he's so busy earning a living," said David.

"I'm glad," said Helen, who put David's hand to her mouth, kissed it softly, and then put it to her cheek. "So soft, a real girl's hand, darling, and I love it. Isn't it wonderful that we met?"

"I'm glad, too."

"Believe me, darling, I've never been so happy before, believe me. A miracle, isn't it, David?"

"It is."

"And I like the name David. When my Azriel was born David was one of the names I thought of for him, but Azriel is nice, too, isn't it?"

"Yes."

"I'm sorry Azriel is asleep now. You'll love him. He's such a devil. And he looks just like you, really he does, the more I look at you, the more I say to myself that you are Azriel's older brother. You know something, David?"

"What?"

"I'm sorry I never met Sylvia. She must have been just marvelous, wonderful, and I'm so glad you were in love with her. I don't like people who were never in love. It makes no difference whether you made a mistake or not, just loving is what really matters, isn't that so, David?"

"Of course."

"The other girl, Alice, I'm sorry for her. She probably was, is very nice, but she, well, she didn't have character. You would have been unhappy if you married her, I know you would have. Do you mind my talking this way?"

"Oh, no."

"And something else, darling, I want to say." She stopped, again put his hand to her mouth and kissed it.

"What?"

"I'm glad the two girls that you loved were both Jewish.

295

I'm that much of a chauvinist. Darling, to me, Jewishness is so wonderful a thing, so holy, yes, holy, so close to all life and all creation, and things that are real and sacred and holy and wonderful, that it's a sin, I think, a terrible sin, to go away from it even for a little moment. I just don't understand Jews who say Jews are just people. They're not. They're more. Like it says in the prayer, *Ahto Shebochartonoo,* You Who have chosen us, we are chosen, we are chosen to lead the world in ideas and in heroism and in spiritual adventures, we got the Torah, only we did, and we have kept it holy for thousands of years. You know something, darling, oh, I love you so much, you . . . " She looked intently at him.

"I love to hear you talk," David said.

"Every time I go into a synagogue, and I go in very often, David, I'm not *frum,* not very, I keep a *kosher* house, I like it, but I'm not very *frum,* but I'm very, very Jewish. Does that sound strange? An actress to feel that way?"

"No, It's wonderful, Helen."

"Well, every time I go in I feel like blessing God for making me Jewish. Coming back to what I wanted to say before, about God. He is not cruel. We really don't know Him, but we also know Him. He is the God of *rachmones,* the God of mercies, the Center of mercy, the Fountain of mercy. My father used to say that no other religion, no other people has a word quite like *rachmones,* it means more than mercy, really, it means understanding and it means justice and it means forgiveness and it means a feeling that you're really, in a sense, not to blame, because you are part of God. You know, darling, because of what my father taught me about God, I can never really be angry with anybody, I mean angry deep down in my heart. I try to see things the way another person sees them. Honestly, darling, I can't be angry even with Mordecai, I can't. He was made the way he was made, and he acts the way he has to act. If anybody is at fault, it's really I, because I shouldn't have married him. But that brings up something else. Was I angry with God, I mean did I say God was cruel? Well, I confess there were times when I almost thought so, but I remembered what my father said, that God is always kind, and we can find His kindness if we will only look. And, of course, I found His kindness

296

right near me, my Azriel, my joy. So you see, darling, never say God is not kind, never." She kissed his hand again.

"I feel like saying something that I don't know if I should say, it may sound funny," began David. "I mean even as I think about it, it sounds strange."

"Tell me, darling, tell me everything."

"Sylvia is gone, and I have been lonely, and I went to the Tobiases to be with pleasant company, and there I met you."

Helen caressed his face. "I'm glad you said that, and I understand why you hesitated, and I'm glad you hesitated."

"And I like what you said about being a Jew. It's so very important to know how wonderful it is. And I think that all the Jews all over the world now know it."

"Darling, I am now feeling something deep, deep in my bones. I know it will happen."

"What?" asked David.

"Zionism will came true very soon. We will have our own country very, very soon. I told my Azriel that before he goes to high school, that will be in less than two years, the Jews will have a country of their own."

"That would be wonderful, Helen."

"It will happen. Do you want some more coffee?"

David looked at his watch. "My God, it's three o'clock in the morning. I better go."

She didn't answer immediately, but seemed to be far away in thought.

"What are you thinking about, Helen?"

She smiled and took his hand in hers. "I know it's late, darling, but I hate to have you go. I was thinking about something else my father told me. Talking about my Azriel reminded me. It was about the Crusades. You know, of course, that that was one of the worst times in the history of the Jews, almost as bad as it was under Hitler, and in some ways, I suppose, worse. Because during the Crusades the Catholic Church was solidly behind the killing of Jews, and the murderous head of them was a monk, Peter. During the Hitler days the Church saved some Jews, though not as many as it now wants us to think. They did talk against Hitler and they did denounce anti-Semitism. But I wish they had done it stronger. They objected to Hitler, and Mussolini, for that matter, not so much because Hitler was anti-Semitic, but because he closed down so many of the parochial schools. The Pope would have kept his mouth shut if Hitler hadn't done that. Look at the Church and Franco's Spain. There is a terrible dictatorship, but the Pope says nothing, because Franco is *frum*. But in a way it was better during the Crusades, in a small and terrible way. The Christians during the Crusades at least gave the Jews a chance to save themselves by getting converted. During Hitler's day they gave nobody a chance. If you were a Jew, you were killed, even if you had been converted to Lutheranism or Catholicism or any other form of Christianity. I think that if there was Jewish blood in you four generations back, then Hitler killed you. Anyway, even during the Crusades very few Jews got converted."

She stopped suddenly and tip-toed over to the door leading into Azriel's room. She opened it gently, peeked in, and then tip-toed back to where David was sitting. There was something lovely, so wholly womanly in what she had done that David felt like embracing her and kissing her.

"I thought I heard some noise in Azriel's room," she said.

"Maybe I ought to go."

"No, darling, I mean, yes, but I want to finish what I started saying. There were very few Jews during the Crusades who got converted. Most of them committed suicide or killed each other rather than be killed by the Crusaders or be forced into conversion. Thousands and thousands of Jews did that. And my father told me about one rabbi, Meshulom b'reb Ytzhock, I'll always remember that name, and he had a wife Tzipporah, and they had one child, a son, whose name was Ytzhock. And the rabbi said to his wife, 'I want to bring him as a sacrifice to God, by killing him.' And Tzipporah agreed but she pleaded with her husband that he kill her first, but he said no, he wanted to kill the son first to make sure that he, the son, does not fall into the hands of those who might force conversion upon him, the son. So he made a blessing upon the son and the son said, Amen, and then the father killed him. And he was about to kill his wife and himself. but the Crusaders broke into their home and they killed both the rabbi and his wife. Isn't it horrible and wonderful, David?"

"It is," said David. "I didn't know that story."

"It's not a story, darling, it's true. I will never forget that, what my father told me."

There was a silence. He said, "I better go now."

They both stood up, embraced and kissed. She whispered in his ear, "You're so good, darling." He replied with another kiss and a promise to call her before the day was over.

"Thank you," she said.

Twelve

In many ways Helen affected David more than did Sylvia
or Alice. She was as lovely as either used to be. Helen, in a
sense, was a mature Sylvia. She was more worldly, more deeply
sensuous, and she was more Jewish in a manner that was significant to David. She represented a kind of Jewish interest
that was quite novel to him, even as she represented a kind of
womanhood that was also quite novel and very attractive to
him. Alice had been brought up in a deeply Jewish atmosphere,
but slowly she abandoned her interest in Jewishness, even looked
upon it as a form of parochialism. The world of socialism and
the world of emancipated youth drew her more, and while he
didn't know, he imagined that she was now likely a Communist
or at least a fellow traveler, and probably not in the slightest
concerned with anything Jewish. It was, indeed, this aspect
of her character that offended David and that was the cause
of their final break.

Sylvia sometimes seemed to be more the lovely woman than
the Jew, and yet the very essence of her wonderful loveliness
was infused with Jewishness: her softness, her understanding,
her silences. But Sylvia's interest in Jewish matters was chiefly
latent, and her knowledge of them was scant. Helen, on the
other hand, was openly and affirmatively Jewish, she was also
womanly and she was worldly besides. To her, Jewishness was

more than a religion, it was a civilization, of which religion was but a part.

As he got to know her better he realized that she and her husband and the other members of the Baruch Haba company and their friends represented the last stages of the *Haskalah* (Enlightenment) movement that had so profoundly influenced East European Judaism. David had heard about it in his father's home: his father was dubious of it, while his mother appeared to be sympathetic, for her own father had been deeply involved in it. There had been fear among the Orthodox that "worldly" learning would lure many of the young Jewish men and women away from Judaism. It did, to some extent, lure them away from some of the religious aspects of Judaism, but in the end it brought new life to their Jewishness, and was in many ways responsible for the intensity of the early Zionist movement. To these Newer Jews, if they could be called that, Jewishness was not just a passive thing, surrounded by hopes of the coming of the Messiah. It was a truly dynamic thing, filled with glory, something that was crying to be made a part of the contemporary world by way of the establishment of a Jewish state, a state with its own government and its own culture and its own *mores* and its own libraries and markets and colleges and universities and, above all, its own destiny.

Helen was this type of Jew, and her womanhood added to the intensity of her conviction. She was now engaged in producing non-Jewish plays by some of the great Russian and German masters, but that was, so to speak, only by default: the Baruch Haba company was in difficulties and for the moment producing plays in Hebrew was out of the question, and she had to earn a living for herself and her son. Hebrew, to her, was a necessary part of the air she was breathing, and so was Hebrew literature and all Hebrew culture. At the same time she was not a fanatical Hebraist, that is, she did not insist that Hebrew was the best language or the only cultural language, she only insisted that it was the dearest language for her, and the dearest cultural medium for her. She wanted Hebrew not only to be the language of the Jewish people for communication of their own specific Jewish needs, she wanted it also to be the means of communicating with the "outside" world, and on an equal basis with other languages.

David was astonished how long it had taken him really to learn that there were many ways of being a Jew, and that the way he was brought up was not necessarily the best.

"It is difficult, darling, very difficult," she said, as they were walking together in Central Park. "Tolerance is like patience, and that's difficult, too. You learn that in the theatre so very much. Sometimes a director will pick out a certain actor and tell him he is good for a certain part, and the actor will say no. Then will come the rehearsals, the actor, you see, has agreed to take the part anyway, he needs the job, or the part looks good. Well, at the rehearsals the actor will have a terrible time, the part will look bad for him, he will be awkward, and the director will tell him he is bad, but he will also tell him that if he tries, if the actor tries, he will be wonderful. I once heard the director Komisarjevsky, did you hear of him?"

"I'm afraid only vaguely, a Russian director . . ."

"Yes. Some say he was greater even that Stanislavsky, some say no. It makes no difference, he was a very great director. Great is a funny word, anyway, darling. It all depends who is talking, and when you're talking. Anyway, I once heard him say, 'Every actor is greater than he thinks, because every human being is greater than he thinks.' That's true, isn't it?"

"A very fine thought," said David.

"And that means that we have to dig into ourselves. And we have to be patient with ourselves and with others. Oh, Komisarjevsky said something else I remember, I remember many things he said, he really was good, he said, 'Remember that light has many colors, and one color is not better than another, they are all part of one reality, light.' Isn't that a good reason for tolerance? Oh, about that actor I told you about. So he complained the part was not for him, that he was right in the first place when he didn't want the part, that he was very bad, and the director agreed with him, but the director kept saying, 'No, you are right for the part, you must be patient, soon you will see how wonderful you are for the part. I'll be patient, and you must be patient.' "

"Helen, I never realized that acting entailed so much of life, that it had to do with philosophy, understanding, poetry, knowing people, their emotions. I used to think that since so many silly girls are actresses, and so many silly men, acting is

302

hardly an art at all, and if it's an art, it's an inferior art. I'm afraid I didn't know, I just didn't know."

Helen smiled. "Darling, you were a snob. And you had an opinion without really having any foundation for it. You were intolerant, and a lot of intolerance is based on not knowing. Actors are artists, and artists are people, and . . . don't you know many writers who are silly outside of their writings, and the same about painters and even philosophers? So why discriminate with actors?"

"There is no reason," said David.

"About being tolerant toward Jews," said Helen, "darling, don't feel too bad about that. I mean I know many people who've felt that way for a time. I felt that way myself. I mean I used to be furious with my father for what he wanted me to do, you know, be very Orthodox, and the fights we had about my becoming an actress." Suddenly she stopped, and a sadness spread across her face.

David was a bit alarmed. For a moment he wondered whether she was suddenly ill. "What's wrong, Helen?"

"Oh," she said, "nothing, I was just thinking about something, and it frightened me."

David had never imagined that anything could frighten Helen. "What frightened you?"

"Oh, it just occurred to me how much closer my father still is to me, and he's been dead for years and years, but he's closer to me than my husband."

"Oh."

"You know something, darling, Orthodox people are really more flexible than you might think, or than others might think, you know what I mean."

"Yes," said David, who recalled some of the remarks his father had made and, especially, that his *alte bobbe* (great-grandmother) had made.

"David, I loved my father, I just loved him, he was so just, so decent, so beautiful, really, I mean it, beautiful. When I would see him in his *yarmulke,* by himself in his room, studying the *Talmud,* and I would see that wonderful glow on his face, I just loved him, I wanted to kiss him so much, but I didn't, because in our house there wasn't very much kissing. That I regret very much, darling, I do. I think people should kiss more when they feel like it, even if later you don't feel the same way about people. You know what I mean?"

"Yes, I think so," said David, who was delighted to hear her say this.

"I'm sorry, David, that I didn't kiss him. I loved him so much. I suppose the Freudians would see all kinds of meanings in that. But they'd be wrong. I just loved him. I didn't want to sleep with him."

David was startled and apparently showed it.

"Does this shock you, darling?," asked Helen.

"I'm afraid it does," said David.

Suddenly she stopped and embraced him and kissed him. "I love you for feeling that way, darling, but you're silly. I only meant that that's what some Freudians would interpret my feeling as being, but they'd be wrong. I just loved him, I respected him, I adored him. Now, can't one adore somebody, respect him without wanting to sleep with him, without the idea even occurring to her?"

"I suppose so," said David.

"It's true. But anyway, I would watch him, studying the Talmud, and I thought how wonderful Judaism is, even though we had all those arguments, and you know something?"

"What?"

"He agreed with me, but he didn't want to give in, not because he didn't want me to feel that I had the better of the argument, but because he wanted to protect the honor of his tradition. Isn't that wonderful?"

"Yes," said David, with a flood of revelation and joy coming in on him . . . now, at long last, he was with a Jew who was closest to what had been, unconsciously, his growing conception of what a Jew should be: of this world, very much of this world, but at the same time very much of the history-drenched Jewish world.

Helen was precisely the type of Jewish woman who pleased him the most now. As they got to know each other more he was pleasantly surprised at the extent of her knowledge of "worldly" matters: she knew Russian literature better than he did. She had read *War and Peace* and *The Brothers Karamazov* and *The Lower Depths,* among other Russian classics, in the original Russian, as well as in English translation. She had read, in Russian translation, Molière and Racine and much of Goethe, and she also knew some American literature. But always her heart seemed to be closest to novels and plays and poems dealing with Jewish themes. She said, "Darling, this is not chauvinism. I just feel these are mine, and I feel closer to them, the way I feel closer to my Azriel than to other children." David liked that very much . . . and he was grateful to her for taking him to literary affairs held by the Yiddish centers and the Hebrew centers and the Russian centers . . . he hadn't known there were such very active centers in New York, and always she seemed to be at home in them.

He was dubious about her attitude towards Yiddish, she liked it, yet she seemed to look down upon it, at least, to consider it as not quite on a par with Hebrew. She said, "After all, Hebrew is Hebrew, and Yiddish is Yiddish. Yiddish was something that developed in *Galuth* (the Exile), but Hebrew is the language of the Bible."

David reminded her that Yiddish had been the mother tongue of the Jewish people for a long time, that Jewish men and women prayed to God in that language, that they had learned about their world and the outside world, most of the time, by way of that language . . . that millions of them went to their deaths in the Hitler concentration camps and crematoriums, pleading to God in that language as well as in Hebrew: they prayed in Hebrew, but interspersed their prayers with outcries in Yiddish, the language they had learned in their childhood, even before they learned Hebrew. Helen readily agreed that the Yiddish language had been sanctified by six million martyrs: "That we Jews can never forget, but the Bible and the Prophets were written in Hebrew. When you talk this way, darling, I feel a little cruel for feeling as I do about Hebrew, but Hebrew is Hebrew and Yiddish is Yiddish."

David smiled. "You agree," he said, "but you really don't feel that Yiddish is very important."

"I suppose so, darling, but I really shouldn't feel as I do. Of course, in my home we spoke nearly always in Yiddish, and when I spoke in Hebrew sometimes my father didn't like it. I mean he felt that it was so holy a language that we should wait till the Messiah comes for us to have the right to talk Hebrew again. But, I suppose, we felt that the Jews were always Jews,

305

and wherever they were, they were still holy, I mean, why wait? That's one thing I liked about Mordecai, he argued with father about this, and he felt as I do. And Melech was the same. They were always Hebraists. And you know something, David?"

"What?"

"A big city like New York, so many Jews, more than in any other city in the world, and so few talk Hebrew, and only one Hebrew magazine, *Hadoar,* that's a shame, isn't it?"

"That part is true."

She smiled again and took hold of David's hand. "Oh, in a sense it doesn't make much difference, I suppose. Jews are Jews. I suppose I agree with what Mordecai once said, he has some good ideas. He said that what hurts him so much when he hears Yiddish is that it's not Jewish, he means that there are so many words from other languages, and that's true, isn't it?"

"It is, but it makes little difference," said David. "All languages borrow from other languages. English is made up of words from Latin and Greek and Saxon and French and Hebrew, too, I suppose, and I suppose from many other languages, but it's still English."

"Yes, but it's different with Hebrew," said Helen, and kissed David's hand. Then she said, "You know something, darling?"

"What?"

"You won't be angry with what I'm going to say?"

"No. Why?"

"You promise?"

"All right."

"In our Baruch Haba Company there is an actor, he's also a director, and a very nice man, he reads a lot, he knows many languages, he has traveled to many places, he really doesn't care for money, a very nice man, he knows the Talmud, he could almost be a rabbi, some of my friends think he once did study to be a rabbi, some say he is a rabbi, I mean he got *smiche* (ordination), you know. Well, he said something not so long ago, he says it many times, he said that America, even though it has more Jews than any other country has ever had in all Jewish history, still has no Jewish community, he means it has no community like there used to be in Russia and in Poland, and like there is, even, in England now, and you know, England has very few Jews. I'm poor at figures. I think England has only a half million Jews, maybe less. Anyway, what he said is that even in England and in the rest of Europe, especially, of course, in Eastern Europe, there is a real Jewish community, a *kehillah,* people feel they belong to the Jewish community, they are Jews, they live as Jews, there are Jews all around them, and they live as Jews, they feel at home most of the time, they do things and they don't do things simply because they are Jews. But here, in the United States, he said, it's so different, so very much different. There is no feeling that there is a Jewish *Kehillah,* there just isn't. There are many Jews, large areas where there are Jews, but no real intense Jewish feeling."

David had never thought of this. For years he had lived in the Jewish community in Boston, where everything seemed to be so Jewish, everything seemed to center about the synagogues and the Hebrew schools and the Jewish holidays and the doings in the Jewish world outside of Boston. People read the Boston English papers but they seemed to feel closer to what was printed in the Anglo-Jewish papers, they seemed to feel closer even to what they read in the Yiddish newspapers that were published in New York City. Yet there did seem to be something in what Helen was saying, though David didn't quite understand it.

"I don't know what to say," he said. "You may be right, but I'm not sure."

Helen smiled. "Darling, I know you would say that, and I'm not trying to make you feel funny about it. I mean I have said the same thing to the Tobiases and to others, and they have said the same thing that you are saying. But this isn't really what I started out to say, David. As a matter of fact, I've almost forgotten what I wanted to say. Oh, yes. But now I'm not sure I want to say it."

"Go ahead, Helen."

"Well, you and all American Jews are so much *Galut* Jews. You're Jews, and you're something else, and there is more of that something else, David, than there is of Jewish." She stopped and smiled.

"Why don't you go ahead?"

"Well, now that I've said it, I'm not so sure that what I have believed for a long time is true, isn't that funny?"

"I don't understand . . ."

"Well, it's simple and foolish of me, I guess. As I looked at you, darling, I saw I was wrong. That's funny. I thought I was right when I talked this way to Mary and the others, there was and there is more *Galut* in them than there is Jewishness, but you're different."

"What do you mean?"

"Well, you're different, and I mean it. For a while, to tell you the truth, I used to think that you were even more a *Galut* Jew than the Tobiases, but now I know I was wrong. You may not know it, but you're very, very Jewish, no matter how many Harvards you go to, no matter how many famous non-Jewish writers you deal with."

"And that's what I like very much," continued Helen. "That's why I love you." She began to smile, and looked at him happily.

"What are you thinking of, Helen?"

"Oh, something I've heard, a story. It's funny—and true."

"Tell me, Helen," said David, who was deeply drawn to her at this moment, for she was girl and wife and mother and human being and all the seasons and all the breezes and all the mornings and all the evenings and all the music of all instruments and of all voices, all of them in one . . . she was the comfort and the softness and the warmth and the hope and the joy of all living.

"It's a funny story, darling, but I think you'll like it. You know something, David?"

"What?"

"Maybe I shouldn't say it. Men are funny. You might think things that are not true. But . . ."

"Tell me, please, Helen."

"I will, but not everything, not now, anyway. I only meant that I feel so different about you, darling. I'm not afraid to tell you everything that comes to my mind. I feel so good with you, David, so very good."

"Was that what you wanted to tell me?"

"No. What I was thinking of is this. A girl told it to me.

308

A friend of hers, a writer, I forget his name, I read some of his things, and I didn't like them, so I forgot his name. He writes about Russia, and he doesn't know anything about Russia. He knows the outside things, not the soul of Russia, and he doesn't know Jews at all. He's very successful, because Americans know so little about Russia, if it sounds all right, people praise it, especially the stupid critics, and a man becomes famous and his book becomes famous, and then he is forgotten." She burst out laughing, but it was not a loud, offensive laugh, it was gentle and kind.

She continued. "This man was Jewish, of course. He lived with this Gentile girl, and I guess he was not so easy to live with. You know, nervous, always talking, talking late at night, and just making life hard for this quiet *shikse,* she wasn't used to this kind of life from a man. Always there was something doing in their home, there was arguing or fighting or loving, and always not quietly, but, you know . . . Jewish men."

"Yes."

"Well, they lived together for a year, no, it was almost two years, and then she couldn't stand it any more, and she left him, just left him. In a short while she married a nice Gentile man, very quiet, I think he was an accountant, or something. You know. He came home on time, washed his face, read the paper, the sports page, I guess, or the financial page, then had his supper, helped his wife wash the dishes, went to a movie with her, or they had people in, or they went visiting, and then went to sleep. A nice, quiet life, no quarreling, no shouting, no insulting, nice and quiet. He kissed her good-bye in the morning, and he kissed her hello or good evening when he came home at night, and he kissed her good-night in bed, on the mouth or the cheek"—at this she stopped and smiled.

She went on. "That's how it was for a few months. At the beginning she liked it, it was quiet, and she told all her friends. 'Thank God,' she said to them, 'now I'm living with a normal man, we're leading a normal married life, talking to each other like civilized people.' Her friends said nothing, they were glad and all that. Then they noticed that she was worried, this non-Jewish girl. They said nothing. After all, things happen between married people. But then they noticed that it was different, this unhappiness of hers. It lasted too long, it seemed more than just passing, you know. Then they noticed other things." She stopped.

"What are you thinking of now?" asked David, who had a hunch that she was thinking of her own marriage to Mordecai. He resented her thinking of Mordecai so often, and he was ashamed that he resented it.

"Oh," Helen said, "you know, Mordecai. Things creep into marriages, you hardly know they are there, and then you discover they were there a long, long time, little bits of sorrow and unhappiness and regret, you know."

"Yes," said David, as his heart sank from hurt and embarrassment and bewilderment at how he was feeling.

"Then her friends noticed that she would sometimes appear at parties or gatherings by herself, not with her husband, and she would say that her husband was busy with night work. It was tax time, and accountants are busy nights around then. But she appeared without him even after tax time, and slowly people didn't ask, and she didn't explain. And then suddenly she said or hinted that she and her husband weren't so happy, and finally she told everything: that she couldn't stand him any more, his quietness, his gentleness, his being normal, it was just driving her crazy. Well, so what do you think finally happened?"

"I can imagine."

"Of course. She divorced her husband and went back to the nervous Jew, and they'll probably be together for the rest of their lives. She'll be unhappy and happy, and miserable, but she'll love it, and she'll love him. Isn't that strange?"

"Yes," said David, spellbound by the sort of woman Helen was revealing herself to be: profoundly dedicated to Jewishness, intensely proud of it, almost a fanatical Hebraist, absolutely sure that the Jews would yet be a nation again . . . and always, even as she spoke about these things that were so dear to hear, always a loving and deeply sensuous woman . . . she would hold his hand often, put it to her mouth, caress his fingers, and caress his cheeks, and kiss him on his cheek . . . and when they were together in her apartment she would hug him and kiss him and feed him and kiss him again.

And there were days and there were nights, and there were

afternoons and there were mornings, and there were evenings when Helen and David found great happiness and deep contentment in each other . . . in each other's talk and in each other's smiles of concern and devotion . . . in each other's arms, and in each other's silences, and in each other's embraces at noon, and these embraces at noon had a loveliness all their own . . . and David learned what he had not known before, that there was a melody to each part of the day and each part of the evening and each part of the night . . . and he learned that every day and every night were so full of goodness and softness and warmth that it was a pity so much of each was wasted by neglect every day and every night.

David often wondered, but softly and quietly did he wonder, that all that had happened had happened naturally, as the day comes out of the night, and as the night comes out of the day, as a flower opens its petals to the sun, as a star makes itself known to the skies, as the summer glides into the autumn, and as the winter glides into the spring . . . and the goodness and fullness and contentment of all being were of marvels all compact.

And womanhood was the flower of nature and of all the seasons and of all the years and of all the nights and the days . . . woman was a constellation of all the glories, and the vast, singing silence of all time and infinity . . . and the damp softness and endearing quietude and assurance and sheer blessing of being that she was and the great and caressing richness of the earth and the air and the stars and the sun and the moon, these were all in her and around her, ready to be enjoyed and relished, ready to be blessed by taking in the manner that was ordained from of old, time back when God first kissed the earth. Woman was the largesse of the earth, the gift of time, the final expression of God's love for humankind. Woman was the healing oblivion of time, the deepest melody of space, the reason for all that cannot be explained, the answer to all the questions that beckon for answers, the logic beyond all logic, the mystery that clarifies even while it mystifies still more. Woman was the gentle sap in every tree and in every flower, woman was the sap in all the earth, was the kindness of eternity, the last and only eulogy and exequy. Woman was the blessing at the beginning of life, and the last caress at the end of life. Woman was youth and growth, maturity and the last vanishing, and woman was the inner song to them all. Woman was the last glad summation of eternity, and the last joyous benediction.

And wonderments and bewilderments came to David's mind, about so much that he had learned and read, about truths that were not true or only partly true, and about dreams that so many foolishly allowed to remain dreams . . . and he wondered about all the waste of emotion and of love and of the delirious gladness that love gives when a man and a woman give at the same time that they take . . . it is a strange union, he thought, a union achieved, so to speak, in passing from the world of prose to the world of poetry, and that union is the one happy oblivion that probably brings us closer to the abiding mystery of creation than does anything else in life . . . and he thought that perhaps this union, or its achievement, was a form of prayer and its immediate fulfillment . . . and he wondered about the writings of the world about love and about men and women, and he was astonished how little they had to say about what actually took place and about the glory that remained and about what that glory added to the daytime life, and what illumination it cast upon the whole world . . . the poems came closer to the reality, but they, too, did not truly get into the essence of the divine oblivion . . . perhaps it was impossible to get into that essence . . . perhaps the cliché of the artistic world was true, after all: that life itself was the greatest poem, and that all that art could do was to suggest the magnitude of that poetry. David wondered which of the arts was blessed with the ability to get closest to that oblivion . . . sometimes he thought it was music, sometimes he thought it was painting, sometimes he thought it was literature. . . . But he knew that not one of these arts could ever give the whole echo and the full, long unending aroma of the union of man and woman.

The sanctity of the body was a revelation to David . . . and so was the basic identity of the body with the mind and the heart and the soul . . . to say that body and mind were two was wrong, at best only an intellectual idea, not a truth of the senses and of the spirit . . . every kiss denied that there was a cleavage between them . . . they were different aspects of one truth, that was what the heart knew, what a union between man and woman proclaimed . . . the body, in any case, was as true as

312

the spirit . . . at times, perhaps, it was truer, even more spiritual than the spirit . . . an embrace, a giving-taking of bodies was the affirmation of spiritual giving-taking, in some way, probably, the essence of the spiritual giving-taking . . . in any case, the one confirmed the other, coalesced with the other, and this was the ultimate democracy, that of body and mind . . . so it had to be, for love without a woman's breasts and abdomen and thighs and arms and cheeks and neck and nose and eyes and fierce quiet kissing with all her holy orifices was hardly love, but something measured and discussed and alien, and not human and not spiritual . . . the body was the cosmic blessing of the spirit, and for the spirit, and the spirit was its seed, and this was the one unity of life, the blessing that issues from the fierce giving-taking of human love.

And each part of woman's body had its own music and its own language and its own independence as a holy province in the democracy of the body . . . and the music of each was a chamber music, soft and delicate and humble and eager for the company of the adjacent chamber music. The eagerness of each member of the body was a song of its own, and the sub-mission of each member was also a song, and the tender silence surrounding a woman in the embrace of love was the most ineffable song of all. And there was unending wonder in each and in the unity to which they all belonged, and this unity of woman's body reflected the unity of the body of the whole world without, reaching high into the heavens and deep into the earth . . . it was a unity that was heavy with the soft damp-ness that spelled the dark secrets not only of the earth but of all fecundity . . . it was a unity that was firm with hope of eternity, and with the promise of an unending future . . . every being, every man, every woman was a proof of immortality, but woman was the surest and most convincing proof of all . . . immortality was a woman, and woman was its full and complete reflection.

A woman spread out on a bed, with her head on a pillow, and her eyes bright with gratitude and promise, and her arms spread out from world's end to world's end was all that was needed to be assured of God and His blessings. A woman deliriously exhausted from love was all the silences of heaven fused into one loveliness. David wondered what impelled God

313

to create woman, for what special blessing? Or was she to be a constant reminder of the glory of God Himself? David's heart filled with delight, more and more, as the days passed and as the nights passed. Helen's home was his home, and his home was her home, and all New York was their home, and their absences were presences, and their presences were a continuing blending of quietness and soft serenity.

But soon a faint doubt entered David's mind, and he wondered what it was . . . and the doubt grew larger and began to gnaw at him, and still he didn't know what it was . . . and soon he realized that Helen knew of his disturbance, and he knew that she didn't ask him because she, too, wasn't sure of its nature . . . and the doubt grew larger and larger, and their embraces became a little tense, and their kisses became less and less delirious . . . and soon David was in doubt whether he should see Helen or stay in his room, and being alone became something to be desired.

And as the doubt grew Helen began to talk more and more about her son Azriel, and she began to reminisce more and more about her husband Mordecai . . . she had spoken little of her son and of her husband before . . . or, perhaps, thought David, she had spoken about them just as much but he had really not listened . . . or, perhaps he thought further, it was her talking about both of them during all that time of loveliness that had, unbeknownst to his conscious self, sowed the seeds of the doubt that was now causing a chill between them . . . and slowly the doubt became clearer to him, though it was still largely vague. He became annoyed with her talking about Azriel and Moredcai . . . and he became annoyed with his own annoyance. She spoke of her love for Azriel, and that was natural and proper, and she spoke of Mordecai's lack of a sense of responsibility, and she was probably correct, but why did she continue to talk about him, especially since she insisted that she wanted a divorce, that she had asked him for a divorce many times, but that he had said he still loved her, and he hoped that in time she would come to her senses? David was bewildered by his own resentment. He knew he had no logical reason for feeling as he did. After all, Azriel was Helen's son and Mordecai was still her legal husband. David kept on repeating this to himself, but no matter how many times he repeated it, he always ended up with the feeling of resentment.

Apparently his new relationship with Helen had created in him a new and strange sense of possession. Then he noticed that the relationship also created in Helen a sense of possession with respect to him. She asked him questions that he felt were his own concern, but that she felt she had a right to know the answers to. David himself felt that she had that right, and yet this, too, he resented. There was a time when David was having worries about his mother and father (both had been ailing), and he was also having troubles with the novel he was writing. David had spoken about these two troubles to her, and for a whole week she had asked him every day, on the telephone, or in person how matters were in Boston and how he was making out with his novel, whether the impasse had been surmounted. She asked because she was interested, and David was glad, as glad as he used to be, months before, when she had asked similar questions, but now there was something added to her asking: she seemed to think that he owed it to her to tell her. There was a day when he didn't feel like saying anything about anything, and she had asked him about his work, on his novel and in the office, where he was also having troubles, and he said tiredly, "Oh, all right . . ."

A few moments passed, and she said, "Well, aren't you going to tell me?"

"Tell you what?" asked David, who had forgotten what she had asked.

"Didn't you listen?"

"Of course, I was listening. Didn't I answer you?"

"You didn't."

"I though I did. I said all right, didn't I?"

"That wasn't an answer," said Helen.

"I thought it was," said David.

"That's the way to answer a child," she said. "I am interested, David, you know that. The least you can do it be polite."

"Wasn't I polite?" He went over to her suddenly, sincerely regretful that he had hurt her, though he wasn't altogether sure how he had hurt her. "I'm sorry. I didn't mean to be impolite, darling." He embraced her and kissed her. "I'm very sorry." David sensed that there was a reserve in Helen's kiss,

315

and he knew that the ardor he had put into his kiss was not entirely genuine . . . and he began to recall occasions of similar reserve on her part in the recent past, and he knew of his own hesitations when embracing her in the daytime and at night-time. Then there was a time when he had failed to call her one day and late that night she called him, asking if anything was wrong. He said no, there was nothing wrong, only he had been busy that day at the office and with some other things. Whereupon she reminded him that he had failed to call her one day the week before, "and I notice you are not in a hurry to call at any other time. You wait till late at night, and I wait up for your call. I do think, David, that's a little inconsiderate. I have a child, and I have to go out to buy things, and sometimes Azriel and I go to the movies, but I don't want to miss your call."

David apologized, and immediately resented his feeling of having to apologize . . . it made no sense, this feeling, yet it was there . . . more and more he realized how binding a kiss was . . . what had first appeared as something freely given now was becoming something of a transaction.

Again David said he was sorry. And he hoped that Helen would accept his apology and continue talking about something else, though at the moment he would have preferred if she simply said good-night. He still wanted very much to see her, and there were still times during the day when he desired her intensely, and during the night, when he wasn't with her, he often wondered whether he wasn't punishing himself needlessly by staying away from her even for one night . . . but he felt hesitant about calling her, he did not feel any more the eagerness of old, though his desire for her was still there.

David slowly began to feel that it was impossible for them to return to their old ways of friendship and loving, and this filled him with sadness. . . . something had gone out, something had come in . . . their relationship had ceased to heal and to caress, it had become an almost continuous state of stress and strain, punctuated by occasional fierce embracing, that was often sudden rather than the consummation of a prolonged and mounting yearning for each other . . . and there was hysteria in it, that only highlighted the chilly background against which it took place. And then she began to ask

316

him what he did at the office in the morning and what he did in the afternoon, and where he ate, and what he was planning to do the next week and the next month, and when he mentioned plans that had been turning over in his mind for some time, she wanted to know why he hadn't told her the first time these plans occurred to him . . . and he hesitated to tell her, and she noticed the hesitation, and she punctuated her distress by saying, "Don't you ever think of me?"

This made him realize that he thought of her more and more as one thinks of something to be combatted, and this made him still sadder, for he could not forget what had been between them, what loveliness and goodness and unbounded joy and delicious giving and taking, and what glorious mad oblivion had bound them together in an otherworldly sweetness . . . and once more he knew that this could not be again . . . love was a one-way caravan, once it retrogressed, it continued to retrogress, turnaround was forever.

At another time she asked why he didn't ask her about her husband, and he said, innocently, "What should I ask?"

"If he will finally give me a divorce," she said, looking intently at him.

The intent look frightened him, for it seemed to say something that was far removed from his mind. There had been fleeting moments in the past when the thought of marriage to her did occur to him, but they had never remained long with him, and now they were never with him.

"I really don't know him," said David, who didn't know what else to say. "I don't suppose he wants to give you a divorce."

"I saw him two days ago, and I think he will consent very soon," she said.

David wanted to say that it didn't matter to him what Mordecai had said. All he said was, "Oh . . ."

"Is that all you have to say?" she asked.

"What else do you want me to say?"

"Nothing, I guess."

Before the night was over they had apologized to each other for their rudeness to each other, and they embraced with a desire that was almost like of old, but soon thereafter the memory of what had taken place between them earlier in the evening inundated David's mind, and he believed that the

317

same memory had also come to Helen. They looked at each other, and there was a sadness between them, a sadness at what the passing days and the passing nights and the passing weeks and months and the passing seasons had done to their love.

Then Helen got complimentary tickets to a performance of a play by H. Leivick, the great Yiddish poet and playwright. She seemed excited, and David didn't quite know why, but he was glad. She was the Helen he had known many months before, she was now far distant from him, but it was a good distance, a loving distance, the same good and loving distance that had drawn them together originally. Now, too, distance was bringing them closer together, for the distance was creating a new and fresh and warm and tender intimacy between them. The new intimate distance had made her seem younger, put new color into her cheeks, and David was glad, and he knew that Helen knew he was glad, and she was glad, and in the subway to the theatre she took hold of his hand, and he was delighted. David wondered and wondered about the mystery of women, and about the mystery of the man-woman relationship, and he wondered if there was anything similar to it in the realm of the planets and of the eras of time, for, somehow, he had lately begun to think of them as persons: Ancient Times was a man, the Renaissance was a woman, the Biblical Period was a man, the Nineteenth Century was a man, the Twentieth Century was a woman up to about the time of the First World War, and then it became a man, and the period of the Second World War definitely was a man. And David thought about the planets and the satellites: Pluto was a man, Neptune, in spite of all the legends, was a woman, Venus, of course, was a woman, but Saturn was a man . . . and David wondered whether the relationships between the planets and the eras of time had within them the same bewilderments as the relationships between human men and women.

At the theatre Helen was even more her former self than she had been. She sparkled and gabbled like a young girl at her first opera or at her first "grownup" party.

"I just love the theatre, David, I just love it," she said.

"Yes. I'm glad."

She smiled. "You like it differently, darling. To you it's just

318

another thing to like, if it's good. But to me it's different, so very much different."

"How?"

"Oh, I just love it, I love it even when it's not so good, I just love being in a theatre. You know something, darling?"

"What?"

"In the theatre is the only real world, darling, the only one. Everything outside, in the street, in the daytime, everything is just shadows. Here you see the inside of the heart of every human being, here the heart dances and the soul sings."

"That's beautiful, what you're saying, Helen."

She took his hand and kissed it slowly. "The theatre is everything."

She continued holding his hand, and a warm and loving silence came between them . . . they were sitting on the far side of a row, Helen close up against the wall, and David, of course, next to her. David felt that while they were in the theatre, with many people walking in and about, both of them were yet in a little private cubicle of their own. Through the corner of his eye David saw Helen's face. He had never before seen it so full and so blooming and so happy.

Suddenly she relaxed her hold of his hand, and she put her hand on her own lap, and David noticed a hardness slowly come to her face, and he heard her pull in her breath deeply, as if it were a prolonged sigh.

David was surprised. He took hold of her hand, but she pulled it back to her lap.

"What is wrong, Helen?"

She didn't answer.

"What is wrong, Helen?"

Again she didn't answer.

Then David saw an elderly man, with a deep-lined face, a frayed collar around his neck, standing in front of them in the row directly before them.

David knew at once who the man was. His name was on his face and in his sunken eyes and in the helplessness around his mouth and in his thinning hair and in his drooping shoulders, and especially in his over-all pleading attitude. David wished the man would sit down, for he seemed tired and ill.

319

"Hello," said the man, facing Helen, and ignoring David.

"Hello," whispered Helen feebly.

"How are you?"

"Good."

"Azriel?"

"Good. This is my husband, Mordecai, this is Mr. David Polonsky."

David extended his hand, but Mordecai didn't notice it, or he chose not to shake hands with the man who was with his wife.

"I wish Melech the best of luck," said Helen.

"Thank you," said Mordecai.

This was the first time that David knew that Mordecai's brother was going to be in the play. Undoubtedly it was through him that she got the two complimentary tickets. David wondered why Helen hadn't told him about Melech. He began to feel that she had deliberately kept the information from him. Perhaps Helen was afraid, if she told David, he wouldn't go with her, and she wanted to see the play. Perhaps her deep secret joy of a few minutes ago was an attempt on her part to find happy oblivion in a faraway world—oblivion from her uneasiness at being in a theatre where her brother-in-law was going to play, and where she was afraid she might meet her husband. David felt himself engulfed in trickery and vague embarrassment. He wondered how he had ever got involved in this sort of thing.

Mordecai looked at Helen, as if from a distance. There seemed to be many things he wanted to say, and David had the idea that there was a shade of contempt in Mordecai's face, as he continued to look at his wife. Now David thought he also saw strength in his face, that Mordecai's face was not as cringing as it had appeared at the beginning. Yet, there was something unpleasant about Mordecai, and this unpleasantness seemed to be mixed with some sort of doom . . . not that Mordecai appeared doomed, but he seemed to be bearing news from the world of doom.

"It's a good play," said Mordecai, "I think it's a very good play." Then, for the first time, he turned to David and said, with sincerity and kindness, "Do you know the play, Mr. Polonsky?"

David was startled that Mordecai knew his name. David had thought that Mordecai had so completely ignored him that he had not even heard his name when Helen had introduced them to each other.

"No, I don't know this particular play," said David. "But I do know many of Leivick's poems, and I think they're wonderful. What he does with the Yiddish language nobody else has done, or, perhaps I should say, has quite done as he has. He lifts it to a high plane. I also like the poetry of Avrahm Reisin."

"Oh, he is marvelous," said Mordecai, with even more kindness spreading all over his face. "His poems are so sad and so beautiful. And his stories, you know his stories?"

"Yes. Especially one comes to my mind this minute. It's called *The Succeh.*"

"Oh that, it's wonderful," said Mordecai, and David thought he detected something in his voice that seemed to say, "You are more intelligent than I thought you were, you surprise me," and this feeling made David feel strange . . . and for a few moments he thought how nice it would be to invite Mordecai to sit down beside him and Helen, but then he realized how silly that would be.

"About Leivick," said David. "There's one poem of his that comes back to mind now, I don't exactly remember the title. I think it was called 'Snow,' how gentle snow is, how gently it covers up the dead, how sad and sorrowful it is."

"Yes, yes, of course, I think that's the title, too, 'Snow,' and it's marvelous, of course," said Mordecai. He became silent, then he said, "It's a shame he didn't write very much in Hebrew."

David couldn't help smiling, but he said nothing.

"Are you a Yiddishist?" asked Mordecai, softly.

"No, I wouldn't say that. I just happen to like Yiddish, and I think that there is a great literature in Yiddish. If Leivick wanted to write in Yiddish, then, I guess, that's all right. Bialik wanted to write in Hebrew, so he wrote in Hebrew, and I suppose . . . " David caught himself and for the first time realized that he and Mordecai had completely ignored Helen. David now looked at her, and he saw that her face had become white, almost ashen, and he wanted to ask her if she was ill, but he didn't.

"Well, it's a good play you'll be seeing." Mordecai now turned to Helen. "Melech was a little disappointed you didn't come to any of the rehearsals. He said he wrote to you and he called you."

"I was so busy," said Helen. "Besides, Azriel had a little cold for a few days."

David knew at once this wasn't so.

"Oh," said Mordecai. "I didn't know. He never told me he had a cold when I spoke to him on the telephone. He's better now, isn't he?"

"Yes," said Helen.

There was a silence, during which Mordecai's mind seemed to be far away, even though he was looking at Helen. David, through the corner of his eye, noticed that Helen was not looking at her husband, but to the side . . . David didn't know what to say or what to do . . . for a moment he wanted to say to Mordecai, "Take my seat. You really belong here," but of course he didn't.

Then Mordecai said, "Well, I think I better go."

"All right," said Helen softly.

Mordecai turned to David. "I'm glad I met you, Mr. Polonsky."

After Mordecai had gone, Helen and David were silent. Both were laden with uneasiness. Helen was looking down at her lap. She raised her head, and a semblance of calm came to her face.

"The play should be starting soon," she said.

"Yes."

"That's one thing I don't like about Jewish plays," she said. "They start on time only occasionally." She laughed awkwardly.

"Yes."

"It's different in other theatres, I mean with plays on Broadway, you know."

"Yes."

"I hope it starts soon."

"Helen, why didn't you tell me that Melech was in the play?"

"I don't know. I didn't think it was important. After all, what difference does it make it he's in or if somebody else is in?"

David said nothing.

"Did it really matter to you?"

"Well, it did, now that you ask."

"Would you have come just the same if you knew? Does it make that difference?"

David said nothing.

"Does it make that difference? Why don't you answer me?"

"It does make a difference," said David, "a big difference."

"Don't talk so loud."

"I didn't know I was talking loud. But it does make a difference, it just does."

"You're still talking loud."

David lowered his voice. "There's something about all this that is strange. I wish I had known."

Helen said nothing.

"Your husband is a very nice man. I felt like asking him to sit down with us, and meet us later, and just sit down."

"You really felt that way?"

"Yes, I did. Very much so."

"Oh."

"I like what he said, the way he talked, everything," said David.

"You did?"

"Yes."

The curtain went up, but David hardly knew what was taking place or what was being said. It seemed to him that everybody was looking at him, judging him silently. The only one who wasn't looking at him was Mordecai—he was looking straight at the play, which was all he was interested in . . . slowly David began to feel as if he were in some barrel of refuse, out of which his head was sticking . . . people were passing him by, saying nothing . . . not far off was another barrel, also filled with refuse, out of which Helen's head was sticking, and people were also passing her by, saying nothing . . . and David recalled that he had been in doubt whether he should go with Helen to this play, he had no specific conscious reason, but there was hesitation deep within him . . . and he recalled that he had always felt em-

323

barrassed when they walked together in the street, especially when Helen put her arm in his, which was often.

He recalled more and more, and he began to feel that Helen had enticed him into all his present entanglement, by saying a little more than was true, and by leaving out much that he should have been told. David wondered whether he was, so to speak, taken in because he was so unversed in such matters, but then he recalled, through his reading, that men infinitely more versed in such matters had also been taken in.

Helen had been keeping silent, as the play was progressing, and he was sure that she was preoccupied pretty much as he himself was. She had tricked him, in many ways, and yet what impelled her to do what she did was her own seeking for peace of heart, and for delight. The disappointments of life make all people somewhat calculating. Life is not fair. At times it seems to be on the side of those who play tricks. Helen was only as other people.

David didn't know how to feel, he didn't know what to think . . . he was trying to be just to everybody . . . he wanted to kiss and to comfort Helen, to tell her that he understood why she had done and not done certain things, but he also wanted to tell her that she had hurt him by what she had done and failed to do. David wasn't sure how she would accept his statements . . . David wanted to shake Mordecai's hand and to spend time with him in the park and in restaurants, and be his friend . . . but how could David achieve all this? David's heart filled more and more with sorrow and bewilderment and with embarrassment and with a sense of being squeezed tighter and tighter in some vise . . . suddenly the curtain rose, the lights burst into brightness, and there was an intermission, and a new heaviness came to David's heart, for now his sorrow and his regret and his sense of engulfment became more and more intense. Through the corner of his eye he saw that Helen's eyes were red.

Thirteen

The *World* continued to flounder. Circulation went down and down, and advertising followed it. But Simmons persisted in holding on to it, and in believing that somewhere there was an editor who could save it. Without telling Bly—who had had the title of editor for many months—Simmons had been looking for a successor. Away from the office, he would denounce Bly in his own slippery way: "He's a fine man, I have nothing against him personally. They don't come any better than he is. And he's a fine editor, too, he has many ideas, he is conscientious. But he's not for the *World*. He's for a more popular type of magazine. He's too good for the *Red Book* or even the *Ladies Home Journal,* much too good for them, but he just isn't made for the *World*. Nothing would make me happier than to get him placed properly. Of course, I wouldn't dream of letting him go without first seeing to it that he gets himself well placed. But he's not for the *World*. It's not a criticism of him that he isn't for the *World,* not at all. It's not a criticism of me, for example, that I'm not made to be a dancer or a prize fighter."

Slowly Simmons began to reveal his feeling about Bly to Bly himself. He began by arguing with him about basic ideas. Bly had suggested that he try to get a series of articles on "The Re-Evaluation of Current Values," a series dealing with dominant values in education, religion, business, the entertainment world, journalism. He said to the whole editorial board, "I have the feeling that we are now going through pretty much the same upheaval in morals and in general values that we did during and after the First World War, and this time it may be worse. I don't really know exactly what I mean, but I feel it. We had the minister over the house the other night, I should say he came over, we're not such good church-goers, but we belong, and, of course, the children go to Sunday school, and we go on Easter and Christmas. Anyway, he's a nice sort, Dr. McAlpin is his name, and he said that psychologists and sociologists are very much afraid of the new growing temper of the country and of the world.

"The A-bomb has made people feel that life is not eternal on earth, as they used to think, you know, life will go on and on. Now they feel that any hour all the countries may blow themselves to bits. Because—and here I think he's right, absolutely right—we have the bomb now, but soon the Russians will have it, and so will the English, and so will the French, and now there'll be only one more war. I mean, or rather he means, that two or three bombs can wipe out a whole nation in a few minutes, and what one country can do another country can do just as well, or soon will be able to, so there you have it. We're all living on top of a volcano, Dr. McAlpin says, and that's a nice, I mean, a horrible way of putting it. In other words, he says, there's going to be despair everywhere, and that will mean immorality, hopelessness, and it will affect business relations, marriage, literature, writers will probably write about mean and cruel things and sneer at old values, and so on. Dr. McAlpin said that some professor, I don't know his name, Dr. McAlpin himself didn't remember it, he said all this, this professor. And I thought that we could get the jump on other magazines by running a series on that, you know top men, Dr. Fosdick in religion, Dr. Fishbein in medicine, maybe Van Wyck Brooks in literature, I don't know this Brooks man, but my wife seems hot about him, anyway, that's my idea."

Betty Garde liked the idea very much and said so. So did Peter Goldstein and Kermit Stern. James Dawson also thought

326

it would be a good idea "from a circulation standpoint. It seems to have homey appeal."

Lester Simmons, however, was not only in doubt; he was sarcastic in his objection. "Hell," he said, "that's long hair stuff. Nobody will read any series like that. Who cares about moral temper of the times and all that kind of stuff? We print that stuff, and we can all look for a job. We need something lively, something like what *Life* magazine prints."

"But the *World* isn't *Life*," said Betty Garde. "I think Bly has a good idea, and we ought to try it."

"I see nothing in it," said Simmons.

Clarice, Simmons's wife, inclined to agree with Betty. "What harm can there be in trying, dear?"

"A waste of time and space and money," Simmons said.

"Why?" persisted Betty. "We all agree, except you. Are we all crazy?"

"I'm against it," said Simmons.

"That's funny," began Betty.

"What's funny?" asked Simmons.

"What's funny is this," said Betty. "We tried your health series idea, and it was a dud, like most of us said it would be. Well, that's in the past. Now we have an idea, Bly's idea, that we all think is worth trying, and you say no, and you don't give any reasons."

"I gave my reasons," said Simmons.

"I have an idea," said Clarice.

"What?" asked Simmons.

"I admit I think Bly's idea is a good one. But, of course, it could be a failure. So, why not just go out for an article in say, the re-evaluation of educational ideas, or literary ideas, or religious ideas, without saying it will be a series, and we'll see how it works out. If it works out, we can say it's part of a series."

"That looks like a good idea to me," said David, who really was not very much interested in what was being said, but he felt he had to say something. "I think Dr. Fosdick might be got to do the article on religion, he seems to have definite ideas on just about what Bly said, and he writes well." Suddenly a fresh idea occurred to David. "We could also have a series on the Jews."

327

"Are you gone completely insane?" asked Simmons. "Do you want the *World* to become like the *Jewish Daily Forward?* Is this a popular magazine or some academic, long-hair magazine, or are we a Jewish magazine?"

"I only meant," said David, who now liked his idea very much, "I only meant that the whole world realizes what a terrible thing happened to the Jews in Europe, and that's a world subject, and an authoritative series, covering every angle, could get us considerable readership, not just Jews, but everybody. After all, when five or six million people are annihilated, no matter what they are, Jews or Eskimos, that's of world importance. Besides, there are more than two million Jews, or almost that many in New York alone, and about three million or so in the rest of the country and that kind of readership is not to be minimized."

"I like that, too," said Betty Garde.

"It sounds good to me, dear," whispered Clarice.

"No, I don't see it at all," said Simmons. "I just don't see it at all. Nobody is interested in the Jews, I mean, it's not a subject for a magazine like the *World*."

"I think it's a good idea, too, David's idea," said Bly. "As a matter of fact, there's no reason why we can't run both ideas in the *World*. The more I think of it the more I am excited."

"Now I know it's bad idea," said Simmons, and quickly caught himself. "I didn't mean it that way. It's just a bad idea, this and the re-evaluation series."

"Then what do you suggest?" said Betty Garde.

"That's what you people are here for," said Simmons.

There was an ominous silence in the office.

"We're going down hill in everything, in circulation, in advertising, people aren't reading us, that's all, they're not reading us, and unless we do something, we'll have a magazine without readers," said Simmons.

Still the others kept silence.

"We need lively ideas," said Simmons, "and we need them in a hurry. Anything at all. The way I feel, I feel almost like printing another mystery story, like the one we printed by Dagobert Prunye some months ago. It was a mystery story, but it got us circulation, readers, that's what we need, and, I tell you again, we need it in a hurry."

"Really, dear," said Clarice, "really, why don't we think a little more about Bly's idea and David's idea? They both look good to me, especially David's idea. Everybody is discussing what happened to the Jews, how terrible it is, everybody. It's not because I, we, are Jewish, but it is a world issue. You yourself said in the Temple only last week, where they asked you to talk about current events, you yourself said that the Jewish issue is more than a Jewish issue. It's a world issue."

"Oh, what I said then doesn't matter," said Simmons.

"Why doesn't it matter, dear?"

"It doesn't matter, that's all," said Simmons. "I was just talking, they asked me to talk, and I thought it would be good publicity for the *World*."

There was a stony silence, as this bit of self-revelation of Simmons's character sank into the minds of the others. Clarice looked down at her lap in embarrassment.

"We could publicize the Jewish series in all the temples and synagogues, and in all the churches, too," said James Dawson, the circulation-advertising man. "The churches are interested, too. They look upon what happened in Germany and in all of Europe when all those millions of Jews were burned to death, they look upon it as a failure of Christianity."

"That's true," said Bly. "Dr. McAlpin said the same thing. The more I think of it the more do I think David's idea is really hot for circulation and for everything, it's just good for the *World*."

Simmons turned to Clarice, his face red. "Whose side are you on? Their side or mine?"

Again there was a silence. It mounted and whirled around the room and filled it with a cloud of embarrassment. Finally, Bly said, "Well, we don't have to settle the business this minute, so why not postpone the discussion for the next time?"

"No," said Simmons, "we should discuss it more now. I want to tell you frankly that we simply must do something now, or I just don't know what will happen with the *World*."

"I don't know, I mean, I don't understand your whole attitude, Lester," began Betty Garde slowly but with belligerence plainly in her voice. "I don't understand your whole attitude. You're acting like a bull in the china shop. Some very good ideas have been suggested, especially by Bly and

David. And by the way, the more I think of it the more do I agree with Bly, that the two ideas, the series on the Jews and the series of re-evaluations, sort of tie in with each other. Because, well, they're all saying it now, the Christian ministers and the Jewish rabbis and just people, I read about it in the *Times* on Monday morning, when they print the reports of some sermons, I mean that what's happened in Europe, I mean what's happened to the Jews, and the way people have almost forgotten about it already, only three years after the war, less than three years, only two years after, really, even less than that, but people have already forgotten, or almost forgotten, and that alone proves something about the decline in morals and general values. And people feel it all over, I feel it wherever I go. There's a kind of despair in homes and living rooms, and the college kids talk about it. The college kids are reading Sartre and Camus, two Frenchmen, and you should see what these writers say: nothing matters, wine, women, and song, for the A-bomb may hit you. Anyway, so I think we ought to try to do both series. If you don't want to take too much of a chance, though I can't see that there would be any chance, we have to print something anyway . . . " Suddenly she stopped, and looked at Clarice, as everybody else, except Simmons, was doing . . . Clarice apparently was trying to control herself from crying or bursting out with some comment.

"No," said Simmons. "I don't see it at all. I'm still thinking about doing another mystery story or two, by Pruyne, or somebody else, just to get the circulation up."

"This I oppose, I oppose it strenuously," said Bly. "It would kill the magazine."

"How can you kill something that is already dying?" said Simmons.

"I don't think that's kind or intelligent," said Betty Garde. "I like mystery stories, I'm not snooty about them, but there's a time and place for everything. Might just as well run a series on the love life of Rita Hayworth, all the movie fans would read it, and then drop the magazine like poison, and the few advertisers we have left would drop out in the meantime. That kind of circulation is not good."

"I don't know what to say," said Simmons, standing up.

"We're in a hell of a fix. The magazine, in Brandt's day, had some standing, even towards the end, but now it's nothing. I don't think a mystery serial or two would hurt us, I really don't, but you fancy people don't think so. Well, we'll see. I'll look around." And he left the room.

Eventually Simmons did give his permission for Bly to start the re-evaluation series, but he still hesitated about the series on the Jews, simply because, to use his words, "That's not for us, that's for some Christian outfit to do. After all, everybody knows I'm Jewish and . . . well, that's for the Christians."

David didn't understand this sort of argument. "What's wrong in a magazine owned by a Jew discussing a Jewish matter, or, rather, a matter that has to do with the Jews directly but otherwise is really of world-wide importance?" And David asked what Simmons would think of The *New York Times* if it deliberately minimized Jewish news simply because Adolph Ochs, and the present publisher, Arthur Hays Sulzberger, were Jews.

"But that's different," said Simmons. "A newspaper is a newspaper, and a magazine is a magazine. In a newspaper news about Jews is buried in the rest of the paper, but in a magazine, it stands out."

He refused to discuss the matter further. But some weeks later he came to the office and called a special editorial meeting. He had gone the day before to a meeting of an advertising organization, of which most of the members were non-Jewish, and they had discussed the murder of six million Jews by Hitler, and, as Simmons said, "They were really upset."

Betty Garde smiled. "What did you expect them to do? Bust out laughing? My God, I begin to wonder if what my rabbi says isn't true, about me and all of us, or most of us, that we're ashamed of ourselves, hold ourselves like *nebiches,* afraid to admit our existence, and are so grateful when some *goy* admits that we are alive. Isn't that right, Bly?"

Bly smiled. "As a Christian, I am free to talk objectively. I agree with what Betty said. And I still think, now that we're at it, that we should start the series that David suggested."

"Well," said Simmons, "I confess I was surprised by what I heard at the advertising meeting, I was really surprised, and

I heard things that really made my hair stand on end . . . how they used to burn Jews, little children and women, naked women, and old men, burn them in big furnaces, and how they used to skin some Jews alive just to get the skin for lamp shades for some pervert of a Nazi woman or general, and how they made many young Jewish girls become prostitutes, forced prostitutes, some of them committed suicide rather than go to bed with the Nazis, and then the Nazis watched them closely, I mean those that hadn't killed themselves yet, and then they, well, they raped them, that's what it amounted to, and after these poor Jewish girls had served their purposes for a month or so, they'd throw them in the furnaces. It makes you sick to hear all that."

"But didn't you know all that?" asked Betty Garde.

"Yes," said Goldstein, "It's been in the *Times* day in and day out for months and years."

"I know," said Simmons, "but . . . "

David couldn't control himself any longer. "You knew it, but you didn't believe it because you wanted to forget about it. And you didn't believe it till you heard Christians discuss it with emotion and with feeling. It's really pretty terrible."

To the surprise of all, Simmons didn't flare up, but said slowly, "That could be, that really could be. I've been doing a lot of thinking."

David was not altogether astonished by what Simmons had revealed about himself. He had heard, at the Tobias home and elsewhere, about the phenomena of self-shame and self-hate among some Jews. Lately David had been reading more and more novels about Jewish life by Jews and non-Jews. He also met several Jewish writers and scholars of note, listened to them, watched them, and he compared what he heard and saw with what he used to hear and see. In his college days and later, when he first came to New York, and later, till about the time of the Second World War and during the war, being a Jew, among some Jews, was something one had to struggle, openly or otherwise, to accept, as a part of one's reality, as a handicap to be conquered. David felt that Jewishness had been a burden especially among "worldly" ones, the college men and women, and those men and women who, while they didn't go to college, were subjected to more or less the same influences at adult education courses. David recalled the various facets of this burden as he saw it in his uncles and aunts and in his classmates at Harvard and in Stock, the former publisher the *American World,* and in Jennings, the music critic, and even, deep in his soul for a while, in Dryfus. David knew that, in some way or other, he had had a little of this burden himself . . . but no, he added to himself, he never had self-shame and self-hatred and any inferiority in so far as his Jewishness was concerned: what he had was a conflict of interest between Judaism and Americanism, and subconsciously he had always tried to integrate them somehow, and then he tried to do so in full consciousness.

Jewishness was something many Jews had to come to terms with, a form of adjustment that was absent to non-Jews. A Jew, therefore, was doubly burdened: he bore the usual burden of humanity and he bore the additional burden of Jewishness . . . *Dos Pintele Yid* was in constant conflict with *Judenschmerz.* This was a major element of "the Jewish attitude." David knew that many anthropologists and psychologists made light of "the Jewish attitude," and in so far as their young sciences were concerned, they were perhaps right in saying that, scientifically speaking, there is little ground for talking about "the Jewish attitude." But David knew that there was plenty of ground for assuming its reality.

At first David was angry with Simmons for what he had revealed about himself, but the more David thought about him the more he realized that Simmons was more to be pitied than criticized. As these thoughts revolved in David's mind and heart he was filled with mounting admiration for the relatively lonely rabbis and community workers and Hebrew school teachers who, through all the centuries of this self-shame and self-hatred, kept the flame of Jewishness burning. It really made little difference whether they were Orthodox or Conservative or Reform, whether they were Yiddishisten or Hebraisten, whether they were secularists or Labor Zionists or Mizrachi Zionists, whatever they were, they still were men and women who had earned the eternal gratitude of Jewish history.

As always lately, when he was in inner turmoil, he sought for comfort and encouragement at the home of the Tobiases.

He came there one night with Dryfus, and he found there
Helen and Ludwig Lewisohn and a man, Loring Weber, a
newspaper man and playwright. David was delighted to see
Ludwig Lewisohn. He had been reading him lately and was
enormously impressed by him, but the nature of the impression
was a strange one. David didn't think very highly of the
artistic quality of Lewisohn's work, especially of Lewisohn's
novels and the stories about the Jews. He thought they were
more editorials than stories. David was embarrassed by the
apparently racist theories behind these stories and novels:
Lewisohn seemed to be saying that the Jews were superior
to all other races, and that Jewish women were better lovers
and wives and mothers than were non-Jewish women.

At the same time David thought very highly of Lewisohn's
two major novels about non-Jews (though there were some
Jewish characters in them), namely, *The Case of Mr. Crump*
and *Stephen Escott*. In both these novels Lewisohn delved
deeply in woman's psychology and into the soul of the South,
and David inclined to agree with the views of Thomas Mann
and Sigmund Freud that both were major works of the literary
art. In short, David was inclined to rate his non-Jewish
fiction more highly than his Jewish fiction, and this worried
David, for Lewisohn, at the time, was considered the major
fictional spokesman for American Jewry. David was awed
to be in his presence.

For a while David wished that he did not come this night
. . . he wasn't prepared for this state of affairs . . . at the
same time he didn't want to keep quiet in the presence of a
man who had given him so much pleasure and whom he
considered of outstanding importance in the contemporary
Jewish world . . . David couldn't very well praise Lewisohn's
Jewish fictional works, at the same time he wanted very
much to tell Dr. Lewisohn how much his *Upstream* and
Stephen Escott and *The Case of Mr. Crump* meant to him
. . . Dr. Lewisohn, of course, would be pleased, but at
the home of the Tobiases he would want also to be praised
for his Jewish fiction, and David couldn't do this with
honesty. As the minutes ticked off, David was more and more
at a loss what to say or do . . . he began to think about Lewisohn's excellent dramatic criticism in the *Nation* and about

his fine writings about Goethe and other German poets and dramatists . . . but there came back to him, over and over again, the deep meaning of *Upstream,* that David had read three times, and that impressed him more and more.

Upstream, David felt, was a major autobiography, in English literature as well as in the literature, in English, about American Jews . . . there was profound understanding in it, and deep pity for the lot of the human race, but, above all, David felt, the book was an almost perfect portrait of the lost generation of American Jews, the Jews who had been ashamed of Jewish traditions, who had wandered off to other isms, such as socialism and communism, and Community Churchism and vegetarianism, and found them all cold and devoid of all comfort, and had at long last come "back home." . . . David looked upon the book as the best answer to all Jews who wanted to hide their background, who insisted that the only worthy object of worship was humanity.

David looked at Lewisohn intently. He was a short man, but with an imposing face and penetrating eyes. David saw vast learning in that receding forehead. He saw a sensitive man, a man who could be generous but one who also could be cruel. David sensed that Lewisohn was still, in his innermost being, troubled, and David wondered whether this commotion was not, in some strange way, behind Lewisohn's racist theories about the Jews. David was in a state of conflict as to what to think about and say to Lewisohn. He wanted to tell him how much he loved his work, and he wanted to tell exactly what doubts he had about the Jewish novels and short stories. And he wanted to say, "Please, Dr. Lewisohn, tell me truthfully and fully, exactly what you think about the Jewish world in America, and tell me also what you would order if you had a say in the organization of the whole world: would you choose to be a Jew, or would you choose to be a, well, a cosmopolite, a devotee of humanity?"

David couldn't help wondering about Lewisohn's marital difficulties. Many had sneered at Lewisohn's inability to choose a woman who was suitable for him, some had called him childish, but David had not been able to do anything but be sorry for Lewisohn, and often, when he thought about Lewisohn in this regard, David had much respect for him.

335

Lewisohn, it seemed to David, only had more courage than did other men, who got tired of their wives. Sometimes the men were to blame, sometimes the women were to blame, but what should one do when it became apparent that both partners to the marriage had made a mistake? The fact remained, however. Many homes were no more than masks for unhappy marriages. Lewisohn only made public his unhappiness.

Besides, since his experience with Helen, David had become still more bewildered about the man-woman relationship. It seemed to him to be a bottomless mystery, a trap for both the wary and the unwary, the source of much delight and also the source of much heartache and regret. Obviously not even the wisest were able to cope with the mystery. Socrates himself knew what a mistake he had made—yet, one had to assume, that for a while, surely before their marriage, he and his wife had been happy. Tolstoy knew he had made a mistake, but both he and his wife admitted that they were gloriously happy in the early years of their marriage. Shakespeare made a similar mistake. Either the bliss of marriage palled quickly, or in marriage the real person came forward—and that real person was deliberately or otherwise concealed during courtship, because of the eagerness of all, especially women, to get married, and all means toward that end were considered fair.

Lewisohn was pulling thoughtfully on his cigarette, his mind apparently far away. Suddenly David heard Helen saying, "I think Chassidism is wonderful, the music, the dancing, the songs, everything. I sometimes think that the Chassidim stand for something very beautiful in Judaism, perhaps more so than do the philosophers, some of whom I don't really understand, but I understand and love the Chassidim, even though I don't agree with them, in some things."

"I have seen the Chassidim dance and sing in Brownsville, in Brooklyn," said Mary Tobias, "Raphael and I, and we were greatly impressed."

"Aren't they like Holy Rollers," said Loring Weber the newspaper man, "like the hillbillies in the South, in the Ozarks?"

"There were several Chassidic groups in Philadelphia," said Dryfus. "Some of them were rather friendly with the younger women, but I find it hard to object to that. Now you all know everything that I know about these people."

"My father is a Chassid," said David, "and I have heard him sing some of their songs, and they're lovely. He has spoken to me about them many times, and I'm very much interested. The founder of the movement, Ba'al Shem Tov, was a very great man."

Dr. Lewisohn seemed to awaken from his trance. "Yes, a very great man," he said. "Ba'al Shem Tov was one of the brightest figures in modern Jewish history. He liberated Jewishness from the dryness of some of the scholars, and he brought it back to the folk. Besides, as Dr. Martin Buber, the great German-Jewish scholar, has pointed out in his classic study of Chassidim, these men, or, rather Ba'al Shem Tov, reminded the Jews that there were various ways of knowing God, by the intellect, but also by the heart, the soul, and that was a good thing, a very fine thing. The Chassidim brought back the song to the Jewish faith. Of course, it was always there, and always will be there, but sometimes it is under-emphasized. Then there is something else about them that I like. It's their insistence upon Orthodoxy, to put it simply and, perhaps I should add, bluntly. What is needed now is to return to the 613 *mitzvoths,* to *kashruth,* to prayer three times a day, and the other wonderful commandments and regulations of traditional Jewish life. There has been too much thinning out of religious belief among the Jews, much too much. It is significant that men like Dr. Franz Rozenzweig felt that, by and large, the elements of Orthodoxy, that these are what is most needed in Judaism now, they alone can fructify it."

Dryfus said, "That makes me a *goy.* I always thought that Judaism was the only form of religious atheism. That is what I like about it. I don't have to believe anything, yet I can be a believing Jew." He looked at David. "Isn't that what you told me?"

David smiled. "Not exactly." Through the corner of his eye he noticed that Helen was looking at him tenderly and smiling . . . he wondered if she had known he was coming this evening. They hadn't spoken to each other for three days. They had had no quarrel, but their relationship was cooling somewhat. He wasn't sure that he had done right by allowing it to cool. At the moment she seemed very lovely in her aloneness, and her warmth and softness and her aroma came back to his memory. He began to wonder what she would think of Dryfus, whom she had not seen before, and what he would think of her. David thought they would like each other, but that somehow they wouldn't get along, and yet, thought David, had Helen and Dryfus met, say, twenty years before, or fifteen years before, they would have probably fallen in love with each other.

"I like the phrase religious atheism," said Mary Tobias.

"I'm sorry, but I disagree," said Lewisohn. "Religious atheism hardly befits Judaism, it doesn't even remotely describe it. Further, it takes entirely out of account the concept of *Atoh Shebochartonu,* Thou Who hast chosen us, the concept of the Chosen People. We Jews are different, in our appearance, one could even say, in our emotional constitution, in our whole *Weltanschauung.* I think, for example, that a Jewish woman not only makes a better lover than a non-Jewish woman, but a better mother. I should say that is pretty well admitted by all people."

"I don't admit it," said Dryfus. "What you say, Dr. Lewisohn, makes me think of Ku Kluxism in reverse."

"If that's what you wish to think, think it," said Lewisohn rather tartly. "I take it you are a Reform Jew."

"No," said Dryfus. "If I'm anything I'm Orthodox, for my people come from Spain, Spanish Jews, and I guess they're Orthodox."

"But do you practice your Orthodoxy?" asked Dr. Lewisohn.

Mary Tobias was getting worried. "Oh, this is not a seminary. Not one of us is as good a Jew as he should be, but, as my father used to say, a Jew is a Jew."

Lewisohn wouldn't let go. "There is such a thing as being too tolerant, too liberal. Reform Judaism or Liberal Judaism or non-practicing Judaism is not what has kept the Jews alive for two thousand years. We would have been assimilated long ago if Reform or Liberal Judaism had prevailed."

"I don't know about that," said Loring Weber. "It could be the other way around, if there had been no Reform or Liberal Judaism, there probably would have been even more assimilationism. I know I couldn't remain a Jew if I had to accept what my grandfather believed in. Besides, I thought that Judaism was more than dogma, that it was a system of ethics mostly."

"It's not ethics that has kept us alive," said Lewisohn with apparent dismay at what he had just heard. "The Chinese religion is mostly ethics, and look where they are."

"They're doing better than the Jews," interrupted Dryfus. "They have a country, it's in trouble, but it's a country, and that's more than we got."

"Oh, well," said Lewisohn, obviously eager to put an end to this kind of argument. "Besides, I have to go. My wife will scold me if I stay up too late. I have to take all kinds of injections." He stood up. "It's not nice getting old."

"I'm sorry," said Mary Tobias. "Can't you stay a little longer?"

David was still astonished that Lewisohn was so short a man. He also looked rather pathetic, with his little paunch, his high forehead, and his short arms.

Lewisohn patted Mary on the arm, "Age is age," he said. "I don't know too much Latin, but this I do remember, from Horace: '*Eheu! fugaces, Posthume, Posthume, labuntur anni; nec pietas moram rugis et instanti senestae afferet, indomitaeque morti.* Alas, Posthumas, Posthumas, the years fly fast, nor can piety ward off wrinkles, or advancing age invincible death.'"

"Oh, Ludwig," said Mary Tobias. "It's not that bad, I mean you look fine. Stay a little longer, please, you only just came."

"You say *a little longer*. It reminds me of a line by Longfellow, 'I stay a little longer, as one stays / To cover up the embers that still burn.' And you know what the sad part is, Mary?"

"What?"

"That I can't say with Joel Chandler Harris, 'I am in the prime of senility.'"

"A little more tea, Ludwig?" pleaded Mary.

"No, thank you very much. I really have to go."

After he had gone, Dryfus said, "Maybe I shouldn't say it, but I think he's a fanatical pedant. I had heard of the great

Lewisohn, and here he was. And something else I would like to say, since I have already said insulting things: I think he's no more Jewish than I am. But wait. I'm Jewish, plenty Jewish, but I don't believe in all those regulations, kosher and all that, and in spite of all that Lewisohn said, I don't think he cares so much about those things either, it's just a talking point."

"What do you mean by a talking point?" asked David.

"You ask the most academic questions," said Dryfus. "A talking point is a talking point, as obvious as that, my dear professor."

"I still want to know what you mean by a talking point," said David.

Dryfus smiled. "I really don't know what I mean. But I have a funny feeling about that man. Listen to me, ladies and gentlemen. He's a disappointed man. He's a lover of German culture, and if the *goyim* had done the right thing by him, right in his eyes, that is, and made him a professor of literature, as he wanted and as they should have, he would be a better Jew."

"I love that man," said Mary Tobias, looking at Dryfus. "Now tell us what you mean."

"I mean he wouldn't be so fanatical. He wouldn't feel he has to prove his Jewishness after more than forty years of being away from the Jews, not being Jewish. He's a walking tragedy, that's what he is, and I love him. *Upstream* is a wonderful book, perhaps his best book. His other things look like hocus-pocus to me, away from the stream of life, fit only for colleges and universities. You see, life is half and half. Half is life, the other is museum stuff, university stuff. And that's where the tragedy of Lewisohn lies."

"What do you mean by that?" asked Weber.

"Well," began Dryfus, "I don't exactly know, but I do know. Poor Lewisohn, and forgive me for talking this way about a man who knows more in this little finger than I will ever know, poor Lewisohn, and I repeat he's a great man, he's as important as Brandeis, in my book, poor Lewisohn is now in the life part of life, and he's talking damn nonsense, I mean his Orthodoxy. But I'm glad he's in the life part of life, otherwise he'd be writing another book on Goethe, and

I'm not so sure Goethe is worth another book. Do I make any sense?"

"I think you make lots of sense," said Raphael Tobias, "a lot of sense. I love Ludwig, he comes here whenever he's in town, though he hasn't been here for months, and we missed him, he has pretty bad diabetes, but I was always sorry for him. I think he's better than he talks. But he's done a lot of good for the Jews, and that's good."

"That's very good," said Dryfus . . . and David noticed that Helen was looking intently at Dryfus, obviously liking him, and David was glad. At this moment David was seized with a desire to embrace Helen and kiss her and tell her that he had been foolish in being so aloof from her the past few days, and apologizing to her for not having called on her this evening and brought her here. It hurt David to think that Helen came here by herself.

"I'm an old newspaper man," began Loring Weber. "I worked for the old *Observer* of blessed memory, and I look at things in a special way. Is Lewisohn news? I say he is. He's a Jew who's come back, and that's news. We're all coming back, well, not all, but many of us, including myself, and Lewisohn is the symbol of us all. And I like him for his women trouble."

"Me, too," said Dryfus.

"Why are you so happy about his women trouble?" asked Helen.

"Well," said Weber, "a man with women trouble is my kind of man, he has imagination, he has values, and by values I mean . . . "

Dryfus interrupted him: "You have said the right word, values. I can judge a man by the kind of woman he associates with. I say that the more raffish they are the better."

"Am I raffish?" asked Mary Tobias, smiling. She turned to her husband, "Am I, darling? I hope so."

"You're raffish," said Raphael Tobias, "very raffish."

"Every woman is raffish," said Helen, "but many men don't know it."

This remark seemed to electrify the room. Everyone seemed to feel that a profound truth had just been uttered. David was proud of Helen. Her remark revealed depths of sensitivity not often to be found in men or women, and it also revealed, or rather hinted at, a sensuousness that he liked, and he recalled, with longing, how lovely and comfortable it was to be with her.

"Don't give away too many of our secrets, Helen," said Mary Tobias.

"Well, my friends," said Dryfus, "I am glad to have heard what I have heard. I now feel happier in this world, much, very much happier. As something of a raffish fellow myself, very raffish, I might say, I could give references, if it were not indelicate for me to do so here or elsewhere, I have often been depressed by the thought that many women were what they appeared to be, dull and respectable and cold and just clods, female clods, who put up with being the mothers of the race and let it go at that . . . and the few women who are, well, maybe I should say honest, are, well, few and even a little bit ashamed of being what they are, I mean, sometimes ashamed, am I making myself clear?"

"Perfectly, perfectly," said Weber, "and please keep on talking, you express my ideas almost as well as I would."

"Well, that's about all I have to say, or almost all," said Dryfus. "And that is one of the glories of being a Jew, raffish women, or the raffishness in women."

"I think I know what you mean, and I love you for it," said Helen, "but I want to hear you say it."

"All right," said Dryfus, "I'll be blunt. I think that Judaism is an honest religion in this respect, it glorifies raffish women, it glorifies the raffishness in women and in men. It seems to say, 'There are no dirty parts in the human body, all are holy, to be relished and enjoyed. The Song of Songs is the Song of Judaism. Men and women go and make love, and enjoy the great gift of God, which is, love making. I think this is just wonderful, what the Bible says. Take the New Testament. I don't like it, because there's no love making in it, so it's inhuman. King David and King Solomon and Father Abraham and all the others, they do plenty of love making, and that's how it should be, but not the damn saints in the New Testament, they're running away from love making. You know something, people?"

"What?" said Helen.

"I think that Jesus and St. Paul and all the others in the New Testament were not Jews, or they couldn't have said what they said about women and about love and about sex, that's all dreadful stuff, I say, inhuman, cruel, and totally un-Jewish." Dryfus turned to Helen. "Have I answered you?"

"Perfectly," she said, blushing a little.

"Now that I like," said Weber.

"You like what?" asked Dryfus.

Weber smiled. "I don't really know. But I do know. I guess what I wanted to say was that Jews never make the mistake of distinguishing between love and sex."

"Only fairies and philosophers and theologians, and theologians are only fairy philosophers," said Dryfus, "only they make that kind of distinction. Although"—his face became mock serious, and Mary Tobias and Helen burst out laughing at the sight of it—"although I will admit, if forced to do so, that one can have sex without having love, but one cannot have love without sex. Still, to be fair to myself and my point of view, it's pretty hard for me to imagine sex without love, either. Now that, my friends, is what I call raffish. And I say that Judaism, thank God, is a raffish religion. The Old Testament is full of love and sex, as I believe I have said, and I don't recall a single instance where the Old Testament, the only Testament that I can read, nowhere does that wonderful Old Testament make any distinction between love and sex. And David and Solomon of blessed and raffish memory knew whereof they spoke in those areas, or, perhaps I should say, single area."

"Now that I like, that I like," said Weber. "That I like very much." He turned to David and said, "So you work for the *World*. I guess that Simmons must be a *goy*, worse, a Jew who's trying to be a *goy*. What a lousy sheet it's turned out to be. Seeing it now really hurts, after what it used to be."

"There are problems," said David.

"The only problem that magazine has now," said Dryfus, "is death."

"It was alive once, though," said Weber.

"Only for a very short time," said Dryfus, "a very short while. Brandt was dead, I assume you refer to the *World* under Brandt."

"Yes."

"Well, he was dead," said Dryfus, "before he had the decency to quit. I used to think that Brandt's real trouble was that he wasn't Jewish, but now I'm not so sure. The *goyim* have no monopoly on dumbness. Simmons is the death of the *World,* as Stock was before him. But an idea has come to me." He became silent.

"What is it?" said Raphael Tobias.

"One of the terrible consequences of the killing of so many Jews by Hitler, six million of them, is that there won't be enough to go around to get some sense into governments and colleges and places like that."

"Well. . . ," said Helen and stopped.

"I have thought of that, too," said Weber, "but I was afraid to say so."

"That's what I wanted to say," said Helen. "There's something about Jews, there is something very different and very special. It's not chauvinism, it's experience, maybe, it's poetry maybe, it's theatre maybe. You can always tell, don't you think so?" She turned to Dryfus.

"Three years ago I would have laughed at you and at anybody else who said this," he said. "I would have said it was shameful chauvinism, not true, unscientific, grownup people shouldn't talk that way, it labels us as parochial. But Hitler and those murders, and especially the silence of the so-called civilized Christian countries of the democratic camp, made me change my mind. The phrase Chosen People means something to me. We're chosen for all sorts of things, chosen to be killed, chosen to be spat upon, chosen to carry the ideals of the human race, chosen to show the way, chosen to outlive them all, the Egyptians and the Babylonians and the Greeks, too, and the Romans, and all the others. I've been mystical about the Jews. I can't tell you how much I and lots of non-Jewish Jews, like me, we used to be non-Jewish Jews, you know what I mean, I can't tell you how much the Jews occupy our minds, the Jews and Judaism and Jewishness."

Suddenly a silence descended upon the room.

"My God," exclaimed Dryfus, "has this place become converted to Christianity? So quiet."

Helen turned to Weber. "What work do you do?"

344

"Nothing." His face became solemn.

"Nothing?" said Helen.

"Nothing," repeated Weber. "But it keeps me busy."

"Keep her guessing," said Dryfus.

"But what do you do?" persisted Helen.

"Well," said Weber, "I should feel insulted. I'm a playwright. I have second-act trouble and third-act trouble."

"Oh, a playwright!" said Helen.

"Ever hear of *Final Edition?*"

Helen stared at Weber. Then she remembered to be diplomatic. "Of course, I remember. How silly of me."

"Oh, that's all right. You don't have to be polite. I'm just another forgotten writer. Well," he looked at the floor, and added shyly, "it ran for six months, and ten years ago that was a hit, but I guess it wasn't a very profound play. I'm no O'Neill. But I'm as good as Maxwell Anderson." He smiled. "But I can't get the producers to agree with me. I've written seven plays in the last ten years, and all I got was a summer tryout in New Jersey, and it died in the swamps there. The Jersey people call their swamps across the river meadows."

All at once David noticed that one of Loring's arms was shorter than the other. David had suspected it before, but now he was sure. David wondered whether Helen had noticed it, whether Mary and Raphael had noticed it. Somehow he was sure that Dryfus knew it all the time.

"They say Broadway is a horse race," said Mary.

No one answered her.

"Have I said something bad?" she said.

"No, not bad. But worse," said Dryfus, smiling. "You've just been guilty of a cliché."

"I'm sorry," she said. "But it's true."

"That it is," said Dryfus.

"Well," said Weber, "Broadway is Broadway, but Hollywood is Hollywood. I've just kissed it good-bye, or rather I kissed it good-bye six weeks ago."

He got up and now his shorter arm was very noticeable. He lit a cigarette and began walking about the room nervously. Actually he was of average height, but David felt that he was getting shorter as he walked about the room.

"Listen to this," said Weber. "One of the big guns calls me

in. All right, I'll give you his name. Morton Slutzky. Big shot. He has the brains of a camel. But, before I tell you about him, I will give him credit for not changing his name. Maybe his wife wouldn't let him. Deborah. She's real fine, how she ever married him is a mystery, but such things are always mysteries. Anyway . . ."

"Isn't he going to produce a play on Broadway soon?" interrupted Helen.

"Yes, I read that, too," said Weber. "I'd been working for his studio, Panorama, for four months, and was wearing out the seat of my pants, most of that time at $1200 a week. That's how they punish you in Hollywood. Then he, Morton Slutzky himself, calls me in, and gives me a script and says, 'Take a look at this. Go ahead.' 'Now?' I said. He said yes, now, so I run through it, and I say to him, 'Looks fine to me.' So he gets angry and bangs the table and says, 'You're crazy, plain crazy. This script wouldn't get us a thousand paying customers over the whole country. We need stuff that will sell. I don't mean cheap stuff, I mean good stuff that will sell.' Well, I look at him, controlling myself as much as I can. I say, 'I still think it's good, as a matter of fact I wouldn't be surprised if it's damn good, if the rest of it is as good as what I've read. By the way, 'I say to him, 'who wrote it?' 'Oh,' he says, 'I might as well tell you, this script's been around here for years. A dead beat wrote it. He used to be a big shot in New York. Now he's just a boozer and a girl chaser, though they tell me he's settled down to one woman, some Irisher, who knows what she is?' 'But what's his name?' I ask. 'Fitzgerald,' he says. 'F. Scott Fitzgerald?' I say. 'I don't know,' he says. 'For Christ's sake,' I say 'don't you even know the name of the man who wrote this marvelous piece?' 'Marvelous,' he mimics me. 'You didn't even read it,' he says. 'Well,' I say to him, 'any damn cluck can see a first-rate man wrote that.' 'So, this Fitzgerald is a first-rate man you say?' he says. 'If he isn't,' I say, 'then you're my father, God forbid,' I say. By then I don't give a damn what Slutzky says or does. You can only take so much vulgarity, so much ignorance."

Weber hesitated, then said, "So that's Hollywood."

There was silence in the room, mounting, pressing, silence.

David sensed that the others had hardly listened to what Weber had said. They were merely watching Weber, and being sorry for his public display of self-pity.

"They're not making really good pictures now," said Mary Tobias, and everyone seemed to be relieved.

"No, they're not," said Raphael, her husband.

Weber sat down, lit another cigarette, then got up and said, "I think I'll be going."

"Oh, no," said Mary. "You've hardly been here."

Weber ignored her pleading. "Thank you for inviting me." He looked at Raphael, said good-night to him, and walked out of the room without saying good-night to anybody else, and with Mary almost running after him to see him to the door. At the door, which Weber had opened, she said, "Do come again, Mr. Weber." But he didn't answer her, and he was off.

Mary slowly walked back to the others.

"Did we insult him? I feel terrible."

"You didn't insult him," said Dryfus. "He insulted us. He wanted us to say he was wonderful, and he especially wanted me to say it, and he knew I couldn't and wouldn't."

"I'm bewildered," said Mary. "We met him at some friends of ours and we asked him to drop over some time. We hardly knew him. He kept by himself. And now this. I feel terrible." She turned to David. "Did we say anything to hurt him?"

"I don't think so," said David.

"All I can say," said Helen, "is that he was probably hurt that I didn't know he was the author of *Final Edition*. As he kept on talking I vaguely remembered someone saying something about it when it was put on Broadway." She looked at Dryfus, then at David. "It was about some cheap tabloid newspaper, wasn't it?"

"I think so," said David, who vaguely remembered having seen a motion picture version of the play, and not liking it.

"It was. And it was as cheap as the paper," said Dryfus. "He submitted the script to various friends of mine. I read it. Just cheap merchandise. He didn't let on he and I met before, about two or three months ago at some party. He was dead drunk. And he got nasty, so I told him off. He's a cry-baby."

"I've never seen so nervous a man," said Helen. "Why does he hate women so much?"

"Why shouldn't he?" said Dryfus. "He's been married to six or seven of them."

"That must be boring." said Helen.

"That's the most profound thing you've said all your life."

"I didn't know you've known me all my life," said Helen.

"Such chit-chat," said Mary. "Anybody here want a sandwich or something?"

"No, no," said Dryfus and David, as they explained they had to leave.

"But you're staying, Helen," said Mary. "You're sleeping over."

"I think I will," said Helen. "I'll be a lady for a night."

"Where have you been?" asked Dryfus outside.

"I was going to call you," said David.

"You got *tsores?*"

"Yes. I always have them."

"The *American World* or personal?"

"Both." said David.

"But, you're doing your own writing, eh?"

"Yes, very much so."

"Then you have no *tsores*. That girl Helen is a smart cookie. She's capable only of hysterical emotion, not love. She's the kind of woman, no matter what she says, who's bound to hurt a man."

"But you never saw her before."

"You don't have to see women, you only have to smell them, briefly. Now Mary Tobias is a fine woman, a fine Jewish woman, all breast, all kindness. Helen may be more Jewish conscious, knows Hebrew, and all that, but as a woman she's a Syrian or a Lebanese. There's no Jewish milk in her breasts. Beware, or she'll hook you. I saw her look at you."

"No chance."

"I hope so," said Dryfus, who apologized that he had to jump into a cab to pick up his wife at some Jewish relief committee meeting.

They promised to call each other soon. David decided to walk back to his room.

Fourteen

A week later, late in the afternoon, Loring Weber called David at the office of the *World* and invited him to dinner that same night. David hesitated. Then Weber said, "You're one of the proper people, you need advance notice. From the way you said nothing the other night I thought you were better than that. But if you don't want to do it for me, do it for my wife. I told her all about you, and she says you're her kind of Jew, whatever that may mean. What kind of Jew are you anyway? Do you carry an eight-pointed star, or maybe it's a nine-pointed star?"

"Well . . ."

"Here, Lottie will talk to you. I warn you Lottie comes from Vienna, she thinks Freud is greater than Moses, and she's only half Jewish, her mother was Jewish, and half Jews are the worst kind of Jews."

Lottie was the precise opposite of her husband in manner. She was soft-spoken, polite, gracious. "Loring really has told me so many good things about you," she said, "and Loring, you know how impulsive he is, suddenly said he wants to see you. I would like to see you, too. From what Loring said, you must be *haimish.* So it would be nice if you came over. I don't know how else I can say it. We have lamb chops and mashed potatoes—enough for more than one extra. If you wish to bring a friend, it will be all right."

Weber broke in. "Plenty of liquor, too, but I suppose you're not the drinking kind."

Lottie was back on the telephone. "So please come, yes?"

Almost automatically David said yes, and immediately began to wonder why.

As David got to know Weber better the more was he puzzled by him, and also offended and fascinated at the same time. Eventually David met his parents and also his two sons, born of different wives. They were all only a little less puzzling than Weber. They seemed to be living on the precipice of an emotional volcano. There was bitterness in their midst, sometimes in the open, sometimes submerged. There was also inhumanity, and a great deal of vulgarity.

As soon as David entered the Weber apartment, Weber exclaimed, "I can't get over it. This morning I saw a ghost."

"A ghost?" said David.

"He means one of his sons," said Lottie.

"Son?" said David.

"He'll be here soon," said Weber, "in a half hour or so. I was in the office of *The New York Times,* seeing somebody in the city room. And a young man comes up to me and says, 'You know me?' I look at him and I tell him I don't know him, but he says, 'That's funny,' and he sticks around. So I tell him to stop bothering me, but he sticks around. Then he says again, 'That's funny.' Then he says, 'You're my father. My mother told me. Goldie. Remember?'"

"Did you ever hear of anything like that?" said Lottie.

"Gilbert is his name. So he says," said Weber. "But it isn't."

"You didn't tell me Gilbert wasn't his name," said Lottie.

"It all came back to me. Goldie was some Brooklyn bitch I married when I was barely twenty. She hooked me. You know. Then the baby came, and we decided to call him Jonathan, and she said she won't stand for that, I said she will. By then I had decided to get rid of her. She was just a sloppy, tricky bitch. I quit when the kid was maybe four months old. She was just impossible. She married some cloak and suiter I learned later. Anyway, she changed his name to Gilbert. Isn't that horrible?"

"What's he doing now?" asked David.

"A copy boy on the *Times,*" said Weber.

"I'm dying to see him," said Lottie. "I'm sure he's nice."

"I've nothing against him," said Weber. "But so help me, he means nothing to me."

"If he's as nice as Morris I'll like him very much," said Lottie, looking at David. "Morris is his other son. By another wife, of course."

The door bell rang. "That must be he," said Weber, as he turned to Lottie. "Push the buzzer. I'm nervous."

"You mean you're embarrassed," said Lottie.

There was an obviously cruel comment in this remark, and David marveled that a wife would make such a remark about her husband in public. But apparently Weber didn't quite hear it or its meaning eluded him for the moment.

Gilbert appeared, and David liked him at once. He was tall, about seventeen years old, soft-spoken, and as he looked at Weber it was clear that he was curious who this man was who had sired him. He was finishing high school and hoping to go to law school. At the moment he was working on *The New York Times* part time.

"How did you find out where I was, who I was?" asked Weber.

"Mother told me. I've been pestering her about you for a long time, where you were, what you looked like, she told me to ask one of your sisters for a picture of you, lots of questions I asked her, then I heard your name in the office the other day, I looked up and you looked just like one of your pictures."

"Weren't you adopted by your mother's new husband?"

"Yes," said Gilbert, with hesitation. "I was. My name is Gilbert Osofsky."

"What do you think of that?" said Lottie, as she faced David. "Ever hear anything like that?"

Weber exclaimed, "You keep quiet! I'm not asking for your running philosophical comment."

Lottie said nothing. She turned to Gilbert and said, "Would you like some orange juice before supper, a large glass?" She turned to Loring. "Are you going to have another drink before supper? Don't you want to freshen up David's drink? May I call you, David, only a few minutes after meeting you?"

"No," said David "one drink is enough for me. And, of course, you may call me David, if I may call you Lottie."

He thought he saw Lottie's hand shake. She began to bring the supper to the table.

Weber poured himself a tall highball as he sat down at the table.

"So you want to be a lawyer?" he said to Gilbert, and David sensed that Weber really wasn't too interested.

"I think so," said Gilbert. "Are you still working in Hollywood?"

"I'm in New York, so how can I be in Hollywood?"

Lottie came to Gilbert's rescue. "Now, you know what Gilbert means. No. Gilbert, Loring has just given up Hollywood, he's writing a play for Broadway."

"That's wonderful," said Gilbert. "I've heard so much about *Final Edition*. I tell all my friends my father wrote it."

As the dinner ended even Gilbert sensed that his father wasn't too glad to see him, and he decided to leave. He asked if he might see his father again, and Weber said, "Sure, any time. Call up first. Lottie'll give you the number."

David was heartsick at the callousness of the man at whose home he had had supper. He was heartsick at the obvious tension between Weber and his wife, and he was offended by the conscious effort on Lottie's part to hurt her husband in front of a stranger. He was sorry for Gilbert, who had spent so many years searching for his father, and now that he found him, he realized that his father not only didn't care about his son but was annoyed with him for having found him.

After Gilbert left, Weber had two more highballs and now he was so intoxicated he could barely go from his chair to where the whiskey and soda were. Several times David made ready to leave, but each time Weber said, "No, no. I have something important to say to you. I have an idea. I think you're just the man for the idea. I know all about you, don't I, Lottie?"

"Yes," said Lottie, quite unconcerned, deep in her private thoughts, as she cleaned up.

"You might be a little more positive," said Weber, and David couldn't make out from his face whether he was angry or facetious.

"Yes, you do know a lot about David," said Lottie, looking straight at her husband, a mechanical smile slowly spreading across her mouth. Suddenly she exclaimed, "You're drunk!"

352

"I'm drunk," he said slowly, as he fondled his highball glass. "A profound observation."

"A child of yours comes up from your past and you can't face it," said Lottie, clipping every syllable as she spoke deliberately. "So you get drunk because you can't face it."

Weber turned to David and said, "See Freud, Dr. Sigmund Freud has just come into my house. Well, he's always here. Every time my dear wife opens her mouth, you can hear Freud talking, she's his dummy."

"And the way you treated that poor boy," said Lottie, her back to her husband. "It was cruel, positively cruel." She turned around, faced him and said, "Aren't you interested in what your own son thinks of his father? And what do you suppose his mother and stepfather will say when he tells them?"

"There you go again, my love, worrying again what other people will think of me. I don't give a damn. Goldie can go to hell, and so can her husband. She's a bitch and her husband can't be any better. Marrying a woman like that labels a man."

"You married her," said Lottie.

"Shut up!" shouted Weber, as he threw his highball glass at her legs, barely missing them.

Lottie at once walked into another room and slammed the door. David said a quick good night to Weber, who mumbled a faint good-night in reply, and he left.

About a week later Loring's other son Morris called David at his office: "Father said he told you about me, that it would be all right if I called, he said you're old friends, you and he, and Lottie said you wouldn't mind. I'm sorry I wasn't around the other night when you had supper with Dad and Lottie, so I thought . . . "

David agreed to see him, though reluctantly. He was uneasy about his whole connection with the Webers, he felt himself sinking deeper and deeper into a relationship with them that was repugnant to him and yet, that somehow attracted him because of its very repugnance.

David had known scoundrels and other dubious people, within the circle of his own family at large and within the circle of the friends and acquaintances who were on the periphery of the family. They were men of slippery moral conscience, such as Beryl Kantor, the foreign correspondent who reported situations in Russia that were, often, largely in his mind, and conversations by men high in Russian political life that were to a very considerable extent imaginary. David had also known men of somewhat easy regard for sexual fidelity in the marriage relationship. One such man was his pious Uncle Pinchus, who was not above pressing his attentions upon young widows and married women who needed only a little coaxing. But the irregularities of such people were, so to speak, within the area of "healthy" aberrations, expressions of the *yatzer horoh* (evil inclination) in all of us. The aberrations in the Weber family were sick. The Webers also represented a relatively new type of Jew to him—a Jew who was more influenced by the anxieties and yearnings in the non-Jewish world around him than by the centuries-old traditions of the Jewish world he was born into.

He thought again about the Jewish community in America. It was not a homogeneous community. It was made up of various kinds of Jews: Broadway Jews, Brooklyn Jews, Williamsburg Jews, Bronx Jews, lower Manhattan Jews, West Side Jews, East Side Jews, Park Avenue Jews, and there were what might be called Bernard Baruch Jews and Felix Frankfurter Jews and Leslie Jennings Jews (Leslie Jennings was former music critic of the *American World*), and College of the City of New York Jews, and New York University Jews. There were other parts of the country which had special types of Jews of their own: Southern Jews, Chicago Jews, Southwest Jews, Montana and Utah and Idaho Jews (David had met some from each of these three states recently and was mystified by some of the things they told him), and California Jews, and Mexican Jews (David had met some of them recently too, and was astonished to learn that Mexico City had a small but compact and quite vital Jewish community.)

Even these divisions (and there were a number more) had subdivisions of their own. Did they all have anything in common? Yes and no. The basic religious tradition, the Torah, they had in common insofar, at least, that they knew about it. Some believed it literally and some accepted it symbolically. But all viewed it with respect and even with some pride. Even the intellectual Jews, the Broadway Jews, the college campus Jews now spoke more freely about Jewish history and traditions, they seemed to be less embarrassed by it than they had been hitherto. They couldn't forget the Hitler horrors, and they couldn't forget the vast indifference of virtually the entire Christian world to them. They suddenly felt alone in a non-Jewish world whose values they had trusted but that now proved to be largely mere words. These Jews naturally tended to get together more and more as Jews, to talk about "the Jewish problem" that had now become close to them. They recalled how more than a generation earlier Justice Louis D. Brandeis of the United States Supreme Court had made a similar discovery, and they also recalled what Prof. Felix Frankfurter, now also of the U. S. Supreme Court, had done. Both had been ardent Zionists even while they were ardent Americans. These two men alone proved how silly the notion of "divided loyalties" was.

These hitherto "uncommitted Jews" began to do more for their people. It was reported that Bernard Baruch secretly increased his contribution to the synagogue in South Carolina that his family had been associated with for generations. Laura Z. Hobson was so shaken by the Jewish experience during the Second World War, that, though she had long been removed from the Jewish world that her mother had known so well and written about with such authority in the Yiddish press, she burst into print with a novel *Gentlemen's Agreement,* a book that was only superficially Jewish, and had little artistic worth, but that nevertheless did tell the world that hundreds of thousands of Jews had now openly affiliated themselves with their Jewish heritage.

These thought went through David's mind as he was awaiting Morris Weber. Morris was twenty-one and looked neither like Gilbert nor Loring. There was something Scottish about him. David couldn't help remarking upon the fact.

"I know," said Morris smiling. "Most people expect my first name to be Malcolm and my second name to be McDougall. Well, I come by my looks normally, I guess. My mother's parents were born in Scotland, Presbyterian, Scotch Presbyterian."

"Do you live with your mother?"

"No. My mother is dead. She died when I was six. I live

with my grandparents, my father's parents. I don't exactly live with them now. I live in a small apartment in Manhattan, but I sort of report to them once a week."

"Yes," said David, who began to notice the same look in Morris's eyes that he had noticed in Loring's eyes.

"Dad was plenty drunk when you saw him," said Morris. "Lottie told me. She hasn't seen him since."

"What do you mean? Where is he?"

"That's not unusual. When he's on a binge, he just disappears. Staying at a friend's, with some woman, or he might even be sleeping it off in a whorehouse. He's a goner."

"What do you mean?"

"He's become hopelessly alcoholic. Lottie is an angel to stand for it."

He then came to the reason for his visit. He had gone to three colleges and had left each of them after a short stay. He'd "just lost interest." He had wanted to become a doctor, then a lawyer, then a playwright, and now he wanted to be a short story writer and a novelist. He wanted advice from David.

"I don't understand," said David. "If you want to be a writer, you write and take your chances by submitting your material to editors."

Morris was dissatisfied. "But isn't there something you can tell me?"

"I have told you all I can say, really."

"That's what my fiancee tells me," said Morris. "She's very hard on me." He hesitated. "I sometimes think she'll leave me if I don't buckle down and write. I've started lots of things, but I can't finish them. I've started more than a dozen stories, and have a dozen first pages, and I've nibbled at a novel."

"What work do you do?" asked David.

Morris became shamefaced. "Well, I don't exactly work. If you mean do I have a job, no I have no job. My grandparents give me a certain amount each week, not much, but enough, and I can get more if I need it, if only I continue to write."

"But you don't write much."

"No."

"Do they know you plan to get married?"

"Well, yes and no. They've met Marcella, that's my fiancee, and I guess they didn't like her on sight. What I mean is they liked her, but not as someone for me to marry."

"Why?"

"She's a Gentile. My grandparents say they've had enough trouble from Gentiles in the family. I guess my mother didn't take too good care of me, so I spent most of my childhood with my grandparents. They're really my parents, because my father didn't have much interest in me either. I can't have a real talk with him even now. So my grandparents didn't like Marcella, because my mother was Gentile and another one of my father's wives was also Gentile. I think my grandparents know that it was not their being Gentile that broke up the marriages, but I can't blame them for feeling as they do."

Morris was getting nervous, twisting a handkerchief into knots, untying them, and then twisting it into knots again. He now looked more often at his lap than at David. It became apparent soon that Marcella was less the object of his love than someone he was using as a cushion for his troubles. David imagined that she was somewhat older than Morris, and was about to ask him what Marcella was doing, when Morris said, "My fiancee has her own problems. She's separated from her husband, has been for over a year. He's willing to give her a divorce, but he says she must get it on her own, and she has no money, so she's saving every week from what I give her and from what she makes, saving up enough to get the divorce. And she has a little boy, four years old, and he's staying with her mother."

"Does Marcella's mother know about you and Marcella?"

"No, not exactly. So I don't know what to do. I thought you'd have some advice."

"Offhand I should say you need a job more than anything else. You'll have plenty of time for writing after work."

"That's what Marcella says. Would you like to meet her?"

David had been awaiting this question, and was ready for it. "I would, very much, but not for a while. We're putting out some special issues, and we're busy every minute practically."

"I understand."

"If you write anything you want me to see, I'll be glad to read it," said David.

"I'll do that," said Morris, and in a few moments he was gone.

David didn't see Loring for about three weeks after Morris had called on him and was content to have it continue this way. But Loring burst in on David, in his room, one Saturday night. He didn't apologize. All he said was: "I get sick staying around the house with Lottie. She's all right, but women are women."

David realized at once that Loring had been drinking. "Come on over to visit my sister with me," he said. "She lives in Brooklyn, and I haven't seen her for weeks, months. Lottie doesn't like Gertrude. She calls her a stuffed shirt, so I keep the two girls away from each other. Hell, when women get a mad on there's no curing them." He laughed. "The funny part is that Gertrude thinks Lottie is a stuffed shirt, and she may be right, what with all her bellyaching about Freud. I'm getting sick of Freud. So come on."

David hesitated . . . he was working on his novel, he also wanted to do some rewriting on an article he had finished several days before . . . he wanted to write some letters home, he wanted to write to his married sister Adele . . . and he wanted just to be alone.

"Come on," said Loring. "My father and mother may be there."

Somehow this news made a difference to David. Suddenly he was seized with a curiosity to see Loring's parents.

As soon as they were out of David's room, Loring hailed a cab and directed the driver to an address in Brooklyn. Loring sensed that David was amazed by this show of extravagance. "I feel like it," he said. "Besides, my father would expect it of me. He once took a cab from Scranton, Pennsylvania to New York City, because he missed the train by two minutes. So, like father, like son."

David thought what his father would say about such a cab ride: "A scandal! A sin, a terrible sin!" Suddenly David asked, "Is your father a Reform Jew?"

"Yes, why do you ask?"

"Nothing. Only, I guess because of my background, I could think only of a Reform Jew having so much money that he

would take a cab ride from Scranton to New York City."
David was a little embarrassed by what he had just said.

But Loring didn't seem to mind. "Yes, he's Reform, and
he's a man of impulses. He's made a lot of money, he's no
millionaire, but he has a department store in Scranton, one
of the biggest in that part of Pennsylvania, and he hasn't had
to work for years. He belongs to a temple, but seldom goes
there, because he thinks most of the people who go there are
vulgar, too much money, not enough culture, and the women
especially bother him, I mean their cheapness. You know
what he says?"

"What?"

"Nothing like a woman temple worker. That's what he
says. He says they all think they're Queen Esthers, and they
think the Jewish people should set up monuments to them.
But he's funny about this. He doesn't like the women, but he
thinks temple is a good thing, and there's never a peep out
of him when mother has the women over to the house."

Loring became silent, as the cab crossed the Brooklyn
Bridge. Through the corner of his eye David, for the first
time, saw a streak of cruelty in his face, but then he wasn't
sure whether it was cruelty or selfishness. David wondered
why Loring didn't ask him about his family. Now David took
another side glance at Loring, and he was astonished how
much more Jewish he looked, yet there was hardly anything
else Jewish about him. If there is such a thing as a Jewish *goy*,
thought David, then Loring was he.

"Your son Morris saw me," said David, merely to make
conversation.

"He told me," said Loring. "He's a no-good kid."

"Oh, I don't know. I saw him only once, of course, but I
liked him. He's having troubles."

"He wants to be babied, and he's sore at me because I
won't baby him. He's lazy and he's mixed up with some bitch."

David continued to defend Morris. He was sure that what
Morris had told him about being neglected by both his parents
was true, and David was on the verge of saying that perhaps
Loring should see more of his older son.

Suddenly Loring said, "Ever hear of Suzanne Pritchett?"

359

"No."

"Well, she was a woman's-page reporter on the *Observer,* and a damn good one. I think her stuff was syndicated, I know it was, and I thought perhaps it might have been syndicated in Boston. She was Morris's mother."

"I see."

"She was the most wonderful listener in the world, and that is where I made my mistake. I thought she knew what I was talking about. I used to talk about Anatole France and Jakob Wasserman, they were my two enthusiasms then, and she would look at me like an angel, as I talked. It was only later I learned she didn't understand anything I was saying. She tried to read, but she didn't have the patience. But it was wonderful to talk to her. I don't know how to explain it. It was wonderful even after I knew she didn't follow me. There was something so very calm about her, and that's how she wrote her column, and women told me that. They said reading her made them feel calm. And men were crazy about her. She had a face like a doll, like a more intelligent Jean Harlow, even though she didn't know very much more than Harlow. She was small, dressed very neatly. All her clothes looked as if they'd just been pressed." He stopped, took out his wallet from his inside jacket pocket, and pulled out a picture. "Here, that's Suzanne the very same day she and I had our first date. Isn't she beautiful?"

David caught his breath. She was beautiful. Her face seemed to be like a carved rose petal, with the sunrise surrounding it. "She's wonderful," he said.

"She was," said Loring. "But women are strange."

"What do you mean?"

"Oh, various things," said Loring, and for the first time David was genuinely attracted to him. Loring seemed to be outside of himself for the moment, he seemed to be speaking for the whole human race, with its woes and its joys and its hopes and its disappointments.

"I'm a cad," continued Loring. "I know it. You probably think so, too. You know why I dropped in on you out of the blue?"

"I was wondering."

"Well, I was going to doublecross you, but it didn't work."

360

"What do you mean?" asked David, who instantly thought of Helen, for he remembered a look that had passed across the room, at the Tobiases, from Loring to her.

"I'll give it to you straight. I thought I wanted to sleep with Helen, she looked like something nice in bed, maybe even for more than one time. I knew she was sweet on you, you could tell it from the way she listened to you, the way a smile passed across her lips, and I liked those lips, too. Call me vulgar and immature, that's what all my wives have called me just before I left them and afterwards, when they discussed me with their best friends or my friends. I didn't want to steal Helen from you, I just wanted to, well, use her a little bit. So I called her." He looked at David. "Aren't you even disturbed by what I'm saying?"

"I don't know. If you want to know the truth I knew it was about Helen from the first . . . and I guess I'm more puzzled than disturbed."

"You're a strange one. I came to you on my knees, and you don't seem to care. You don't drink, you're not jealous, you don't want to hit me. I know damn well you slept with Helen, and yet . . . you're a strange one."

David felt his face turn crimson. "Helen said no to you?"

"The first human reaction out of you. You're right. She said no. She wouldn't even let me see her in her apartment. She saw me in a restaurant. And she was very cute about it."

"How?"

"The Hollywood bitches and the New York bitches and all the bitches of the whole world could learn from her. She only said, 'You're wrong about me. You don't want me. You want another girl.' I congratulate you for having such a girl. Aren't you going to ask if she mentioned your name or if I mentioned it?"

"Not especially. You can tell me if you want to."

"Well, she said nothing about you, but I knew all the time she was thinking about you."

"Oh," said David, who somehow didn't care at the moment.

Again Loring became quiet. David noticed that he was still holding Suzanne's photograph in his hand. Without looking at it again, Loring put it back in his wallet. David was hoping that it would be quiet in the cab till they reached their desti-

361

nation. Then Loring said, "She was one in a million, Suzanne was. Until we got married. Then the trouble started, or a little later. Ever have trouble with a woman?"

"Yes," said David, who immediately recalled Alice of many years before.

"Then you know," said Loring. "The first few weeks were really out of this world. And it wasn't just sex. That way she was something of a disappointment. She was very strange that way. She would be very loving and very passionate before we really got together, and then she would be only so-so. Maybe she lost interest, maybe it was my fault. But I don't really know. I don't think that mattered so much, I really don't think so, because we kept on talking and loving afterward, and the loving afterward was just as wonderful as the loving before. She would say such wonderful things, and just be wonderful. Then we learned Morris was coming, and we were thrilled. You got no children?"

"No."

"They're wonderful," said Loring, and David couldn't help smiling at the insincerity of this remark.

"I mean at the beginning, before they begin smelling and yelping. I guess I mean before they come out." He stopped and added, "I've just learned something about myself. I guess I just like the idea of having kids, but not the kids themselves, once they're here. Lottie says maybe I'd feel differently if I had a girl baby, well, maybe, but I'm not so sure. I think she just told me that so that she and I could have a baby together. Women are tricky. I don't want any more, and I told her if she has any, if she fools me, she'd have to support it, girl or no girl. But I don't think she can have any anyway. She was married before, some lousy Viennese painter, and she told me he wanted kids and she wanted kids, so it stands to reason there was something wrong with her, eh?"

"Oh, I don't know. It could have been his fault," said David.

"No, that I don't believe at all."

"Why?"

"I just don't. Besides, Lottie always has colds down there, hell, she's always going to the doctor."

"Then one day," continued Loring, "I noticed that Suzanne wasn't listening to me the way she used to. So I ask her if she isn't well, being pregnant and all that, you know. She didn't answer, so I ask her again. I remember it as if it happened yesterday. She bursts out crying. I come over to her, and put my arm around her, but she pushes me away. That never happened before either. I get angry and I shout, 'Why the hell don't you say something? If you're sick, say so, if not, talk.' Then she turns around and gives me the godamndest tongue-shellacking you can imagine. She bawls the pants off me for having neglected her, for not having asked her once what the doctor was saying, and she tells me she almost lost the baby and that she started to talk to me about it once but that I was drunk, and she said she was sick and tired of being my slave, and she wanted to be treated like any other wife, and you know the rest."

He wiped his brow. "I still get hot when I think of it," said Loring. "I heard her use words I never thought she knew. So I tell her she can choke with the kid, and that was the beginning of the end, no, it was the end. But at the beginning she was the most wonderful woman I've ever known."

"Did you see her after that?"

"Not really. Just to get my things. I left her some money and told her to shift for herself."

David was shocked by the cruelty of what he had just heard. Here was an evil and brutal man, the like of whom David had never before met.

"She called me a few times after that, asking me to come back, but I wouldn't, I just wouldn't. The kid would be sick or she needed money or she just wanted me back, but I said no."

"What about Morris?"

"I don't know. My parents took care of him. Suzanne committed suicide when Morris was only six years old. I suppose he told you about that."

"Well, he did, in passing," said David.

"I know. He loves to talk about his mother's suicide. He gets some psychopathic satisfaction out of it."

Loring's sister, Gertrude, was tiny, dumpy, and lethargic. She was apparently content to live the life of a housewife in Brooklyn, the wife of an accountant and the mother of a gawky twelve-year-old daughter, who was some inches taller than her mother. "So how's the big world in New York and in Hollywood?" she said to Loring, almost in the same manner she would use if she had asked him what time it was.

"All right, all right," Loring said, and that was the complete answer he deigned to give to her question. He barely paid even this much attention to her husband. "Everything all right, Barney?" was pretty nearly all he said to Barney.

But he was very attentive to his parents. He inquired several times about their health, apologized for not having called them more often, and reported at such length and so lovingly about Lottie that David wondered exactly why he was being so untruthful: were his parents fonder of his wife than he himself was? Did they threaten to disown him if he divorced her or mistreated her? By this time David had begun to have definite ideas about Loring's calculated practicality.

Mrs. Weber, a woman of generous bodily build, said very little except to compare the weather in Scranton with the weather in New York City, to become quietly exuberant about a fund-raising affair Hadassah had put on in Scranton, and to agree with her husband with his ideas as to what should be done to make sure that Germany does not attack the democracies again: his idea was to break up the country into a dozen or so smaller countries, the way it was before Unification under the Hohenzollerns. Loring's father looked like a *Yahoodi* (German Jew)—at least like the Reform Jews David used to see at Temple Israel, a Reform synagogue in Boston, where David used to visit on the High Holy Days, when he was a young boy. Mr. Weber spoke quietly, somewhat nonchalantly, a trifle pompously. He used strange words, or he pronounced old words strangely. He did not say *hoiz* for house, as David's parents did; he said *haus,* as the Germans did. He spoke of *kartofel salad,* for potato salad, and he pronounced the two *a's* in salad as the *a* in *arm* is pronounced; whereas David's parents, on the few occasions when they did speak of this dish, spoke of it as if it were spelled *potate seled.* And Mr. Weber, as well as his wife, used such words as *wunderlich* and *umbeshcriehn* and *Grossmutter,* which David had not heard at all in his father's house.

Mr. Weber obviously was a man of culture. Though he had

been in the department store business most of his life and had done well in it, it was clear that he had continued to read books and magazines and newspapers—and among the books were the novels of Sinclair Lewis and Thomas Mann and Somerset Maugham and Thomas Hardy—and he subscribed to the *New Republic* and th*e Nation* and the *National Geographic* and the *Atlantic* and *Harper's*.

"Once," he said, "I subscribed also to *Foreign Affairs*. I thought if I read it I would understand better the international mess in the world. You know, articles by the Foreign Secretary of Great Britain, by our own Secretary of State, by the Prime Minister of South Africa, and by a lot of professors of international law and history and politics here and in other countries. That's what I thought, but then I realized that these men weren't saying anything. They were in favor of peace and for solving problems around the table, and they talked about the past, Metternich and Richelieu and Kutuzoff and Garibaldi, but I still wasn't any clearer about things going on now. So I stopped subscribing to the magazine."

He seemed to want to talk more about books and ideas, but his wife and daughter kept on interrupting him: "Don't get so excited, you know it's not good for you. Discuss things, but quietly. You're already getting red in the face, and you know what the doctor told you."

"What the doctor told me is nonsense," said Mr. Weber. "Discussing books doesn't hurt the heart or lift the blood pressure."

"Then what does it?" said Gertrude.

A deep thoughtfulness came to Mr. Weber's face. "What causes high blood pressure? I don't know, but the doctors don't know either. I believe it's aggravation, but there's aggravation and there's aggravation, and that's another puzzle. Everything is a puzzle. All I know is that there's too much worry in the world."

"You have nothing to worry about, dad," said Gertrude. "You're retired, take it easy."

"Eh," said Mr. Weber in disgust. He turned to his wife, first, then to his son, then he walked over to the window. His back faced them all, and his back was eloquent with silent disappointment with his family, and David thought that mixed with this personal disappointment was also a disappointment with all of life. Here he was, without financial worries, with time to read and think and listen to music, but his own little garden, he seemed to be saying to himself, was filled with weeds: regrets, aches, despairs.

He faced his family again and said, "Worries are strange things. I was reading recently about Herbert Spencer. Even when he was a man of distinction, famous, people discussed him all over the world, his ideas of evolution and social statics, he was worried about his heart, even though there was nothing wrong with his heart. So, sometimes, even while he was crossing the street, he would stop in the middle of the street and count his pulse. So he lived to a ripe old age, seventy-three, which for those days was very old." He turned to David and said, "We have no great system builders any more, do we?"

"No, I guess not, Mr. Weber, not in the sense that Herbert Spencer was a system builder," said David. "Your idea is an interesting one. The age of the system builders—Kant and Fichte and Spinoza and Leibnitz—is gone." He turned to Loring, and said, "That's an interesting idea of your father's."

Before Loring had a chance to say anything, his father said, "No sense in asking him. He doesn't even know who Spencer was. How I pleaded with him to read Spencer and Hume and the other great English philosophers, Locke and Bentham. Loring was always interested in the lighter things."

Loring got up, his head almost resting on his chest. "That is true, dad, and I was wrong. But there's no point in rubbing it in after all these years."

Mr. Weber ignored his son. He said to David, "Of course, in this country we've had William James and John Dewey, rather, I should say, we still have Dewey. But James looks like a good-natured and well-read preacher to me, a little more scientific, perhaps, than Emerson, but pretty much like Emerson. And Dewey, well, I don't know what he's talking about."

"Dad always talked this way, even when I was little," said Gertrude.

"He did," said Loring, who seemed to be eager to please his father.

"This sort of talk or thinking still keeps him up late in

the night," said Mrs. Weber, "and he gets up so early in the morning, usually at four."

"I like to get up early," said Mr. Weber. "When I was active in business, I would get up early to get in some reading. I'd come home late at night very often, and I'd be tired, so the only time I had for reading was in the morning."

"No, I think there's another reason, dad," said Gertrude.

"What?" said Mrs. Weber.

"Dad must be a morning baby," said Gertrude. "Now, don't laugh. I read this in some magazine only last week."

"Screen Romances?" asked Loring.

Gertrude merely gave him a look. "No, my wise friend, I think it was *The New York Times Magazine Section.* It said there that some statistics recently showed that babies born late at night are night owls, stay up all hours of the night, and babies born in the morning get up early in the morning. So dad must be a morning baby."

"Superstition," said Mr. Weber. "Old wives' tales."

"I don't know," said Mrs. Weber smiling. "Old wives' tales sometimes have good ideas in them. I know my grandmother, *selig,* always would give us raw lemon to eat and very strong tea with lots of lemon juice to drink when we had colds, and my father used to roar at this foolishness, what he called foolishness. But now doctors prescribe ascorbic acid for colds, and ascorbic acid is only lemon juice."

Mr. Weber turned to David. "What do you think of Hemingway, Ernest Hemingway?"

"Frankly, not very much," said David. "He is skilful with conversation, but only a certain kind of conversation."

"That he is," said Mr. Weber. "Simple people, but he isn't deep. I should think he isn't even a novelist, I mean, a real novelist, like Thomas Mann or Heinrich Mann. After reading, say, Thomas Mann, you know something about people. I have read *The Magic Mountain* many times, in English, in German."

"He must have read it twenty times," said Mrs. Weber.

"That's all I heard about when I was young," said Gertrude. "Thomas Mann, Thomas Mann, all the time. The book you used to talk about had another title, what was it, dad?"

"It had another title, because it was another book," said

Mr. Weber slowly, and with obvious despair about his children. "Perhaps you remember, Loring?"

"*Buddenbrooks,*" said Loring.

"Did you read it?" inquired Mr. Weber, with a quiet belligerence in his tone.

"I did," said Loring.

"And?" said Mr. Weber.

"I didn't like it," said Loring. "Wordy, dreary, it could all be said in one-tenth the space."

"Hemingway is better?"

"Yes. *A Farewell to Arms* is a great war story and a great love story," said Loring.

Mr. Weber threw up his hands in disgust. "That I call a real aggravation," he said. "That's what gives me my heart condition, my blood pressure, that and other aggravations, many other aggravations."

"Why did you have to say it, Loring?" asked his mother. "You know how your father feels about Dr. Mann."

"He asked me," said Loring, "so I told him. As a matter of fact, he didn't have to ask me. We've talked about this before, so he knows perfectly well what I think about Thomas Mann."

She sighed, then said, "I don't see why any one should get aggravated because somebody disagrees with him about a book."

Mr. Weber threw up his hands again, in disgust. "You don't see," he said, "you don't see. Is there anything else worth being aggravated about?"

"Dad, why be aggravated about anything?" said Gertrude, who apparently was less afraid of her father than were the others. She also seemed to be doing the talking for her own family, for her husband barely said a word. Now and then he smiled, but it was not clear from his smile whether he agreed or disagreed with what was being said.

For a third time Mr. Weber threw up his hands. There was a tense silence in the room. Then Mr. Weber said, "I was reading in an article where a professor, who was along in years, in his late sixties or early seventies, he said that as a man grows older he longs for death, death becomes something desirable. That's how I feel now."

"Oh, dad, don't talk that way," said Gertrude. "You're so depressing."

"Now I'm getting aggravated," said Mrs. Weber, sighing. "You children don't know. Your father says this to me many times a day. It makes me shudder."

"No, it's not the way it used to be," said Mr. Weber. "We do more things now, have improvements, more progress, radio, we'll soon have television, lots of things, many more things than they had when I was a young man, a young boy, but there are not enough things, less, as a matter of fact, that make life worth living."

"This, too, I hear all day long, children," said Mrs. Weber. "He keeps on asking me, 'Is life really worth living?' I can't answer him. I know it's worth living, and that's all. It isn't anything you have arguments about. I get so nervous, really, one might . . . I'm afraid to say."

"I wouldn't worry, mother," said Lottie's husband, in the one extended speech throughout the evening. "It's only his way of saying he has time on his hands. Besides, we should always remember that people who talk this way live long lives. All hypochondriacs outlive normal people. They fret and fuss and take care of themselves."

"Still, I think he shouldn't talk this way to mother when they're alone together," said Gertrude. "It's creepy."

Loring got up from his seat, lit a cigarette, and walked about the room. "Such talk, such talk," he mumbled. He turned to David. "Ever been to such a place before? Like a psychopathic ward." He laughed. "Just like a psychopathic ward."

"I wouldn't talk if I were you," said Mr. Weber.

"Why?" asked Loring.

"Nothing," said his father, not deigning to answer him.

"Loring asked you something, dad," said Gertrude. "Why don't you answer him?"

"Some questions have no answers," Mr. Weber said. "Besides, some questions shouldn't be asked. This reminds me of what George Bernard Shaw once said. Somebody asked him what he thought of marriage, and he answered something like this: 'This is a question that no married man ever asks of another married man, and no single man ever should ask of a married man. Wise married men, when confronted with such a question, remain silent.' That's what he said, or something like that. I think he also said, 'Some truths must forever remain private.' "

"I don't see anything profound in that," said Gertrude. "Do you, Mr. Polonsky? Or shouldn't I ask a single man, I assume you are single?"

"Yes, how did you know?" asked David.

"I don't know, just guessed," said Gertrude. "Maybe it was your silence, I don't know."

"He talks to me about that, too," said Mrs. Weber. "About marriage, about children, he wants to know why, I mean about marriage why people have children, whether they should have them. It's so funny hearing this all day long, even when people come to the house. I'll be perfectly frank with you, I feel relieved when he puts his records on, then at least he doesn't talk his philosophy. I feel so defeated, I guess that's the word."

Gertrude became serious-faced. "Don't we please you, dad, Loring and myself?" A mechanical smile came to her face, as she turned to David. "Don't let this upset you. We always carry on this way."

"No, we don't," said Mrs. Weber emphatically. "Goodness, Gertrude, how can you say that. Mr. Polonsky might think God knows what sort of people we are, abnormal."

Gertrude's husband said to David, "I'm used to it now, don't feel funny."

"Such talk, such talk," Loring continued to mumble. "If I put it in a play people would say it's unreal. Well, sometimes I don't know what's real, what isn't real. Maybe they're the same."

"Of that I'm sure," said Mr. Weber. "The real and the unreal are both real. What's in the mind is real, whether it has any relationship to the outside world or not. Sooner or later the outside world does what the mind says it should do. The whole world is one big mind. The English philosopher Berkeley said that, or something like that."

"I think I'll make some coffee, and we'll be back to normal," said Gertrude. "I have no liquor, Loring, so get that out of your mind. I'm not like Lottie who caters to your every whim, whether it's good for you or not."

"That remark was uncalled for," said Mrs. Weber. "Lottie is a nice woman, considering."

"Considering what?" said Loring.

"It was only an expression," said Mrs. Weber, as she wiped an imaginary speck of dirt from her lap.

"Lottie is another one," said Mr. Weber, and stopped.

"Another one what?" asked Loring.

"Nothing," said Mr. Weber. "I don't want to discuss it. Women are strange, men are strange, but women are stranger. As Nietzsche said, I don't see what's in it for them?"

"What's in what?" asked Gertrude.

"Life," said Mr. Weber.

"That's a laugh," said Gertrude. "I admit I don't read heavy books, I like cooking, and I like sewing, but not too much, but Thomas Mann bores me, and, for that matter, Hemingway does, too. At least when I read what my dear brother calls the slicks and the pulps, you know, the *Ladies Home Journal, Good Housekeeping,* magazines like that, I'm not fooling myself I'm reading something profound, even if I was looking for profound reading. I read it just to pass the time, it's pleasant, and I know when the author is lying, or not saying what he should be saying. Life is no bed of roses, I know, even a dumb woman like me knows it. But I don't see how Thomas Mann and Hemingway know any more or tell any less lies. You talk about *A Farewell to Arms* and what's the name of that Spanish novel of his you made me read, Loring?"

"For Whom the Bell Tolls."

"Yes, They were just claptrap, not much better than what I read in the *Journal,* and the people who write for the *Journal* at least don't make any pretentions. Catherine, is that her name in *A Farewell to Arms?"*

"Yes," said Loring.

"She might as well be advertising Chanel No. 5 or some bras or some school for the deaf and dumb. There never was such a woman, except in the mind of a man like Hemingway who doesn't know anything about women. You men should hear women talk in the women's wash-rooms, and then you'd know women. God, I wish I could write."

"Gertrude, what's come over you?" said Mrs. Weber, who looked at her husband, who was obviously very much impressed with his daughter.

"She's talking sense," Mr. Weber said. "Go on. I like very much what I'm hearing."

"Oh, I don't know," said Gertrude. "I've said enough."

"No, go on," said Mr. Weber. "Please."

"Haven't you heard enough?" said Mrs. Weber.

"Not enough of this," said Mr. Weber. "I feel a little better already. Go on, Gertrude."

Loring lit a fresh cigarette. "Such talk, such talk . . . ," he mumbled.

"Women talk among themselves, when they feel they can trust each other," continued Gertrude. "Women are afraid that if they tell the truth to other women, sooner or later, it will get to the man they're in love with, and they don't like that. A woman would rather have a man love her than have him know the truth, about the truth of women in general."

"I'm learning something," said Lottie's husband, who at the moment seemed very childish and helpless to David.

"You don't have a thing to worry about, dear," said Gertrude.

"That's good," said her husband, who smiled sheepishly, and now he looked even more childish to David.

"And that Maria girl in Hemingway's other novel is a laugh, too," said Gertrude. She stopped suddenly. "But that's not what I wanted to say. What was it?"

"Mr. Weber said," said David, "that he wondered what women got out of it all, and . . . "

"Yes, that's it," said Gertrude. "I hope you don't mind my saying it, dad, but this kind of idea makes me laugh, too. Men are always thinking that women get the dirty end of the stick in life, that they have to take a lot from men, they have no fun, and like that. Women get plenty out of life. They get love. When a man tells a woman he loves her, and means it, she has enough to last her for a lifetime. And a woman bears children, and that's something nobody can take away from women. And a woman spends more time with her children than does her husband. And no man has ever fooled a woman about anything: even when he thought he was fooling her. Women know the power of silence. A woman is silent so long as she thinks it's to her benefit to say nothing. When she starts talking that's the time to worry. I'm sorry I shot my mouth off. Let's have some coffee, if the water hasn't boiled away."

"I don't understand such talk," said Mrs. Weber. "Gertrude, I never heard the likes of this from you, I never would have believed it. You, of all people!"

"I'm sorry, mother," said Gertrude, who wasn't at all sorry.

Mr. Weber turned to David, "You're Jewish, of course."

"Yes," said David.

"The Jewish question," said Mrs. Weber to herself.

"What about the Jewish question?" said Mr. Weber in a somewhat belligerent tone. "Do you want me to keep quiet and you take over?"

Mrs. Weber said nothing, apparently realizing that she had been as outspoken as she dared to be for the time. And David realized where Loring got his brusqueness from.

"Some women have a habit of interrupting whenever a man speaks," said Mr. Weber. He turned to David. "What do you think about the possibilities of the establishment of a Jewish homeland in Palestine?"

"I don't know what to say, Mr. Weber. It's so breathtaking a possibility, that I just don't know."

"Have we a chance, Mr. Polonsky?"

"I don't know. I certainly hope so, Mr. Weber."

"I do, too."

"Have you changed your mind, dad, about Zionism?" asked Gertrude.

"That's one of the things that's been aggravating me lately," said Mr. Weber. "We German Jews have been all wrong about Zionism, most of us."

"I always worked for Hadassah," said Mrs. Weber softly, as if she were not sure that she dared speak up.

"Yes, you did," sair her husband roughly. "But you didn't know what you were doing or why or anything. It was a social matter to you. The other women were doing it, so you did it. I said nothing about all those meetings, because, well . . . oh, what's the use. But, Mr. Polonsky, I take it you're a Russian Jew. Of course." He laughed. "We *Yahoodim* have looked down upon you, and all the time you were our superiors. That's a joke, a bitter joke."

David was attracted by Mr. Weber despite his rudeness to his wife, despite the cruelty he displayed toward his son and sometimes toward his daughter. There was something brilliantly genuine about him . . . there was failure and tragedy and disappointment all over him, and this somehow gave him stature . . . indeed, he gave stature to the whole room where they were sitting . . .

"Well, Mr. Weber," he said, "I'm sure you haven't forgotten that Dr. Theodor Herzl, the father of political Zionism, was a German, well, a Viennese Jew, so you don't have to feel so humble, I mean German Jews as a group."

"Yes, he was a very great and tragic figure. My father, *selig,* had a chance to meet him at the first Zionist Congress in Basle, Switzerland."

"Didn't he?" asked David.

"No, he didn't. My father was pretty dumb in many things, the way nearly all the German rabbis were, though my father was not a rabbi. They all thought that Dr. Herzl was insane, parochial. Isn't that terrible?"

"Well," began David, "Zionism did look hopeless at the end of the last century.

"That's another thing that aggravates me," said Mr. Weber.

"I'm sorry, dear," said Mrs. Weber, "but I do wish you wouldn't use that word again."

"What word?" asked Mr. Weber.

"Aggravate."

"Oh," said Mr. Weber, and immediately ignored her. "It does aggravate me. You Russian Jews saw it right away, how wonderful an idea it was. As a matter of fact, you saw it before Dr. Herzl did. I've been doing a lot of reading into Jewish history and Zionist history lately. You Russian Jews had an organization called Lovers of Zion, before Herzl even took his Jewishness seriously. You saw that Palestine was and always had to be a Jewish land. You were close to destiny."

"You're really excited about it, dad," said Gertrude.

"What an idea Zionism is!" he said. "What an idea! Impossible the dumb German rabbis said, stupid, and the rest of it, so did my father. Yes, Zionism is stupid, just as stupid as history, as destiny."

"We haven't got the country yet," said Gertrude. "Of course, I'm all for it."

"We'll get it," said Mr. Weber. "Otherwise the whole Hitler business makes no sense. I can see it happening."

"That's another thing he's always saying now. 'I can see it happening.' So I ask what, and he doesn't answer me."

Gertrude smiled. "I can't help it," she said. "It's funny, dad walking up and down the apartment saying, 'I can see it happening.'"

"Well," said Mr. Weber, "that's about the only thing left now that makes life worth living."

"Dad, please," exclaimed Loring. "Don't you see this kind of talk annoys mother?"

"She doesn't have to listen," Mr. Weber said. "She can go to another room."

"Dad! Don't say that!" said Gertrude.

"Don't take him too seriously, children. I've been hearing this for almost fifty years," said Mrs. Weber.

"Such talk, such talk," mumbled Loring.

"I've been reading the Talmud lately," said Mr. Weber. "A wonderful book. I've spent all my life selling knives and paper and pencils and shoes, and never looked in the Talmud, next to the Bible the greatest book ever written by man. I have to read a translation, of course, and the volume I'm reading is a condensation. I can imagine how wonderful it is in the original Aramaic. Anyway, there's a passage there where it says that two rabbis are arguing for pages and pages if life is worth living, and then they get tired, and they come to the conclusion that since we're here anyway, let's make the best of it."

"It is funny," said Gertrude.

Mr. Weber continued, as if he hadn't heard his daughter. "That and music and books, that's all that's left."

"You're making me nervous, too, dad . . . *that's all that's left* . . . you mustn't think that way."

Suddenly Mr. Weber turned to Loring, "What's going to become of Morris?"

"He's old enough to run his own life," said Loring.

"Have you prepared him to run his own life?" asked Mr. Weber.

"Oh, dad, you starting that again?" asked Gertrude.

"You're right, daughter. I shouldn't. My son's two children

375

might just as well not be. Morris a wastrel, his own father didn't see him for years, and still wouldn't, if mother and I didn't take him to our home, and now he's running around with some no-good woman who isn't even divorced yet."

"Goodness!" exclaimed Mrs. Weber. "Where did you find that out?"

"It's true," said Mr. Weber. "He told me. And she has a child. They're probably living together, she and Morris. Do you blame me why I am aggravated?"

"Nothing I can do," said Loring.

"No, nothing you can do," said Mr. Weber. "Children, children, they walk all over you when they're young, and they break your heart when they're older."

"Oh, to hell with it," said Loring. "Come on, David. This place is driving me nuts. I came over here for a friendly visit, and this is what I get. Come on, David." He walked out, and David followed him, after saying a quick good-night. Once out in the street Loring mumbled that he had to go somewhere, and almost before David knew it, Loring had left him.

Fifteen

When David came back to his rooming house, he found a message from Mary Tobias to call her at once. When he did he was told to go immediately to Helen's house: "Something terrible has happened. I'm afraid Mordecai is dying, and Helen is frantic." By the time David came to Helen's house, he found nobody there, only a note telling him to go to a hospital not far away. There he found Helen and Mary and Raphael Tobias in the waiting room. "They're not letting us up," said Mary. "He's getting oxygen. After a while they will let us up. They'll let us know. A nurse will tell us."

David was wondering where Helen's son was, and was about to ask when Helen looked at him and said, "Thank you for coming. I asked Mary to call you. I don't know why I asked for you, but I wanted friends, and I thought . . ."

"Of course," said David, and immediately felt that his whole relationship with Helen had been exposed. He looked at the two Tobiases, and saw nothing there, and at once he felt better: it was clear that whether they knew or not, it wouldn't matter to them.

Helen said, looking at David, "I didn't tell you, I guess, but Mordecai has been very sick for a long time. The doctor said it was very serious but not very critical. His liver. At first they thought it was hepatitis, some sickness of the liver. He was

377

yellow for a while, two, three years ago, and that was a sign that it was hepatitis, or it could be. He had pain in that place. Then he got less yellow, but he still had pain, and then he got pain in the upper stomach, and then in the chest, and he couldn't eat, only some things. Doctors really know so little. Some said he should eat only dairy, some said meat, some said eggs, I don't know. He used to make something of his own, milk and honey and bread soaked in milk, and that he could eat. And Passover wine, that he liked." She smiled painfully. "Remember, Mary, two years ago, how much wine he drank?"

"Yes," said Mary, "and he looked so well, too."

David was puzzled and pained that Helen had not told him that the Tobiases were friendly with Mordecai . . . and he wondered whether all such relationships as had been between Helen and him had, of necessity, big gaps of lack of knowledge . . . no matter how intense the passion, no matter how happy the relationship, it was not a relationship of complete give and take, of complete confidence . . . and perhaps, he thought, that was one of the major unpleasantnesses of such a relationship . . . physically, emotionally, even spiritually, it was most intimate and satisfying, but it was surrounded by cold winds.

"He looked fine to me, too," said Raphael.

"But I knew and he knew," said Helen. "And he prayed and I prayed. They found a sign of cancer in two or three examinations they made, and also the heart. I never knew he had a bad heart, I always thought that in the heart he was strongest, he said he was so good in the heart that he didn't know he had a heart. I always have had pains in my breasts and right here in the middle, and I was always afraid I had heart sickness and high blodd pressure, but the doctors said it was nothing, only nervousness, gas, I don't know what. But Mordecai had a bad heart, the doctors told me, and they told his brother. Mordecai didn't know it. So he fainted this afternoon. His brother called me. I wasn't worried. He has fainted before, you know that, Mary . . ."

"Yes."

"I didn't think it was anything. We all faint, get dizzy, and we go on. Even in the street. Nothing. With him it's happened before, too. But when I came this time, I saw it was different.

He was blue. Anyway, we took him to the hospital, and the things they told me."

"He's very sick," said Mary, softly, to David. "But it's not all hopeless. Helen, it isn't. You heard what the doctor said. He said his pressure was down, his pulse was regular, and they're giving him oxygen just for protection."

"I know, I know," said Helen, "but he looked so bad."

"I didn't think he looked so bad," said Mary. "Anyway, the oxygen will make him look better, and it will make him feel better."

"He was perfectly conscious," said Raphael. "He said hello to me, he knew who I was."

"He knew everything that was going on," said Mary.

"But I never saw him look like this," said Helen. "It wasn't the same Mordecai, it wasn't."

"He's looked better," said Mary, "and he's looked worse. Besides, by looks you never can tell."

"Looks don't tell everything," said Raphael.

"No," said David.

"How long does it take to give oxygen?" asked Helen.

"A half hour, sometimes an hour, two hours, sometimes they keep them under a bag of oxygen for a whole day," said Raphael. "So it means nothing that they haven't called us. They might even ask us to go up while he's still in the oxygen tent, but at the beginning they don't want him to be disturbed."

A nurse came into the waiting room. "You may come up, if you wish," she said, "but only for a little while."

"How is he?" asked Helen.

"I'm only the floor nurse," she said. "The ward nurse will tell you."

As they went into the ward David's heart sank: it was a humiliating place for a human being to be . . . it was a long and drab-looking room, with cots on both sides, some surrounded by screens, some exposed, so to speak . . . nurses were constantly coming in and out, stopping at a bed and then leaving to go to another bed . . . there were some men, in white jackets, at the farther end of this room, that David imagined were doctors . . . soon only one of the group remained, and he walked over to one of the beds.

"He's seeing Mordecai," Helen said. "That must be the oxygen tent they have over him."

"You have marvelous eyes," said Mary.

They were now at Mordecai's bed . . . Raphael, Mary, and David stood to the side, as Helen walked over to him. The doctor had left.

"How are you, Mordecai?" she said.

"Good," he whispered.

"You look much better," Helen said.

Mary walked over and said, "Hello, Mordecai," and she turned to Helen and said, "He's got more color in his face, don't you think?"

"Yes," Helen said.

"I think I'll just be here," said Raphael to David.

David said he would do the same . . . and there David and Raphael stood, and soon Mary joined them, a few feet away from Mordecai's bed, and all the time Helen stood beside him, looking at him . . . a nurse came to the bed, took Mordecai's pulse and temperature, and walked away . . . Helen did not ask her how Mordecai was . . . soon Mordecai closed his eyes, he had gone off to sleep, and Helen continued to stand by the bed . . . an orderly came by and gave her a chair, and he said, "You might as well sit down."

"I'll be going soon," she said to him.

"Stay as long as you want," he said. "Might as well sit down."

She sat down and continued to look at Mordecai, whose chest went up and down rhythmically . . . David was glad he was breathing so regularly and, apparently, so vigorously . . . it seemed to mean that at least his heart was working properly . . . but there was the cancerous condition: what was being done about that? David decided he wouldn't ask the Tobiases or Helen.

A doctor came over, smiled at Helen, and put his stethoscope to Mordecai's chest . . . he also pushed gently at the region of his stomach . . . Helen followed the doctor, as he went off, and then the two stopped and talked.

"I think he looks pretty bad," said Mary.

"I'm afraid he does," said Raphael.

"If there were only something that could be done," said Mary.

"I'm afraid there isn't," said Raphael. "His heart, cancer, high blood pressure. All the doctors say in such cases is rest and hope."

Helen was with them now. "The doctor said he's doing as well as could be expected, considering everything. He's been doped, so he's resting. He said he could sleep this way for hours and hours. Thank God, he has no pain. But he did say his liver is swollen, and that's not good. And he said the spleen was tender, and that this could mean it was infected, and he said he had a little anemia."

Mary looked at Raphael, then said, "In a hospital lying on your back all day and all night, you can get weak from that alone."

"But he looks so bad," said Helen. "His color is so yellow, green."

They were in the street now.

"Do you want to stay with us, Helen?" asked Mary.

"No . . ."

"You can bring. . . ," began Mary.

"No, thanks, I just want to be alone. They said they'd call me if . . ."

"Then we'll take you home," said Mary.

"No, thanks," said Helen.

"I'll walk her home," offered David. "It's on my way, anyway."

David and Helen walked slowly and silently. After a few blocks she put her arm in his, but there didn't seem to be any personal emotion in her action.

"If there's anything I can do," began David.

"Thank you. I'm glad you came. Maybe I shouldn't have asked Mary to call you. I was hysterical, I guess."

"Oh, no. I was glad to come."

"I knew you would come, David." She hesitated, then she said, "I felt you're the only one I can really talk to. I mean you would understand. But now, I don't know why, I don't feel like talking. Maybe I will a little later."

"You don't have to talk, you don't have to do anything."

"Thank you."

They walked on in silence, then she said, "I feel strange about what I'm going to say, David. I'm not sorry, in a way,

381

that Mordecai is going to die. The doctor told me long ago, two, three years ago, that he couldn't live very long. Cancer, his heart, his liver, anemia, there's something wrong with his stomach, too, his spleen, everything isn't right. The doctor said his mind won't be the way it used to be, and that's the worst thing of all, the mind, isn't it?"

"I guess so."

"But I'm sorry for him, so sorry, David, you just don't know." She stopped for a few moments, then she added, "I'm sorry for him and for me, too. We never should have got married. It's my fault, as much as his. I never could be a wife to him, never, really. I just couldn't. I knew it the first night. I know it's horrible to talk this way, David, but it's true, it's true. I can't help it. Do you hate me for saying this, David?"

"Why should I hate you?"

She looked at him seriously, as she stopped walking. "You don't hate me, David, please tell me, you don't, do you?"

"Of course, not, Helen."

She continued to look at him, then she started walking again. She said, "It's so pathetic. All the time, in his whole life, he has lost everything he wanted, everything, David." She seemed to be stifling a sob. "There is no Hebrew theatre anywhere now. His company died here. Nobody cares about Hebrew. And he wanted me so very much. I know it, David. But I couldn't want him the same way, I just couldn't."

"These things can't be helped," said David.

"But it's even worse," said Helen, and stopped.

"What?"

"He's going to die just as Hebrew is going to be revived, and there'll be a Hebrew theatre in Palestine, and there'll be a revival of Hebrew all over the world."

"I don't know what . . ."

"That's one of the things Mordecai and I always fought about. Maybe it was one of the most important things that we fought about. I kept on saying he shouldn't feel depressed, that Hebrew is not dead, that there'll be a Hebrew theatre, and I also told him that the Jews will have a nation again, and that's when he laughed at me. I don't suppose you believe this either, I mean do you believe it?"

"Well . . ."

"It will happen, David, it will happen very soon," said Helen. "I'm sure of it, I am as sure of it as I possibly can be about anything. And that's what makes me so sad for Mordecai. And it's in a time like this that I find it so difficult to believe in God. It's funny. I believe in God when I think of Palestine and the Jews, that they'll soon have their country, only a God could do that, only the Jewish God. But when it comes to dying, to Mordecai, I can't believe, I can't understand why a God should want to do that to Mordecai, or why a God should do terrible personal things, to people, to children, I just can't understand it."

David passed the street where he ordinarily turned in to go to his room. He continued walking with Helen, who was silent now.

Then she said, "I worry about you and me. I think I hurt you, and I know how I hurt you, but I sometimes think that a woman has to hurt a man, even when she loves him very much, I mean she hurts him not wanting to, she hurts him because she loves him so much, you know what I mean?"

"Well . . ."

"I think it was Chekhov who said it, or maybe it was Tolstoy, I don't remember, one of the great Russian writers, the Russian writers know a great deal about women, more than any other writers, except maybe Jewish writers, but the Russian writers know a lot about women. So Chekhov said that a man feels oppressed when he's in the presence of a woman who loves him deeply, he feels better about her when he's away and enjoying her love from the distance, he also said that a man can't stand too much love for a long period."

"There's a lot of sense in that," said David.

"Everybody knows that love means two different things to men and to women," said Helen. "Men are puzzled by things that seem perfectly natural to women."

"What do you mean?"

"Well, like now. We've just come from Mordecai. He's dying, he's my husband. I am terribly concerned about him, I'm sorry for him. But I still don't love him. I love you, I feel very much drawn to you right now, and it's perfectly natural to me. But I suppose you can't understand it, you probably think I'm cruel, terrible, and things like that."

"Well, yes . . ."

"I knew it."

"I mean . . ."

"Don't begin explaining and apologizing, David. Your first answer was the honest one. Men are not always happy when loved. Loving is a woman's affair, they feel it's nice but for women mostly, women who are interested in that alone."

"Well . . ."

Helen took hold of David's arm, and then grasped his hand. "Darling, I don't mind, I really don't. I feel so confused now I can afford to be honest, and I am comfortable in talking this way, because, I guess, you wouldn't dare to argue with me now, even though you probably think I'm awful for saying I love you when my husband is dying." She took David's hand and kissed it. "I do love you, David."

David squeezed her hand. He also wanted to kiss her, but something held him back.

"You know, darling, one of the things I love about you, even though you're angry with me right now?"

"I'm not angry, Helen."

"Puzzled."

"Yes, puzzled, now that you've said it, Helen."

"What I love so much about you is that you're so Jewish, so honest with your feelings, with your convictions, even with your male sense of morality."

"What do you mean, Helen?" asked David, who now realized how marvelous a woman she was, with all her confusion and even with all her trickiness . . . surrounding her female-hood was a being of great dignity and stature and perception, and also loveliness.

"What do I mean by morality, David? I mean only that women subscribe to a different kind of morality than men. They subscribe to the morality of the heart, first, and when that fails them, they subscribe to the same kind of morality that men believe in. Women learn very early, darling, that the heart does not always protect, because men don't always believe in the laws of the heart, and when women learn that they say to the men, 'All right, then we call upon your sense of decency, which is your inferior morality.' Do you understand, darling?"

"Frankly, no—and yes."

384

"That's an honest answer, David," said Helen, and kissed his hand again. "You have lovely fingers. A woman's fingers."

"Oh . . ."

"Yes. I'm so very glad you decided to take me home. I was hoping you would. But, darling, I ask you to make me one promise, no, two promises."

"What?"

"When you come to my house, which will be very soon, you won't come up, and you will kiss me deep and long, and then go back to your room."

"Yes, if that's what you want."

"It's not what I want, it's what I prefer."

David wasn't sure he understood what Helen meant . . . suddenly he did realize what she meant. "Of course."

"You know, darling, we are in the street, but I feel so close to you, so very much closer than ever before, so very, very close, David." She pressed his hand to her breast.

"I do, too, Helen," said David.

They were at the door of her apartment house. "Now say good-night to me," said Helen.

He took her in his arms and pressed her close to him, closer and closer, and then he kissed her long and deep on the mouth.

"Thank you, David," Helen said and walked into her apartment house.

David looked at her as she disappeared. He felt as if he had entered into another realm of being.

Sixteen

Two weeks later, in the morning, Helen called David and told him that her husband had died shortly after midnight, and that the funeral would be from a certain chapel that very afternoon. She did not ask him to come to the funeral, but David went. The room where Mordecai was laid out in a coffin was narrow, though the ceiling was high. There was only one window, and on the sill, in the center, was a huge pot of flowers. Helen had greeted David, taken him to the room where Mordecai was lying, in an open coffin, and walked out. David was alone with Mordecai, and he felt strange, almost as if he were intruding upon Mordecai's privacy.

David looked at Mordecai. He appeared peaceful. This embarrassed David, for in that calm face there seemed to be a knowledge that hurt David. He felt an arm touch his, and he saw it was Helen who had come in again. The two remained standing, silent, and soon she led him out of the room. When they had come into the hall she said, "Thank you for coming."

David looked at her, not knowing what to say. She looked composed, there was a shine in her eyes. She put her arm in his and introduced him to some of the people there, and again David found himself alone. He felt he didn't belong here, his mind went back to the room where Mordecai was lying. He felt closer to him than to any of the people around him.

"Mordecai knew how sick he was," said one of the people within David's hearing.

"He did?"

"Oh, yes."

"How do you know?"

"How do I know? I know. He had great courage. But he knew."

"Ah, such a thing to know."

"He knew."

And David wondered how many other things Mordecai knew, and a new wave of embarrassment went through him. He saw Helen going from one group of people to another, and he saw her son following her. The son looked exactly like Mordecai, and David wanted to talk to him, but he didn't know how. He wished that Helen would bring the son over to him, but she seemed too busy.

A man said to David, "Terrible, isn't it?"

"Yes," said David

"And right now, too, when there is so much talk about the Jews and Palestine and Hebrew, terrible, terrible for him to die now."

"Yes," said David, and the man walked off, still mumbling to himself, "Terrible, terrible."

Another man walked over to David. He seemed to be in his sixties, he had a kindly face, and he seemed to be preoccupied. "A fine man he was," said the man. "A very fine man."

"Yes, he was," said David.

The man looked off into the distance dreamily. "I was hoping, but it looks like it won't be. Well, Mordecai would understand."

"What do you have in mind?" asked David.

"We were hoping, a few of us, that some of the people who are at the United Nations now would come over and maybe say a few words. Mordecai would have liked that. Some of us even thought that maybe Dr. Weizmann would come over. He's in this country now, you know, at the United Nations."

"It would be nice," said David.

"Well, some things have to come ahead of other things," said the man. "But sometimes I wonder."

"You wonder about what?"

"Maybe I shouldn't say it. I wonder about what should come

first and what should come next. And maybe some things can come first together. After all, Mordecai gave his life to Hebrew, to Palestine, to Jewish things, and that's what we're all struggling for, for Hebrew, for Palestine, for a country where we can have our own culture, pure and not mixed with other cultures. After all, that's what Zionism is. A country worth fighting for is more than just a country."

"That is true."

"Maybe I shouldn't say it," continued the man, "but I should think that they could have sent somebody over, not Dr. Weizmann, that I understand, but somebody else. But, who knows? It's very serious what is happening there, in the United Nations. So maybe Mordecai will understand. Nu . . ." And he walked off.

Helen was with David again. She put her arm in his. He wanted to press her to him, and at the same time he wished that she didn't put her arm in his. She had done it with other people, men and women, but David considered himself in a different category.

"You know who that man is who just spoke to you, David?"

"No."

"That's Avrom. He has done more for the Hebrew stage than anybody else in the past fifty years. He used to be a business man in Russia, leather, I think, shoes, too. He had factories in Germany and in France and England, he still has, I think. And he loved Hebrew and the theatre, and he loved Mordecai. He tried to get Dr. Weizmann to come here to say something, but I don't know, Dr. Weizmann is so busy. But isn't it wonderful for him to do this?"

"Yes," said David.

The Tobiases joined them now. Helen excused herself and walked off.

"I don't know," said Mary. "It's hard to believe. We knew he was very sick, but his dying, that's different, it's so hard to believe."

"Did you meet him, David?" asked Raphael.

"Only once," said David.

"He was very sweet," said Mary. "He took the domestic situation very hard, but that was an old story."

"I heard he left a play in Hebrew," said Raphael.

"I heard that, too," said Mary. "You know, David, he looked so shy and timid. But you should have seen him on the stage. We once saw him in *Der Golem*. He was absolutely terrific. You wouldn't think it was the same man. Like a giant, and such speaking, so tremendous, he looked as if he were seven feet tall, didn't he, Raphael?"

"I've never seen such a transformation in a man," said Raphael.

"I don't know what to think now," said Mary. "He led such a sad life, and he was in pain at the end."

"Even before he went to the hospital the last time," said Raphael. "I used to see it on his face. Now and then a twitch would go across his face, or he would move here and there in the chair, he couldn't find a comfortable place, it looked."

"Yes," said Mary. "That is true, but it's so sad. I know it happens with people, but when it happens to a man like Mordecai. And he had so many problems, I mean, inner ones. You know, Raphael, I've been thinking, I meant to say it to you this morning, at breakfast. I always had an idea that, in spite of everything, Mordecai was Orthodox."

"I guess you're right," said Raphael. "He used to talk so . . ."

"That's just what I mean," said Mary. "When he would tell us about the way his father would carry on the *seder,* and when he would tell us about his *cheder* days, his eyes would positively glow with joy."

"He would sing those songs, too," said Raphael. "And what a voice he had! It was really fantastic. He used to sit in that big chair, you know it, David, don't you, the big one in the corner, near the little statue of Lincoln?"

"Yes," said David, whose mind now was so confused and who was so embarrassed by being told so many wonderful things about the man with whose wife he had had such intimate personal relations . . . he didn't remember the chair at all, but he repeated, "Of course, I know that chair."

"He would sit there," continued Raphael, "slouched, his head resting on his chest, and he looked almost as if he were asleep. Suddenly, he would wake up, and he would talk about his boyhood days in the synagogue and in the Hebrew school and just among the Jews of his little village, and then he would sing songs—religious songs and folk songs and sometimes he would sing Russian songs, and he sang in Hebrew and in Yiddish, but I guess he loved the Hebrew language best of all."

"And I remember his theory about the Russians and. . . ," began Mary.

"He may have been right," said Raphael.

"I guess he was, but I confess the first time I heard it I thought it was just his love of the Jews and his hatred of the Russians who hated the Jews, *pogroms,* you know."

"It was a valid theory. The vanquished often conquer their conquerors," said Raphael. "It happened with the Greeks and the Romans. The Romans virtually destroyed Greek nationalism, but it was the Greeks who gave the Romans their civilization. The Romans were proud of this influence of the Greeks, they openly studied the Greek philosophers and writers, and even copied their architecture and sculpture. That doesn't mean that the Romans did not have a philosophy and literature of their own, and also an architecture and sculpture, but the heart of it all is Greek. So a good deal of the same thing, I guess, took place in Russia, though, of course, on a much smaller scale. After all, the Romans didn't hate the Greeks the way the Russians, or a lot of them, hated the Jews. Besides, in the days of the Greeks and the Romans religion didn't play such a big part in dividing peoples and causing hatred among them, the way it is now, I guess that's Christianity's contribution to civilization, it has made religion a cause of war and hatred and killings. Anyway, there's no doubt that Jewish customs and songs and writings did have an effect on Russian songs and writings. That would make a good piece of research."

A silence descended upon the three. Then Raphael said, "It's amazing, really amazing."

"What do you mean, dear?" said Mary.

"The Jews. There's something mystical about them. I can feel it even here."

Mary slowly put her arm in her husband's. "I feel it, too," she said.

"Wherever they are they carry more with them than themselves," said Raphael. "I don't know what it is. I'm only an architect. But I feel it. I mean this something else that they carry. Maybe it's history, maybe it's religion, maybe it's poetry,

maybe it's destiny. I'm using words I don't ordinarily use."
He looked at his wife, almost apologetically.

"Go on, dear."

"Well, that's all I mean. Like here now. Mordecai is dead.
But it is really true when I say that what he stood for lives on.
All these people are proof of it. But I really don't need this
kind of proof. I feel it inside. The Jews are strange and wonderful. I've been wondering about it since Helen first told us about
Mordecai. It's religion and it isn't religion. Mordecai wasn't
religious, and in a way he was, like we said a short while ago.
And I suppose most of these people are not religious, I mean,
observant Jews, but they are religious, in so far as the Jews
are concerned. They believe in the eternal worth of the Jews,
what the Jews stand for, and they believe that this worth will
win out, triumph, and I guess that's what religion is, believing
in something you can't see or prove in the ordinary ways of
proving."

"That's true," said Mary.

"It's very true," said David.

"I was thinking," began Raphael.

"What, dear?"

"The Jews may be the only ones who will come out the
winners out of this war, I mean the winners, in a ghastly sense.
They have been the worst losers, six million killed is a number that the human mind can hardly grasp. Still—and I hate
to say it this way—they will win. They will win their country."

"You really feel that way, dear?" asked Mary excitedly.

"I do."

"I have been feeling this way, too, but I was afraid to say
it," said Mary. "I feel it deep inside of me. Do you, David?"

"Very much so," said David.

"It's so historic, so romantic, I mean so historic," said Mary.

"After two thousand years," said Raphael. "But I am positive about it. It's amazing how an idea gets hold of you. You're
sure it will come about, even though you can't prove it."

"I know," said Mary.

"This will sound strange," said David. "But I think the Arabs
feel the same way. They know they're fighting a losing battle,
that's why they're so furious, making all sorts of threats, using

tricks, making promises, and all that. They know they're licked."

"You are right," said Raphael.

"Mordecai felt that way," said Mary. "He was so dedicated, almost fanatical."

"I'm glad he was fanatical," said Raphael. "On things, matters like this, on all important things you just can't be practical. You can be practical only about unimportant things."

A man came to them and said, "Please go into the chapel, over there."

Slowly the hall emptied . . . and David could almost feel the silence left behind them following them into the chapel proper, which was filling with people, but which was quiet. The casket was directly in front of the platform, parallel with it. There was a black covering over it, with a Mogen David (Star of David) right in the center. Mordecai was alone . . . his friends were in the same large room with him, but he was alone. One could almost sense thoughts and memories about Mordecai floating about the room, and David hoped that they entered into that coffin where Mordecai was . . . a woman rushed down front to find a place on the first row of seats, then a man followed her.

Now a group of men came on the platform, one of them wearing a *yarmulke*. A man, of about the same age as Mordecai, stood up, walked to the center of the platform, and said, "My friends, we are here to say good-bye to a man whom not one of us who had the privilege of knowing will ever forget. He was our conscience, he was our strength, he was our guide. Such faith as he had not one in a million has. But faith is not enough. The Hamans of the world also have faith. With faith must also go values, worthiness. Faith alone, as I say, is not enough. One must have faith in something worthwhile, something holy, something noble.

"Mordecai had faith. He had faith in the Jewish people. He was two thousand years of Jewish history. He had the patience of two thousand years of history—of suffering and joy and triumph and more suffering. He was as sure that the Jewish people would continue, that Jewish history would be eternal, as he was that the sun would rise tomorrow, and that spring would follow winter.

"It was his faith that kept him alive. It was this faith that was his life. The Jewish people was his religion. He believed. He believed in the Jewish people, and he was happy.

"But Mordecai knew that in this world human beings cannot be God. They must limit their activities to things that appeal to them most, to actions where they feel they can be most successful, where they can do their best. And he found that his heart was most at home in the theatre, but a special kind of theatre, the Hebrew theatre. This was the great love of his life.

"And he was happy in his love. Many people go through life without a great spiritual love, but it is this spiritual love that gives meaning to life, perhaps its deepest meaning. And this love Mordecai had. We all learned from him. We all learned of the wonder and greatness of his spiritual love. Those of us who had doubts sometimes needed only to be in Mordecai's company for a few moments, and we were shamed. We all became bigger and stronger and prouder in his company. We are all stronger this very minute, when he lies before us. His example will always encourage us."

A young woman, very beautiful, stood up, and in a simple, quiet, way, said, "I presume to speak for the young men and women of my generation, who owe so much to our leader who has passed on. He inspired us with a deep love for Jewish history, for Jewish traditions, for the Jewish stage, and, above all, for Hebrew as the language of Jewish culture. With all the sincerity I am capable of, I want to pledge our undying devotion to the memory of our leader, and I want to give our pledge to carry on his great dream." She stopped, bowed, and, with dignity, walked backward to her seat as a special mark of respect to the deceased.

Now a third person, a middle-aged man, got up and began by talking in Hebrew. David was surprised by how much he understood, but he was also depressed by how much he didn't understand . . . many years before, when David had gone to Hebrew school, he would have understood every word of Hebrew that was spoken—he could have delivered a speech in Hebrew himself. Then the man began to talk in English: "We Jews are not a nation of worshipers of human beings. We have no heroes, as the non-Jews have. We have many

393

heroes, of course, but we do not commemorate their birthdays or their deaths. We remember their golden deeds throughout the year, and such worship as we bestow we bestow only upon God. We have no Moses Birthday, no Rabbi Akiba Birthday, no Vilner Goan Birthday,. And we have no images of these great men in our synagogues. We have no images in our synagogues. The spirit has no image. We are a people of the spirit.

"We remember our great men every day. Every day is a birthday to us, a day of remembrance of glorious deeds. And every day, for us, will be a day of remembrance to us of what our great leader has done for us. His example will be our great memory. We felt so close to him, all of us. He was our better self. Talking to him was like talking to ourselves. He was Mordecai to all of us, because he was all of us, the part we try to be and that he alone had the strength and greatness to be.

"Since the terrible news reached us all, I have been thinking. I have become a Chassid for a while, and I have the authority of Mordecai himself that we are all Chassidim at heart. We all want to be close to God, to the Great Mystery, if you wish. We all believe in miracles. As Mordecai used to say, Jews have to believe in miracles, for they are themselves a miracle.

"And I have been thinking how like some others of our heroes Mordecai is. God, or the Great Mystery, if you please, has apparently decided to do with Mordecai what He had done with Moses and with Dr. Herzl and so many others. And what I am about to say, I know, will please Mordecai, and it will also make him a little sad. We are living in a very historic period, I might say a very historic day. There is something going on now at the United Nations which will decide the future of the Jewish people.

"And I have no doubt about the outcome. Mordecai himself had no doubt. We often talked about it. He talked about it with many of us. As he said, the Jewish people had come out of the desert, and were heading back home, back to their own land. And Mordecai had no doubt about the outcome of what is going on at the United Nations. 'The times are with us,' he said. 'History is with us. I can see the handwriting on the wall.' Yes, my friends, it is a question of another week, another month, perhaps several months, though I don't think so. And

394

we shall once more have our land. And we shall once more have our culture. And once more Hebrew will be the chief and most sacred language of the Jewish people. Hebrew will be spoken on the streets of the old-new land of the Jews, it will be spoken in the schools, in the stores, in the parks, everywhere. And it will be spoken on the stage, in the theatre that was so close to the heart of the man we are honoring now, and who honored us with his friendship.

"How happy Mordecai would have been to have heard Hebrew spoken on the stage of our rewon nation! But it was not fated, as it was not fated for Moses to see the land he had hoped to take his people to, and just as it was not fated for Dr. Theodore Herzl to see Palestine as the rewon Jewish homeland. Mordecai is in good company. He is in worthy company.

"Mordecai was one of the many who made a dream come true. He was one of the greatest of these many. As we say our last earthly farewell to him, we want to assure him that the dream he dedicated his life to will always be our guide."

There was a hush in the chapel. The man with the *yarmulke* stood up and chanted *El Molay Rachmim* (Lord All Merciful), the traditional chant at a funeral. He finished, and four men came to the casket and slowly wheeled it to the door . . . then Mordecai's family, Helen, their son, the brother, others followed. David waited till nearly all in the chapel had joined the procession, and then he left . . . by the time he was in the street, the casket had already been placed in the hearse, which was far ahead . . . David waited . . . people were going into cars . . . then the procession of cars, led by the hearse, began to move . . . David watched the line of cars, till he could see it no more . . . a few people remained, talking . . . a quiet descended upon the street . . . and David turned to go back to his room.

As he walked home he felt ennobled for having been at Mordecai's funeral, for having heard what had been said . . . he felt he had participated in something good and profoundly human, and also profoundly historic . . . and a new and deeper pride entered into his heart, a pride of peoplehood, of being a part of the Jewish people and the millennia-old tradition, a pride of being a palpable instrument of destiny, a pride of being an integral part of the flow of eternity . . . and he sensed that great events were on the horizon.

Seventeen

The catastrophe that had befallen the European Jews at the hands of the Hitler government had aroused little more than a flicker of protest from the non-Jewish world. There were glorious exceptions, even within the Nazi-controlled countries, where non-Jews risked their lives day and night to hide Jews from the Nazi officials. Denmark and Holland were havens of refuge for fleeing Jews, and so were Norway and Sweden. But the non-Jewish world as a whole was virtually silent. When the Nazis offered to exchange large numbers of Jews for tractors, the Christian world did not respond. When the Nazis offered to allow large numbers of the Jews to go to whatever land would have them, for a relatively small consideration, the Christian world again did not respond.

And yet the horror of the extinction of six million Jews did eventually seep into the conscience of the world. As the conquering democratic armies swept across Europe and opened up the concentration camps and investigated the crematoria, where millions of Jewish men, women, and children were burned to death, and photographs of what they saw began to appear in the press, the non-Jewish world was filled with a sense of shame and guilt, and there arose a conviction, in certain quarters, that "something has to be done." Preachers, at long last, began to discuss the Jewish problem from their pulpits, there were more letters in the newspapers, there were more articles in the magazines, and the halls of Congress as well as of the State legislatures echoed to speeches about the plight of the Jews in the countries formerly dominated by Hitler.

There was another development that was most important within the Jewish world itself and also had influence in the non-Jewish world. Hitherto the Jewish world had been divided into two camps with respect to the solution of the Jewish problem. The Zionists maintained, that in a world such as prevailed and such as was likely to prevail for a long time into the foreseeable future, no solution was possible without a Jewish homeland, and that this homeland had to be the traditional one, Palestine. Another camp maintained that the Jews were not a nation but a spiritual community, whose function it was to lead the world spiritually by precept and example. To this latter group, for a long time, belonged a substantial portion of Reform Jewry in America and also a substantial portion of religiously non-affiliated Jewry—the intellectuals who were conscious of their Jewish origins but only superficially. Many of the latter were for assimilation, and others looked upon themselves simply as cultural Jews. By and large Jews of Eastern European origin were inclined toward the Zionist position, while the Jews of German and Austrian origin were inclined toward the opposite position. There were many anomalies in this division of attitudes. Perhaps the most interesting of them was that the leader of political Zionism, Dr. Theodore Herzl, was an Austrian Jew. He did not originate the Zionist idea, which had been a basic concept of a large section of the intellectuals of East European Jewry, but it was he who gave it unity, world dignity, and it was he who integrated the basic philosophical concept of Zionism with the political realities of the world.

What Hitler did to the Jews brought about a sharp change in the point of view of Reform Jewry and of religiously non-affiliated Jews. Whereas before Hitler Rabbi Stephen S. Wise was one of the few Reform rabbis who espoused the Zionist idea, much to the dismay of his fellow Reform rabbis, there were now hardly any Reform rabbis who spoke against Zionism. Events had shaken them. Some Reform rabbis still looked upon Judaism as basically a spiritual civilization, with barely any political significance, but now they were faced with a complex of undeniable facts that made the Zionist solution a practical one: no other nation wanted to offer the pitifully few remaining European Jews a home. There was, then, only one place for them to go, namely, a Jewish homeland. There was no Jewish homeland. There was, then, only one thing to do: establish a Jewish homeland. A fantastic project? Perhaps, but Britain had long ago, in the Balfour Declaration, promised the Jews, with all sorts of circumlocutions, to provide them with Palestine as their homeland. It was time that Britain made good its promise. And now that the United Nations was being established it was an excellent time to work for a Jewish Palestine.

Nearly all American Jewry was united in the belief that sheer humanity made it necessary for the Jews somehow to get Palestine as their national homeland. Palestine would be a place where any Jew, as a Jew, could find a home. But suppose all the remaining Jews of Europe wanted to go to Palestine, and with them also many of the Jews of the United States and of the South and Central American countries: could so arid and so undeveloped a land take care of four, three, two or even one million people? It probably couldn't. Therefore, the land had to be developed. But such development needed money, and quickly, too, and American Jews were the only Jews who could afford the necessary money. Then American Jews would have to supply the money.

Meanwhile, the American Jews would have to collect large sums of money at once to take care of the bare physical needs of the wandering, emaciated, bewildered Jews who had escaped Hitler's concentration camps or somehow survived them. Immediately there began a stupendous drive over the country for money to help the European Jews, and millions of dollars were collected.

Hitherto non-Jewish Jews became more conscious of their Jewishness. They read the Jewish news in the newspapers with greater interest. They read more books that dealt with the Jewish problem, more novelists and short story writers and playwrights began to write about Jewish characters and Jewish situations. These spread across the land the substance of the story of Dr. Theodore Herzl. Not all the facts were accurate, there was some romanticising, yet the spirit of the man was truly promulgated. Similar romantic reconstructions of the life of Eliezer Ben Yehuda, the great Hebrew lexicographer, were spread across the land. There were accounts about such heroes of Zionism as Dr. Shmarya Levin and Nahum Sokoloff and Dr. Max Nordau and Pinski. But over them all was the story of Dr. Theodore Herzl. There was something in his life that appealed especially to the returnees among the American-Jewish intellectuals and non-intellectuals.

David began to hear about Dr. Herzl in groups where hitherto hardly anything was heard about any Jewish subjects and personalities. He heard stray bits of fact, stray bits of legend, and people were discussing heatedly what was going on in the United Nations. There were reports in the newspapers that the whole Palestine Issue would soon come up, that there were maneuvers behind the scenes by those countries friendly to the Jews, and by others who were not friendly. The first group of countries were for having the United Nations Assembly vote for giving some part (perhaps all) of what was now British-mandated Palestine to the Jewish people as their national homeland. Among the countries that felt this way were France and virtually all the South and Central American countries. But England did not hide its opposition. This was a great disappointment to the people in whose company David spent most of his leisure time. It was a great disappointment to David, too.

Over the years he had had the feeling that England, the Mother of Parliaments, the land of Magna Charta, the land of John Locke and Edmund Burke and John Stuart Mill and of Shakespeare and Shelley and Keats, was also the land of friendship for oppressed peoples. Further, there was the fact, that England had had a Jew as its Prime Minister. True, he was a converted Jew, but he was a Jew nevertheless. Non-Jews considered him a Jew, despite his conversion, and he himself appeared to think of himself as a Jew, at least, he was fully conscious of his Jewish heritage. Yet this same England, the England that had given the world the Balfour Declaration— the first statement by any nation, after two thousand years of Jewish exile, that the Jews had a moral and historic right to Palestine as their national homeland—this same England was now siding with the Arab countries, who unanimously were violently opposed to giving the Jews sovereignty over any part of Palestine.

David discussed this matter with Dryfus, who had become deeply interested in Jewish matters.

"I never thought I'd feel this way," said Dryfus. "I always laughed at the word *mystical,* but now I myself feel mystical."

"How?" asked David.

"Well, about the Jews. I don't know how to describe it. I feel I am certain about something about to happen, but I can't prove it in the ordinary ways."

"What ordinary ways?"

"I don't know. There used to be ways of proving things, you know, facts, but now I'm not so sure they are the only ways. I used to laugh at people who said there are all kinds of truth, and some truths you can only feel. But now I'm with the people I used to laugh at. That's strange. I never knew before that Jews were so mystical."

"I don't understand," said David.

"Well, there are a lot of things about the Jews that are beyond the laws of nature. Now, that sounds strange. But it's true. I don't know how else to say it. I'm mystical about the Jews. I'm mystical about Dr. Herzl." Dryfus stopped, smiled, and said, "This will surprise you, David, but I wouldn't dream of calling Dr. Herzl plain Herzl. I wouldn't dare. That gives you some idea of how mystical I've become."

"Yes . . ."

"All I mean, I guess," said Dryfus, "is that destiny, whatever it is, is on the side of the Jews, though the poor Jews have to pay plenty for it."

"What do you mean?"

"You sound like a district attorney."

"I don't mean to."

"I know. What do I mean? Well, I mean that something wonderful is going to happen to the Jews. There's something in the air."

"I feel the same way," said David. "A lot of other people feel the same way. But what I don't understand is Great Britain."

"Well, I don't either," said Dryfus. "And then, I do. Britain, as Napoleon, or somebody else said, is a merchant. It has no temporary morality, just as a grocer has no temporary morality. I guess, now that I think of it, that's what Napoleon said, England is a corner grocer or something like that, not a merchant. Well, a corner grocer has no morality. What gives him a penny profit is moral, what doesn't isn't moral. Right at this moment, I don't really know all the facts, but I know enough, Britain needs oil or something from the Arabs, so it's with the Arabs and against the Jews. But there are people in Great Britain, maybe Winston Churchill himself, who know damn well that the Jews are Britain's real friends, not the Arabs. It's an idiosyncrasy, this way Britain has of doing business. It's a whore at times, but at bottom it's a lady. Now that makes no sense as far as women are concerned. With women, a whore is a whore and that's all, but with nations it's different. A nation can be a whore at night and a lady in the morning or afternoon. I still think that Britain is with the Jews, in the long run. I know, the long run could mean the lives of hundreds of thousands of Jews. Well, all I can say is that you shouldn't blame Great Britain. Blame God. He's the one who makes no sense. Anyway, I'm not too worried about Britain. In the end it will be on the side of the Jews."

"But the United Nations," said David, "how will Britain vote? To give the Jews some sovereignty, or will Britain vote to give in to the Arabs?"

"I don't know," said Dryfus. "I suppose Britain will vote for the Arabs, but I think the resolution for giving sovereignty to the Jews will pass."

"What makes you so sure?" asked David.

"Mysticism."

"Mysticism?"

"Yes. I feel it. I'm positive."

"I hope you're right."

"Don't you feel the same way?"

"I do," said David, "but I was afraid to say so."

"That makes it unanimous," said Dryfus. "Millions of Jews can't be wrong about what they mystically feel certain about."

"Well, maybe . . ."

"But you're sure, aren't you?" asked Dryfus.

"Yes."

"That's all that matters."

"Dr. Herzl must have been right. I've been reading what he predicted, that the Jews will have Palestine as their national homeland in fifty years, and he said this just about fifty years ago."

"Yes, I read that, too," said David, "and I've had the same feeling. There seems to be some sort of plan."

"What do you mean?" asked Dryfus.

"Well, you may laugh, but I'm thinking about God. Destiny, or whatever you want to call it. All sorts of things have been running through my mind. I remember reading somewhere or maybe I heard it in my father's house, that whoever harms the Jews will pay a heavy price. God is on the side of the Jews. Now, I never thought I'd say that. It's chauvinistic, superstitious, and all that. And I don't mean it in a chauvinistic or superstitious sense. I don't know just how I mean it. But I feel something is happening. And it makes me feel proud."

"I know," said Dryfus.

Then David told Dryfus about Mordecai's funeral services, the mystical feeling that went through the hall.

"I read the obituaries in the *Times* every day, sometimes that page is the most interesting one in the whole paper, a damn sight more alive than the editorial page. And I read a small item about your friend, so I asked my theatrical friends who knew him, and they said they were at the funeral, and they felt exactly the same way you felt."

"Are they Jewish, these people who. . . ?"

"I don't associate with people who are not Jewish," said Dryfus, with a twinkle in his eye.

"Oh . . ."

"I was at the United Nations the other day," said Dryfus, "listening to all the arguments about the partition of Palestine. It was wonderful, I tell you, it was just wonderful. Here they were talking about a country that's been dead, as the phrase goes, for two thousand years, and they were talking about it. A country full of fleas and Arabs and swamps and deserts and tombs, but how alive! It's absolutely fantastic. And I want to tell you something else."

"What?"

"It was good to see those Jewish faces," said Dryfus, "the

402

faces of the people who were arguing the Jewish case. I liked especially the face of Rabbi Abba Hillel Silver. I liked the look in his eyes. I liked his dignity. I think he represents the World Jewish Congress or some other such organization, no, I think he represents the Zionist Organization of America. There he sat with history, Jewish history, which is a special kind of history, all over his face, there he sat, listening to the opposition arguments, and I could see right through his forehead, and I saw with absolute certainty that the Jews were going to win their case. And as I was watching him another face came to my mind."

"What face?" said David, who was greatly moved by Dryfus's quiet exuberance.

"During the war I saw a picture in the newspapers, you probably saw it, too. Maybe we talked about it. Anyway, it's always stuck in my mind. It was a picture of a Jew, with a beard, and a Nazi soldier was pulling his beard, or maybe he was just laughing at him, anyway, the Nazi soldier was sneering at the Jew, with the beard, but the Jew looked straight into his face, with such pride and dignity as I have never seen on any human being's face, and I was proud of that Jew, and I was proud that I also was a Jew, that I belonged to the same people that Jew belonged to. I saw that Jew on Abba Hillel Silver's face, and that Jew's face was the face of the whole Jewish people. It was wonderful."

"I remember that face, too," said David.

David had talked to Phil Sirkin about what was happening at the United Nations, and Phil made no secret of his interest and involvement. "It's funny," said Phil, "I never thought it would come to this. The Jews haven't got Palestine, and it looks like a tough struggle ahead, but I know enough history to know that it's never before come this close. Not just with the Jews, as a people, as a nation, you know what I mean, but with any other people. God, after two thousand years!"

"You can feel the excitement all over New York," said David, "especially, of course, the part where Jews get together."

"Yes, that's so. That's about all the lawyers are talking about. The legal aspects, but other aspects, too, of course."

"What does your father say, and your mother?" asked David.

"Well, that's the funniest thing," said Phil. "Real funny. My father, like all Orthodox Jews, was against the Zionists, you know, atheists and all that, smoke on Saturday, don't *daaven* (pray), and all that. But he seems to have forgotten all that, and he reads the Yiddish newspaper through and through, wanting to know what's going on at the United Nations. Hell, he buys two papers, the *Forward* and the *Morning Journal,* you know, he thinks maybe one has something the other hasn't got. And the two of them, my mother and father, discuss what they read. And another thing, you should see them listen to the radio. I bought a little radio sometime ago, and they hardly ever listened to it, just now and then. I had it in my room, most of the time, because they didn't care for it, I had it first in the kitchen, you know, where everybody could listen. But then, like I say, I took it into my room, you know, to hear news late at night, and to hear some music, on WQXR, the *Times* radio station, marvelous. But now, when I come home, there are my father and mother listening to the radio for news about the United Nations, and they listen to the same news over and over again. And my father keeps on saying, 'Ah, *hallevai*—I hope we win. May the good Lord give strength to President Truman, he looks like he's on our side.' And he's worried about Eddie Jacobson."

"Why?" asked David, who was delighted that so close a friend of President Truman's was his old-time business partner.

"Well," said Phil, with an understanding of his father's point of view and even a warmth for him that David had not thought was in him, "well, it's like this. My father says that Eddie—he calls him Eddie, like an old friend—Eddie, says my father, is in a difficult situation. He naturally wants that partition resolution to go through, after all, he's a Jew. But he can't talk, because he doesn't want to lose the President's friendship, you know, it's a pretty delicate situation. On the other hand, he probably knows, like so many people know, that there is a faction in the State Department that is pro-Arab, and these pro-Arab people—I think, Loy Henderson is one of them, he's Assistant Secretary of State, or something, for Far Eastern or Middle Eastern Affairs, something like that, and he and his kind might be filling Truman's ears with all sorts of lies. And if Eddie hears of this, how can he keep silent? At the same time how can he talk, he being only a friend?"

"That's right," said David, who had heard this line of reasoning, but didn't interrupt Phil, because he was pleased and surprised by his excitement about "the Jewish problem," which only a short while before had seemed to him so "parochial and local."

"My father is the same way," said David, who recalled the letters he had been receiving from him lately—and also from his mother.

Phil hesitated a bit, then said, "I'm frank to admit that I've changed myself, well, a little. To be perfectly frank, when the Palestine question first came up before the United Nations, I didn't think much of it, I mean, I said that some Jews were pushing the Zionist cause, you know, we Jews can do that, you know that . . ."

David pondered the phrase "we Jews" . . . he had never before heard Phil use it . . . at long last, it seemed, Phil was openly identifying himself with the Jewish people.

"Yes, I guess we do sometimes push things," said David, but quickly added, "You know what I mean. This is different."

"Sure it's different. I saw that right away, well, not right away, after a while. The Palestine issue became a world issue. It sure is strange, after two thousand years. You know there's a kind of tension in the air. And something else," added Phil and stopped.

"What?"

"Well, I now feel sort of proud I'm a Jew."

"Yes."

David had been getting more letters and postcards from his family, asking him if he knew anything "special" about what was going on at the United Nations: "After all, you're right there, and you hear things."

David told them that he knew no more than they did, but they persisted. Not only did his father and mother write, but also his brothers and sisters: "If you hear anything important, please let us know. After all, Boston is Boston, and New York is New York."

405

David was especially moved by the letters from his parents. "Do you go among Jews, David, do you hear what they say?" asked his mother. "How I envy you, to be in New York now, where you can go to the United Nations whenever you want to."

David couldn't go to the United Nations whenever he wanted to. He had work on the magazine. He did go to the United Nations twice, but on both occasions the Palestine issue had been postponed to a later date. He did go to the home of the Tobiases, who went regularly to the meetings of the United Nations, especially Mary. Mary went almost every day. She was there when Dr. Weizmann addressed the Assembly, she was there when the representatives of Guatemala and Honduras presented their arguments in favor of the partition of Palestine, with one part going to the Jewish nation: "I can't tell you how thrilled I was, tears came to my eyes, when I heard these Christians speak about the Jewish nation. It's simply wonderful, I get tears in my eyes even when I say it now, right here."

On the *American World* there was a young college graduate who assisted the editors: he did research, he checked proofs, he saw the magazine through the press. His name was Daniel Zuckermann. He had come to the magazine only a few weeks before, but he was of so friendly a nature that it seemed he had been employed there for many years. He had come from a weekly devoted to exposing the tyranny of Soviet Communism. The *Free Flame* was largely a one-note magazine. Its editors tried to make of it a general magazine, dedicated to promoting liberal ideas in politics and economics, but always it reverted to its one note: anti-Communism. Its articles on anti-Communism, in the main, were excellent in both content and execution. For the authors were nearly all men of learning. Several of them had been ardent members of the Communist Party in the United States, and a few had been members of the Bolshevik party in Russia in the days before the Revolution, and afterward. They had all been disillusioned, and so they wrote "from within." Their articles were often commented upon by the leading newspapers and magazines of the country, and abroad, too. It was rumored that the *Free Flame* was read very carefully by the United States State Department and by the foreign offices in every other major democratic nation. The

Soviet Embassy, in this country, apparently also read it carefully, for now and then it would issue a sharp denial of charges made in the *Free Flame*.

The magazine, of late, had been spreading out a bit—including in its coverage Latin America and Africa. Not that it had not dealt with these continents before, but it had previously done so only cursorily. Now it began to deal with them on a larger scale. The basic idea was that Soviet Communism was now beginning to spread out over the whole globe, with a greater intensity than it had done before—and that soon or late Soviet Russia would try to surround the United States with enemy bases. Russia would slowly infiltrate into the governments of the Latin American countries, and it would also agitate in these same countries against "the Colossus of the North."

The *Free Flame* also had a "literary department," which was edited by a former Communist. That's where Daniel Zuckerman's heart was. His aim was to become a literary critic. He had tried to get a job on *The New York Times Book Review,* the New York Herald *Tribune Books* and the older monthlies, such as *Harper's* and the *Atlantic,* but he was unsuccessful. It was his father, who in his younger days, had been "active in the labor movement," who got him his job on the *Free Flame,* for he was close to members of the editorial department. The father was now a jobber of furs, and thus was a capitalist in the eyes of his former colleagues. Actually, he had long before lost interest in "radical" ideas, but he still was attracted to his old associates, and he saw them now and then socially. Sometimes he also would donate money for this or that "cause," and on more than one occasion he made a contribution for the upkeep of the *Free Flame.* He seldom read the magazine. Secretly, he found it dull, and its whole philosophy now seemed childish to him, far removed from the realities of life, as he saw life.

It was in his radical days that he had met his wife, who had been a union organizer among the Italian garment workers. She was Irish Catholic by birth and very pretty, though she was a bit of a cripple: one of her legs was shorter than the other. In their innermost beings both were drawn to the customs of their respective religions, she to her Catholicism and he to his Judaism, but outwardly they sneered at "all this superstition." Less than six months after they met, they were secretly married by a municipal judge. His parents didn't like it, her parents didn't like it, but no violent objection was made on either side. As his father said, "And if I object, what good will it do now? Eh, *es fadrisst* (it is painfully regrettable)." His wife was so hurt that she said very little.

Both parents felt to blame themselves. They had both been brought up in Orthodox homes in Russia, but when they came here, they lost most of their religious convictions and after two or three years of going to synagogue only on Rosh Hashonoh and Yom Kippur, they stopped going to synagogue altogether, and slowly they violated the *kashrut* regulations: they served butter and meat at the same meal, they mixed their dishes, they celebrated Passover simply by buying a five-pound box of matzohs—and pretty soon they didn't object too violently when their children began to bring bacon to the house . . . and they didn't object when their children joined socialistic organizations . . . and they didn't object when they began to bring non-Jewish friends to the house. Now they felt they were justly repaid for their neglect.

"Ah, I can't tell you how bad I feel," said the father to the mother.

"To me it's a terrible thing, I'm almost ashamed to see the neighbors," said his wife.

In time a child came to the couple and the parents on both sides began to feel a bit better about what had happened. This first child was Daniel, who endeared himself even more to the grandparents because he was sickly for a long time. But while the two pairs of grandparents were inclined to forget, at least now and then, the fact of the inter-marriage, Daniel's father himself, in his innermost being, early had doubts about it. His doubts grew as he went up in the business world, and as he severed virtually all ties with his socialistic past. His old socialistic friends at least outwardly accepted his inter-marriage: they had to by principle. But his new business associates looked askance at it. They said nothing, of course. But Daniel's father sensed their disapproval. Actually, he felt, they not only disapproved, they thought he was silly. He could almost hear them saying, as he had heard them say about another inter-marriage, when these same people did not know about his own inter-marriage:

"Eh, a *shikse* is a *shikse,* some are very nice, some not so nice, just like Jewish girls, some make fine housewives and mothers just like Jewish girls, and some don't, just like Jewish girls. And a little fun now and then with a *shikse* is not bad, either, but something serious, no. Why look for trouble? Marriage is a gamble, why take more of a chance. It's crazy."

Daniel's father, at first, had to struggle with himself with respect to his wife: she became a little distasteful to him, he still liked her but she seemed to be a symbol of his "lack of sense." But slowly he found that it wasn't too difficult for him to accept his lot, and now he found he liked her more than before, for she really was a good wife and a good mother.

However, just as he was beginning to sink in the groove of the acceptance of his marriage, the "outside world" began to instill him with new doubts. He once overheard his mother say, "I still can't say I'm happy about what he did, but I must say that his wife is a fine woman, quiet, *tchichtig* (immaculately clean), and just a fine woman. And as for her son Daniel, and any other children, after all, when they grow up maybe they'll become Jews. At least, she's not teaching them to be Catholics, that I will say for her." The mother knew that according to the ancient law (*Halachah*), a child's religion is determined by the religion of its mother. But she soothed her thoughts on the subject by saying to herself that the mother in this case really was not a Catholic—born a Catholic, but not a practicing one. Besides, she further said to herself, the mother had, in effect, been excommunicated from her church for marrying a Jew and for marrying without the benefit of a Catholic priest.

This "trouble" wasn't too serious. The Catholic in-laws were beginning to "move in" on the couple. It was all so strange. They had "carried on" much less than did their Jewish in-laws. They visited the couple often, their relatives invited them often to their homes. Daniel's father was conscious, in some mysterious way, of what they were all saying about him. He didn't actually hear them say this, but he could almost hear them say it. "Well, whatever had to be had to be, but you have to admit that Jews are family people, they look after their families, wives, children, and so on."

As soon as Daniel came, however, his father immediately

noticed something. His wife's parents at first said openly, "You mean you're not going to give him any religious recognition—have him baptized or circumcised or something, and what harm would it do if little Daniel were baptized, afterward, when he grows up, he could do whatever he wants, as you two have decided? After all, a child needs some grounding. You don't have to make a fuss over it, but we really don't see how a ceremony of baptism could do any harm. It could be done quietly and quickly, and that's all."

Daniel's mother objected strenuously. "I made a promise and I'll keep it. What our child does when he grows up is his business, but now we won't decide for him. It's unfair."

Then the mother's parents began to try to influence Daniel's father. "Since you don't believe in anything of this sort, how can you object if the child is baptized, since you don't believe in any of this anyway, and the child is not harmed, is it?"

The father said no. "He'll be brought up as a human being, not as a Christian or a Jew or a Confucian or anything." Deep in his subconscious he would have preferred that his child's name were at least mentioned in synagogue on Saturday and thus got involved in the Jewish faith. Also in his subconscious he did feel that by not having Daniel "registered" in some way in any religion, he, the father, was doing something "not right." But he was sure of one thing: he would never allow little Daniel to be baptized. There were times when he wondered to himself whether his wife felt that little Daniel should be baptized, as he, the father, felt that Daniel should have his name blessed in the synagogue. Now and then, while lying in bed with his wife, he sensed that she was not sleeping and he wondered whether she was thinking about this very same matter. This added a sour taste to his marital life, and soon the sourness became bitterness. For months there was tension in the home, and the father was beside himself with bewilderment.

Daniel did not have the usual childhood and adolescence. He had Catholic friends and Protestant friends and Jewish friends, and much as he tried he could not be on the most intimate terms with any of them, for they spoke of things that had almost no meaning to him. When the Catholics spoke of their various saints he didn't know what they were talking about. One Catholic boy once asked him what his favorite saint was, and Daniel didn't know what to say. He had no favorite saint; he had no saints at all. The Catholic boy insisted that Daniel must have a favorite saint. "I have one, St. Francis, that's my middle name, my saint's name."

Daniel asked his mother what his favorite saint's name was. His mother was made uncomfortable by the question; it reminded her of her own childhood when she had a favorite saint and when this saint had brought her considerable pleasure: it was good to a child's heart, she thought, to have the feeling that some supernatural being, way out there, was in an intimate relationship with him, looking out for him, guiding him, and in special communication with him. This pleasure was being denied her child, but she had made a promise to her husband, and she would keep it.

"Oh, dear," she said to her son, "you have no favorite saint. We don't have any here, I mean in our house. Your father has no favorite saint." As she said this she realized how impossible it was for her to say that she herself didn't believe in saints and that she didn't have a favorite saint, either.

There was another time when Daniel came home with tears streaming down his cheeks. "Mommie," he pleaded, "am I Protestant or a damn Jew?"

His mother was heartbroken when she heard this. She didn't know how to answer her son.

"You're a human being, darling," she said, "and anybody who calls you names isn't worth your attention. Now wipe your face and be a little man."

Daniel went to the bathroom and wiped his face. The streaks of the towel were visible on his cheeks, but the cheeks were not clean, and, thought his mother, neither was the deep pain in his heart wiped off. What could she say to comfort him? She didn't know, she merely hugged him to her breasts, and her heart was heavy, for she knew that she was failing her son, he demanded more than a hug. Another painful thought came to her: should she or should she not tell her husband what had happened? He might be offended, he might be bewildered . . . perhaps she should say nothing, but if she said nothing, she would perhaps be doing the wrong thing: for her son, for her husband, for herself. She realized that her education had not prepared her for this situation. At the table that night, she told her husband everything (while Daniel was in another room). For a while her husband said nothing, then he said slowly, "It's not so serious. What you told him is the right thing. He'll meet up with this sort of thing later, so he might as well get used to it now."

This logical answer didn't satisfy her, and she was sure it didn't satisfy her husband. Daniel grew older, and now he had a sister, two years younger, and the sister was a problem. Her name was Eunice, and at an early age she revealed a certain snobbish tendency: she liked to play with children of rich people, she began to lie to them that she had "a large trust fund in my name, left to me by my mother's mother," and she told of the vacation plans of her parents, which included "staying for a while at our summer cottage in Bar Harbor, Maine." All these things were not true, of course, and her parents told her so, and scolded her for telling such fantasies, but even as they were telling her they knew that she was listening only with one ear and that she would continue telling such fantasies. She went to a public high school and her parents thought that this would cure her of her snobbishness, but it didn't, for she continued to write fantasies to her friends who were going to private high schools: that her parents were going to buy her a sports car, that "next year" she would go to Europe, "probably Italy and Spain, mostly. I don't believe in just traveling in high speed from one foreign city to another."

Then she began to show anti-Semitic tendencies. When she had just entered public high school she once said to her father, "Are you really Jewish, Dad?"

"Yes, didn't you know?" asked her father, who was by now completely baffled by his daughter.

"You knew that, Eunice. Why do you ask?" said her mother, who somehow looked upon Eunice and her snobbishness as largely her personal problem.

"Yes," said Eunice rather haughtily, "but I wasn't sure. I was just thinking."

"You were thinking what?" asked her mother.

"Now don't get so belligerent," said Eunice. "I am an individual and I have a right to talk in this house."

Her mother looked at her husband, who obviously was wondering what to do with his daughter . . . and who also looked whipped by the problem, a matter that hurt his wife very much . . . she hadn't known that an inter-marriage would entail such problems and of such intensity and complexity . . . she was sure that her husband hadn't known this either . . . and the thought passed through her mind that she and her husband had hardly discussed Eunice by themselves, when they were in bed together, and she was frightened.

"You are an individual but you're still our daughter," said her mother, "and you should be polite. Besides, you're old enough to know better."

Eunice got up, sighed, looked at her parents, as if she were saying, "Oh, God, you old fogies, too bad I have to tolerate you. I guess I better not say anything, that's safest."

"Where are you going?" asked her father.

Eunice looked at him, but said nothing, then she looked at her mother and said, "I'm going to the movies with the gang."

"Why didn't you answer your father?"

"I thought I did."

"No, you didn't," said her mother.

"I said I was going with the gang to the movies," said Eunice, "and Daddy heard."

"You know perfectly well what I'm talking about," said her mother.

"Go on to the movies," said her father slowly. "I hope you'll grow up some time."

Eunice left abruptly. Her mother wanted very much to talk to her husband, but as she looked at his sad and bewildered face, a lump came to her throat, and she rushed off to the kitchen for fear that she would burst into tears.

Not long afterward Eunice came home from school and said to her mother, "Mom, what am I?"

"What do you mean?" asked her mother.

"I mean, am I Christian or Jewish? I know you're Christian, you look it, anybody can see that, but . . ." She stopped.

"But what?' asker her mother, glad that her husband wasn't present to hear what his daughter was saying.

"Well, I mean about Daddy. He looks Jewish. I know, you told me long ago that he was Jewish, but I was just wondering what I am?"

"What brought this up?"

"Oh, nothing."

"That's not true. There's a special reason why you bring this up. Tell me. I want to know."

"Don't question me so, mother. After all, I'm not a criminal. I just want to know. I have a right to know, I was just talking. Goodness gracious . . ."

"Tell me," insisted her mother.

"Well, you know Gerald."

"Gerald who?"

"I thought I told you about him. Gerald Wilkins. We're going steady, not actually, but sort of."

"Yes."

"Well, he's sweet on me, and he said his parents were Christian, Baptists, I think, and he said he heard I was Jewish, and I said I wasn't, but I wasn't sure."

"You're half Jewish," said her mother. "You know that. Your father is Jewish, and I'm not, I mean he was born Jewish, and I was born Catholic, but we don't observe any religion in our home, you know that. We wanted you children to choose your own religion, if any, when you grow up."

"I know, but what am I?"

Her mother wanted to say, "Nothing," but she sensed that this would not quite be true; besides, she couldn't say this to her daughter. This snippy, offensive girl who was bringing agony to her heart, was, after all, her daughter, and her husband's daughter.

"You're a girl, whose father was born Jewish and whose mother was born Catholic, and when you grow up you can choose whatever religion you wish. That's what you can tell your Gerald."

"I have," said Eunice, and stopped. Her mother marveled at the duplicity of this fifteen-year-old offspring of hers.

"And what did he say?"

Eunice hesitated.

"Tell me what he said."

"He said I was Jewish no matter what I did later," said Eunice, and burst into tears. "Oh, mother what shall I do?"

Her mother didn't know what should be done, but she was heart-broken by what Eunice had left unsaid, namely, that she, Eunice, was ashamed that her father was Jewish. A few days later the two discussed the matter of the father's Jewish origin. The father was not present, the mother had deliberately picked a time when only she and her daughter would be at home, and this made the mother feel guilty: a family problem in which her husband had a right to be consulted was being discussed without him. The mother told Eunice that religious origin was of no consequence in a democracy, that anyone to whom religion was as important as it was to Gerald was probably one whose friendship was not worth cultivating, that what counted in a person was his "real worth". Eunice agreed and she apologized for having made a scene a few days previously, but her mother sensed that her daughter was not really convinced, and she was positive when Eunice asked a few days later, "But dad doesn't really believe what his parents taught him, I mean, in a way, he's not really Jewish, is he mother?"

Eunice and Daniel continued to bring up the matter of their parents' mixed religious origins, and their parents continued to be "logical" with them. Then the two children stopped discussing the matter with their parents, but the parents knew that they had failed them, that they were not satisfied with the explanations and guidance offered them at home, that they were now meeting "the problem" in their own ways, which they did not plan to discuss with their parents. At first this was a deep pain to the parents, but then they gradually learned to live with the unpleasant fact: they accepted it largely because they had to accept it. Yet the pain never quite left them, and often it was uppermost in their minds.

Eunice "went out" at first with boys of various religious origins: Jewish, Protestant, and Catholic. Then she stopped seeing Jewish boys, and soon she virtually stopped seeing Protestant boys. Both parents noticed this but said nothing because they didn't know what to say: it would have been against their philosophy of letting their grownup children choose their friends. Now they were not at all sure that this philosophy, which made so much sense before they had children, was really so intelligent. While they were wallowing in their bewilderment the children continued to go their own ways.

The parents were not troubled so much by Daniel, who was a rather introspective child and seldom went out with girls. They were deeply troubled, however, by Eunice who was now seeing only Catholic boys and at times boasted about it to her mother when her father was not present. The mother was troubled by many things with respect to this development. She was conscious of a vague feeling of satisfaction that her daughter was showing a partiality to boys of her own, the mother's, faith at birth, but she was also conscious that if her daughter were going out only with Jewish boys, her husband would secretly be pleased, though he would not say so to his wife. There was something else about the new development that worried the mother very much, namely, the obviously increasing enmity that was growing up between the daughter and father . . . the daughter seemed to look upon the father as the cause of her problems, and the mother also sensed that the daughter was becoming more and more anti-Jewish.

The mother herself had noticed in her own parents' home that anti-Semitic feeling was being inculcated: the Jews were depicted as the people who crucified Christ, the priests now and then threw out hints that the Jews were the "real enemies" of the "true faith" . . . Protestants, true enough, denied a cardinal element of the Catholic faith, that the Pope was the supreme authority in matters of faith. Still, the Protestants did believe in the divinity of Jesus Christ, and they did subscribe to the teachings of the New Testament. The Bible used by the Protestants was the King James version, while the version used by the Catholics was the Douay version, but they both accepted the New Testament just the same. The mother remembered hearing one priest say that while there were doctrinal differences in the two translations, long stretches of them were virtually alike. Thus the Protestants and the Catholics had much in common, but the Jews were totally different: they denied the whole basic Christian doctrine of the divinity of Jesus Christ, and Catholic priests pointed this out, sometimes openly, sometimes indirectly. She remembered hearing all sorts of sly comments about Jews: that they were sharp business people, that they cheated more often than did Christians, whether Catholic or Protestant (this was not said in so many words, but that was the meaning that the mother obtained).

At the same time she remembered that nuns used to come to her parents' home . . . one of them was a first cousin . . . and there were times when these nuns said that Judaism and Catholicism were closer together than were Protestanism and Catholicism . . . it was all very strange . . . but the more she thought about it the more was she inclined to think that this relative friendliness toward the Jews was, as a friend of hers, also a Catholic, had said, "just public relations, news releases." Apparently the Catholics occasionally expressed a friendliness toward the Jews merely to emphasize their hatred of the Protestants: they hated the Protestants so much that they were *almost ready* to say that they liked the Jews, even the Jews, more, but it was only *almost*. Actually, thought Daniel's and Eunice's mother, both the Catholics and Protestants hated the Jews, were nearly always uncomfortable in the presence of Jews and all of them, without any exceptions she knew of, would have been horrified, in more or less degree, if a child of theirs married a Jew. The worst horror of it all was that she herself, the wife of a Jew, had some of this anti-Jewish feeling: again she admitted to herself that she was secretly not too perturbed that her daughter was now going out only with Catholic boys.

She didn't know what to do, what to say. She discussed it with her husband, and she remembered the look on his face, as he said, "I know it, I'm not surprised."

"What do you mean?" she had asked.

"Nothing," he said, and walked off.

In time the situation with the daughter became an accepted part of the family life. The problem appeared to be insoluble. The daughter, after a while, did see some Protestant boys, and on two or three occasions she did bring home a Jewish boy, but the father and mother knew that while intellectually Eunice was more tolerant now, deep down in her heart she still resented her father's Jewish origin. There was heartache in the house almost every moment, silent heartache and silent disappointment and silent resignation.

Then something happened that disturbed the family deeply: Daniel began to have fainting spells, he would occasionally have a very fast heart beat that no doctor could find the physical cause of. One doctor, a general practitioner, a Jew, suspected that the home atmosphere was to blame and he suggested that Daniel go to a psychiatrist. He did this, and it became clear to the psychiatrist soon enough that the tension at home was more than the sensitive Daniel could bear. Daniel said little, but he sensed what was worrying both his parents, and he suspected that his sister Eunice, consciously or unconsciously, went out of her way to hurt her father. Daniel wanted to tell Eunice not to do this, but he desisted, first, because he knew that Eunice would tell him to mind his own business; second, she would deny the accusation outright; and third, she would laugh at Daniel—and he wasn't sure he could bear any one of these reactions. So he kept his thoughts to himself, and then, one Sunday afternoon, as he heard his parents arguing about Eunice's disrespect toward her father ("Only you can stop her from treating me like her enemy," the father had said to his wife), Daniel walked into the living room, determined to say something to his mother, in agreement with his father, but instead he fainted and dropped on the floor.

Daniel was being analyzed at the time he applied for a job on the *American World,* and he continued to be analyzed for many years afterward, at longer or shorter intervals. He was assigned at first to be a general assistant to whatever editor wanted to use him, but slowly he became David's assistant almost solely. The very first week Daniel told David about his home situation, and he also told him about his analysis. He asked David to suggest some readings in Judaism to him. Daniel found the readings interesting and he asked for more. David suggested that he read a one-volume edition of the Talmud and also some of the writings of Rabbi Milton Steinberg, Rabbi Abba Hillel Silver, Rabbi Solomon Freehof, Dr. Solomon Shechter, Maurice Samuel, and also some translations of Bialik, Ahan Ha'am, Sokoloff, and Theodor Herzl. Daniel was especially taken with the writings of Rabbi Steinberg, particularly with his novel, *As A Driven Leaf,* but what appealed to him most of all was Dr. Herzl's *Jewish State.* "There's something wonderful about the whole idea of reviving a nation that, politically-speaking," said Daniel, "has been dead for two thousand years." And Daniel revealed that his father had been taking him on walks lately and talking to him about Zionism. The United Nations at the time was beginning the discussion of the proposal to partition Palestine into an Arab State and a Jewish state, and various other proposals for dealing with the "Palestine problem."

"My sister isn't interested," said Daniel, "but I am."

"Is your mother interested?" ventured David. "I mean does she talk about Palestine with your father?"

"No," said Daniel. "Anyway, not much, if at all."

Another time Daniel revealed to David that his father was bringing home Yiddish papers, solely to read about the debate on Palestine in the United Nations. "The papers looked sort of funny in our house," said Daniel.

"What do you mean?" asked David.

"Oh, just funny. We haven't had such things in our house."

"Does your mother object?"

"No, she says nothing. But the idea of Zionism is an interesting one, a very interesting one. My father told me when he was very young, years ago, he once belonged to an organization called Labor Zionists, in Hebrew they're called, well, I can't pronounce their name."

"Poalay Zionists."

"I think that's the name. I asked him if he still belonged, but he said no, and I asked why he left, and he just shook his head. But he does know a lot about the thing, Zionism, he told me all about Dr. Herzl, after I told him I read the *Jewish State,* he was surprised but pleased, too, I think, and he told me about Dr. Weizmann and about a Dr. Levin."

"Dr. Shmarya Levin."

"That's the one."

After a while Daniel stopped talking about Zionism and about the debate in the United Nations, though they did come up now and then in their talks together when the *World* was negotiating for an article on the Near East.

David himself, however, was daily becoming more interested in what was happening in the United Nations. He read *The New York Times* carefully, reading and re-reading the news stories about the debates in the United Nations. He went to some of the debates, but to his great regret, on all these occasions the anti-Jewish point of view was being presented, either by the Arab countries or by England. Then David decided that he could almost get as much about what was going on by reading *The New York Times* and listening to the radio. He would come home from work, eat his supper quickly, and then turn on the radio if the debate at the UN was being broadcast. One evening he was at the home of the Tobiases. Mary

Tobias insisted that David stay so that they could all hear the UN debate.

The three of them sat around the radio. To the delight of all it became obvious that tonight the case for the partition of Israel was going to be presented. There was a wonderful and lovely feeling floating over the room, and the wonderment and the loveliness entered into the beings of all. David looked at the radio—it was a cabinet model, and David was glad: the occasion was too sacred for a mere small box radio . . . there was considerable static on the air . . . it was not clear who was presenting the position of the United States . . . David thought it was Herschel Johnson, but the others were not sure . . . and then Johnson or whoever it was began to speak:

"I wish to present the position of the government and the people of the United States with respect to the proposal now before us. We support it for various important reasons. There is first of all the sheer matter of historical justice. The Jewish race has suffered long enough without a country of its own. The United States is of the opinion that two thousand years of persecution is enough. The elders of the Jewish race believe that the establishment, or perhaps I should say re-establishment, of a nation of their own would offer a solution for their most pressing problems at the same time that it would rectify a gross injustice of history. The government and the people of the United States agree with this position of the elders of the Jewish race.

"But in a sense, and I might say, an important sense, the government and the peoples, at least of the Western democracies, are already committed to the establishment, or, rather, re-establishment of the Jewish state in what is now Palestine. I might remind the Western democracies, and the English government, in particular, with all respect, that there is on the record the Balfour Declaration, which definitely and specifically and, in the opinion of the government of the United States, clearly guarantees and vouchsafes to the Jewish race the re-establishment of their national homeland in Palestine. We do agree with the English delegate that the Balfour Declaration does not state the precise nature of the re-establishment of the Jewish state, that it does not state a specific time or manner. With respect and concerning the time, the government of the

420

United States thinks that the time is now. Forty years is long enough for a promise to be held in abeyance. It is now time that this promise be fulfilled. With respect and concerning the manner of the fulfilment, that, it seems to us, is fully covered in the proposal now before us. We think that the manner thus made and delineated and detailed is fair and just to all concerned.

"We are asked to consider a plan for the partition of Palestine, with due regard to the legitimate interests of the people of Arabic origin who are now resident there. The proposal fully states, and certainly implies, that all religious shrines be respected and guarded and in every way be considered holy by the two respective peoples, the Jews and the Arabs, who form the major ethnical groups under consideration. On this score I do not think, and the government of the United States does not think, that there can be any two opinions. Holy places to all religions will be kept holy and inviolate. The elders of the Jewish race have given us this promise in the clearest terms. And I am sure that the Arabic peoples, when the time comes, will give us the same assurances. I cannot conceive of any ethnical group desecrating the shrines of any other group.

"The government and the people of the United States have had only the most cordial relations with the governments and peoples of all the Arabic lands, and it is the sincere hope and wish of the government and the people of the United States to continue this cordial and mutually beneficial and satisfactory relationship. The position of the government and the people of the United States does not imply any diminution of cordial feeling to the governments and peoples of those Arab countries who now oppose the proposal for the partition of Palestine. We are against nobody. We are for justice, long-overdue justice for an ancient and great race of people, who have given us so much of human treasure in the way of thought and ideas and philosophy and art. The Jewish Bible is the Bible of us all. I am sure that the representatives of the Arabic nations, once they give full and calm consideration to the merits of the proposal now before us, when they do so, they will see its justice and its practicality.

"The view of the government and the people of the United States will be further elaborated and made clearer, and supported, with ample evidence, by other members of the United States delegation here, but, in conclusion I wish to add a few words of my own, on my own responsibility, though I dare say my government will not object to that which I am about to say. What I do wish to say now is that I am filled with a feeling of awe and historic significance, that I am greatly stirred by the mere argument on the proposal now before us. There is a certain judgment of history, rather, I should say, of destiny, what, I imagine, historians would call manifest destiny, in what is taking place here. I belong to a denomination of the Christian religion, Presbyterianism, or some people call it Calvinism, and we are trained in the teachings of the Old Testament as much as we are trained in the teachings of the New Testament. My grandfather was a minister in the Presbyterian Church, he had a little parish in Old Lyme, Connecticut, held his pulpit for thirty-five years, and he raised his whole family of eight children there, and he is buried in the little cemetery attached to his little church. And on his grave stone are inscribed Hebrew words, by his own wish and desire, and those words, I'm sorry I don't know Hebrew well, or at all, as a matter of fact, but my father translated them, as I recall it, in Hebrew, 'Lover of the human race and of peace.' I am proud of that. I am very proud of that. To me it represents all that is wonderful about our religion, about Judaism. And I have been thinking about that inscription lately, and I have seen much significance in that inscription. And that is an additional reason why I personally am so eager about the proposal now before us, why I feel it is so just, because I feel that the passage of the proposal will add to the peace and the love of fellow men in the world.

"And I remember other things about my grandfather, or, rather, I should say about my grandfather as my father told me things about him. He was a remarkable man, my grandfather was. He, my grandfather, had a special attachment to the Jewish race. Not only because it was from them that Jesus sprang, but also because he was so attached to the teaching of the Jews, and he said that a great deal of the writings of some of the Christian Fathers was a perversion of what Judaism was. My grandfather was deeply attached to what he called the true, genuine Christian tradition, which, in his lights, and in mine, too, is imbedded best in our denomination. But I am

422

saying this not to advertise, so to speak, any denomination, but only out of respect to my grandfather and also to state publicly how I personally feel, and I dare say that my government and my fellow Americans will and do feel as I do. What I wish to point out is that my grandfather constantly spoke of the grave injustices that have been inflicted upon the Jews, and he felt that Our Lord would have wept and, indeed, does weep whenever a Jew is harmed. Jesus loved the Jewish people; they were His people, and he urged that the Christians follow the Jewish Law and the Jewish prophets, and that this love of Our Lord for the Jewish people was later turned into hate by followers of Our Lord.

"I have been thinking how pleased my grandfather would have felt now, if he were alive, because of the proposal now before us. I like to think that my grandfather reflected and does reflect the feelings of the overwhelming majority of Christians the world over. Gentlemen, rather, ladies and gentlemen, I submit that we Christians owe a debt to the Jewish people, not only for the Bible, not only for having given us Our Lord, but for having repaid them for these glories with murder and assassinations and pogroms. It is not for me to speak about the people of the Mohammedan religion, but I dare say that they too feel an obligation to the Jewish people, for their religion, too, is grounded in Judaism. We now, all of us, the world over, we all now have an opportunity to right a long-standing wrong against the Jewish people, we now have a chance to practice as well as preach true Christianity, true love. It will indeed be a most historic and thrilling moment in world history that, after two thousand years of persecution, the Jews have at last achieved some measure of rest and peace in the world. I plead with you, let us not fail the Jewish people once more, as the world has so cruelly failed them for twenty centuries. Let us not fail them in their cruellest hour. Let us not fail our own deepest convictions. Let us not fail our own sense of justice and truth and mercy and kindness, but above all, justice. Let us not fail human history. Let us not fail our destiny in this fateful hour. Let us not fail our children, Let us not fail our grandchildren. Let us not fail the future."

There was a hush in the room, as the speaker stopped. There

seemed to be a similar hush in the meeting place where he had spoken. Then a burst of applause came from the radio. Raphael Tobias looked at his wife. Mary put her hand on Raphael's. The hush continued.

Then Mary said, "It's hard to say anything. I feel as if I were present at some great event. Something has happened. The man was so sincere."

"I've never heard so powerful, so moving a presentation of the Jewish position," said David.

"It was wonderful," said Mary.

"Wonderful," said Raphael.

"It's all strange," said Mary. "In a way he said nothing we haven't heard before, you know . . ."

"That's true," said Raphael, "but . . ."

"But it was new, in another way," continued Mary. "It sounded like something I have never heard before. It sounded like a judgment, the final judgment of, . . ."

"The final judgment of history," said David.

"Yes," said Raphael. "For a non-Jew to talk that way! Some of it was beautiful poetry."

"Especially the end. 'Let us not fail our own sense of justice. Let us not fail our children and our grandchildren . . .' And you know, I had the feeling," continued Mary, "I had the feeling he was not talking from prepared notes, but spontaneously."

"That made it all the better," said David.

"It's England that I don't understand," said Raphael. "They're for the Jews, they're against the Jews. Their whole tradition is really pro-Jewish. Disraeli does mean something. But they play politics, I guess that's it, but I don't understand what politics they're playing in this case. England wants to be on the safe side with the Arabs, on account of oil, I suppose, but oil will soon not be necessary, I hear, the atom will take the place of oil, I mean atomic power will eventually, and maybe sooner than we know, will replace oil and coal. But I have a feeling that England will double-cross the Arabs, too, the same way it has double-crossed the Jews, for its own temporary selfish interests. But it would be so much better if England were on our side now."

"I know how you feel," said Mary, "but maybe we won't need England, I mean we won't need England's vote."

"Russia is still pretty much of a mystery as far as where its vote will go," said David.

"They're pretty good at double-crossing, too," said Raphael. "Russia double-crossed the Western democracies at the time of the Hitler-Stalin Pact, and then it shouted holy murder when Hitler double-crossed Russia."

"Russia will be on our side," said Mary.

"What makes you say that?" asked Raphael.

"I feel it," said Mary.

"It could be," said David, "and the only reason I have is that being on the side of the Jews would give Russia a chance to go back on whatever word it gave the Arabs. I heard that the Russians are trying to woo the Moslem world, and one way of making the Moslems see things the Russian way is to show them that Russia is in a position to hurt them, and the establishment of a Jewish state would hurt the Moslem world. I mean it would make all the Arab countries look ridiculous very quickly. The Jews will build up their country, and show up the Arab countries for the slave kingdoms they are."

"I hope what you say turns out the way you say it," said Mary. "It sounds crooked enough, what you just said, the way you explained it, for the Russians to do just that. Of course, if Russia goes our way, then the other satellite countries will go the same way, Poland and Czechoslovakia and Rumania and Yugoslavia, and that will clinch the vote for partition."

"Well, not quite," said Raphael, and immediately went into an elaborate discussion of the position of the Latin American countries. These countries, he pointed out, were almost completely Catholic, and the Catholic hierarchy had a powerful say in the civil governments, and the position of the Catholic Church, in Rome, was highly problematical. Several Protestant leaders, all over the world, had come out enthusiastically in favor of the re-establishment of some semblance of a Jewish state, but not one important Catholic leader had said a single favorable word. The theory, according to some people that Raphael had talked to, was that the Vatican, by the very nature of its creed and tradition, had to oppose the establishment of any Jewish state on the ground that the Jews were doomed to wander all over the world, without a home, subject to insults and privations, so long as they refused to accept the doctrine

425

of the divinity of Jesus Christ. Several of their popes and saints, especially St. John Chrysostom, St. Bernard, and St. Gregory of Nyssa, had called upon the Christians to treat the Jews with the contempt that was their lot, and to make sure that they never enjoyed any real comfort. There were times in the late Middle Ages when some of the civil authorities, especially in Spain and Portugal, had decided to treat the Jews as co-equal citizens, with the right to enjoy many of the priviliges of full or semi-full citizenship. Whereupon the Papacy had severely criticized the civil authorities for permitting such "laxity."

All this made Raphael wonder what would be the stand of the Church in Latin America, whether the Vatican would tell the Latin American Church what to urge upon its people and its governments. Raphael also wondered how strong a hold the Catholic Church really had upon the various Latin American governments. It was obvious enough, from history, that Catholic leaders sometimes spoke to deaf ears when they tried to advise civil authorities. A country that is predominantly Catholic in religion is not necessarily a country that is governed by Vatican ideas in its domestic or international affairs. There was the case of France, which was sixty or sixty-five percent Catholic, yet modern French history was characterized by its opposition, often of a violent nature, to Vatican policies. The church and state were sharply separated for a long time in France, and, indeed, the Church enjoyed even fewer privileges in so Catholic a country as France than in England or the United States. Catholic priests did not have any immunity from conscription in France, and neither did they get any preferential treatment once they were in the army or navy. They remained privates, if they did not merit any higher rating, and they were promoted only if they earned promotion—along with non-clerical soldiers. But in England and the United States Catholic priests, along with ministers of other religions, did not have to serve in the armed forces. And even better examples of the separation of church and state in a Catholic country was Italy, where some ninety or ninety-five per cent of the population was Catholic, yet the Italian government pursued its own policies on the home and the international fronts, with little regard to what the Vatican wished. The various liberal governments before Mussolini prided themselves upon their anti-Vatican platforms, and

426

Mussolini himself would hardly deign for long to discuss anything of political moment with the Pope.

All this was true, but it would be very good if the Vatican could say something favorable about a Jewish state. "I should think the Vatican would know that the Jews would take better care of their holy places than would the Arabs," said Mary.

"The Arabs, the Turks, have taken good care of these places," said David. "I don't think that can be denied."

"I suppose so," said Mary.

"The Catholic Church has a special objection to the Jews," said Raphael, "a very special objection."

"What's that?" asked Mary.

"You know what," said Raphael.

"The Jews killed Christ?" said Mary.

"Of course," said Raphael. "All who are non-Catholics are damned and doomed, and will go to hell, and all that, but for the Jews it will be worse than for anybody else. All Christians, at least of the usual sects, believe this in one way or another, but the Catholics alone have it as an integral part of their whole creed. They teach it to their children, in Sunday school, later in adult classes, their priests talk about, or hint at, it. I don't mean that the priests necessarily tell their people in so many words that the Jews are especially to be hated—the Popes and the saints did say just that during the Middle Ages, before and after—but in more recent times, with the spread of democracy and more human decency, it became impossible to talk this way, but they get their point across. Anyway, that's why the Catholics dislike the Jews more than they dislike Mohammedans. We killed their Redeemer."

"But we didn't," said Mary. "Not as a people."

"Of course, we didn't, as a people," said Raphael. "As a matter of fact, the Jews, even as a few individuals, may have had nothing to do with the killing of Jesus, who was probably apprehended, tried, and killed by the Romans, with no Jews participating in the trial at all. Besides, even if Jews did take part, that is no reason for blaming a whole people, and condemning them to eternal misery. That makes no sense at all. It's like blaming the American people for killing Abraham Lincoln, just because one crazy man, Booth, shot him."

"Then why do they do it?" asked Mary.

"Well, I don't know," said Raphael. "Nobody knows. I read something about this recently, I think it was in a book by a Professor Joseph Klausner, a man of very great erudition, I think, it was in his book, *Jesus of Nazareth,* I saw it somewhere recently. Dr. Klausner says that three of the Gospel writers, Sts. Matthew, Luke, and Mark specifically absolve the Jews of any complicity as a people in the death of Jesus. Only one of the gospel writers, St. John, blames 'the Jews,' but even in his case it can be proven that he didn't mean 'the Jews' as a people. You'd think that's authority enough for the Christians to stop talking about the Jews killing Jesus, but they don't."

"I think the Church won't say anything to the Latin American governments," said Mary.

"Maybe not," said Raphael. "The Church is very practical and diplomatic, I mean it looks far ahead, and does not hesitate to adjust itself to changing conditions, if it will work out, in its opinion, to its own good."

David walked over to the radio and kept on turning the dial so see if there was any more news about the debate. Finally he did come upon a station where a discussion was going on about the debate. An Arab diplomat, or perhaps he was somebody associated with an Arab delegation, was speaking. He spoke grammatical English, he had an Oxford accent, and obviously was a man of education. He was plainly trying to appear to be fair. He said he understood why the Jewish people looked forward to Palestine as their homeland once more, but he quickly added that the Jews had no right to it:

"The Jewish people have forfeited their right to their land, to resettling their land. In all these years very few of them have so loved their ancient land as to come over to settle it. The few that have come over have hardly distinguished themselves, and this I say with sorrow, for I count among my friends many Jews, and I want to be on friendly terms with them, as I'm sure they want to be friends with me. The Jews who have settled in Palestine have often bought land at ridiculously low prices. Jews are better business men than Arabs, that is well known, and I do not say this in criticism of them, but a fact is a fact. Thus there are now more Jewish landowners in Palestine than there are Arab landowners."

The speaker was interrupted by another speaker—apparently

a panel discussion was going on—who said, "I'm sorry, but I wish to point out that while my good friend, Dr. Gamal Fey, is stating facts some of which are accurate, he is, unwittingly, I'm sure, leaving out other facts that put his own facts in a more accurate light. There are more Jewish landowners than Arabian landowners, but all the Jewish land put together is a very small fraction, less than one-half of one percent, I believe, or in that neighborhood, of the total land available, and most of that land is owned by a handful of wealthy Arab landowners. What I wish to say is that Palestine, and indeed all Arab lands, are places of desolation economically and places of the absence of economic as well as political democracy. All the Arab lands, and I say this fully aware of what I am saying, are run by small oligarchical families, who lord it over their people, most of whom are illiterate, disgracefully housed and clothed, forever living in a state little removed from serfdom. I do think, and I see no reason why I shouldn't say this, that the Arab intellectual leaders, are not often as, well, entirely frank and open with the Western world, with respect to this Palestine problem as they could be. They often give us half the facts, and sometimes even less."

A third man began to speak. It was obvious that he sympathized with the Arab position. He said, "I think my pro-Zionist friend should also tell the whole story, practice what he preaches, as the saying goes. The Jewish people did once inhabit Palestine, but the total number of years they inhabited Palestine as a sovereign nation was only two or three hundred years, I think, I'm not sure of the precise length of time, but it was in that neighborhood. History has deprived them of their land. Perhaps I shouldn't say it quite this way. In any case, the Jews lost their land to the Romans, and they spread all over the world, and, as Dr. Fey has pointed out, very few of them have seen fit to come back. For practical purposes, we may say that none of them has come back. And who has lived in the land all these years? I ask, who? Who has tilled the land? Who has given the land whatever semblance of a habitable country it is now? Who has given it its present complexion, good, bad, or indifferent, as some may say? Only the Arab people. They have lived here for two thousand years, they have raised generation after generation of people here, whole lines of families. By their very blood, by their very toil they have earned the right to possess the land, as their own native land, as their motherland, as their fatherland. To them, and to them alone, belongs the land. It would be the highest injustice against them, it would be the highest injustice against international law to deprive the Arab settlers of any portion of their land, now or at any time."

He raised his voice, and a certain shrillness came into it: "I feel I can say that if this partition proposal passes, there will be grave difficulties in that part of the world. The Arab peoples are not unmindful of their rights, and their governments cannot be expected to be silent and acquiescent in case partition passes. I am not speaking for the government, any single one of them, I am only a resident economist, Arab economist, associated with the Arab league, a group of independent nations, combined to preserve their interests."

The moderator interrupted. "If I may say so, while I realize the emotional tensions involved between you two Arab gentlemen, and you two pro-Zionist gentlemen, one of them Jewish and one non-Jewish, I don't mean personal tensions, of course, I mean tensions engendered by the nature of the proposal now before the United Nations, our aim is only to spread light, still and all, we should try to keep the talks, the whole discussion on a calm and friendly level, without personalities, I am sure you will agree with me . . ."

He continued to talk. A smile seemed to spread across the room, encircling the faces of Raphael and Mary and David.

"The Arabs are admitting something," said Mary. "I wonder if they know just what they are admitting."

There was some more static on the air, and it was difficult to make out who was talking now and what he was saying. Soon the radio went silent.

"Maybe it will come back by itself," said Raphael. "That Arab sure admitted a great deal. They seem to feel that things are not at all going their way. That's news to me. I was beginning to think that things didn't look so good for our side. Now, it looks better. Maybe they got wind that the Russians and the other Iron Curtain countries are going to vote for the resolution to partition."

"Of course, it could be only a threat," said David. "Maybe they hope that word gets around that if the resolution is passed, the Arab countries won't agree to it, will denounce the resolution, will not accept the decision, and so on."

"That could be," said Raphael. "The Arabs are very tricky."

Now clear words began to come from the radio.

"There are some matters," he said, "about which there can be no two opinions. They are matters of fact, to be noted by all who care to examine. It is true, as one of the learned gentlemen here has said, that there have been relatively few Jews who have settled in Palestine. But that wasn't because they had small regard for their ancient land. Actually, no other people in all history has had a longer memory of its ancient homeland than have the Jews. For two thousand years they have prayed, three times a day, for the return of Palestine. That has been their eternal dream, that has been the dream that has kept them united and also buoyant down the millennia of the years.

"Then why have so few of them gone to Palestine? The reasons are clear enough. The very same people who are now wondering why so few Jews have come to Palestine refused to allow the Jews to come to Palestine, or they made it most difficult for them to settle there as citizens. Always there have been obstacles put in their way, by the Turkish government, or by the English mandatory government, or through the pressures of the Arab countries upon the Turkish and the English governments. There have been other reasons, too. One of them is that the Jews in the rest of the world outside of Palestine have been poor, destitute, with little excess money to make it possible for them to make the long voyage to Palestine. That the hearts of these people still were in Palestine is fully attested to by the fact that these people have had what amounts to Zionist organizations from decades back. Every Jewish home has had its *pushke* (coin box) for dropping in an occasional coin for this or that foundation for the improvement or the development of this or that project in Palestine. The Jews have had many such foundations. They have also had an international bank for the sole purpose of unifying and coordinating the funds collected by various agencies. I can say categorically as a student of history that no people in all the known annals of the human race has had so long a memory of its heritage, so widespread an eagerness to keep its identity intact, so profound a desire to constitute itself once more as a nation among the

431

nations, as a culture among the cultures, as a civilization among the civilizations.

"But there is more that I wish to say in answer to some of the remarks made here by the gentlemen who are attempting to persuade us here and our vast unseen audience of the justice of the Arab position. Like my Arab friend here, and I call him a friend with all sincerity, I'm not an official of the Jewish groups now presenting their position at the United Nations. I am, however, on the staff of one of them, serving entirely in an advisory capacity, making available to my Jewish colleagues whatever historical knowledge I have that will help bolster their position, in which I am deeply interested, to which I am deeply committed, and which I think the whole world, both non-Jewish and Jewish, has a historical stake in.

"I have before me figures of what the few Jews have accomplished in Palestine in the past three decades alone. I do not wish to burden you here or to burden the radio audience with statistical facts. If you will write to me in care of this station I shall be glad to send you a copy of the document I have before me now. Merely send 10 cents in postage, and we shall gladly send you a copy, as I have said. Several Jewish organizations have paid for the publication of this document, and we are eager to present this information to the public, so that they may better form their opinion. We ask for nothing more than that you read the facts, all the facts, and discount all unsubstantiated propaganda—and make up your mind then, and only then. What are some of the salient facts revealed by our statistics? The average per capita income among Jews in Palestine is 250 times what it is for the Arab population. I repeat, 250 times the income of the Arab population. There is virtually no crime whatsoever among the Jewish population, whereas stealing is rife among the Arab population. The government figures attest to that. Jewish government figures? No. There is no Jewish government as yet. But the figures of the Turkish government, and the figures of the English mandate government.

"I am not done. The death rate of the Jews in all age groups is almost incredibly lower than it is among the Arab population. Fifty times as many Arab children die before they reach the age of one year as do Jewish children. The incidence of eye diseases is twenty times lower among the Jews as among the Arabs. The same with skin diseases and stomach diseases and ear diseases. Longevity? Here I can give you the precise figures. The longevity among the Jews is 54 years; among the Arabs it is 33 years.

"What else? A great deal else. The Jews introduced industry to Palestine, they modernized much of the transportation system. What else? They introduced many facts of modern medicine. There are several medical and dental clinics in Palestine now. And everyone of them is Jewish sponsored. Every single one of them. I do wish to add here that individual Arab intellectuals and public-spirited men and women have generously offered financial and other assistance in the erection of these medical clinics, but their governments, local or national, I mean the very Arab states who are now opposing the partition resolution, gave no assistance whatsoever. Are these medical and dental clinics—and I might add, the hospitals that, so to speak, mother them, about which I could say a great deal, since they form one of the most glorious achievements of the few Jewish colonies in Palestine—are these medical and dental clinics open only to Jews? Of course, not. They are open to everybody, regardless of race or creed. Go to the clinics, go to the hospitals, and you will see Arab children, Arab men and women being treated as equals with Jewish children and Jewish men and women. And I wish to say one more thing. Several of our doctors and several of our nurses are Arabs, and the Jews are proud of that fact.

"I say categorically that if it were not for the Jews—few as they are—Palestine would now be in exactly the same economic and sanitary and educational condition it had been in before the Jews came here in any appreciable numbers. Palestine would be on a plane with Iran and Iraq and Yemen and Saudi Arabia—where illiteracy is rampant—in Yemen alone the rate of illiteracy is more than 90 per cent, that is, at least 90 out of every 100 people cannot read or write. Among the Jews of Palestine the rate of illiteracy is exactly zero. And many Jews know not only Hebrew but Yiddish and Russian, and some of them know English and French, too, depending upon the country they came from. In conclusion, and I wish to thank this station for the opportunity to present our case, in conclusion, I ask, what are the Arab governments afraid of? Are they afraid that the almost miraculous progress of the Jewish communities, if translated on a national level, when a Jewish state is established, will arouse the depressed Arab peoples to ask for more justice, for better living conditions, for more culture and freedom, for less serfdom, for greater democracy? Is this what is behind their senseless opposition? I say senseless, and I say it advisedly, not in order to hurt or insult. I say senseless, because it seems to me that if the Arab governments and peoples should cooperate with the Jewish peoples, the two together could so transform the Middle East in every way, politically, economically, medically, and in every other way, that it would once more become an area of joy and delight and happiness and contentment and brotherhood. Let us live together for our common good. Let us not battle each other for our common hurt."

Again the radio became a blur of sounds, for a while went silent, and then went into a blur once more. Raphael moved the dial and volume knobs here and there, and then said, "Maybe I better leave it alone, like before, and maybe it will get better of itself. Of all the times for the radio to go blank, it had to pick now. This man is wonderful."

"I'm just thrilled," said Mary. "I didn't know we've really done so well in Palestine, I really didn't. Amazing."

"I've been thinking," began David.

"About what?" said Mary and Raphael.

"Well," began David, "about myself, about us here, about other Jews in this country, in England, elsewhere. I mean, how little we know of what has been done in Palestine. We have left it for a few dedicated Jews to do most of the work, to endure hardship, to be in constant danger of attacks by Arabs, by others, and now we'll reap the advantages, so to speak. They, these people, did it for us, and we are delighted. They want us to be delighted, of course, that's why they did it, they'd feel they were failures if we didn't feel delighted, but I feel funny. I guess I don't make sense."

"Oh, you make plenty of sense," began Raphael. "I was saying the same thing to Mary, wasn't I, Mary?"

"You have, dear."

"As we're getting closer to the vote in the United Nations on

434

the Partition proposal," continued Raphael, "a funny sense of guilt, mixed with delight, is coming over me, and," he smiled, "I sort of wish I could make up for my neglect and indifference, too, I guess, in the next few days, so that when the final vote takes place, I'll feel better about it. By the way, I hear the vote may come on Friday or Saturday this week."

"I heard that, too," said David.

Now the radio could be heard again, though not too distinctly . . . slowly it became clearer . . . the announcer was speaking: "You have heard both sides of the argument, perhaps it would be more accurate to say debate, about the Palestine Partition, and the gentlemen who have spoken to you are certainly fully qualified. I thank them for giving of their time so generously, and I am sure all of us have learned a great deal from them. Thank you again, and good night all."

As he walked home that night, David's heart was full, and it was also heavy. It was almost unbearable for him to be alone now. The memories of his youth came back, many of them: his years at the Boston Hebrew School, the speaking of Hebrew in all the classes . . . *Yvrith b'yvrith* (literally, Hebrew in Hebrew) . . . the singing of *Hatikvah* (the Zionist anthem) . . . and he recalled how honored he felt when he had been chosen as the student welcome speaker when Nahum Sokoloff and Dr. Shmarya Levin came to the Hebrew School . . . and he recalled the thin, heavily bespectacled little man, Eliezer Ben Yehuda, who sat at a student's desk in Hebrew School Yvrioh: this man who was devoting his whole life to the composition of a Hebrew dictionary . . . and David thought of all the holiday festivities that used to take place in the Hebrew school . . . and he thought of Alice . . . and he thought of his parents: especially his mother, who was an ardent Zionist.

David recalled that years before, right after World War One, one morning, his mother came back from the grocery store with a copy of the Boston *Post* in her hands . . . she pointed to the streaming headline announcing the Balfour Declaration, in which the British government clearly stressed its conviction that the Jewish people had a right to the re-establishment of their national homeland in Palestine . . . "Look, David," she had said, and couldn't go on . . . David looked, and he couldn't go on, either. He read on and on, and his heart became fuller and fuller. He turned to his mother, and he saw that her eyes were red from joy.

"It's true, David, isn't it?"

"It's true."

"Without any buts?"

"No buts."

"Ah, *derlebt* (literally, thank God, we have reached this happening). Ah! Dr. Weizmann, it mentions him, doesn't it?"

"Yes, very much so. The Declaration is a letter to him, not exactly, but sort of."

"Ah! He used to come to visit my father, *olav hasholem* (may he rest in peace), and I remember their discussions, far into the night, far, far into the night, and I used to try so hard to stay awake to hear them. It was such wonderful talk, David, such wonderful talk. And now it's happened." She hesitated. She looked to the side, then up, then to the side again, and David saw what a beautiful face his mother had: he had never before seen so many invisible things in it . . . and she said, "I know, I know. It will be years before we actually have our land. I know. But Jews are used to *tsores* (troubles, difficulties). We'll manage to conquer them, we'll manage, I'm sure. Ah, if my father were now alive . . ."

David walked on and on, alone . . . but as he recalled his days in Hebrew School, and especially as he recalled his mother that morning, he was not alone any more . . . and he walked on and on, and a wonderful loveliness came to him, and the sky looked warmer and nearer, and the stars seemed closer, and they all seemed to know what he knew, and they all seemed to be as sure about what would be as he was.

Eighteen

David was alone in his room. He had called the Tobiases, wishing that they would ask him again to come to their home to hear the proceedings at the United Nations in Lake Success, Flushing, Long Island. Tonight the historic vote would probably be taken. Tonight perhaps the two-thousand-year-old dream of the Jews, the re-establishment of their national homeland, would be realized. But the Tobiases had a family obligation, and now he was alone in his room. He didn't want to miss any of the speeches, and he certainly didn't want to miss the vote . . . he also wanted to hear whatever commentary the various stations would be making. So he bought some sandwiches, some fruit, and a large container of coffee.

He turned the radio on, and a celebrated news analyst was presenting the situation as objectively as he could. It was clear to him (as it was clear to David and to other Jews) that the Arabs appeared sure of victory. With the recent addition of Afghanistan and Yemen to membership in the United Nations, the Arab-Moslem group was sure of eleven votes in the General Assembly—and it appeared confident of votes from the Iron Curtain countries. A victory for partition necessitated a two-thirds majority vote, and since the Arabs already had eleven votes, even before the voting began, the Jews had to get twenty-two votes to offset them, and for each vote that went for the Arabs, the Jews had to get two more—and at the moment it was highly problematical that they could get these votes. Actually the Arabs needed only another nine votes to kill Partition.

The Jews were not without friends. There was Granados of Guatemala, who was fervent in his advocacy of the Jewish position. Smuts of South Africa and Pearson of Canada were almost as fervent, while Evatt of Australia and Masaryk of Czechoslovakia were close runners-up in their sympathy and positive action. But to offset them were the men of the major powers, Great Britain, Russia and France. There was also the question of what influence these countries would have upon their friends—how much influence Great Britain would have upon New Zealand and the Netherlands, how much France would have to say in the decisions of such lands as Luxembourg, and what Russia would do in getting its satellite and other countries to vote in this or that direction.

The cases of the Latin America countries and of Great Britain were especially baffling. The officials and people of the United States were for partition—after a period of some indecision—but where Cuba stood was doubtful, and similarly dubious were the positions of Brazil and Argentina and Peru and Ecuador and the other lands of Central and South America. The Arab nations were working mightily behind the scenes to get these lands to vote against Partition, making all kinds of promises with respect to Arabian oil. The Jews could do little such persuading. They had no legal being, they had no ambassadors. They had to depend upon friends in other countries.

The Jews were not at all sure of Russia. Russia had jailed many Jews for their Zionist activities, charging them with "cosmopolitanism," which apparently meant split-allegiance; Russia would not countenance such split allegiance, as did the United States and Great Britain. The latter two countries saw nothing wrong in their citizens expressing an emotional attachment to the land of their fathers, but Russia would not stand for similar dual loyalties in her country. Russia might thus tend to oppose Partition. There was also its friendship with the Arab states, which was entirely based upon the need for oil.

There was one other thing to consider, said the commentator, and that was Russia's persistent desire to embarrass the

Western democracies. If it could do so by voting for Partition, without endangering its interests, it would certainly do so. "Russia," he said, "is totally unpredictable. The Russia that made the Hitler-Stalin Pact and then joined the democracies in the war against Hitler can be expected to do anything. If diplomacy is the art of clothing the cynical and hypocritical with the garb of unctuous morality, Russia may well be considered a prime example of such diplomacy. At the same time, in the interests of truth, it must be said that other countries are also capable of such cynicism. No country has a monopoly of international hypocrisy. Whether such hypocrisy is good or bad for the world is beside the point. The fact is indisputable."

David suddenly recalled that it was Friday night—the Eve of the Sabbath. There seemed to be some mystical meaning to this. The final vote on Partition would probably be taken tonight. The General Assembly of the United Nations, with fifty-seven nations represented, was called to order. The gavel thumped and as it did so the clang of destiny seemed to come over the air waves. Then the chairman said, "We shall have a roll call of nations on the partition resolution. A two-thirds majority is needed for passage. Delegates will answer in one of three ways, for, against, or abstain."

There came over the air the word, "Afghanistan."

Immediately the delegate of Afghanistan arose, and in a squeaky but firm voice said, "Afghanistan votes against."

David knew that this Moslem country would vote against partition, everybody knew it, but David's heart sank . . . he had been lying on the couch, as he was listening . . . now he sat up, but soon he decided to lie down again.

"Argentina."

David held his breath. Commentators had said various and conflicting things about which way the Latin American countries would go. Argentina was one of the largest Latin American countries, indeed, the second largest, and it could be that what it did would have an influence upon its sister Latin American countries.

"The government of Argentina wishes to abstain."

Again David's heart sank, but not as low as before. An abstention was not a vote against, but it wasn't a vote for, and it meant that the Jewish cause was up against greater difficulties.

439

Australia was the next country to state its vote. Its representatives had for long expressed their friendliness toward the Jewish delegation at the United Nations, and yet when its chief representative Evatt announced, "Australia votes in favor of Partition," David felt relieved—and he was sure that Dr. Weizmann and the others watching the proceedings were also relieved.

Then Belgium announced its vote: "Belgium votes for partition."

Belgium was a small nation, and perhaps it sensed a kindred spirit in the Jewish small state yet-to-be.

David looked at the list of states and noted that Bolivia, Brazil, and Byelorussia were next in line. He sat up in his bed. These were very crucial votes. The two South American states might set a trend, and Byelorussia would clearly indicate which way the Iron Curtain countries would vote. The Latin American countries did have much in common, but they were not under the thumb of any one country.

"Bolivia votes for Partition . . . Brazil votes for Partition . . . Byelorussia votes for Partition." And then, as if for good measure, came the voice of Lester Pearson, "Canada votes for Partition."

Tears began to come to David's eyes . . . if only Sylvia were with him now . . . the Iron Curtain countries were going to be solidly behind Partition, that was certain . . . and the South American Countries were turning in a good showing: Costa Rica, Ecuador, Guatemala, Haiti, the Dominican Republic were all in favor of Partition, and there were more to come . . . only Cuba, so far, voted against partition, and Honduras, which obviously had been "worked on" by the British and the Arab countries, abstained. Cuba and Honduras were disappointments, but the favorable vote of France did much to counterbalance the disappointment. India, the land of Gandhi, voted against partition, and this, too, was a great disappointment, but then came Liberia, Luxembourg, the Netherlands, New Zealand, Norway, Panama, Paraguay, Peru, and the Philippines: all voted for partition.

"We have won," said David to himself, though he kept no count, but he was sure the Jews had won.

And the vote continued: "Poland in favor . . . Saudi Arabia

against . . . Sweden for . . . Syria against . . . Turkey against . . .
Ukraine for . . . Union of South Africa in favor . . ."

Then there came over the radio, as if from far away, and
with the clarity of destiny: "Union of Soviet Socialist Republics."

The announcer of the radio station whispered quickly: "This
is a crucial vote. The Soviet chief delegate, Andrey Vishinsky,
is rising, and there is a stony and fateful silence all over the
Assembly chamber. Mr. Vishinsky is beginning to speak: "The
Union of Soviet Socialist Republics votes in favor of Partition."

Then, in quick succession, came two votes, both more or
less known beforehand, but now they joined the stream of
history: "His Majesty's Government wishes to abstain . . . The
United States of America votes for Partition."

Yemen voted against, as was expected, Yugoslavia abstained,
obviously because of the large Moslem population in its borders, but Uruguay and Venezuela voted in favor.

All the Arab states could muster, outside their ranks, were
two votes, or thirteen in all, while the Jews mustered thirty-three.
It was a stupendous victory for the Jews, said a commentator
who came on immediately after the announcement of the victory was made officially:

"At this moment it is impossible to gauge properly the importance of what has just happened. Jewish history has been
made. Human history has been made. The heart of all the three
major religions of the West—Judaism, Christianity, and Mohammedanism—has been beating feebly, so to speak, but hope-
fully for two thousand years, but now it is beating vigorously.
It is born again. I trust I am making sense, and not offending
any people. I surely do not mean to. But my very confusion, if
I may call it that, and I guess it is, is an indication of the historic nature of the events we have just witnessed. Perhaps the
mind of man is having difficulty in comprehending the event,
for I do not recall any other event like it in all human history,
but then, I am not a historian. Still, I can report that there
is a strange sense of destiny here. It's all over the Assembly
chamber, on everybody's face. The Jewish delegation is in
sober jubilation. I say delegation, yet, in actuality, they represent no government as yet, but they do represent an ancient
people, the most ancient here, I imagine.

441

"And I say sober, because these people, Dr. Weizmann and the others, know full well what still lies ahead of them. One moment, there is some pandemonium here. It looks as if the delegations of all the Arab states are marching out of the Assembly chamber, in a block. Some are shouting as they leave. Perhaps we can get the words of their shouts. Yes. 'We will never accept this resolution! . . . There will be war! . . . Death to the Jews! . . . A monstrous, illegal vote! . . . We shall declare a holy war against the Jews till they are driven from the land! . . . War against the Jews!'

"And I imagine these Arab delegates mean everything they say. The vote is a devastating defeat to them. They managed to get only two votes from outside their circle: Greece and Cuba, and it is a mystery how they did it. It is also significant that France deserted England, or rather Great Britain. And so did the nations of the British Commonwealth desert the mother England: all of them, almost, Canada, Australia, New Zealand. The action of India against Partition is strange, indeed, in view of Gandhi's known friendship for smaller nations and minority groups. On the other hand, Indian diplomacy has mystified the Western world, since it became independent.

"We have just received word from Tel Aviv that the city is alight with such joy and dancing and merry-making as has never been seen there before. It is easy to see why. No people has more cause for rejoicing. But even as the Jews in Tel Aviv and other cities in Palestine exult, the same people know the hard and difficult times ahead. No doubt some of them can hear Arabs in neighboring lands shouting, 'Perish the Jews! Death to the Jews! War Against the Jews Forever!' "

The commentator continued to talk, but David's mind now wandered off into a region that he did not recognize . . . he saw before him a desert, wide and sandy and bright with the sun's light and heat, limitless on all sides . . . and yet there was a coolness hovering over the heat . . . and soon a breeze came, but still there was no one to be seen . . . soon voices could be heard coming from aside, the voices mounted and deepened . . . now women's voices could be heard above men's voices, now men's voices could be heard above women's voices . . . and now violins played: what they played was not recognizable, and yet it sounded familiar . . . and now David saw trees slowly

442

rise up from the ground, and houses, and stretches of water . . . and now he saw men and women, boys and girls rise up on the streets, and it was these men and women, these boys and girls who were singing, and as they sang they worked: on the fields and around their homes, and in factories . . . and more and more men and women and boys and girls seemed to be coming from alll around to join those already there . . . and the sun shone, but it was not hot, and the day became longer and longer, and David began to wonder what had happened to the night, but the night did not come . . .

Now, in the midst of this thriving city of people and light and coolness and warm goodness, a hill sprang up, and soon it was a mountain, and the top of the mountain was circled with tall trees . . . and soon, from the midst of the trees, there rose up a man, with a powerful face and a long but neat beard, and he held up two tablets, and he showed them to all, round and round he turned to make sure all saw the tablets . . . and now the man rose higher and higher, but he had left the tablets on the mountain, and as he rose higher and higher, slowly vanishing, music from men and women, from boys and girls, and from instruments followed him . . . and soon a glorious sigh of joy came from the mountain and from the people below.

David suddenly came out of his reveries, and again he heard the commentator: "This is the Eve of the Sabbath for the Jewish people, so their joy is now subdued, for it is forbidden to make merry on the Sabbath, at least in a worldly way. But we can well imagine what will take place tomorrow night, on the departure of the Sabbath, and what will take place on the days following. One of my associates has been trying to get one of the Jewish delegates to come to the radio to say a few words, but so far we have not succeeded, but we hope to have one of the Jewish folks here at the mike shortly.

"The question of the implementation of the Partition resolution is serious, indeed. That there will be hostilities no one here doubts, but neither does any one doubt that the Jews in Palestine will give a good accounting of themselves. They have on their side the majority vote of the General Assembly, that is, world opinion. But they have other things. They have hope and glory and they have a cause, the most glorious and won-

derful a people can have, their very existence. And they have
arms and they have soldiers, soldiers who know what they are
fighting for. Many of them no doubt have fled from the Hitler
gas chambers, and they surely have something to fight for, a
homeland for themselves and for their children. No one here
knows how much arms the Palestine Jews have, but one can
be sure that the Jewish leaders have taken everything into
account. They have something to fight for, and they are ready
to fight. The next few days will be crucial, indeed. Already
word has reached us of Arab attacks upon Jewish colonies in
Palestine. There have been casualties on both sides. What a
tragedy it is that at this time there should be killings as so
historic an event has taken place. I have been hoping that one
of the Israeli gentlemen would be here by now, but I guess
they are occupied elsewhere, though I am sure one of them
will be here soon. There is, of course, also the matter of this
being the Eve of the Sabbath.

"I have just been handed a slip of paper telling us that the
Arab delegates are still threatening all sorts of reprisals, that
they are carrying on in the United Nations lobby, shouting
at newspaper men that this, in their view, gross injustice to
them will be avenged by blood, a holy war, and so on. This
is not a surprise, I mean, these threats, such threats have come
from the Arab delegations throughout the week and even before, but now that they are out in public, for the whole world
to hear, so to speak, they are ominous, indeed. But, as I say,
the Jews are probably prepared, and one may say that public
opinion, at least in the form of the United Nations, which
does represent the concerted views of the whole world, or a
goodly part of it, will have something to say about whether
or not a vote of the General Assembly can be flouted. Well,
this will be all for now. I feel I have been present at a most
significant turn in the stream of history, most significant, indeed,
and I am sure you do, too. Good night."

David walked out of his room . . . he looked at his watch . . .
he didn't realize that it was so late, nearly midnight . . . he was
astonished that the people walking up and down the street
were so sober, so glum, almost: didn't they know what had
happened but a short while ago? . . . he stood at a corner,
the more closely to watch the passing faces: they were still

sober and glum and apparently indifferent . . . he could barely believe it . . . he looked at his watch, it was much too late to call the Tobiases . . . he only wanted to say how wonderful the news was . . . that was all he wanted to say . . . he wanted to say it to somebody, even to one of the passers-by, but something held him back: they might consider him strange . . . he walked to a cafeteria, it was crowded, so he stepped out on the street again . . . his loneliness was increasing and becoming almost unbearable . . . he so wanted to talk to somebody . . . he walked to the Grand Central Station . . . the central lobby was deserted . . . the lights were a little dim, the cleaners would soon come in and wash the huge marble floor.

Suddenly he decided he would call his parents in Boston. His father answered the telephone.

"Wasn't it wonderful, what happened?" said David.

"There's wonderful and wonderful," said Moshe to his son.

"I just thought I'd call up," said David, who remembered that his father was far from being the Zionist that his mother was.

"It's good that you called," said his father. "We are not yet asleep anyway. Aidel was here, her husband, the others, we were listening to the radio. Nu, now we have to trust in God, what with the Arabs making all those threats. Nu, *beshert* (literally, it's fated). Here is your mother. You all right, David? Good, good."

David's mother was on. "You feeling fine, David?"

"Yes, yes, Mother. Wasn't it wonderful?"

"David, I cried from joy," said his mother. "What can I say? It was so . . . like something fated. I am so happy . . . happy is not the word . . . how can I describe it? If only my father were alive now, if only! I wish I could hear it all again."

"That's why I called, Mother. I wanted to say . . . well, that it was wonderful."

"I was telling your father. I keep looking at the picture of Dr. Herzl in the kitchen, you know, and I hope he knows. Did you hear what one of the radio people said, that Dr. Herzl predicted it would happen fifty years from his time, and it did."

"Yes, Mother. Wonderful."

"All the Jews should be talking now, I mean . . ."

"Yes."

445

"I was hoping you would hear it. I didn't say anything, but I was hoping, and I knew, David, I knew, you were listening, and I was hoping you would call, David."

"That's why I did, Mother."

"I know."

"Are you all right, Mother? I mean the pain . . ."

"It's nothing, A little pain sometimes, everybody has it. It's late, so go back to sleep."

The operator interrupted: "You're three minutes are up."

"Good-bye, Mother, and say good-bye to Father and the others."

"Thank you, thank you, David, for calling. And eat well and go to sleep, and thank you."

Nineteen

The morning newspapers had front-page stories about the United Nations vote. David read the stories in *The New York Times* and the New York *Herald Tribune,* but he was disappointed: they missed something, they missed all that had gone though his heart and soul the night before, all that had gone between his father and mother and himself when they talked over the telephone. He bought the two leading Jewish newspapers, the *Forward* and the *Day,* but the editions he bought had nothing about the vote, obviously they had gone to press before the time of the ballotting. There was still another disappointment: the Tobiases hadn't called him this morning . . . He couldn't contain himself any longer, and he called them, but there was no answer: they had probably gone away for the weekend on some family obligation. He felt deeply depressed, he needed someone to talk to, preferably a woman.

Suddenly he recalled Helen: they had had arguments, he had been offended by some things she had said and done and somethings she had not said and not done. He was ashamed that she came to his mind only as a last resort, so to speak. She was worthy of greater devotion. The more he thought about her the more appealing did she become: all her warmth and all her out-going comfort and all her giving companionship, and all that she had meant to him as they had embraced each other came back to him. He looked small in his own eyes, for not accepting Helen for the wonderful woman she was, and for not seeing that what he had considered as faults were, perhaps, no more than the faults of all womankind.

She answered the telephone at the first ring: "Oh, David, you won't believe this. I was hoping you'd call. I knew you would. I was waiting at the telephone for your call. I knew it was you. Darling, darling, it's wonderful, what happened, isn't it?"

"It's good to hear you, Helen, I'm sorry . . ."

"Oh, David, don't be sorry. I was to blame for everything. Let's forget it all. You know, darling, there's going to be a big celebration in St. Nicholas Arena, uptown, in New York, tonight, at seven, I think, as soon as the sun goes down. Thousands and thousands and millions of Jews will be there. Let's go together, darling. I want to dance with you, I want to kiss you, right in the street."

"But . . ."

"No buts, David. Listen to me. I have to go soon, something about my son, I have to take him to the doctor, nothing serious, then I have to go with him to his father's sister because . . . but why bother you, it's family things. But I'll be through at six, around there, and I'll meet you, or you come here, darling, have a quick supper, or something, then we'll go to that place, St. Nicholas, you know where it is?"

"Oh, yes, 66th Street at Broadway, they have prize fights there and meetings. All right, I'll pick you up at your house. I'll bring some sandwiches."

"Oh, no. I'll make something. You bring nothing, David, just yourself. I love you, I just love you. I knew you'd call. Oh, I forgot something."

"What?"

"*Mazel tov* (literally, good luck, congratulations). I made up my mind I'd say *mazel tov* to everybody I meet on the street for the next week, day and night. It's a holiday, isn't it?"

"Yes, but . . ."

"It is a holiday, David, the biggest and the best the Jews have had in two thousand years. *Gott in Himmel!* Such a holiday this is! I just can't say how big, so big it is, the biggest.

You'll be here around six. Good. I send you a big holiday kiss till then, darling."

But it was many hours till six, and David couldn't be alone. He decided to go to synagogue. He wanted to go to one of the small synagogues in downtown New York. He felt that he would be more at home there today. He didn't know just which synagogue he would attend. He took the subway downtown, and in a short time he saw what looked like a line of people going in one direction. He followed them. Soon they came to the vicinity of the *Jewish Daily Forward* . . . and soon he found himself in front of a large synagogue, with about thirty stairs leading up to its door . . . the line of people was entering the synagogue. David looked up and saw a huge round stained glass window, directly above the central door, and the central design was a Mogen David, the star of David. The front wall apparently had not long before been sandblasted, for its light yellowish bricks seemed freshly washed. David looked at the people entering the synagogue. They seemed to be far from impoverished.

David couldn't make up his mind whether this was really the sort of synagogue he wanted to enter today. He had wanted something more modest, the sort of *shul* his father attended. But suddenly he decided he might as well enter, and as soon as he entered he was delighted. It was a truly beautiful Orthodox synagogue, with the *bimme* (roughly, platform) in the middle, and a woman's section above. The synagogue was like those he had gone to as a boy in Boston, like the one his father went to now: not in size, or in splendor, but in *minhag* (custom of worship). The *Oren Kodesh* (Holy Ark, wherein the Torah rests) was simple but immensely impressive. There was a large ornamental chair to the right of the Ark, and another to the left, and at once David knew that there the president and vice-president of the *shul,* respectively, sat. And David liked that very much.

It all reminded him of the *shul* where his great uncle Mottel used to be the vice-president . . . yes, the old North Russell Street *Shul* was built on the order of this *shul* . . . it wasn't so grand, but it was, so to speak, a smaller version of this one . . . and pretty much the same sort of people attended, well, not

449

exactly: those who were all around him now, David thought, were better situated financially than were those who attended his great uncle's *shul,* but both groups were a rung or two or three above, say, the class that David's father belonged to—yes, several rungs above. In other words, those who came to both *shulen* were *balebatim* (literally landlords, that is, men of some means, not necessarily wealthy, however). As David looked about he recalled Alte Bobbe, his great-grandmother, whom he used to escort to *shul* Saturdays and holidays . . . how wise and knowing she was, and how often he had thought of her . . . and with what joy she used to look down from the balcony upon her son, Mottel, who was sitting in the vice-president's chair . . . and all those long-passed days came back to him with their poignant memories and all their vague yet deep meanings.

The services began exactly in the manner in which they had begun in his father's *shul* . . . the *daavening* (praying) was the long *daavening,* and David liked that . . . today surely was a time for long *daavening,* for there was so much to give praise to God for . . . the *ba'al shachris* (lay leader for the early part of the prayer) had a good voice, and it was plain that he wasn't going to hurry his part of the services.

"*Gut gedaavened* (literally, well prayed)," David heard one man say.

"Very good," answered another. "I always did say that he would make a good *chazan* (cantor). Anyway, today is not just a *Shabbes.* It is truly a *Shabbes Hagodel* (literally, a Great Sabbath)."

"So it is, very much so."

The synagogue was still filling up. David turned to a man sitting beside him, and said, "Like on Rosh Hashonoh, so full it is getting."

The man, who was well in his sixties, and who had a goatee, pretty much like David's own father's, said, "Nu, it really is a Rosh Hashonoh for Jews today, the greatest in two thousand years."

The prayer continued, and slowly the *chazan* walked up to the *bimme,* and after him came members of the choir; they made a semi-circle around the *chazan.* Now the *moosaf* (second part of the services) began. The *chazan* was excellent, and so

450

was the choir. David liked especially the way the *chazan* and choir sang the *Shma Ysroel* (Hear, O Israel). They didn't thunder it forth . . . they did it quietly, instilling it with meaning and with holiness: it almost seemed to be coming from on high and from far away . . . it was soft and warm and at the same time piercing . . . then came the weekly reading of the Torah, and David's heart swelled with pride as he heard the reader say the ancient words: they seemed to be especially appropriate today . . . and the singing of the portion by the reader added a loveliness to all that was taking place . . . and the services of the reading of the Torah proceded in the same manner as it has proceded in synagogues for some twenty centuries. The Torah was then put in the arms of a man, who had taken a seat on the *bimme* . . . and the whole congregation became quiet.

The rabbi now walked up to the platform where the Holy Ark was, and looked about him. David liked him at once. He was medium of height, in his late fifties or early sixties, he had a generous gray beard, and there was something very kindly in his face. He had on a long *talis* (prayer shawl) such as David's own father wore—David's father thought it was discourteous to the Almighty to wear one of the modern abbreviated *talaysim*. The rabbi held on to the *talis* with both hands, and slowly began to speak:

"Mazel tov."

A pleasant sigh spread throughout the synagogue.

He continued, "For two thousand years we have been ending many of our prayers with *Leshono habo b'Yerusholayim* (next year in Jerusalem), and now it has come to pass, thanks to God. We are now, or soon will be, a nation again among other nations.

"What shall I say? What can one say at a time of great joy, perhaps the greatest a Jew can have, except *Gott zei dank,* thank God? We Jews differ among ourselves. The principle of free speech, I sometimes think, was born among us. We even argue with the Uppermost, as witness the Book of Job. We differ as to many things, but we do not differ as to the great joy that has just come to our people. Orthodox, Reform, Conservative, we are all sons of Israel, we are all happy. From now on, in a deep sense, we are all Zionists. It has been said

451

that Jews unite only when there is a gun at their people's head. It is also true that Jews are all happy when something wonderful has happened to their people, whether this wonderful thing agrees with their philosophy or not. Last night we became a united people the world over.

"Jews, what can I say? I have no prepared *droshe* (sermon), and now I feel worried, for I have not seen so many people in *shul* on an ordinary Shabbes except on Rosh Hashonoh and Yom Kippur. That is good. Already we can see one wonderful result of what happened yesterday. People are coming back to *shul*. Yes, it is very good, seeing all of you. The *shul* is the center of the Jewish soul. In times of grief and misery, Jews flock to the synagogue, and in times of joy they flock to the synagogue.

"I am your rabbi, and I want to confess to you that last night, from the strict point of view of Jewish law, as interpreted by our Orothodox tradition, I desecrated the Sabbath. It is not permitted us to turn on the radio or to talk on the telephone. I know that some of you here do not observe these two rules meticulously. But I do. Last night I didn't. I turned on the radio. I called up friends, including another Orthodox rabbi, and he said that if I hadn't called him, he would have called me. I think God will forgive me, for our God is an understanding God. And the great rabbis of our past, the *gaonim,* the *lamdonim,* would have understood. They probably, I dare say, would have done what I did, what I am sure other rabbis did.

"I am standing near the Torah, the symbol of all that we are, the very heart of all that we are. Without Torah there is no Judaism, without Torah, Judaism would have perished long ago. Torah is life, Torah is Jewish life, Torah is kindness, Torah is gentleness, Torah is *rachmones* (mercy), Torah is humanity, Torah is the universal rule of life. Torah takes in the whole of life, the whole of humanity. In the days of the Temple in Jerusalem, we made one sacrifice in prayer for our own well-being and peace, but we also made seventy other such sacrifices for the welfare and peace of the seventy other nations that were then on the earth. Torah thus is the very essence of spiritual democracy, and spiritual democracy is the essence of all other democracy, including political democracy.

It is therefore no accident, but in the inevitable nature of things that the line around the Liberty Bell in Philadelphia is from Leviticus XXV, 10: 'Proclaim liberty throughout the land unto all the inhabitants thereof.'

"How did I desercrate the Sabbath, or, rather, why did I feel free to desecrate the Sabbath? I am going into this matter because what I am about to say is an important element of Judaism, and that, after all, is what we are celebrating, the revival of Judaism as a national state, to be respected by all the nations. It has been said that Judaism is a religion of laws, not of mercy. That is not true. Judaism is the very heart of mercy. *Rachmones,* pity, sympathy, compassion, is the most common, most characteristic word among Jews. Ah, if only those who charged us with being merciless had practiced some of their vaunted mercy upon us!

"The Sabbath, as we all know, is in many respects the holiest of Jewish holidays. The Sabbath as a day of rest is ordered in the Bible. The Sabbath, in many respects, is what differentiates us from animals. It is a day, not only for rest from work, from toil. It is also a day of rest from being, so to speak, a non-human. Animals work, too. They work all the time. But work is only part of a man's life. His main life is his relationship with God, his consciousness of his divinity, his being made in the image of God, as it says in Genesis. On the Sabbath we rethink our divinity. On that day we are closer to our God, and therefore all the more human. Therefore, it is forbidden to Jews to work on that day.

"But there are exceptions. To save a life it is allowed to desecrate the Sabbath. To save a people it is allowed to desecrate the Sabbath. To keep a man alive so that he can satisfy his desire to study Torah it is also permitted to desecrate the Sabbath. I wish to tell you a story, a legend, that is told about one of our greatest teachers. Its *ikker* (core, heart) is the very essence of Judaism, from so many wonderful angles. I tell it to you for that reason, and once I have told it to you we will have before us another glory of our faith, whose great victory in the world at large, among the nations of the world, we are celebrating. We are happy. Here is only one reason why we should be happy, for what this story, this legend, this essential truth tells is one of the things that the nations of the world, last night, voted should go on, unto eternity, unmolested, and that we Jews from now on will see to it, in the open and with pride, will be unmolested from the enemies, not only of our faith, but of all decency and truth and justice. The vote last night, let us not forget, fellow Jews, was not a gift, though we are, of course, immensely grateful. The vote last night was a simple statement of long overdue justice to us, to our history, to our tradition, to the conscience of the world.

"What is the story, the legend? You have all heard of Hillel the Elder, one of the glories of rabbinic history. He was a manual laborer, doing whatever came his way, for to the rabbis all honest work was honorable, he was a manual laborer, generally earning one half of a dinar, gold coin, a day. Half of this he would give to his wife for the family expenses, but the other half he gave to the *shames* (sexton) of the *Beth Hamidrash* (House of Study) so that he would be allowed in to study with the great scholars, Shemaya and Avtalyon. But then there came a day when Hillel found no work, so he had no money with which to get to hear and participate in the studying in the *Beth Hamidrash*. The day on which he could find no work was Friday, *Erev Shabbes* (Eve of the Sabbath), and it was also the month of Teveth, a very cold month, and it was freezing. But Hillel would not be discouraged. Quietly he climbed to the roof of the *Beth Hamidrash,* and sat upon what we now call the skylight, and with all his might he strained to hear the studying. Hillel heard enough to be able to follow the studying, but so intent was he upon what he was hearing that he hardly realized that he was being covered with snow, and he almost froze to death. As a matter of fact, he fell asleep on the skylight, in the snow, cold as he was.

"Early the next day, on Shabbes, when they came into the *Beth Hamidrash,* Shemaya said to Avtalyon, 'Isn't it strange how dark it is now? Usually at this time of day, our House of Study is well lighted. Did you notice whether it was cloudy outside? I thought it was rather clear.' So both rabbis looked up into the skylight, and of course they beheld the figure of a man. At once they went to the roof—even though it was Shabbes, for the life of a human being was involved—and there found Hillel almost dead from the cold. In the *Beth Hamidrash* they took off his clothes, bathed him, massaged him, and sat him next to the fire so that he would warm up. Now what did these great rabbis say? They said that anyone who was so eager to study Torah, as Hillel was, obviously merited that the laws of the Sabbath be for the while overlooked so that he may be saved for more study of the Torah. So human is Judaism, so delighted is it with the act of learning, one of the noblest of all activities. Indeed, as I have told you often before, one sect of Chassidim places study, learning, studying the Torah on a level with prayer.

"I am sure that Shemaya and Avtalyon and Hillel himself would have been eager to hear the radio last night, would have blest every word of favorable voting as it came over the air, and would have called up, on the telephone, other rabbis to rejoice with them. And, further, last night my mind wandered happily—I was so filled with joy I could hardly sleep . . . I said *Tehilim* (read the Psalms) far into the night . . . my mind, as I say wandered, as a joyful heart always wanders, is always restless, and I entertained myself with many pleasant Jewish thoughts: I imagined how the angels must be singing, especially those nearest to the Uppermost . . . and I imagined how our great prophets must rejoice, especially *Eliyohu Hanovi* (Elijah the Prophet). And why Eliyohu? Forgive me, my fellow Jews, for telling you of my boyhood, only one instance. Eliyohu was my favorite prophet, especially on Passover, you know, when the door is opened for Eliyohu, for him to come into the house. I used to tremble when I opened the door for him, and I used to imagine I saw him, with a smiling face, a fine, kindly face, and I wanted to talk to him, but I didn't dare. He was a favorite of mine, to a considerable extent, because he was associated with Passover, the festival of freedom, freedom from slavery, freedom to be ourselves, to be a nation and a people among nations and peoples. We Jews were the first freedom fighters, and we never forgot our dedication to freedom. That is why every Friday night, every Saturday, in almost all our services there is a reference to *zacher yetziahs Mitzrayim* (to recall our deliverance from Egypt), for it was in Mitzrayim, in Egypt, that we were slaves.

"And what did this memory, this constant recalling do to us? It made us free men forever. Even in Exile, yes in Exile, too. Jews have borne themselves proud down the centuries of their Exile. Their religion made them proud. Their God made them proud. They were people of quality, and they knew it. They knew that they were the people who set the standard of quality the world over and down the centuries of time. I am not one to claim all qualities for the Jews. Non-Jews are also God's children. That is one of the glorious teachings of our Torah and of our sages. And yet, as we look at the records of history, we do see that Jewish tradition, in many respects, was superior to other traditions. The Greeks? A great people, no doubt, and we owe them an incalculable debt. But their democracy was a sham democracy, based upon human slavery and the concept of the congenital superiority of some people to others— not mental superiority, but innate spiritual superiority. The Jews have ever denied this. We are all on a plane before the Almighty. We all have a right to freedom and liberty. The Books of Leviticus and Deuteronomy are filled with rulings on these matters. And the Romans? They are justly celebrated for the code of laws. All men are equal before the law. This is a Roman concept. But the Jews preached it before the Romans. And the rabbis, as you can see by reading the Mishna, said that even God Himself is subject to law, He is subject to the rules of right and wrong, He cannot transcend them, for otherwise He would not be God. Godliness is the very embodiment of the good and the right and the beautiful. It is unthinkable, in Jewish tradition and religion, for God to act as the Greek and Roman gods carried on. Their very acts deprived them of their claim to divinity.

"And now Eretz Yisroel is ours," continued the rabbi, after a brief pause. "Ours. I know that much hard work and even fighting still have to be done before Eretz Yisroel fully becomes ours. But it is ours in the eyes of the world and this makes all the difference. Eretz Yisroel is ours. It's hard to say the words without being made speechless by the wonder of them, the sheer glorious and unending wonder. Never, never have the Jews given up their dream of a rewon Palestine, no matter how long their exile, no matter how intense their suffering.

"Today is Shabbes. And I am reminded of what Dr. Theodor Herzl said: 'Zionism was the Sabbath of my life.' What a beautiful thought. And it was fated that Zionism should be realized on the Sabbath. One of the things I did last night was

456

to re-read Dr. Herzl's *The Jewish State,* one of the most prophetic of all books. He was a *novie* (a prophet). He predicted that a Jewish state surely would be realized in fifty years from the time he said it, shortly before his death, and so it has happened. *Dos Pintele Yid* (literally, the Jewish point, trademark, that is, the Jewish heart) was large and grand in him. Listen to the universal human being, that is, the Jew, speak in him: 'I believe that a wondrous generation of Jews will spring into existence. The Maccabees will rise again. Let me repeat once more my opening words: the Jews wish to have a state, and they shall have one. We shall live at last as free men on our own soil, and die peacefully in our own home. The world will be freed by our liberty, enriched by our wealth, magnified by our greatness. And whatever we attempt there to accomplish for our own welfare will react with beneficent force for the good of humanity.' "

The rabbi stopped, sighed, then said slowly, "May he have a *lichtiggen Gan Eden* (a bright Garden of Eden). He gave his life to his people, dying at the age of forty-four. But his name will live forever. Eretz Yisroel is ours. It was always ours. It was always in our hearts, and what is in our hearts is ours. Such love as the Jewish people have had for their ancestral land has never before been known in history. We were exiled first to Babylonia, but our hearts were in Palestine. King Joconiah and his court brought earth and stones from Jerusalem for the purpose of building a *shul* in Babylonia, so as to comply with the passage. 'For thy servants take pleasure in her stones and love her dust.'

"Yes, Yisroel has ever been in our hearts. We have thought about it, we have prayed for it, we have fasted for it, we have never forgotten it. And we have been joyous about it. Yes, joyous. Judaism is essentially a joyous religion. In the Bible there is only one fast day mentioned, Yom Kippur. But it is for only one day. After every fast comes a period of rejoicing. We Jews have faith in God, that He will bring good conclusions, as He always does.

"There is a beautiful tale told in the Aggada. Rabbi Akiba and his students and associates came to Jerusalem and were thunderstruck by the desolation, the waste, the *poostkeit* (empiness) all around them. Only animals roamed about. The rabbi's

457

students and associates tore their garments. They cried in their pain. But Rabbi Akiba appeared composed. His associates were astonished and asked him to explain why he didn't mourn as they did. Said Rabbi Akiba: 'As the portentous prophetic words came true in all their terrifying fulfillment, then all the more sure are we that the tenderly cherished prophecies will be fulfilled completely.' And the rabbi's associates were comforted and consoled.

"Eretz Yisroel is ours. But how dearly we have paid for it. Think of the thousands and thousands of Jewish men and women who were massacred by the Romans and the Greeks and the Egyptians. Think of the thousands and thousands of Jewish men and women and children who were massacred by the Crusaders. Think of the thousands and thousands of Jewish men and women who preferred to be burnt to death to accepting any other faith than their own. Think of Spain and think of Portugal. Think of the thousands and thousands of Jewish men and women and children who were massacred by the Russians and the Rumanians and the Poles and the Turks. Think of the blood libels and what misery they brought us. Think of all the centuries when we were considered second-class citizens, or no citizens at all—even in countries, in civilized countries, like England and France and certain parts of our beloved United States, too. Think of Buchenwald and Auschwitz. Think of the six million who were destroyed by the Nazis, while a Christian world did less than it might have.

"Eretz Yisroel is ours. This is indeed a day of rejoicing. But in our rejoicing let us not forget the millions and millions of Jewish men and women and children, down the centuries, who have given their lives that we might now celebrate. Eretz Yisroel is ours. It is also theirs. Let us say *Kaddish* (prayer for the dead) for them."

A tense holiness and a sorrowful silence filled the synagogue. The entire congregation stood up. The rabbi went to the Holy Ark, opened the *paroches* (the curtain) and the Torahs were visible, resplendent in all the wonderment of the occasion. The rabbi stood aside, still facing the Torahs. And the whole congregation began to say the Kaddish, with the cantor leading:

"Yisgadal Veyiskadash shmay raboh, beolomo dibroh chiroosay . . . Glorified and sanctified be His great name in the world

458

which He has created according to His will. May He establish His kingdom during your life and during your days, and during the life of all the house of Israel, speedily and soon, and say ye, Amen.

"Yehay shmay raboh mevorach lolam oolalmay olmayoh . . . Let His great name be blessed for ever and to all eternity. Blessed, praised and glorified, exalted, adored and honored, extolled and lauded be the name of the Holy One, blessed be He . . . May He Who makes peace in His heights bring peace upon us and upon all Israel; and say ye, Amen."

The *Amen* was said firmly, clearly, and there was determination in it . . . and following it was a hush, as if it had descended from heaven. And now the cantor continued with the remainder of the Sabbath service.

Twenty

Helen was in utter jubilation. She seemed to have become ten years younger. Her whole face seemed to have blossomed out, and her breasts and her arms and her hips, her whole body . . . and there shone from her eyes a spirit and a delight that filled David with wonderment and also delight. Here, in front of him, was a new yet an old Helen: the Helen that he had sensed the first time he saw her, the Helen that he had embraced in the warm dark of the night . . . and yet there was something new and different now: as he looked at her he heard echoes of his youth in Hebrew school, he heard distant music that he had heard in his dreams when he had been a boy in Boston.

She continued to throw her arms around his neck and to kiss him and kiss him, as she did on his arrival at her house. "Darling, darling, isn't it just wonderful?"

"It is, Helen," he began, when she threw her arms around him again and kissed him again and again.

Dinner had been prepared before, as he saw from the table. "This is just nothing, David," said Helen. "Quick, you know, because we have to go to the celebration. But tomorrow and the whole week we'll have real dinners and everything, yes, darling?"

"I'd like that very much."

As they ate she continued to look at him and to smile at him, almost like a little girl, so excited was she. "You know something, David?"

"What, Helen?"

"You're beautiful."

"Oh, now, come on . . ."

"You are, David. You look just like a little boy, so sweet. I want to sit beside you. I'll move the chair over, no, you sit, I'll do it."

As she sat down close to him, she again threw her arms around his neck, but this time she did not kiss his mouth, but dug her nose into his neck. "Oh, darling David, is it really true that we have a country again?" She turned to face him, looked intently at him, her nose almost touching his nose. She continued: "It's hard to believe. When I was alone, I just didn't believe it, when I heard it over the radio. You know, David, it's hard to believe things when you're alone, did you know that?"

"Well . . ."

"It is, David, it is." She kissed him quickly on the lips, and continued. "And when I talked to other people about what happened, I wasn't sure, still or yet, whatever the word is. But when you called me, and said what you said, I knew it was true. You make things true, darling, did you know that?"

"Well . . ."

She kissed him quickly on the mouth again, and said, "It is true, you make things true." Suddenly she became business-like. "We have to hurry. I'll get the coffee."

She brought the coffee, and said, "This is very strong. I did it on purpose. You know why?"

"So we'll be up a long time, dancing and singing. This is a birthday party, the first birthday of the new State of Israel or Palestine. I hope they call it Israel, don't you?"

"That would be good."

"Yes, I like Israel better, too, David. Yes, today every Jew everywhere, in the whole world, has a birthday, isn't that right, darling?"

"Yes, I guess so."

She put her finger to his mouth, and smiling, said, "You don't guess, darling, you know, don't you, darling?"

461

"I know," he said, and threw his arms around her neck and kissed her long on her mouth.

"Thank you, darling, for the birthday kiss," Helen said. "I'll leave the dishes. I'll clean them tomorrow. You want another coffee? It's very good, isn't it? Good and strong. Yes?"

"Yes, it would be good," said David.

"I think there's time, don't you, David?"

"Oh, I don't know. We'll try to squeeze in the hall somehow. Who's going to talk?"

"Oh, I don't know. Everybody I guess, darling, you know, the important people. They ought to let the ordinary people talk, they know how to say they're happy better than the important people. Important people aren't happy naturally. They're always making speeches, even when they make love." She put her hand to her mouth, like a little girl saying something she shouldn't say . . . and she looked very lovely in David's eyes. He walked over and embraced her and kissed her. "Helen, you're wonderful. I like what's got into you, Helen. I like it very much."

"You'll never make speeches to me, will you, darling?"

"I promise I won't."

"I wish they'd let me say something tonight. I have so much to say. But you'd have to be right next to me. Otherwise I couldn't make any speech, couldn't say a thing. I guess we better go now, yes?"

On the subway uptown Helen kept on talking: "It's hard to believe, dear, isn't it? But it's true, isn't it?"

"Yes," said David.

"There's one thing I'm sorry for, David."

"What?"

"About Mordecai, my husband. It's so sad, so terribly sad he isn't here now. He would have been thrilled."

"Yes."

"Always he thought about it. He was such an ardent Zionist. It's terrible the way things sometimes happen."

"Yes," said David, who was pleased to hear her talk that way.

"You know what I'm thinking of now, darling?"

"What?"

"I wish that all the Jews who ever lived were now here,

462

with us, alive, you know, even for a little while, so they could know."

David was so startled by the idea that he kissed her hand. "That would be marvelous, Helen, just marvelous."

"So why can't it be?"

"I don't know, Helen."

"I know."

David then began to tell Helen about what happened earlier that morning, how thrilled he was at the synagogue, how especially thrilled he was by the rabbi's talk and by the *Kaddish.* As he finished he noticed that Helen's eyes were getting red.

"What's wrong, Helen?"

"Nothing, only . . ."

"Only what?"

"I wish I were there, too. The *shul* is the place to go to when this happens, it's the only place to go to. The Torah is there. I'm ashamed I didn't think of it. It's terrible what being civilized does to a person, isn't it? And I didn't think of it."

"Well . . ."

"It's terrible, David, that I didn't think of it. When you go against the people, it's never good, not natural, not good."

"You're still a good Jew . . ."

"I am, David, I am. I know. But I should have gone to the synagogue. We'll go together next *Shabbes,* yes?"

"Yes."

"Because this will be a long birthday celebration, for our new-old country, it will be a long celebration, yes?"

"Of course, Helen," said David, as he kissed her hand again. "Of course, it will be a long celebration."

She kissed his hand. "Darling, I wish my father and mother were here now. They were both such lovers of Palestine." Suddenly a big smile came to her face. "It's so wonderful, imagine, so wonderful, imagine, here we are going to a celebration of the new state of Palestine, no, Israel, that's better, isn't it, David?"

They came to Lincoln Square, where St. Nicholas Arena was. The square was crowded with people, young and old, men and women. It was so crowded that the buses had to crawl along. There were many police all about. There was

463

talking and singing . . . joyful faces all about . . . Helen and David wended their way to the Arena, but a line of police was stationed at the door, and they said, one after another almost, "Closed! Full up! No one admitted!"

"Marvelous," said Helen softly, "marvelous."

"What do you mean, marvelous?" said David. "It means we can't go in."

"I know, I know, darling. But it's good we can't go in. I like a hall to be filled for such an event. I love it."

"You're right."

Suddenly David heard someone shouting, "David, David!"

David turned around, and he saw Daniel, his assistant on the *World,* approaching him through the thick crowd.

"Gee, it's good to see you," Daniel said. He was alone.

David introduced him to Helen. "Well, you couldn't get in, either."

"No," said Daniel. "I just missed it. I almost made it, though. The cops closed the door just as I was about to enter."

"How do you like it?" asked Helen. "I mean . . ."

"Wonderful. I never thought . . . Really . . ."

Helen turned to David, then to Daniel. "I never thought this would happen either. Jews, after all . . ."

Daniel interrupted her. "You should see my house. My father is out of his mind with joy. He's probably around here somewhere, probably inside. Not probably, I'm sure he's inside."

"What happened?" said David.

"He hasn't gone to sleep, he's been listening to the radio all night, listening to the same news reports over and over again. He's bought the Yiddish newspapers, all of them, and the English papers, all of them, and reading them and reading them, not just to himself but to us kids and to mother. Like I told you, she's not Jewish, but she sort of got on to the excitement."

"What do you mean?" said David.

"Well, he began by walking up and down the apartment, saying out loud, 'We did it, goddamn it, we did it!' That's what he's been saying, shouting, saying it right out loud."

David looked at Helen who was beaming with pleasure. "What else did he say?" asked Helen.

464

"Well," said Daniel, "Like what I said, I mean what I told you. Oh, yes, other things, like 'Think of it, after two thousand years! Now, of what other people can this be said, of what other people, tell me?' He said this looking at my mother, who's Irish and English and Scotch, mostly Irish, and she didn't know what to say. But he kept on asking her, like he was teasing her, in a friendly way, you know."

"Tell me what your mother said," said Helen.

"After a while, naturally, mother had to say something, because father kept looking at her, and I could see that mother was pleased by father's excitement, she had never seen him so excited, and neither did we kids. So finally she said, 'Yes.' And he said, 'See, I told you,' and then she said 'Yes' again." Daniel smiled. "What else could she say, after all, you know what I mean?"

"That's beautiful," said Helen. "And why did you come down, Daniel?"

"I guess because I got excited, too. Like I told David, I've been reading up on Zionism lately and other Jewish things. Father got me interested. In our house, we were sort of let alone about religion, as I explained to David, but since the Palestine issue came up at the UN father talked a lot to me about Zionism and other Jewish matters, and I got interested. And when this happened last night, it really was exciting. I was hoping father would take me along when he rushed out, but he didn't, he didn't mean anything, he was so excited, he just ran off, and I've been hoping I'd run into him, but I guess I won't, in this crowd, and he's probably inside anyway. It's just wonderful." He paused, then continued, "Mother is listening on the radio, she's pretty excited, too. Our house sure has become some place. But so has this square, too, I've never seen so many people here, in this square, or in any other square, not even when they have fights at the Arena."

"I hope you find your father, Daniel," said Helen.

"I might at that. Nice meeting you," he said to Helen and to David and ambled off.

Helen squeezed David's hand. "Isn't it wonderful?"

"He's a nice boy. Lots of problems, as you can imagine. I guess you can tell by what he's said."

"I know, David, but this will cure most of his problems.

465

What happened last night is going to cure a lot of problems all over the world, I mean Jewish problems, and it will cure problems among non-Jews in what they think about Jews."

"I hope you're right, Helen."

"I know I'm right, darling."

They walked on slowly, in silence, through the crowds, sometimes so hemmed in that they could hardly move a step. They listened to young men and young women talking, they watched them smiling, saying nothing yet saying a great deal . . . there were few older people in the center of the crowds, but soon, as they came to the sidewalks, especially as they walked in the two little parks at both ends of Lincoln Square, they saw that slowly older men and women were appearing, holding on to each other, and out of their faces came a quiet delight.

"It's a miracle," whispered Helen.

"Yes."

David noticed that policemen were re-routing traffic at the lower end of the square, and soon he realized that they had also re-routed it at the upper end, for now no vehicles of any kind were passing through . . . and slowly the whole square became a mass of humanity.

David looked up at the lower end, and saw the large statue of Dante, with the poet standing erect, a book in his arm, and looking down upon the people. He wondered what he was thinking of now . . . in the dark it was not wholly possible to make out the clear outlines of his face, but David thought he sensed a brooding all about the statue.

"You thinking about Dante, darling?" said Helen.

"Yes, but not seriously. I mean . . ."

"I know what you mean, David."

"What, Helen?" David felt he was closer to her now than he had been for months . . . there was something so open, so utterly honest, so utterly womanly about her face and her whole bearing . . . and there was so much love in her now, so clear and open a desire to give and to receive love . . . and she was completely Jewish . . . on her face he saw his mother and his grandmother and his great-grandmother, his Alte Bobbe, and from her face he heard melodies, rather, one long soft lovely thankful melody that issued from the Psalms and from the

466

Talmud and from the Temple and from the little *shulen* down the centuries of Jewish history in Exile . . . and the melodies were from the festivals and the High Holy Days . . . and on her face he saw Friday night and the lighted candles flickering gently.

"I mean, David, that he doesn't belong, he really doesn't, darling. This is a family festival, the greatest festival of the largest family in all history. It's for us alone. It's sacred, isn't it, darling?"

"It is."

"I mean, David, nobody else can understand, really, not this. Here, art doesn't help. It has to be in you, you have to be born with it, don't you think so, darling?"

"You're probably right."

They walked on and on, again in silence, listening, watching . . . listening, listening: "My father should now be alive. It makes me choke up when I think of it. In Europe he died, and he always said, 'It will happen, I know, we will have Palestine back' . . . It's hard to believe it, I pinch myself . . . I say to myself, 'Is it true, really true?' And I look at the paper and I say yes, and I'm still surprised and happy, of course, you know what I mean . . . I was holding a cup of tea when the news of the final vote came over the radio, and I dropped the cup, and my husband was so excited, he was listening with me, he dropped his eyeglasses, and he came over and kissed me like the way he did years before, I tell you it was just wonderful . . . so many Jews being happy, in the open, outside, I mean, there must be hundreds, no, thousands, in the middle of New York City, on a Saturday night, just being together and being happy, talking and laughing . . . To me it's like a dream come true, more, like the greatest dream come true . . . Crazy ideas, I suppose, are the most wonderful ideas, I mean Herzl's idea about Palestine . . . yes, and he was such a young man Dr. Herzl, when he died, forty-four, I think, no more, he died of a broken heart. Now being a Jew means something, it makes you feel, for the first time, you don't want to hide, you know what I mean, you feel like saying, 'Listen, in case you don't know, you, I'm Jewish, did you hear the radio last night?' You know what I mean. . . . Right here, it looks like our country already, like in Jerusalem. It's funny and wonderful, being here with so

467

many thousands of Jews, makes you feel different, sort of more relaxed than otherwise, you know what I mean, I guess that's how it will be in Jerusalem when the government is organized. . . . I was foolish when I was young, you're young and you don't know any better. My parents were Zionists and they spoke Hebrew at home, read Hebrew, you know, and they wanted me to study Hebrew, but I said no, so now I don't know Hebrew, wasn't I foolish? But it's never too late . . . I hope we're sending plenty of ammunition to the Jews in Palestine, they will need it. I hear the United States government can't do it openly, you know what I mean, though I don't see why not. And I hear that President Truman is very friendly, he's really a wonderful man, can you imagine what Dewey would have done? . . . You don't have to worry, the Jews knew all the time what they'd be up against, so they're probably plenty prepared for the Arabs. Anyway, you know Weizmann is a chemist, sure, one of the greatest in the world, and he's probably invented things to take care of the Arabs. He must be a brainy, wonderful man. Imagine how he feels now, Dr. Weizmann, it's just wonderful, after all those years, what do you think he's saying to himself right now, do you think he's like the rest of us, hardly believing it could have happened? I'll tell you truly, I was hoping, of course, naturally, what Jew wasn't hoping, but after two thousand years of hoping, with nothing happening, you must know what I mean, you sort of begin to doubt, you know what I mean, and then I heard it happened, it sounds, well, it's just a miracle, that's the only word, it sort of makes you feel we Jews are, you know what I mean. My daughter says I'm behaving like a child, I'm excited, I'm so nervous, you know what I mean, I keep on thinking of my Hebrew school days, so many years ago, when we carried the Jewish flag in our Bar Kochba plays, and on holidays, you know, who would have thought then that it would come out true, who would have thought it? . . . There is something truly mystical about all this, really mystical, I never thought I would say a thing like this, but I have to, you know what I mean? . . . Yes, I do, I was thinking the same thing, only I was a little ashamed to say it, but I guess it's true. And another thing, I might as well tell you. All sorts of pictures come to my mind: Mt. Sinai with Moses and the Ten Commandments, you know, and the forty years in the desert and Passover and all those things, wonderful things, really. You know what I did last night, Mildred? You wouldn't believe it, but I did it. I knew the vote, the final vote, was coming up, so I lit candles in the apartment, I felt like it, I went out and bought some candles, and I put them on a piece of glass, glued them on, with Scotch tape, and I lit them, and I stood there, and I prayed to myself that the vote would come out right, and it was the only time I really prayed and it was the only time I really understood prayer, prayer is a deep wishing and trusting in the good forces of the world, that's what it is, and it made me feel good, because, you know why, because the prayer put me in touch with outside forces for good, and I guess those forces are what is meant by God. I know I'm repeating what my rabbi, years ago, used to tell us kids in Hebrew school and what he sometimes preached on Friday night and on Saturday, but I didn't really believe then, or understand, but last night I understood . . . Right now, I wish I had more sense years ago, Muriel, I mean I wish I had more than two children, I wish I had at least half a dozen, so some of them could go to Palestine and settle, and anyway, so there'd be more Jews, that sounds funny, but you understand. It's just incredible and wonderful, just wonderful, and so suddenly it happens. No, it wasn't suddenly, really, Herzl and Weizmann and all the others were working all the time, while we were doing nothing, so it wasn't sudden. I only wish the Jews have enough guns, those Arabs are really crazy, a holy war they have announced, did you hear that on the radio? And when they have a holy war they kill everybody, men, women, and children, this Mohammedanism is the killingest religion there is, they massacre with swords and knives, they're real brutal, barbarians. But they're no good, I don't mean the poor people, they're slaves to the kings and the landowners and the no-good politicians, they, the no-goods and the kings, they tie up with all the other no-goods, like Hitler and Mussolini and Stalin. Yes, and talking about Stalin, he's not to be trusted, believe me, I'm over sixty and I remember. A Russian is a born anti-Semite, these Russians will hate Jews all the time, and the sooner the Jews leave Russia the better . . . If Stalin will let them. That's right, if he will let them . . . ah, suddenly everything is different. One day it's a plain Friday, a day in the week, then it's Saturday, and all history is changed, and all history for the Jews is changed, we're a real people now, like other people, all this in one day, no, one night, that's how things happen, it's hard to believe, it's wonderful. Ah, I wish to do something to help those soldiers in Palestine. You'll be told how to help, there'll be plenty of ways to help, God knows they'll need help, not just money, but food and medicines and clothing, and, of course, guns and guns and guns . . . Look, look . . ."

Coming up, from downtown, were two truckloads of young people singing "Hatikvah", "God Bless America," "Hapalmach," "Yayin, Yayin," "Afen Pripitchok," "Kinereth,' and other Jewish religious and secular and Palestinian songs . . . and as the trucks came closer and closer their songs seemed to become lovelier, and David thought that the singers were trying to put more and more meaning into their songs as they neared St. Nicholas Arena . . . Helen was holding his arm tight, and through the corner of his eye he could see that her eyes were bright with the tears of deep emotion.

Suddenly the two trucks stopped in an open space not far from Dante's statue . . . there was some commotion, and soon there was a clearing, and the two groups of young men and women made a large circle and they were dancing and singing . . . and on and on they sang, and danced the *horah,* the Israeli dance that the Israelis had made popular and were spreading through the world . . . and now, as if out of nowhere, there could be heard an accordion and a trumpet and a drum, and the accordion and the trumpet and the drum joined in with the singers, and the area became a sweet bedlam of song and delight and utter joyousness and complete and absolute Jewishness . . . and the wondrous confusion went on and on, far into the night . . . and now the crowds began to thin out . . . and the instrumentalists could not be heard any more . . . and the singing and dancing subsided, till they, too, could not be heard any more . . . but what remained was not a cold emptiness, but a warm glow of completion and satisfaction and delight and happy Jewishness.

Helen and David remained in Lincoln Square. It was late, past midnight. They sat on a bench directly below the statue of Dante. There were fewer people now, so that the square began to look deserted. A chill wind came to the square, and swept up and down and around it, and somehow it seemed to add a sorrow to the whole area and to what had taken place before.

Helen took David's hand in hers and said, "I feel strange, darling."

"I do, too, Helen."

"I want to dance and talk and dance all night, David, that's what I thought people would be doing here, and we just watched."

"I know."

"We only watched."

"But it was wonderful, Helen."

"Very, very wonderful, darling. We were really dancing when we were watching."

"Of course."

"But why, David, are all things like this? I mean why don't they go on and on, I mean why don't they go on the way they started?"

A shudder of delight went through David. Helen was saying what he had always, for so many years, been thinking and wondering about: why don't things go on the way they started? Why do all things get lost in time? What happens to them in the vast spaces of time. David kissed Helen's hand slowly, and she kissed him slowly and pensively on the lips.

"You've just said something wonderful, Helen, you don't know how wonderful."

Helen said nothing, she was looking off into the distance . . . and David was glad that she said nothing . . . her silence added a wonderment to what she had said . . . David looked at her and sensed that for the first time he had met a woman who had all the loveliness he had dreamed about and all the softness and all the warmth and all the womanly intuitions . . . and as he looked at her he knew that she was deep in the mystic world where he had often been, and he knew what she saw there: an unending road of glory, unutterable in its magnificence, and by its very glory and magnificence filling this world with an unending sorrow and a strange certainty and even comfort, a comfort that had no bounds and was incapable of description and occasionally was suffused with sadness and that yet

471

was a comfort . . . and this comfort was the comfort of a sense of union with that mystic world, an even greater comfort than that which came from the embrace of one's beloved.

Greater? At this moment David wasn't sure, for the comfort he now got from being near Helen was unlike any other he had ever known. And he began to wonder whether this comfort wasn't a foretaste of the comfort that came from that mystic world, where Helen and all her loveliness were now wandering, where they were gliding into the arms of infinity . . . he was certain that something truly new and liberating and comforting and complete in its intimacy had just come into his life . . . and there was something else about Helen that was so wondrous, and he tried to capture it in his understanding, to say the words to himself that would define this wonderment and make it more his own.

He put his hand on her breast and kissed her on the lips, and she kissed him in return slowly, and she breathed into him, and he was delighted, and now she kissed him slowly again, and she pressed his hand on her breast.

"Darling."

"Helen."

"You know what I was seeing a little while ago, David?"

"What?"

"I was seeing the Jews crossing the Red Sea, and I was seeing Moses and King David and . . ."

He kissed her on the mouth and tried to inhale her words. She smiled, and kissed him in return.

"And, David, I saw the prophets and the kings and the great rabbis and . . ."

"I saw them, too, Helen."

She pressed his hand and then put it to her lips and kissed it. "And I saw the great Jews in Babylonia and in Persia and in Spain and in Russia and in France and in England. And I saw Dr. Herzl."

"I did, too, Helen."

"I know you did, darling," she said and smiled at him.

"You did?"

"Yes, and you know I knew."

He kissed her on her lips and on her eyes. "I'm glad you did. I mean I knew you knew."

472

She moved closer to him and gently pulled his thighs to her.
"Are you cold, Helen?"

"Not now, darling." She hesitated, then said, "I'm glad we sat down here. I just wanted to be here as long as possible, just to remember and remember, didn't you, darling?"

"Yes."

"I'm so proud, so very proud, David, so terribly, terribly proud." She kissed him and took a gentle bite of his hand. "That's how proud I am. I am as proud as only a Jew can be today. You know something, darling?"

"What?"

"I think today everybody, everything is Jewish, the stars are Jewish, the moon is Jewish, the sun is Jewish, everything, everybody, you know what I mean, darling, don't you?"

"I do, Helen, very much."

"Oh, David, it's been such a wonderful birthday for the Jews today, such a very wonderful birthday. I never want to go to sleep, I just want to think about this birthday."

"I do, too, Helen. With you."

"With me?"

"With you, darling."

"With us," she said, and put her arms around his neck. "I love you, I love you, David. Hasn't it been wonderful, this birthday, it's jumping, singing inside of me."

She hesitated. "And it's been a wonderful birthday for us, David. We just learned to know each other."

"It's been the most wonderful birthday I've ever had, Helen."

"With me, too."

And they put their arms around each other's necks and they embraced and they kissed and they smiled at each other and they were unendingly pleased with each other and they pressed their bodies to each other, and they pressed their lips to each other and they explored each other's faces and they came to blissful rest on each other's necks . . . and she knew and he knew, and what they each knew was one, and above all, they knew that this was their common birthday . . . and she knew that her long waiting had come to a wonderful end, and he knew that in finding her he had, at long last, found himself, with a sure knowledge of where he was and what he was and what he wanted to be and do, and he knew and she knew that

473

what each wanted was what the other wanted . . . it was the
end and it was the beginning, and it was a beginning that
would have no end . . . and it was a beginning that had its roots
in the earliest times of history and of Jewish events . . . and
it was a beginning that was two thousand years in starting . . .
and it was a beginning that was intertwined with the soft warm
glorious wonderment of all womanhood and the soft glorious
wonderment of night and day and all the seasons . . . it was a
beginning that was complete with pride and assurance . . . it
was a beginning that was rich with birth and song and continuous joyousness and mystic bedazzlement . . .

"Helen . . ."

"David . . ."